W9-DCL-191

THE

CRISS
CROSS

This is a work of fiction. All of the characters, organizations, and events portrayed in this novel are either products of the author's imagination or are used fictitiously.

The Criss Cross. Copyright © 2004, 2011 by Crystal Lacey Winslow. All rights reserved. Printed in the United States of America. No part of this book may be used or reproduced in any manner whatsoever without written permission except in the case of brief quotations embodied in critical articles or reviews. For information, address Melodrama Publishing, P.O. Box 522, Bellport, NY 11713.

www.melodramapublishing.com

ISBN-10: 1-934157-42-2

ISBN-13: 978-1-934157-42-8

Mass Market Edition: February 2011

10 9 8 7 6 5 4 3 2 1

Interior Design and Layout by candacecottrell.com

THE
CRISS
CROSS

CRYSTAL LACEY WINSLOW

Buy

for Melodrama

THE CRISS CROSS

Unbeknownst to you, you are about to meet someone in a few seconds that could have an astounding effect on your life. If you could fast-forward ahead and see how this encounter will end, would you? Alternatively, would you savor the mystique and let life play out as it was meant to be?

Have you ever been in a situation where the relationship was so turbulent when you looked back at it, you could not think of one good reason why you and that person's paths had crossed?

I am here to tell you that every chance meeting is not by chance at all. Our lives are pre-planned. Our destinies are tattooed indelibly on our souls. Whether we exacerbate our situations or ameliorate them is solely our own mechanism to enhance or diminish life.

Sometimes we can become so inundated with the minuscule things in our lives, that when the criss cross approaches, we are usually too preoccupied to recognize we are about to be bamboozled. When two people's paths criss cross, there is bound to be a point of impact. You need to be perceptive while deciphering how to put the pieces back together. The question is—are you?

Lacey

PROLOGUE

NIKKI LING

WINTER 1988; FLUSHING QUEENS

It was my eleventh birthday, and my sister and I were hungry. It was nearly noon and we hadn't had anything to eat in days. My mother was in her room with the door locked as usual with Mr. John. My mother's friends were always named "Mr. John."

"Noki, be quiet and come over here now," I whispered. Noki's eyes grew wide with curiosity as she tiptoed to me. I kneeled and looked through the large peephole on the old-fashioned door. There, I was able to see my mother and Mr. John naked. Mr. John was standing up with his legs spread apart and my mother was on her knees kissing Mr. John's pee-pee. Mr. John was holding my mother's head tightly. My mother's head was moving back and forth rapidly. My mother always said in the room she had lots of fun, but their faces looked like they were in pain. I knew they were doing grown-up things. Soon enough, Mr. John let out a loud moan and said, "Swallow it cunt!"

My mother soon released her mouth and spat out a white, gooey liquid onto the bedroom floor. Mr. John slapped my mother hard on her face— right before my very eyes. Her hand immediately shot up to shield her from further blows. I balled up my fist and banged on the door.

"Leave my mommy alone!" I screamed.

"Shut up you little brat before I make *you* suck it!" he roared, and then let out a hideous cackle. My mother jumped up and stuffed the peephole with tissue.

"Let me see now," Noki begged.

"It's too late, Noki. I hate him anyway, don't you?"

"I dunno. If you hate him, then I guess I hate him too."

How could I take my mind off what I'd just seen? I walked to the kitchen. I was upset about Mr. John hitting my mother, so I decided to do something fun.

"Noki, come in here. I got a surprise for you," I said. I was excited because it was my birthday. My sister Noki was four years younger than I was. She was so cute and chubby and looked exactly like my mother. She had straight, silky, black hair, olive skin, and Japanese eyes. There's not a hint of African-American in her features.

I, on the other hand, look like my father. I'm 11 years old, and already 5' 5" tall. Mother says I'm going to be tall and slender like my father. I have his dark-chocolate skin and full African lips. I have mother's silky hair and Japanese eyes. Mother calls us Yin and Yang.

"Come eat," I said and continued, "Then we will have some cake."

My sister's eyes widened at the mention of food. She ran to the table but was immediately disappointed.

"I'm hungry, Nikki," she cried. She balled up her little fists out of frustration and rubbed her eyes. I sat her down and placed a bowl in front of her. The bowl was filled with water.

"Noki don't cry. Let's play make–believe. Let's pretend

we're eating Nabeyaki Udon and then we'll have cake and you'll sing 'Happy Birthday' to me."

"I wanna eat!" she wailed even louder, her fat cheeks jiggling with every word. I cupped my hand over her mouth. Mother was already angry. We knew we had to be quiet when Mr. John was over. Sometimes, we would be beaten with a switch for disobeying her rules.

We heard the bedroom door open—Noki shut–up abruptly! We watched Mr. John leave our apartment. Mother lingered in the shadows, and then joined us in the kitchen.

"You are too defiant Nikkisi–too strong for a woman. You will have to learn to be subservient in order to find a husband. Your independent spirit will be your downfall. You're just like your father." She spoke to me in Japanese. She understands the English language but never speaks it.

I was ashamed that my mother was disappointed with my behavior. I put my head down to avoid eye contact.

"Hold your head up high Nikkisi. Never bow your head to anyone *except* your husband. Do you understand me?" my mother admonished.

"Hai," I said, which means "Yes."

I thought about my father and how things had changed in the year since he died. Mother didn't have a job or money to take care of us. Soon she had to give herself to Mr. John.

"Mommy, do you have money now so we can get somethin' to eat?"

She didn't answer. However, with tears streaking her face she gently placed two $20 bills in my hand, then bent down and kissed my cheek. She stared at me a moment, then kissed Noki.

"Let me hold the money," Noki cried. She loved to handle money; it made her happy.

"Mommy, please don't cry. We can—" Mother didn't stay to hear the rest of my sentence. She turned and walked into the bathroom. She always bathed after Mr. John left.

While she bathed, Noki and I talked about what we'd buy to eat.

"I want Oreo cookies, and frankfurters, and ice cream, and Now and Laters, and Lemonheads." Noki was now suddenly full of life.

"Noki, what would you do for a million–trillion–thousand–dollars?" I asked.

"I would trade my right arm and left leg," she reasoned. Then she said, "What would you do for lots and lots of money?"

I thought for a minute. "I don't know what I would do. But I know I wouldn't do what mommy does!" Noki stared at me. She did not quite get it—and I did not want her to. "But I'd be willing to do anything to protect you, Noki. Always remember that."

"I will Nikki. Do you wanna play with our Kokeshi dolls?" she asked.

"Yes," I said. I was glad that Noki had taken her mind off of food. My mother had bought us the dolls after our father died to help cheer us up. After a while of playing, we both looked down to see water creeping across the kitchen floor. We jumped up, ran to the bathroom, and opened the door. Mother's lifeless body floated in a tub full of bloody water.

It's an old Japanese belief that a woman who disgraces and dishonors her family must take her life and the lives of her children as well. My mother would never harm Noki or I. She loved us too much.

IVANKA ZAMORA

WACO, TEXAS; 1988

"Ivanka, come to mother. It is time to go to your horseback riding lesson, darling."

"NO!" I screamed. I was tired of horseback riding, swimming, violin, piano, and archery lessons.

"Ivanka, don't you dare disobey a direct order. The equestrian training will give you culture. You are from a fine Southern family with old money. We have a reputation to uphold," my mother scolded.

I stomped my feet and ran through the large corridors. The enormous columns upheld the manor nicely and added elegance to the lifeless estate. As soon I got to my room, I slammed the door and locked it. Then I let my stereo system blare the words from Psycho, a new rock band. *"I got a gun, and I'm going to kill the bastard. Blow his brains out and let it splatter everywhere!"*

I sang in unison, "I got a gun and I'm going to kill the bastard. Blow his brains out and let it splatter everywhere!"

I was screaming while my mother banged on the door. She eventually got our butler who had the master key and let her in. I spun around immediately and experienced a rage I could not control.

"Get out!" I commanded with such vehemence it startled my elderly mother. She put her hand over her chest like a dignified woman.

"Ivanka, what on earth has gotten into you lately? This poisonous music . . . your awkward hair colors . . . those preposterous clothes you wear. Dear child, you are thirteen years old and growing into a woman. It is about time you take responsibility for your actions. I will speak to your father about this as soon as he comes home from Europe."

"Fuck you!" I yelled. The threat of mother telling father I had disobeyed her sent me into a frenzy. I loved and admired him so much. He was much younger than my old, feeble, wealthy, *tattle-telling* mother. I ran back downstairs and into the kitchen with my mother right on my heels. In a blind fury, I grabbed the hammer from underneath the sink.

"Where are you going with that, young lady?" my mother questioned. I ignored her and walked directly over to her precious, white, poodle named Queen Elizabeth. With one swift movement, I lifted the hammer and slammed it upon her head! Her head cracked open like a walnut. Blood squirted everywhere and she let out an eerie whimper. This provoked me. I stared at the dog's head and saw blood oozing out. She started panting and gasping for air. Queen Elizabeth was petrified. I took a step closer to her and she let out a high-pitched squeal.

I was in control. I kept bludgeoning her head with the hammer until I was exhausted and soaked in blood. Just like the song, her brains splattered everywhere. Pieces of brain fragments had got caught in my hair and around the head of the hammer. Queen Elizabeth's left eye was dislodged from her eye socket. The annoying eye kept staring me. Mockingly. The dog was still alive. I took this as an insult. I took the back of the hammer and ripped her eye out of socket as if I'd just cracked open a can of beer. My mother screamed in horror as the good ol' Queen made a weak attempt to get up. Her once white, fluffy coat was soaked in blood. With her brains oozing out the side of her head, she crawled a few steps towards my mother who was still standing there mortified. I lifted my hammer again and let it crash down upon Queen Elizabeth's head for the last time. She was dead. The bastard dog was dead! The scene was humorous in a menacing way.

I let the hammer drop and make a loud thud on the floor and stared at my mother. My chest heaved in and out. As I perspired profusely, my purple hair stuck to my forehead. I felt euphoric. I intently gawked at my mother with my piercing gray eyes, she openly gasped. Then, slowly, she clutched her pearls and backed out of the foyer.

"Don't ever fuck with me again or you'll be sorry!" I threatened. My mother didn't say a word.

KAPRI HENDERSON

MARCY PROJECTS–BROOKLYN; 1988

It was a cold D'cember evenin and I hadda feelin' shit wasn't gonna go right. Knowledge Born and I had just fucked and he had a bitch feelin' right. But what he wanted to go down was crazy, yo.

"Kapri, I need you to do me this solid. Now I dun told you da bitch I usually use ain't no where 'round and I need you to make this emergency trip for me outta state," he reasoned.

"Knowledge, why you tryin' to play me? I'm supposed to be ya girl. How you gonna let ya girl take cocaine 95-south on a Greyhound bus. What if a bitch git caught? Then what, nigga?"

"You ain't gonna git caught! Shit always go accordin' to plan. Anyway, you seventeen. Can't nuthin happen to ya ass. You a minor AND a *girl* minor. Besides, you 'posed to be my downassbitch! You gotta ride or die fo a nigga. When you wanted dat Ellesse sweat suit who bought it? When you hadda have that nugget watch who made it happen? Damn, I'm your man right? You ain't down fo ya man?" he asked.

He was standin' in front of me butt-ass naked. Huge dick solid–slightly bow legs and flat-top hair style. His dark chocolate complexion and pearly white teeth made a bitch lose her mind. My nigga was fine.

I thought for a moment of what the outcome could be. Then, I thought for another moment of how much paper I could git from this transaction and said, "Hell yeah! I'm down fo my nigga. What I gotta do?"

"What da fuck I say! Now git your silly ass over here," Knowledge Born snapped.

"When I git back, Knowledge, I want you to git me that Honda Scooter– just like da one Lisa man bought her!"

"Come here," he said, ignorin' me. I walked over to him, and he made me open my legs. Then he shoved a half-ounce plastic baggy of pure coke in between my pussy. When I started squirmin' he barked on me, "Keep still!"

Then he continued, "Now listen. You gonna carry an overnight bag and cop a round-trip ride to Washington, D.C. You git on the bus and sit in the front so you can be the first one off da bus. You 'n shorty—"

"I ain't takin' my baby!"

"Word?"

"Word up!"

"I ain't got time to be—"

"I said I ain't takin' Kareem." I countered.

"Nah, you gonna take Kareem so no one will be suspicious. I'm gonna give you an address where you will take a cab. Let da cab wait for you. Drop the coke, git my dough, and bring your narrow black–ass back home."

ONE

NIKKI LING

1992

I had been living with my foster family for about three years. The parents were a religious "God-fearing" family, with issues. Martha, my foster mother, was the only member that was actually nice to me. She really treated me like I was a distant relative, which was nice, sometimes. The only thing I disliked about her was that she didn't have a backbone. She'd turn a blind–eye to everything her bad–ass teenagers did as well as to her no-good husband. She was such a hypocrite.

Her biological daughters, Renee and Elizabeth, didn't like the fact that their mother was treating me kindly. So every time Martha turned her back, they'd jump me, pulling my hair, scratching my face and biting me! They were also experienced fighters, especially Elizabeth, who was only thirteen. She had the biggest hands I'd ever seen and was quick to ball one up in a fist and punch me until I was visibly bruised.

Renee, who was the eldest at sixteen, would always instigate the fights. She'd just start picking on me, saying things like, "You think you so pretty 'cause you have long hair. You ain't pretty. You ugly. Anyway, don't nobody like you. They say you big and goofy."

"Who said that?" I asked. I hated when people made fun of my height. I had already felt awkward, being the tallest girl in my school. And I hated even more when people didn't like me because of my features. Because I looked different than the other black students, I was alienated from my peers. I didn't have any friends.

"Shut-up stupid!" Renee continued, "Everybody said that. Your own momma didn't like you that's why she threw you away," Renee screamed.

"She did not!" I yelled back.

"She did not," Renee mimicked. Then her sister Elizabeth chimed in, "She did not."

"Why don't you just git out?" Renee asked.

"I don't have anywhere to go. I can't go and live with the foster parents my sister is living with because they don't want me."

"See, just like I said, nobody want you!"

I began crying, because what she was saying was true. And I knew it. Nobody wanted me.

"Well, as soon as I turn eighteen, I'm leaving here to live on my own, so you don't have to worry."

"Eighteen!" They both said in unison. Then Renee continued, "You ain't stayin' *here* that long. You be fifteen soon, why can't you leave then?"

"Yeah, why can't your ugly-self leave then? I'm tired of every time I get a pair of Nike sneakers, you always beggin' my mother and she has to buy you a pair too. You a bum and a beggar. You stupid, ugly girl," Elizabeth said.

"I don't beg anyone. The State gives your mother money for me. That's my money she spends on my things. And that's probably *my* money that she spends on you and Renee too!"

"What chu' say Mutt?" Renee said.

"You heard me –" I tried to challenge, but was met with a solid fist before I could finish my sentence.

Elizabeth's large hands began to pound on my head and back, while Renee jumped on me and kicked and scratched at my face. I fought back as best as I could, but I was no match for two sisters.

For the first time, I realized that I might not be able to beat the two of them, but perhaps if I concentrated on one, I'd have a better chance.

Although Renee was the oldest, she was smaller than Elizabeth. Therefore, I concentrated all my fighting efforts on Renee. When she bit me, I bit her back–only harder. When she punched me, I punched her back–only harder. Soon I was pulling at *her* hair and digging my nails in *her* face. I was so enraged from years of torture and physical abuse that I didn't realize that I was now fighting the both of them. I just started going crazy like a wild maniac. I started screaming, "I'll kill you! I'll kill you! I'll kill you!"

Then *they* started screaming too, "Ah-h-h-h, get off me. Get her off me!"

Within moments of the commotion, their father, Reverend Daniel, came running in the room to break up the fight. When he pulled us apart, my adrenaline was pumping; and I tried to lunge at them again. They both flinched and hovered behind their father. At the end of the day, they were both cowards.

"Kick her out, daddy. Make her leave now!" Elizabeth screamed.

I had them both scared and it felt great!

Reverend Daniel punished all of us equally by having us read Romans 4:7. *"Blessed are those whose lawless deeds are forgiven."* Then we were to write an essay explaining why we shouldn't fight each other. Finally, we were all restricted from watching television for one week. *Big deal*, I thought.

I went into the bathroom to dress my wounds. Of course, my eye was a little swollen, my lip busted, and my hair was pulled out in some areas. However, that was a small thing compared to the victory I felt in my heart. I was a fighter.

TWO

NIKKI LING

One particular Friday morning, Elizabeth came and woke Renee and me up early. She whispered, "I got a plan to make some money."

"How?" Renee whispered back.

As I listened intently, Elizabeth explained that her eighth-grade class was going on a trip to see the Intrepid ship in the city. She explained that if we go to our local bodega and steal hero sandwiches, we could sell them for half price to the students.

"We have to make sure we order ham and cheese hero sandwiches wit everythin' on them. They cost $3 dollars. We can then sell them for half price," Elizabeth exclaimed.

The thought had gotten me excited. I was never given an allowance like Renee and Elizabeth. So the last time I handled money was the day my mother died.

"Elizabeth, that's a great plan, but how do we steal from Gino's? He's crazy!" Renee said.

"I know . . . but we just have to be careful. Come on . . . get dressed. We don't have all day."

I was a little hesitant that the girls would include me in on a plan that involved money. When Elizabeth looked at me and said, "Come on Nikki...don't you wanna make some money too?" I jumped up and started getting dressed quickly.

Gino's was a local deli and supermarket located behind the projects.

The owner's name was Gino. He was Italian and known for beating your ass instead of calling the cops if you stole something from his store. Walking in, I was intimidated. Elizabeth took the lead. She walked towards the middle of the store to the deli department. She approached the counter and ordered four ham and cheese heroes with everything on them just as she said she'd do. I quickly calculated that was a quick $6. I decided to order *five* sandwiches. I wanted to keep one for me.

With our hero sandwiches in our small shopping baskets we left the area and headed towards the back of the store. There I realized why I had been invited.

"Open up your school bag Mutt so we can dump our sandwiches in," Renee whispered, looking around to make sure no one could see us.

My heart started beating fast.

"The only thing going in my bag are my sandwiches," I challenged.

"You have to do it because Gino will be suspicious of me and Renee," Elizabeth said loudly.

"Too bad," I said firmly and realized we were running out of time. We needed to hurry up or else we'd get busted.

"Look, she not gonna do it. We'll deal with her later," Renee warned, "We'll just stick the sandwiches down our pants and make it look like we're having a baby. If we get by the door and Gino asks us to open our school bags... nothing will be there."

"That's silly. You can't stick it in your pants and look like you're pregnant. You didn't come in here pregnant. They'll surely stop you. Look, we can stick them down our sleeves—" I tried to finish when Elizabeth pushed me. I was going to push her back when someone came up the aisle and we all dispersed.

Renee and Elizabeth went one way and I went another. I walked to the refrigerator where they had sodas and started to stick each sandwich down my jacket sleeves. When I was done, I slowly walked out the front door. My heart was racing as I passed by Gino who was guarding the door. He smiled. I smiled back. When I got outside, I ran all the way back to the projects. I never looked back to see if Renee and Elizabeth were behind me.

THREE

NIKKI LING

Yo, Nikki, whatchu got?" Big Monica asked as she came out the building.

I had a small crowd of students around me who were paying for the sandwiches.

"I got some hero sandwiches for sale. You got a buck fifty?" I said trying to be down.

"Word, I got you," Big Monica said and purchased my last sandwich.

As I sat on the bench, I noticed Renee and Elizabeth hadn't come back yet. As I waited for them, I opened up my hero and started to eat my sandwich. The cold ham and cheese tasted so good. I had asked for extra mayonnaise and tomatoes. It was perfect. As I took another bite, I felt a firm grip on my arm. I was lifted off my feet, spun around and my hero fell to the ground. It was Gino. He had Elizabeth in a headlock and Renee was crying hysterically.

"You's better pay me for that sandwich!" Gino threatened.

"I . . . I . . . I . . ." was all I could say. I trembled from fear.

"Quiet! I want my three bucks, or I'll slam your face in the ground. Don't nobody steal from Gino," he warned.

Thinking quickly, I reached in my pocket, peeled off $3 dollars and handed it to Gino. He snatched the money and then let go of Elizabeth's head.

"If I ever catch any one of you's in my store again, I'll smash a brick over you's head. I don't take no bullshit!"

"But she got more—" Renee said.

"Quiet! I don't want to hear no more from a rat," he said, "Your friends ratted you out! Italians hate rats. If you twos were my friends, I'd have your tongues cut out. Canaries you twos are."

When Gino left, Renee and Elizabeth took that opportunity to try and get my money.

"We have to split your money, Mutt," Renee said. "We should all get $1 dollar each!"

"Dude, if it were up to you, I wouldn't have any money," I spat.

"Don't get smart!" Elizabeth yelled. She was embarrassed at being caught and ruffed up by Gino. She wanted to take her anger out on me.

"You ain't nobody's momma," I said and smacked her with all my strength. Stunned, she tried to back away, but I wouldn't let her. I met her left cheek with a right hook. As the kids came out of the building on their way to school, they immediately ran over and gathered around to see the fight.

"Fight, fight, fight, fight . . ." they all chanted.

"Stomp her out, Nikki!" someone tried to coach me, and I listened as best as I could. I was learning how to fight with more than my mouth and it felt great.

At this time, everyone was late for school but no one budged. People opened their windows and watched the fight from their apartments. The projects loved a good fight.

I attacked Elizabeth mercilessly and Renee just stood and watched but didn't jump in or break it up. As I began to whip her ass, Reverend Daniel walked quickly out of the building on his way to work. He glanced over and saw us fighting. He, too, didn't break it up. But later that night I was punished. Reverend Daniel said that I was becoming a real menace.

"You're treading on thin ice, young lady," he threatened.

FOUR

NIKKI LING

Sometimes their father would break up the fights. Sometimes he wouldn't. I slowly adapted to how consistently inconsistent he was. So, I tried to stay out of his way and never allowed myself to be left in a room alone with him. He's never tried anything, but since I was approaching fifteen in a couple of days, he's been leering at me. Brushing up against me when we pass by each other. And saying sexual adult things when no one was listening.

His attention towards me developed almost overnight. I remember waking up one morning and felt top-heavy. My once-flat chest had developed into large, firm breasts. Everyone noticed immediately, so Martha took me shopping to purchase a few bras. At fourteen, I had size 34-D cup breast. That coupled with my dark chocolate skin, Japanese eyes and long- silky hair, I was stunning.

One afternoon after school, I ran back home to watch a "Beavis and Butthead" video, but that was easily spoiled because Renee and Elizabeth came in and quickly changed the channel. This pissed me off because the channel they turned to wasn't clear. So, I got up and tried playing around with the hanger that was replacing the antenna, but I wasn't having any luck.

"Could I put the video back on? We can't even see the picture. Plus, you guys aren't even watching it," I asked.

"But we can hear it," Renee replied. So, I walked back and flopped on the couch; the plastic covering made an annoying noise. Within seconds, my legs were sticking to the seat.

It was a Friday and they were both going to a party in the neighborhood.

"Could I go too," I asked as they were getting dressed while discussing what the highlights of the party might be.

"If they wanted you to go, they would have invited you," Renee said. This was true.

"So, why is Elizabeth going? She wasn't invited," I challenged. They both just ignored me and kept getting dressed.

Listening to their conversation, I realized that the party was in Building 30, in Linden Plaza, in East New York, Brooklyn. The reason this was so big is that out here where we live, Linden Plaza is considered the place to be! Rich millionaires who drove fancy cars lived there. Mercedes-Benz, Lexus, and BMW's were all parked downstairs in the parking lot. And all their baby mommas wore nice clothes and nice gold jewelry. "The City in the Sky" is what I call Linden Plaza. When I first moved here, I asked Martha why she hadn't rented an apartment there. She told me you had to have a good job *and* good credit to get into that development. I promised myself that when I was older, I was going to get a nice apartment with a terrace in Linden Plaza and find a nice husband who will take care of me just like my father took care of my mother.

Unfortunately, for now, I had to live with the grim reality of living in the Pink Houses Projects on Loring Avenue across the street from the laundromat. It was a real tough neighborhood.

Even the schools were tough. Renee and I went to Franklin K. Lane High School and Elizabeth went to Intermediate School 218. None of us brought home good grades, and we all made excuses. I didn't excel in school because I didn't want to. They didn't excel in school because they were as dumb as the day is long.

"Mutt, why don't you scabeatit!" Renee said interrupting my thoughts.

"Dude, I keep telling you to stop calling me Mutt. My name is Ling. Nikki LING."

"I want fi chicken wing fried rice," Elizabeth said imitating an Asian person.

"Oh, so not funny. It doesn't hurt my feelings because I'm *black* just like you. So you can make all the Asian jokes you want!"

"You ain't black with hair like yours and eyes like yours."

"My mother said I'm black. My skin is black and my father was black. So I'm black!" I screamed.

"You think you cute," Elizabeth said and rolled her eyes.

"I do not," I said and put my head down.

"I should get a knife and cut ya face!"

"I'm telling Martha what you said!" I yelled.

"Go ahead!" Elizabeth challenged.

As the bickering began, the telephone rang and interrupted our argument. I went to answer it.

"Hello," I said.

"Hi, Nikki? What are you doing?"

"Hi, Martha. I'm not doing anything."

"Where are the girls?"

"Getting ready for a party."

"A party? Well, that sounds nice. Why don't you go with them?"

"They won't let me," I sulked.

"Oh, those girls are so stubborn. Well, why don't I bring home a movie and make some grits and fish. Would you like that?"

"Sure," I replied. Why couldn't she make them take me to the party?

"Where's Reverend Daniel? Is he home yet?"

"Not yet, I'll tell him you called. Good–bye." I hung up the telephone and returned to the living room to watch them get dressed.

Renee was around four feet ten inches, brown–skinned with short over– processed hair. She always kept it greasy and always dressed half–naked. She had a cute face with round eyes and two prominent front teeth. She looked like an adorable chipmunk but with a not-so-adorable personality.

She was wearing a pair of *borrowed*, dingy, DKNY jeans and a bra– shirt that was too big for her small breasts. Meanwhile, Elizabeth, who was slightly taller with longer hair, but not as attractive, was wearing her boyfriend's Karl Kani two-piece jean suit.

After they left, I went back into the living room, changed the channel back to my cartoons, and subsequently fell asleep. At some point, I was awoken by Reverend Daniels' hand sliding up my blouse and cupping my breast. Startled, I sat up and was pushed back down with his other hand.

"What are you doing?" I cried. He didn't answer me. Instead, he forced all his body weight on top of me and pinned me down. With one swift movement, he had my jeans unzipped and was positioning himself in between my legs.

"Stop it," I yelled and kept twitching my body so he couldn't position his penis near my vagina. Nevertheless, he was much too strong and experienced. He had my jeans and panties down before I could stop him.

His stiff penis kept pushing at the entrance of my vagina with such force, I could hear him straining as he pushed harder. Sweat started to pour off his forehead into my eyes, which mixed with my own tears, leaving me visibly blinded. Soon, his diligence prevailed and his penis forcefully pushed through and broke my virginity. The sudden pain astounded me and it felt like my heart had briefly stopped.

As he pushed in and out, the soreness and stinging sensation made me want to kill him. I was so angry and disgusted with the whole scene. I started pounding as best as I could on his back begging him to stop. But, he ignored my weak pleas. After that, I just stopped fighting and let him finish.

Soon, his fat, out-of-shape body stopped jerking and he just laid his sweaty, funky body on top of mine, until I pushed him off me. He grumbled something incoherent underneath his breath, and then stood up and zipped up his pants—all the time he looked at the floor.

As I got dressed, he tried to explain.

"Nikki, I would appreciate it if you didn't mention this to anyone. Just let it be our secret. The Lord will bless you girl for helping me release some of my frustration. The devil –"

"Forty bucks," I said interrupting his pathetic apology.

"Excuse me?"

"I said $40!"

"You want me to *pay* you? You must be joking."

"Dude, I take my work seriously."

"What work?" he asked in amazement, and then continued, "I did all the *work*."

"Don't flatter yourself. Now as I said, $40."

"If you wanna be on punishment for the next three weeks, keep talking nonsense, young lady," he threatened.

"Okay . . . but first thing in the morning I'm going to the 75th precinct and tell them what you did to me!"

With one swift movement, Reverend Daniel slapped my face. "Now stop talking such foolishness, chile. I took you off the street and put a roof over your head, and this is how you repay me? You're going to threaten an old man like me with jail!"

Although my face was stinging, I didn't flinch. "Give me my motherfucking money!" I yelled and for the first time used profanity in front of an adult.

He looked in my eyes and realized I wasn't joking. He knew I'd keep true to my words. I had nothing to lose. He slowly pulled out his wallet and peeled off a bill. "I only have twenty. I'll give you the rest later . . . or next time."

"Sonuvabitch! Do I look like I'm in the bargaining business?" I shouted. My jeans were still open and I was buttoning up my shirt. Just as he started to protest, Martha walked in on us. She looked at me, half dressed, then to her husband, who was sweating profusely. Reverend Daniel's dress shirt, which barely covered his fat stomach, was hanging loosely. His clothing was unruly and he had the look of disgust plastered on his face.

"What's that smell?" Martha asked anxiously.

"Martha, give me $20!" Reverend Daniel demanded.

She quickly reached inside her purse and gave him a twenty. He, in turn, handed it to me. I snatched it out of his hands and continued to get dressed.

"Like mother, like daughter," he spat with disdain. His words stung because I had no idea they knew the details of my background and my mother's death.

Reverend Daniel excused himself to his room and left Martha and me alone. I knew she knew what had just occurred and would be kicking me out as if it were my fault. I didn't care because I had already made up my mind to leave.

"So, you almost ready to watch the movie? I'll go and start dinner," she said, her voice wavering with each word. Her eyes darted back and forth nervously.

Hot tears streamed down my face. Couldn't she at least *pretend* to care for me? Care more about me than her fairy-tale family life. As she stood in the living room, I walked back into the bedroom and started to pack a small duffle bag with the few things that I did have. I had my new forty bucks, and my new plan to contact my sister, Noki. I needed someone who loved me in my life.

As I walked past Martha, we made eye contact. Her

eyes spoke regret to me, but it wasn't enough. I went to the elevator and, of course, it wasn't working. I had to walk down six flights of a piss-infested staircase.

I left the Pink Housing Projects on a mission to start a better life for myself with my sister. I was determined.

FIVE

NIKKI LING

As I walked up Grant Avenue in East New York, Brooklyn, I realized I had nowhere to go. Not one relative had come forward to adopt Noki and me. We were alone. I purchased one subway token and boarded the A-train. While on the subway, I needed to clear my head. For hours I rode the train from the first stop, Mott Avenue in Far Rockaway to the last stop 208th Street in Manhattan.

During the two-hour commute, I fell asleep. As a safety precaution, I had dressed in layers, hid my money in my bra, tied my hair up and hid it underneath a baseball cap that I pulled down real low. I had gotten about six hours of sleep before I heard police harassing a vagabond in the next car. I took this opportunity to get off the train at Eighth Avenue and 34th Street. It was 4:00 a.m.

Outside, in the cool night breeze, I aimlessly walked the streets. I was tired, cold and hungry. I realized I still had close to $40 in my bra. As I passed a 24-hour diner on the West Side Highway, I decided to stop and get something to eat.

The diner was crowded for such an early hour in the morning. There was one waitress on duty and one cook. I ordered a cheeseburger deluxe and went to the bathroom. The bathroom smelled so much of piss that it almost made me lose my appetite. I walked into one stall and pulled out $4 to pay for my meal. I didn't want to take the chance of someone seeing me pull out all of my money and rob me. When I came out, the food was on my table. I quickly ate my meal and left.

Outside I walked down the West Side Highway and saw things I had never seen before. There were men dressed as women in wigs, high heel shoes and lipstick. There were women cat-calling men. They were on different street corners wearing skimpy clothing and ripped stockings, and they would get into cars with strange men.

As I took in the whole scene, a tan car approached me and someone inside rolled down the window. I peered in and saw a middle-aged, overweight, white gentleman. He had missing front teeth and greasy hair.

"Do you need a ride?" he said.

"No thank-you," I replied and quickened my steps.

He continued to ride alongside me. "You sure? I won't hurt you. In fact, I want to help you," he said and smiled a toothless grin.

He reached into his pocket and flashed what appeared to be a $100 bill. I realized I had nothing to lose and some money to gain. Reluctantly, I jumped in the front seat . . .

SIX

NOKI LING 1992

The yellow school bus pulled in front of our Long Island cul-de-sac home just after 3:00 p.m. I raced in and dropped my books in the foyer before continuing to run up the steps to my bedroom. I wanted to watch "Beavis and Butthead" on MTV.

Lucy, my stepmother, came in shortly, holding the cordless telephone in her hands. She was a nice-looking, petite, Japanese woman who was very domesticated.

She taught me that women should wear nice clothing and expensive jewelry, drive elite cars, have a master's or doctorate degree, and marry the richest man.

Once you accomplish this, you stay at home and raise children. That was her intent, but her dream was almost shattered after she was married and the doctors told her she would be barren. After giving up hope of ever having a family, she and her husband decided to adopt foster children, but so far, I'm the only one. I guess I'm a lot to handle.

"Noki, Nikkisi is on the telephone for you. Do you want to speak to her?"

I just shook my head "No," as I was still watching cartoons.

She quickly dismissed Nikkisi, and then returned and began conversation.

"Are you sure you and Nikkisi have the same father?" she asked.

"Yes," I said still watching the television.

"Well, how do you know that to be true?"

"Because my mother told me so."

"Well, in my opinion, someone who committed suicide in front of two small children is hardly a mother."

"She was sad that my father died."

"Do you ever wonder why you don't look like you have a black father?"

"I look like my mother; Nikkisi looks like our father."

"Your mother told you that too?"

"Yes."

"Are you glad that you don't look black?"

"When I was younger I wanted to look more like Nikkisi. But, now—"

"Now, you're happy you don't?"

"Yeah . . . I guess."

"Not yeah, Noki. It's yes. Always be precise and decisive."

"Yes."

"You know you will never meet a rich husband if you keep telling people your father is black."

"I won't?" I questioned.

"Noki, listen to me. I think it would be wise if you told people that we are your biological parents. Because, before the new millennium, I predict that Japan will run this country. Although I am a second generation Japanese American woman, I embrace my culture. We are three times smarter than the average American and more advanced in technology. You will meet a rich, Japanese man who will buy you all the nice things you so love. Now, Nikkisi, unfortunately, will remain in the ghetto with her black compatriots."

"Nikkisi is living in the ghetto?"

"I think so dear. Does that bother you?"

I thought for a moment and realized that I didn't really remember Nikkisi too well. In the beginning, I missed her, but now, after living with my foster parents, and they gave me everything I could ever want, seeing Nikkisi isn't that important. My childhood memories are sad, sporadic visions of always being hungry and never having any money to buy food. I honestly said, "No, it doesn't bother me at all."

"Good. Noki, when I made mention to you that you should tell people that we are your biological parents, how did that make you feel?"

"I'll say it. You guys are really nice to me," I responded wishing she would get out my bedroom so I could finish watching cartoons. Nevertheless, she continued, "Well, I'm so glad you are open for suggestions. It makes me feel good that you heed my advice and value my opinion. But, I would just like to reiterate my suspicion that I don't think the man you call 'father' was that at all."

I turned around briefly, because I didn't understand her concerns about my parents.

"I told you that Nikkisi and I have the same father! Why don't you just shut–up already," I yelled. She had ruined my cartoons. I had lost concentration.

"Well," she said, unfazed with my outburst, "You would think that the daughter of a prostitute would certainly be a little wary with claiming men as her father. You are wiser than that Noki. Surely, you realized with a mother like yours, anyone walking this earth could have fathered you. And I'll bet my last dollar—it wasn't a black man."

"What did you say?" I stammered.

"Well, dear, I think you heard me quite clearly."

All the color drained from my face. My past fast-forwarded, and I remembered the different men coming in and out, Nikkisi always peering through the peephole, and how sad my mother always was when her men friends would leave.

"How do you know this to be true?" I asked.

"Why, the adoption agency told us. They were concerned that you may need some additional counseling."

"I don't believe you."

"Why would I make that up?"

"Do you think I'm supposed to believe everything I fucking hear?" I bellowed. I was so embarrassed and angry with Nikkisi. I'm sure she knew, and she never once uttered a word about our whorish mother. Sporadic images started to filter through my mind. I remembered all the men that would come and go. The strange noises coming from out of my mother's bedroom. How we never had any money until *after* "Mr. John" left. Like, how humiliating is this information?

"Don't raise your voice at me, dear. Now, cut off the cartoons, go, and wash your hands for dinner. It will be served shortly."

I calmed down quickly because I was hungry. Lucky for me, I thought quickly. My mind rapidly moved from thought to thought. When I was little, the doctors thought

I had Attention Deficient Disorder. As I got older, it was ruled out.

"Mother, do you think I can go to Jane Whitman's house tomorrow. She's invited a couple of school friends over."

"Will boys be there?"

"Um-m-m . . . I don't . . . well no. No boys. Just a few girls," I lied.

"Noki, I don't want you there. She's a bad influence. I know what goes on over her house. Kissing and touching and messing around with boys. I told you we have to marry you off a virgin."

Inwardly, I laughed because I'd already given up my virginity in the bleachers at school to a black boy from a prominent family in the neighborhood. I didn't dare mention this fact.

Since I was still upset because I couldn't have my way, I said, "I can never do anything around here! I'm a prisoner in my own home. I hate you!" I screamed and ran in the bathroom and locked the door. I was good at melodrama.

Soon, she slightly tapped on the door and said, "Don't be upset dear. Tomorrow we will go shopping at Neiman Marcus. I'll buy you that great new outfit we saw in Teen Vogue. Would you like that?"

Wow! That outfit cost $500! It was a very elegant skirt and blazer. When I go back to school with that outfit on, everyone will be jealous!

I slowly came out of the bathroom, gave my mother a big kiss on her cheek, and told her that I'd join them for dinner in a moment. Once she was gone, I went into her bedroom and located her Louis Vuitton pocketbook.

Then, peering over my shoulder to be sure no one was around, I pulled out her wallet and took three $20 bills and stuffed them in my bra. My palms were sweating and my heart was palpitating fast, but I loved the adrenaline rush thievery gave me.

Next, I happily skipped downstairs to dinner only to be disappointed.

"What's this?" I asked. The housekeeper had prepared oshi sushi, mitsuba, and azuki bean salad.

"It is dinner Noki," Chin, my foster father said.

"Raw fish and steamed vegetables are what you and Lucy eat. That's not dinner for me. I want steak and French fries, chocolate cake, and a milkshake. Tell our maid to get her ass back in here and make me something to eat!" I bellowed.

"Noki, we've decided to put you on a diet. You're a little too plump for a girl your age . . .," my mother's voice trailed off.

"I'm almost twelve. This is baby-fat!" I challenged. They both just put their heads down and that meant the discussion was over. I picked up my glass of tea and slammed it into their china white colored walls and the glass pieces scattered everywhere.

"Noki, stop this violent behavior now," my stepfather said.

"I hate you! I hate you! You're not my *real* parents. I want my *real* parents," I yelled.

After my temper tantrum, I ran upstairs and locked myself in my room.

Soon, Tomoko, our housekeeper came up with a cheeseburger and French fries for me, plus the chocolate cake I'd requested. My outbursts, which I indulged in moderation, were the quickest way to get my way. I had my foster parents wrapped around my little fingers.

SEVEN

KAPRI HENDERSON

UPSTATE CORRECTIONAL FACILITY 1992

I don't know if a bitch could say that she could ever get comfy behind bars. I had been locked down for a while and that nigga Knowledge didn't come check a bitch once.

The whole time I kept true to the motto, "ride or die fo my nigga."

Five-0 kept wantin' me to snitch on his *bitch-ass*, but I couldn't go out like that. I thought that nigga would love me for life, wanna marry me in jail, the whole nine yards. Everythin' they ask a bitch to do for them when they locked down.

Once I was sentenced, all his bullshit lies came to a halt. It hurt my heart 'cause if this was his situation, I woulda held him down.

Now my kid, Kareem's in some foster home. I'm locked down. And Knowledge is wit the next bitch. Talk about a ghetto soap opera.

I had just come from the shower and had washed my hair. I was about to go and make Keisha braid it for me in corn-rolls. Maybe add some beads. I have a reputation to keep up wit. These bitches keep tellin' me how cute and fly I am. I have shoulder length hair, brown skin, a pug-shaped nose, and full lips. My best asset is my ass.

It big and round! Niggas go crazy over my shape. I came through and showed everybody love.

"Whadup?"

"Whadup yo," everyone greeted. I was the big cheese in my cellblock. I had to fight many bitches to get my respect. Quickly I learned to spit a shank out my mouth and bust a bitch down. Gave one dike, a tough actin' bitch, a "buck fifty." That was one hundred and fifty stitches in her face. Dat's how I get down. After that I had bitches cleanin' my sneakers wit their toothbrushes, givin' me their commissary money and makin' me grilled-cheese sandwiches on the radiator.

I'm not tryin' to act like shit is sweet, but I make the best outta my situation.

Everyone was readin' mail, playin' cards and gossipin' in the recreation room.

"Yo, Keisha, could you braid my hair for me?" I asked. "Make it look fly."

Keisha looked shook-up. She was new here and terrified of everyone. I had already made it known to everyone that she was off limits.

"Sure. I'll hook it up," she replied.

"No doubt. Good lookin' yo, let's go back to my cell" I said wit a smile.

"Well I can do it right here," she said.

"Naw, let's go back to my cell. There's too many mutherfuckers out here who ain't wash their funky asses, smellin' like spoiled fish," I joked.

"Fuck-you Kapone," Trina said. They called me Kapone instead of Kapri because I had shit on lock just like Al

Capone, the infamous mobster. "I already did dat," I said and flickered my tongue in and out rapidly. Everyone burst out into laughter. I mean, it's not like I'm gay or anythin'. But in jail, you gotta do what you gotta do. I know niggas who did five years or more upstate and said they ain't ever ran up in a nigga, or let a nigga give them head. Or played with a nigga's bootie hole. Pa-leeze. Those mutherfuckers are lyin'. After you adjust, it's time to get your freak on.

I looked at Keisha, who was standin' in front a me. She was dark- skinned with big, pink lips. Nice body, sweet ass. She wore her hair in a tight ponytail every day. She never switched up and tried a different hairstyle. Just kept it simple. I liked that about her. It was all her hair too.

Keisha followed me back inside my cell and I sat in between her legs and let her hook my hair up. The whole time she was yappin' her mouth about her life outside of jail, her boyfriend and her two babies. I'd say, "Word," every now and then, but truthfully, I didn't really give a fuck.

Once she was done, I turned around and said, "Eat my pussy."

Startled, she stared directly in my eyes and tried to smile faintly. Then said, "I'm not a lesbian Kapri. I'm sorry if you thought that. But, I love my man."

"Bitch, eat my mutherfuckin' pussy before I make it so you don't ever see that mutherfuckin' man of yours. You silly, dumb bitch. You think I'm a fuckin' lesbian?"

She didn't answer me. She just began cryin'.

"Shut the fuck up," I screamed on her but she kept actin' stupid. When she saw me reach for my shank, she slowly backed away. She was cryin' so fuckin' hard she got the hiccups and her nose was runnin' all over the place.

"SHUT-UP!" I yelled so loud I thought the guards would come bustin' in. But I had Trina lookin' out for the guards, so I knew we wouldn't git caught.

I pulled my Khaki pants down to my knees and laid back on the bottom bunk. Then I motioned her to come over. She took baby steps over to me, and I then reached up and pulled her forcefully down. Then I put the cover over her head. She started doin' a real fucked-up job. She stuck out her tongue and took short, quick licks. Then I punched her in her mutherfuckin' head and she put a lil' effort in it. She began to suck my clit a little, and then she stuck her tongue in my pussy.

"Not your tongue bitch! Stick your finger inside my pussy until I get wet and then suck my juices up," I coached.

All I kept thinkin' was, if she sucked her man dick as poorly as she ate pussy, her man wasn't missin' shit while she was locked down.

Soon, I dismissed the crybaby and began writin' Knowledge. I never mailed these letters 'cause I didn't have an address to his new crib, but writin' 'em made me feel like I had someone on the outside that cared about me.

EIGHT

IVANKA ZAMORA 1992

It was a hot and muggy afternoon in July and I had just arrived at my psychiatrist's office. It was as hot as I imagined hell would be as I stepped outside of our air-conditioned Lincoln Town limousine.

My appointments were consistently scheduled every Thursday for an hour. Compliments of my mother. The wicked *bitch* of the South.

The only enjoyable thing about this psycho bullshit is that I get to pop pills legally. My shrink writes out a prescription for Prozac, giving me a six-month supply twice a year. That, mixed with the marijuana, alcohol and other illegal drugs I take, makes a girl high all the time.

His plush office, decorated with the proceeds he received from dumb parents like my mom, was quite impressive. He had oversized leather sofas, imported end tables, and authentic Picasso paintings. All this for an alleged wise-ass who can't even get into my little brain, the brain of a minor.

As I walked into his office, Mr. Cohen, my psychiatrist, stared at me in shock. Now how unprofessional is that? After seeing me for years, with multi-colored hair, purple lipstick, numerous body piercings, and grunge clothing, why would seeing me with my head and eyebrows completely shaved, take him off guard? Shouldn't he have an inkling that I'm a multifaceted person?

After his initial reaction, he greeted me. "Ivanka, please have a seat.

How was your week?" he asked clicking on his tape recorder.

"It sucked," I announced.

"It sucked. How so?"

"My mother wouldn't allow me to go to the Psycho rock concert."

"How did that make you feel not being able to go?"

"I went to the concert, just without permission. I love disobeying the old crow. But, truthfully, it was my father's displeasure with me that annoyed me."

"So you hold your father in higher regard than your mother?"

"I adore my father. I'll never hurt him. But, my mother . . ." my voice trailed off purposely. I could see I had him going.

"Do you ever imagine yourself hurting your mother?"

"Yes, sir."

"Could you describe for me what your method would be?"

I pushed forward in my seat, looked him straight in the eyes, and began my story. "Sometimes I dream about waking just before dawn and creeping into her bedroom. She and my father have separate sleeping quarters, so he won't have to witness her murder. Mother will be breathing heavily through her nostrils, a sound that infuriates me, as I take the newly sharpened butcher knife with its shiny blade and bring it to her wrinkled throat. Just as I'm about to drag the knife over her throat, she will awaken. Her gray, filmy eyes will dart to the knife and then back at me, and her weak heart will give out on her from fear. She will hold her chest while gasping for air, mouthing the words, 'Help!' Just before she dies of a heart attack, I will slit her throat. Gobs of blood will ooze out onto her Presti designer silk sheets. We will make eye contact one last time, and she will try to speak. Maybe ask me 'Why?' Her words will be incoherent as she gurgles them in her own blood. I will then walk over and kiss her cheek, leaving my signature, purple lipstick printed on her face. She will die with a look of shock plastered on her face."

Doctor Cohen looked perplexed after listening to my remarkably graphic murder fantasy.

"How often do you think about murdering your mother?"

"Well, let's just say it's on a consistent basis. Specifics aren't really necessary now are they?"

"Well, could you tell me precisely when these fantasies began? Was it after you killed her dog or before?"

"So, you think that I was practicing on the dog? Maybe getting up the courage?"

"Is that what you were doing?" he asked as he adjusted his eyeglasses on his nose. He was leaning far back in his spiraling leather chair with his legs crossed effeminately.

"I killed the dog because I wanted it to die at that very moment. Real murderers don't need practice. They have instinct."

"So, you consider yourself a murderer?"

"Don't you? Consider me a murderer? Isn't that why I'm here?"

"Well, killing a dog and killing a human are quite different situations."

"I'm still an amateur. Is that what you're telling me?"

"Don't misinterpret my response. If your mother had reported the incident, you may very well have gotten in a lot of trouble young lady."

"I don't live off of maybes. But don't fret doc, I'm planning to up-step my game."

"To kill a person?"

"All talk and no play makes Ivanka a very boring adolescent."

"So you plan, or rather have thoughts about killing your mother? Do I understand you correctly?"

"Actually Doc, I've been planning on killing you!" I said. My voice was unwavering as I stared directly into his pathetic eyes.

"And how would you plan on doing that. You can't come into my bedroom and slit my throat. An intelligent young lady like yourself should know that."

"Your murder is going to be different. Have you ever heard of 'thrill kill?'" I said, but without waiting for him to answer, I continued, "Your murder would be a thrill kill for me. I would waltz in here for my usual Thursday appointment. Sit down and talk for a while. Then as I'm leaving, I'll pull out my personal ice–pick, newly sharpened, and jab you in your pathetic guts. Just as you're about to cry out for help, I'll jab you again. This time in your jugular. Blood will squirt everywhere from the numerous pricks I will inflict upon your person. Your hands will immediately go up to your neck to stop the flow of blood. There, your hands will sustain defensive wounds as you try to shield me from inflicting further injury to you. Soon, as your body loses too much blood, your knees will get weak. You will collapse on your imported Italian rug and die. I will walk over to you, bend down, and plant a fat, wet, kiss on your cheek leaving behind my signature purple lipstick. Then, I will walk out of here unfazed, after taking a shower in your personal bathroom."

Doctor Cohen, after turning stark white, looked at his watch and concluded our meeting.

"Ivanka, I'm going to up your dosage in your prescription from 50 milligrams to 200 milligrams, which is the maximum dosage. This session is concluded. Thank you."

NINE

NIKKI LING

My sister and I moved to a small kitchenette apartment on Jefferson Avenue in Bedford-Stuyvesant, Brooklyn. The rent was $300 dollars a month. The apartment's living room was medium-sized. There was one closet and a small bathroom off to the right and the kitchen was to my left. I had purchased my sofabed from a bargain furniture store, and the mattress was thin and lumpy. Noki and I slept together, and every night she complained. So I had decided to sleep on the floor until one night I felt something run across my arm. I jumped up, screaming hysterically when I saw a large rat running into our closet. The next day I inspected the apartment and found a large hole in the wall. It appeared that the landlord had plugged the hole with a steel-wool pad, but eventually the rat ate through the barrier and came in. It ate through our bread, cereal, and any groceries that we had out. After that incident, I had to crawl back into bed with Noki who was furious.

Since I was only fifteen years old, I didn't have a work permit to get a *real* job, so I had to make money the only way I knew how, and Noki didn't approve. Actually, Noki didn't approve at all of the way I was handling our lives.

Realistically, she had a right to be angry. I'd called her for two consecutive months, begging her to run away and come live with me in Brooklyn. I promised her that I'd take care of her and told her we shouldn't be separated. She'd always deny my request. She always seemed standoffish and aloof when I called, which hurt me deeply. I remembered her as being so sweet and sensitive when we were little. Sadly almost every day of my life, I longed for the past.

Then one day I called, and she told me that she wanted to come and live with me. I was astonished. Just like that, she had changed her mind. She hopped on the Long Island Railroad and I met her at Atlantic Avenue station in Brooklyn.

When she arrived, I thought she would be glad to see me, instead, all she did was complain. She made me feel like I'd taken her from a life of opulence to live in what she called the "ghetto" with me. I made Noki a promise on that very day that I'd make a way to earn more money to give her the life she so deserved.

When I asked her what had changed to make her want to come and live with me, she'd never respond. I had an inkling that something happened at her foster parents' home, but Noki wasn't revealing any secrets.

It was early afternoon and I had to go food shopping. Noki wrote out a long list of things she wanted me to get. Most of the list consisted of junk food. At first I wanted to protest because I didn't think her weight was healthy. Noki was 4' 8" and weighed 125 pounds. But then I decided that we've had very few things that gave us pleasure in our lives, so I couldn't bring myself to deny her.

Quickly, I walked up Nostrand Avenue towards my apartment because I had spent my last $50 and needed to make some money. As the heavy bags pulled at my weak limbs, I ignored the hecklers—none of whom ever asked to help me with my groceries as they pleaded for my telephone number.

As I walked, I concentrated on my next move. Lately, I had been going to the city and jostling people for extra money. Taking people's wallets had actually happened without premeditation.

I was in a supermarket trying to steal something to eat because I was broke when I saw this woman take out her wallet and count at least $100. Something inside me said I needed that money. I followed her around for about twenty minutes before I seized my opportunity. She had become occupied reading the back of a cake box, and I quietly walked up behind her and gently slipped my hand into her pocketbook and slid her wallet out.

My heart was racing as I walked rapidly from the scene of my crime.

I remember being elated that I had enough money to buy some food and save a little cash for bills I expected in the near future. Then, I became sad because I had stolen from a person. A human being. Someone who earned that money. What if some tragic event would befall her because I had taken her money? Somehow, I felt that my actions were going to haunt me for the rest of my life.

"Noki, I'm home," I said as I opened the door just in time to see Noki and some boy butt–naked on the sofa.

"Noki, n-o-o-o-o," I screamed. I was appalled to see my baby sister being used and manipulated by some boy.

"What are you doing to her?" I accused, but before he could respond, Noki said, "We're having sex! What does it look like?"

"How old are you?" I asked the boy, ignoring Noki's smart mouth.

"Who me? I'm sixteen," he responded, trying to get dressed.

"Noki, did he force you to have sex with him?" I asked, ready to call the police.

"Ha! I've been having sex for months," she gloated.

"But, you're just a baby," I said as large tears streamed down my cheeks. Somewhere, amidst all this dysfunction, Noki had lost her sense of self. She was better than this. She was better than me. She was better than our mom. I so desperately didn't want Noki embracing the same fate that had befallen my mother and me.

"Mentally, I'm twice my age! I'm tired of you treating me like I'm a baby. I'm practically taking care of myself around here. You're never home. I can do whatever I want."

Noki was still butt–naked as she preached and it was painstakingly obvious she wasn't shy about nudity. Her long, silky, black hair, just barely covered her small breast. Her cherubic face conveyed a childlike innocence while her round, plump, overweight figure was that of a woman.

"Noki, what are you doing when I'm not here?" I said. "Don't answer that. Just get dressed. We will discuss this later. Please tell your friend to leave and to never return to my house again or I will have him arrested."

"How would you like it if somebody arrested you for being a prostitute?

Huh…how would you like that!" she spat.

"Yo, you a ho? Word. Wait until I tell my mans and them," the boy replied.

"Tell them! Tell them she's a prostitute," Noki retorted and then burst out into wicked laughter.

"Shut your fat mouth!" I yelled at Noki.

"Baishunfu!" she said, taunting me by saying I was a prostitute in Japanese.

"Shizuka ni!" I screamed telling her to shut-up.

"Nai!"

Out of frustration, I turned around and left the apartment before I slapped Noki silent. Her smart mouth was going to make me seriously hurt her one day.

TEN

NIKKI LING

After the sex incident with Noki, I realized that maybe I didn't know my baby sister as well as I thought. This really made me feel down. I was caught in a difficult situation. I needed to go out and make money, but I was afraid to leave Noki alone. I didn't want my sister getting pregnant and having babies. I tried to make her promise me she'd stop sleeping with boys, but she flat out refused. There was nothing I could do.

One morning after Noki left for school, I made the decision to call her foster parents. I started thinking that I may be a bad influence on Noki and that she may be better off back with her foster parents. Her stepmother picked up on the third ring.

"Kon'nichi wa," she said.

"Good afternoon Ms. Tanaka. This is Nikkisi."

"Nikkisi, I would really appreciate it if you didn't call my home," she said coldly.

"I know you're probably mad that I made Noki run away but that's why I'm calling. I'm thinking about sending her back."

"Back? Noki isn't welcome in my home. She's a disgrace to our culture." Her voice was filled with pain. Noki had done something terribly wrong.

"Mrs. Tanaka, what has Noki done that's so bad. Can't you forgive her?"

"Kesshite!" she screamed, finally losing her dignified composure.

"Your sister is nothing but a little whore," she continued, "I caught her in bed with my husband. I guess the apple doesn't fall far from the tree . . .,"

Mrs. Tanaka's statement about my mother had astonished me. Was there a sign etched in our foreheads that our mother was a prostitute? I wondered if she had said this to Noki.

"Mrs. Tanaka please don't hate Noki. I'm sorry that she did something bad but she doesn't know any better. It makes me sad knowing how painful Noki's betrayal must feel. I hope you can find it in your heart to forgive her. And I just want to say that I wish I could have met you." I meant this honestly.

"You and your sister are like apples and oranges. I'll be the first to admit I may have chosen the wrong child."

Mrs. Tanaka went on to say other mean things about Noki. I listened intently and apologized for Noki's indiscretions. After we hung up, I realized that Noki was my responsibility, and I intended on giving her a better upbringing. Just as I was getting ready for work, Noki came in.

"Where are you going?" Noki inquired.

"I have to go out and make some money. You need things for school and we have to pay bills."

"You're going out prostituting?" she asked.

"Well, it's a little too early in the day for that now, isn't it?" I sharply replied. She knew I was going to jostle, not to walk the beat. My clothes were evidence of that. I had on jeans and sneakers. Very nondescript. She just wanted to belittle me, which had become a daily exercise for her lately.

"How can you stand to look in the mirror?" she badgered.

"If you really want to know, I hate looking in the mirror. I hate that I have to do this. I hate that our parents are dead. And among all this hate the only thing I love is you," I said as tears streamed down my cheeks.

"You don't love me, you love that money!" she spat.

"Why are you so mean to me? You constantly hurt my feelings. I don't do this for me. I do it for US!"

"I can take care of myself. Why don't you let me come with you?" she asked.

"Now how stupid is that suggestion? What I do could get me locked up in jail. Do you think I want that life for you? I want you to have better than I have."

"Stop speaking as if I'm the only adolescent in the room. You're only a few years older than me. I know what you do is dangerous and I think I could be of some help."

"I said no!" I said and stormed out of the house.

I hopped in a taxicab and asked to be dropped off on Pitkin Avenue in Brooklyn. It was a little shopping area for bargains where my foster mother would take us. This is where I'd get my steady flow of cash.

I'd been out there for around two hours, just trying to spot my mark, when a middle-aged man took out his wallet to get change for the telephone. When he did that, I spotted his money.

While he was on the telephone, I came up quickly behind him, took my two fingers, and just barely caught the end of his wallet in his back pocket. I'd never jostled a man before, so he was a challenge. His jeans were tight and his wallet was heavy. Just as the wallet eased out of his pocket, I lost my grip and blundered. This alerted the man and he quickly spun around, feeling his back pocket for his wallet. When he didn't feel it, he grabbed me by my wrist and twisted it.

"Police," he called. My heart was palpitating quickly, and I knew I had to think fast.

"You little thief," he yelled. Then continued, "I should beat ya ass!"

Just then, I decided that I should give him his wallet and beg to be let go. Before I made that choice, Noki came from out of nowhere, walked right past me, and scooped up the wallet. She left undetected into thin air.

When the police got there, I was ultimately let go. Of course, I played innocent—the wallet was never found—and there were no witnesses.

I ran home and as soon as I walked in, Noki already had the money divided. She decided she deserved *half* for her role in today's event.

ELEVEN

NIKKI LING

FALL 1998

A kiss on the hand feels very good, but a diamond tiara last forever," Marilyn Monroe said. I was listening to an old movie on television as I was getting dressed for my date. I had a fixation on Marilyn because I understood her plight, and admired how she had men in the palm of her hand, yet she wasn't happy. She was the epitome of sexiness, shyness, strength, and vulnerability all encapsulated into one being. She and I had lots in common, I thought.

My date arrived promptly at 9:00 p.m. I exhaled as I approached the door. I decided to take one last look in the mirror–although I didn't doubt I'd achieved perfection. My silky–straight long hair was dangling provocatively by my ass and my dark–chocolate skin was glowing. The dress I'd chosen to wear for the evening was long and elegant. I had found it in the Tahari section at Saks just hours earlier. It cost nearly $2,000. My heels were the latest black and gold Jimmy Choo, and the only make-up I wore was a peach-colored lip-gloss and a little blush on my high cheekbones.

"Hello, Salvatore. Please come in," I graciously said and guided him into my apartment.

His walk was the walk of a self-confident man. His steps were heavy. He was unusually attractive with his dark olive skin and broad shoulders. My dates were never eye candy. They were usually old, fat, and lonely with insatiable, kinky sexual appetites.

"You look simply, simply, stunning," he complimented as he took off his topcoat.

Ignoring his flattering remark, I said, "What do you want?"

He looked directly in my eyes and said, "Everything."

"Well, I do everything *except* swallow. Is that acceptable?"

"But you will at least take it won't you?" he asked nervously.

"That's extra."

"I'm sure you know money is no object," he boasted.

"Good. $10,000 up front for one ejaculation or an hour maximum– whichever comes first."

"I thought the cost was $5,000?"

"Listen, dude, I'm not in the bargaining business. I take my work very seriously. As I just explained, jerking off in my mouth is extra."

"An extra $5,000?" he asked in disbelief.

"Precisely," I stated, not wavering in my numbers.

"I see you're just as business savvy as you're gorgeous. But your technique is what matters the most. You better be worth it!" he spat. A dark cloud had seemingly come over him, and it gave me goosebumps on the back of my neck. I hoped he wasn't going to be trouble.

Salvatore was a new client for me, recommended by one of my regulars. He was in New York on business. Married.

Wealthy. And the governor of Texas.

He opened up his briefcase and counted out $10,000. As I went to get the money, he threw it *all* in my face. As the crisp hundred–dollar bills came cascading to the floor, I thought, "Let the games begin."

Directing him into my bedroom, I quickly prayed this wouldn't take long.

I actually had two master bedrooms in my over-priced Upper East Side apartment. One I *entertained* in, the other, I slept in.

Once inside, he got aggressive. "Strip!" he commanded.

"Whatever you say big–daddy," I whispered in a baby like voice.

"Shut-up! Your voice is irritating you sluttish bitch," he badgered.

Silently, I quickly pulled off my dress and lingerie— but left my heels on. I stood back and waited for him to give me another commandment. I realized he was controlling and didn't come here for dim lights and romance.

"Squat down and open your mouth," he ordered.

I seductively went down to my knees and opened my mouth as he suggested. I sat poised in this position as he pulled out his penis and began to urinate in my mouth. I nearly choked, because foolishly, I assumed he wanted a blow job. Once, I got my composure back, it was in vain because he decided to get juvenile and make circular motions with his penis. Therefore, I got urine in my eyes, hair, and dripping down my body.

I was a professional first, livid, second.

After he was all peed out, he let out a rambunctious roar. I stood up and wiped his urine from my eyes with a silk handkerchief, and I remained silent. Depending on my client, I'm prepared for most anything kinky. But it's usually my celebrity clients that like to give golden showers. This one took me by surprise because men in positions of authority like a governor or senator usually like to be dominated in the bedroom. Foolishly, I assumed he would have opted to be tied up and spanked. My political clients are almost always submissive.

After loosening up, the governor decided to take off his suit jacket and loosen his tie. Then, he was ready for more action.

"Suck my big dick!" he leered.

As I squatted back down in my five inch-heels, I simultaneously reached up to grab hold of his dick. For a moment, I couldn't find it. To my amazement, this six-foot, broad-shouldered, gorgeous guy had the smallest penis I'd ever seen. It was almost microscopic.

Trying to hold my composure to keep from bursting out into laughter, I engulfed his puny penis aggressively. It was almost like sucking my index finger.

Using my expertise, I licked and sucked his dick until I had him moaning in ecstasy. I had the vein bulging and his legs trembling within minutes. He was holding my head tight, pumping his ass in and out with a mechanical movement.

It was eerily quiet, except for a few grunts and moans that escaped his mouth. The silence was fucking with me. It allowed me to concentrate on what I was doing.

With great relief, I brought him to a climax and he screamed, "Ahhhhh," like he'd just been shot. I let his hot juices enter my mouth, and when I was sure there was nothing left, I discretely went to the trash can and spit out his semen.

I stood before him, completely naked and said, "Thank-you Salvatore. I hope to see you again. You can see your way out." In twelve minutes, I had made $10,000.

As I was on my way to my bathroom to clean up, I noticed Salvatore hadn't left. I turned around only to be startled that he was less than an inch from my face.

"You find something funny?" he questioned.

"I wasn't laughing," I stated.

"You're a lousy liar, just like you're a lousy lay!"

He was very intimidating as his eyes hooded over and his lips were pursed so tightly together they formed a straight line.

I tried not to show fear, but I was visibly trembling. I'd never had a problem with an appointment since I became a high-priced call-girl. When I was prostituting and walking the streets, I'd be slapped around every now and then. Since I moved to the Upper East Side and only dealt with elite, recommended clients, everything usually went well.

"Well, give me a call sometime tomorrow and we'll set–up another appointment. Maybe next time we can be a little more creative. I have many things I would like to do to you. Play around a little..." I said, letting my voice trail off.

"Really? Can you *play* dead?"

That was the last thing he'd said before his fist smashed into my high cheekbone.

TWELVE

NOKI LING

1998

*C*hanel. *One of the most prolific designers of our time,"* I thought as I stood outside the enormous glass window. It was a cold day in October and the air was moist and brisk. I had on my full-length Fendi mink coat that swept the ground as I walked. Prada stilettos adorned my feet. I had to look the part. The part of someone who could *afford* absolutely anything inside of there.

As I strolled inside, a uniformed doorman held the door. I smiled warmly. The store was small and quaint. On the first floor, Chanel pocketbooks graced the shelves. The leather *smelled* like I couldn't afford it.

"Hi, my name's Samantha. May I help you?" a friendly saleswoman asked.

"Nai . . . excuse me . . .No. Lit-tle En-glish. I no need help. I will summon you later," I said with a think Japanese accent. I then smiled, did a customary bow, and walked away. Then Samantha left me alone so I could browse the store.

Immediately, I spotted the most gorgeous, dreamy, black and white Chanel pocketbook. I had to have it! I eased into the section and picked it up. The price read $1900. To my surprise, I also noticed that the pocketbook didn't have a sensomatic alarm on it. As I studied the bag, there was an equally gorgeous blue and gold colored pocketbook with a gold strap chain. Unfortunately, this bag had a sensomatic alarm on it. Usually I would not have flirted with the danger of snapping it off, because it was eerily quiet in the store. But somehow the scenario challenged me and quicker than you can blink an eye, I had removed the sensor without detection. In a brash move, I quickly grabbed both pocketbooks, lifted up my skirt, and shoved the bag inside my girdle. I was wearing a girdle underneath my skirt and around my thighs leaving room for merchandise to be stored. Since the material in the girdle is tight spandex, once the merchandise is forced inside, it conceals it nicely. That coupled with the thick mink coat, all usually went well. The only downside is that you walk a little awkwardly. But an experienced thief, as I claim to be, can walk and play the part of an upstanding citizen.

I guess I lingered in the section too long because Samantha and I made eye contact. She smiled and decided to come over. I could tell she was a little perplexed as she looked at the missing spaces that once held the handbags. Just as things were about to get uncomfortable, a petite, blond came over and intervened. She held two handbags and thrust them at the saleswoman.

"Samantha, I'll take these. Charge them to my father's account," she said.

"Oh. Okay. Where—"

"I took these from over there," she lied and pointed to the empty spaces.

"Oh," she smiled with a gesture of relief. "I'll go and ring these up right away."

"You do that," the petite, white lady snapped. Her attitude had changed quickly. Once we were alone, her piercing gray eyes studied me. I didn't have a clue what she wanted or why she'd came to my assistance.

Why had she helped me?

"I saw what you did," she whispered.

"Me speak lit-tle En-glish," I stated.

"Oh blow me, bitch! I want half of whatever you got in there," she threatened.

"What makes you think I'm going to give you one of these pocketbooks?" I protested.

"Because I just saved your ass!"

"I still have to walk out the front door," I reasoned.

"So, I'll walk out with you."

"Why would you do that? It doesn't make sense. If you can afford to purchase these bags why would you steal them?"

"I can't afford anything. This is my father's money. Besides, my life has never made any sense. It's all about the thrill."

"If you want a thrill, then you shove a bag down *your* skirt. Otherwise, don't ride me. I'll put a thank-you card in the mail," I stated and tried to walk away when she grabbed my arm.

"Listen you selfish, fat umpa lumpa! You have about ten seconds before Samantha prances her ass back over here and I blow the whistle on you. So either I'm down or you go down! The choice is yours."

I know I should have been grateful that this stranger helped me but I detested sharing.

"Oh, all right. Once we get outside I'll give you a handbag," I said reluctantly giving in.

Samantha walked back over with a Chanel shopping bag with the two items for the mysterious stranger, and just as she promised, we walked out of Chanel together like old friends. My heart was racing as we passed by the doorman who was standing next to a security guard. I was sure I was going down. If the white lady had any anxieties, her facial expression didn't reveal them.

"Good night ladies," the doorman said.

"Good night," we both replied in unison.

Once outside and safely away from the store, I walked with the stranger a few yards to where she had a chauffeur driven limousine awaiting her. I was impressed. I unloaded my merchandise and tossed her the blue and gold Chanel pocketbook.

"So where to now?" she inquired.

"What do you mean?"

"Are we going to more stores to steal more items?" she said.

"You've got to be joking?"

"I lie but I don't joke," she replied coldly. I was immediately fond of her.

"So, what's your name?" I asked.

"What do you want it to be . . .?" she said as she tapped on the window to cue her driver, and we drove off down 5th Avenue.

THIRTEEN

NIKKI LING

"**K**ayla . . . can you come over . . . to my apartment now?" I cried into the telephone.

"Omigod, Nikki, are you all right?" she responded.

I was barely audible. My face was pulsating and my head was throbbing. That bastard Salvatore had worked me over something awful! The dude was purely psychotic. He had just flipped out on me, kept inferring that I was laughing at his penis.

"I had a date tonight . . . he just started hitting me . . . I thought he was going to *kill* me. I thought I was dead," I sobbed into the telephone.

"Why do you call these creeps dates? Nikki, I know what you do and I'm not judging you but–"

"Dates, appointments, fucks, Johns–why the hell does that bother you so fucking much? I just told you I got my face beat in and all you can do is correct my lingo. Kayla, I need you right now," I yelled.

"Damn, girl. I'm sorry. I'm jumping in a cab right now. *And*, I'm bringing a knife."

"Shit, I got plenty of knives in the kitchen. Won't do me any good though," I lamented.

"When I get there, come down and pay for the taxicab. I'm dead broke, okay?"

"Sonuvabitch! How do you expect me to come downstairs and let the whole goddamn world see that a trick just beat the shit out of me. I live in an upper-class high-rise, Kayla. Shit like this doesn't go on."

"Okay . . . okay. I'll stop at an ATM and head right on over. Sit tight. I love you."

"I love you too."

Kayla hung up the telephone but not before giving me a headache. She was my best friend and always there when I needed her. She hated what I did, but she understood I had to make a living. I usually called her right before a date came over and again once they left. She always wanted to make sure that nothing drastic had occurred while I was making money. Sort of like a pimp. Only she didn't get any royalties off my indiscretions.

I had met Kayla while I tried a short stint in college. I tried to make an honest woman out of myself, but it just didn't work out. I took to her immediately. The first day of classes she walked in, surveyed the room, then came and sat next to me. Kayla has a Colgate smile that tugged at my heart. She has a short hair cut, extremely light skin, a small button nose and thin lips. She's not gorgeous but she's extremely attractive. She stands 5'2" and has a curvy figure.

Soon, I'd let my guard down and started divulging buried secrets about my past. And much to my amazement, she didn't judge me.

Originally, she thought that I had rich parents paying my tuition and footing the bill for my Upper East Side condominium, but I ultimately told her the truth. Ever since that day, we became almost like sisters.

I dressed my wounds and took a hot bath with Epson salt, to ease the pain in my muscles. It would be almost an hour before Kayla arrived. I was so happy to see her; it almost took the pain away. She came right in because she had a key.

Kayla walked over to me as I sat on my $6,000 Thomasville sofa; she kneeled so she could get a look at my face.

"Geez, Nikki . . . look at your face. He could have killed you," she said. Kayla's eyes welled up with tears and her thin lips quivered. "I don't think I can stomach you doing this any longer. Do you ever want out?" she asked.

"Every day," I said and looked away. "I'm 21, I don't want to do this forever. I want a husband and children. I want to be normal . . . ,"

"You'll have that. Don't worry," Kayla said.

"Kayla, could you ever . . . would you . . . all this money," I stammered.

"No. I don't think I could ever sell my body but I haven't walked in your shoes."

"Thank God for that," I said and burst out into tears suddenly feeling sorry for myself.

"Don't cry Nikki. You have a choice to make. I think it's time to give up this lifestyle! It's too dangerous. I've been having really bad feelings lately," she admitted.

"What do you mean?"

"I'm scared that someone may hurt you."

"Kayla, don't get paranoid. I'm sorry if I got you all worked up right now."

"Why can't you just stop?" she pleaded.

"Kayla, I don't do this because I want to . . . I have to. I can't live off my looks alone. I have bills to pay."

"So get a job," she countered.

"Doing what? My skills are in the bedroom. It's too late for me to go out looking for a normal job or starting some trade school."

"It's never too late."

"I need financial security," I tried to explain. "Don't you think I'd stop in a New York minute if I could? But I can't. I need the money."

"You have money."

"I have money today but what about tomorrow? You know money has a way of evaporating when you have bills to pay and I can't risk that. Have you ever gone weeks without any food? I used to drink glasses of water trying to stop my stomach from growling," I lamented.

Kayla shook her head and looked away.

"Damn," she exclaimed looking at the $10,000 decorating my living room floor. I had never picked it up. I had come a long way since charging $40.

"So this wasn't about money?" she asked.

"Nope. It's like I told you. Dude just flipped out. He kept saying I was laughing at his penis."

"Were you?" she accused.

"Hell no! I mean, I wanted to . . . but, I'm a professional, Kayla.

Look at you, ready to blame this on me."

"Look at your face and the way this apartment is messed up. I'm surprised he didn't take his money on his way out. It looks like at least four grand on the floor."

"Try $10,000."

"Get the fuck outta here!" she exclaimed.

"I don't play," I said jokingly, then continued, "You should have seen me. Dude hit my face and my body started moving like I was doing the Harlem shake. Go Nikki . . . it's ya birthday."

"How can you joke at a time like this?"

"Darling, laughter gets me through my days."

"Are you going to tell Noki?" she asked.

I hated when people asked questions they already knew the answer to. Like why waste my time because you want to hear yourself talk?

"Of course not. You know she doesn't condone this. And I don't want to hear her mouth," I said, now wondering why I had invited her over anyway.

Sensing my angst, she said, "Come on and get in bed. I'm going to fix you something to eat and get a cold compress for your face."

I smiled because I loved how much Kayla loved me.

FOURTEEN

NIKKI LING

Most would have taken this recent physical abuse as a sign to pull down the curtains and close up shop. But not me. I wasn't a quitter. I chose to purchase a mysterious gypsy's veil with a sexy skirt and decided to do a little role-playing for my dates. None of them complained. I would let the Arabian music play while I danced around seductively, shaking my hips, and doing belly rolls just like Shakira, the singer. I was good at reinventing myself, a chameleon-like quality I'd inherited from being a victim of my childhood. When you're the child of a prostitute, every day is make-believe.

Today, I actually slept past noon because it was Sunday—my only day off. I made it a rule to *never* take a date on Sunday for religious reasons, and it seemed like a logical rest day.

On the inside, I was down. On the outside, I looked like shit. That pissed me off because I would have to explain the bruises to Brian. Brian Carter was my exclusive boyfriend who had recently started an urban clothing line, as well as a small record label. We've been dating for five years.

Five years ago we met when I was sixteen years old, and Brian was eighteen. I was an amateur pickpocket, and he was hustling the suckers in Three–Card–Monty. It was love at first sight. The first day I met Brian a crew of guys rode down my block on motorcycles. When he saw me, he stopped and let the others ride ahead. At first I thought he was the new up-and-coming rapper/actor Tupac Shakur. There was a strong resemblance.

He stood 5' 11" and was slightly bowlegged. He had dark chocolate skin, round expressive eyes, a straight nose, juicy pink lips and a strong jaw bone. He asked did I want a ride and I declined his invitation. He could see in my eyes that I was curious, so he persisted. When we got to know each other, I asked him to teach me how to ride. At first he refused. He felt that a girl couldn't handle a powerful motorcycle. Soon I was riding better than Brian and saving money for my own motorcycle. We formed a bond that couldn't be broken by anyone. Brian is the only man who cares about Nikki Ling.

At first, I was ashamed to tell Brian I was prostituting on 42nd Street in Manhattan, but eventually I did.

My pimp at the time had problems keeping his hands to himself, and I'd have black eyes on a regular basis. Brian had thought I was seeing someone else and threatened to break off the relationship if I didn't come clean about the abuse. I kept telling him I had been jumped at school.

"So, you keep letting the same girl whip your ass every week?" he asked.

"I keep telling you Brian, she's really big."

"Nik, you damn near six feet tall! I know there ain't too many bitches out here bigger than you!" he said sarcastically.

"Dude, I'm tall, not big. She's husky like a man. She could probably beat you up too."

"I don't know about all that. I'm comin' up to your school tomorrow and I'm stepping to this girl. She say one smart thing and I'ma jab that bitch!"

Brian's eyes grew very small, and he started biting the corner of his mouth. He did this out of habit whenever he was angry.

Soon the conversation escalated to his getting some neighborhood girls to jump my fictitious classroom bully, and I finally broke down and told him the ugly truth. I started off slowly, "Brian do you love me?"

"Nik, you know how I feel about you."

"You know I've been sixteen for four months now, and I can take care of myself."

"Yeah, for now. But one day I'm going to be rich and I'm going to take care of you. You won't have to jostle anymore."

"I know," I smiled, then continued, "but digging in people's pockets don't always pay my bills. Plus I have Noki to look after."

"Yo, that little girl is a brat. She's selfish and it seems like she hates you. I'd give her ass right back to her foster home. That's why you always broke. Sending her to that fancy ass catholic school . Meanwhile, you going to a public high school in the 'hood."

"Don't talk about my sister, Brian. That's the only family I got!"

"Well, she doesn't see it that way."

At this point, Brian had me frustrated the way he kept dogging Noki. So in a rage I blurted out, "Sonuvabitch! If you would shut your big old mouth up for a minute and let me tell you that I've been prostituting for big bucks, and it's my pimp that keeps giving me black eyes, and I haven't been to school this whole goddamn semester. Now there! No secrets. You know everything."

I suddenly burst into tears, afraid that I had just ended a relationship with the only person that loved me.

"You mean to tell me," he paused for a moment, "That you've been letting some bitch-ass nigga take your money and beat you down!"

"Ya . . . ya . . . yes," I stammered.

"Oh, no, this shit gotz to stop. You gonna take me to his punk–ass right now."

"For what?"

"Because you're quitting today!"

"I can't quit. I need that money."

"That's exactly why you're quitting."

At first, I didn't understand his logic. But soon I did. Or at least I thought I did. So, I said, "So I should quit and you'll take care of me?"

"Nik, I'm still tryin' to do me. You gotta do you for now. You gonna stop workin' for this pimp and work for yourself. If you get into any beef, I'll be there. I got your back."

What Brian said made lots of sense. I was both happy and sad. I was almost hoping he'd be angry that I was prostituting, but not angry enough to leave me. But just enough to want me to quit.

FIFTEEN

NIKKI LING

Reluctantly Brian and I hopped on his motorcycle and I rode us over to my pimp's Upper West Side apartment, but he wasn't there. As soon as we stepped outside, my pimp, Ice, came strolling down the block with one of his two girls draped on each arm. One girl was named Sandy. She was his bottom ho. That means she's been with him the longest. She's white, petite and looks just like Marilyn Monroe. She gets preferential treatment from Ice and has the best apartment. Every time you turn around, Ice is giving her a little extra money to go shopping and buy things she needs. She and I have had several fights. She hates the fact that Ice pays for my sister's catholic school. Even though she knows that I bring in just as much money as she does, she feels that I haven't earned the rewards that she's entitled to.

The second girl's name is Trina. Trina is from Memphis, Tennessee. At thirteen, she ran away from a two-parent home in the suburbs to come to the big city to make it as a model. She claims she stole $50 from her mother's purse and purchased a one-way ticket on Greyhound from Tennessee to New York. Ten minutes after she got off the bus, she met Sandy. Sandy was responsible for recruiting Trina for Ice.

Trina has brown skin, oval eyes and is not tall enough to have aspirations of becoming a model. But her face is pleasant enough. Three years later, Trina is still working for Ice.

As we approached Ice, he had on a pink polyester suit, leopard tie, and pink alligator shoes and his Jeri-curl was dripping with activator.

My pimp was forty, but that didn't scare Brian. Brian approached him and began to threaten, "Yo, pops," Brian began, "You see slim here? She don't work for you no more. And if you ever put your hands on her again, you gonna have problems."

"You jive turkey, who you think you is comin' on my turf talkin' shit about my bitch. I own that ho," he stated.

"Listen, I'm only gonna say this once. Nik isn't down with you no more. So you need to chill out and find someone new."

"Nik? That ho named Peaches. Peaches, you better git ya narrow ass back on the block and make my money b'fo I match ya black eyes with a slit throat. You low-down, dirty, slitherin' snake. Tryin' to crawl to the next pimp without asking me to exit. Now man if you want that ho, that ho gotz to choose you," Ice stated. Then he continued, "Peaches, you done gave this jive-turkey my papeh?" he slurred. He spoke slow and moved his body with every word. He thought he was so cool.

"Look pops, I ain't no pimp and she ain't your ho. This my girl. So if you see her out-don't make no trouble, and you won't get none. You got that?" Brian said aggressively. I was so proud of him standing up to my pimp without showing any fear.

"That's what's this is about. Some little boy caught up

in a ho. Man, you don't know who you messin' with. Hold my jacket," Ice said and passed his overcoat to Sandy.

He pulled out a switchblade and swung the blade at Brian. Brian ducked and the knife cut the air. Ice didn't give up. He swung the knife again and this time the blade sliced Brian in his face. Brian swung back, but Ice was too quick with his blade. He cut Brian on both arms before Brian was able to rebound. Brian punched Ice in the nose, and Ice dropped the blade and fell to both knees. Brian landed a few more punches before Sandy reached in her purse and pulled out a switchblade. Before she could slice Brian, I pulled out my pepper spray and sprayed Sandy in her eyes. She screamed out of pain, dropped her blade, and called me every obscenity in the book of ho vernacular. Trina just stood frozen. She will catch a real ass-whipping tonight for not helping to defend Ice.

I was able to pull Brian off Ice before the police came. As we ran down the block, Ice threatened to cut my throat when he caught up to me, which I never allowed to happen.

SIXTEEN

NIKKI LING

Brian took me on his motorcycle to my little apartment on Jefferson Avenue in Brooklyn.

I told him we probably only had a few hours to pack all my belongings and go. He was a little confused about why I had to move. So, as we packed, I filled him in on my lifestyle.

"A lot of people think they know the politics of being a prostitute from watching movies or catching a quick episode of Starsky and Hutch on TV."

"I mean . . . it's not brain surgery. I beat the guy up . . . you don't have to run."

"Brian, when I first started taking money for sex, I didn't have a pimp. I was smacked around a lot and most times, I wasn't paid. My life was always in danger. Then I ran into Sandy, and she convinced me why a girl always needs someone to watch her back. Ice was like a boyfriend to me . . ."

"A boyfriend?" Brian spat.

"Yes. He paid all the bills and protected me when I needed it. I felt safer. I had always been yearning for someone to take care of me just like my father had done for my mother. So when I was introduced to Ice, it all seemed to make sense."

"Well, you've got that in me. I mean I don't pay your bills . . . but one day I will," Brian softly replied and put his head down.

"Not a boyfriend like I have in you, Brian. I love you. I thought I *needed* Ice. Listen, all of us girls consider each other Wives-in-Law. That means we all share the same man. Ice. Our pimp. We all play different positions. Sandy is Ice's bottom-ho because she's been there the longest. She oversees the girls and brings in a lot of money. Her specialty is robbing tricks. Sandy will go out and walk the street and catch a sucker for anywhere from $5,000 to $10,000. She's never out on the street for more than two hours a night. If you bring in that kind of money, Ice will let you come in a little earlier.

Then there are girls like Trina. Trina likes to walk the street too, but she never catches any tricks for big bucks, or so it seems. So, she's usually out for eight to ten hours. Rain, sleet, snowstorm . . . Ice keeps her out there. Only Ice thinks that Trina doesn't have game, when in fact she's gaming him. She confided in me that she stashes money away regularly. She's saving to move to California. So with every trick, she stashes half of her money. Turning in half your money means more hours walking the street."

"Why does she have to stash? Don't you determine how much money you give the pimp?"

"Not at all. You give your pimp 100% of your earnings."

"What! What the fuck is wrong with you? Please tell me that you are just as smart as Trina and you've been stashing," Brian exploded.

"Brian, calm down," I said as I stuffed more sweaters into a duffel bag. "No, I didn't stash. And yes, I gave Ice all my money. I was too afraid to stash. That could ultimately get your throat slit. These pimps are vicious. But I did do my own hustle that Ice didn't know about. I jostled during the day when I should have been getting my rest. If Ice knew I had that talent, he would have put me to work doing that too. See ... I'm not as brainwashed as you may think I am."

"Lucky you ..." Brian said dryly. "I still can't believe you risk your life every night and don't have control over your money."

"Well, I've got privileges. Ice paid for my apartment here and Noki's catholic school. He gave me money for clothing, food, and toiletries. Most girls have to live together in one of Ice's apartments in the City. That way he can keep an eye on them. It gives him more control. I told him that I needed to keep my sister far away from that lifestyle and he let me. Plus, I was able to work in Midtown, which is safer, in a massage parlor. They call us "Flat-backs." It's like a regular job. Nothing illegal goes on ... except prostitution. No robbing tricks ... no drugs ... nothing. My life isn't in danger like it was when I was walking the street. The cops do random shakedowns all the time. And when they roll in, we'd better just be giving a massage."

"So if there are so many rules and regulations, why can't you just quit? Leave. Why do you have to run?"

"There's no out."

"Nik, you're nothing but a melodramatic brat," he stated.

"I'm not being dramatic. You can't just leave Brian. If a girl wants to leave, she has to leave with nothing. You can't pack up because there will be someone in the house that will stop you. Then your pimp will come and beat you close to death. I'm lucky because I was able to keep this apartment. So I can at least take most of my things. But

we had better do it quickly because Ice will be here shortly
. . . with some of his hoodlum friends. They will have guns
. . ." I said. The thought sent chills down my spine, and I
started packing quicker. Brian did too.

I went to the top of my closet and pulled out my stash.
It was close to $1000. Brian and I only brought what we
could carry and had to leave behind the rest. He took me
to Noki's school where I told her we were moving. Brian
helped us into a cab, but I didn't have a clue as to where
we were going.

The night that Brian was cut was the last time I'd ever
work for Ice, or any other pimp for that matter. I officially
went into business for myself.

SEVENTEEN

NIKKI LING

I'm still in the same business but ready to settle down. The only thing is that Brian isn't ready yet. He said he's on a "paper chase" and doesn't want to be distracted by a wife. His two companies have flourished nicely, so that's where his commitment is at the moment. So, I've been waiting on my man to make even more millions, enough to satisfy him, so in turn, he will marry me.

My telephone rang and interrupted my thoughts. I glanced down at the clock and assumed it was Brian calling after his usual workout at the gym.

"This me—this you?" I seductively whispered into the telephone. I always answered my telephone like that.

"Nikki, darling, I need to make an appointment," Jack said. Jack is a South African diplomat who has been a steady customer for three years. He has millions and is very sweet.

"Okay, Jack, hold on a moment while I get my day planner. What day do you have in mind?"

"Tonight."

"Jack, you know I don't work on Sundays."

"Yes, I understand that, but please make an exception. I need you . . ."

"And I need a day off. I'm sorry Jack, but rules are rules."

"I'll pay you double," he stated.

"Look, dude, I'm not in the bargaining business. I take my work very seriously. Rules are made to be enforced. So, as I said, tonight's a no–go."

"Okay, darling, tomorrow night, same time," he said and then hung up without letting me confirm that I had an opening. Lucky for him, I did.

After having a relaxing night, I decided to take my morning jog over to my sister's house.

The weather was great, so I told myself that I would come back, get my motorcycle and head over to Linden Boulevard in Brooklyn and take part in some of the motorcycle sports that are held every Sunday. Usually, everyone met up in McDonald's parking lot and did a few shows before the cops came and chased us away. I rode with three other girls. Our skills surpassed most of the men. They nicknamed us "Lady Night Riders."

Riding on Linden Boulevard was a bitter-sweet pleasure. I enjoyed the ride but hated going back to the old neighborhood. My past was so painful . . .

My sister had a great apartment that I was paying for in Soho. It was a little distance from her prestigious college, Barnard, and the atmosphere was diverse and safe. Noki was so brilliant that at 17 she was already in college. I was so proud of her.

Once I got there, I rang the bell and was buzzed in. I jogged up two flights and then walked in. She was walking around in stilettos, her silk kimono, bra, and panties as usual. A person couldn't convince Noki that she wasn't sexy. Her jet-black hair was pulled back in a tight ponytail and her olive skin was glowing. From the neck up she looked beautiful. From below the neck her weight was unhealthy. She had wide hips and huge thighs. Her flat-butt was unflattering but I couldn't convince Noki to eat better and exercise.

"Hey, Noki, what's up?"

"Nothing," she responded sourly. She was never happy to see me unless I was giving her money.

"What's the matter?"

"Why do you always ask me that?"

"Perhaps because every time I come to see you, you seem upset. And I'm starting to wonder if I trigger those emotions."

"You're paranoid, just like your mother."

"First off, she was your mother, too. And I don't recall her ever being paranoid."

"What do you want, Nikki?"

"Want? When do you ever give for me to want? What I would like is for you to acknowledge that I came all the way down here to spend some time with you before I go to work."

"You call prostitution work?"

"Well it pays my bills as well as yours."

"Well, I'm in college so I can get a respectable job. Not lying on my back counting down the days until I get AIDS."

"Well, I use protection. And I hope you don't think that only whores, as you call us, get AIDS. I hope you use protection."

"Don't ever discuss sex with me, Nikki," she exclaimed. "If you don't mind, I want you to leave. I'm expecting someone shortly."

As Noki and I were involved in a heated discussion, someone came in with a key. I was startled because I was never given this privilege. In fact, he had a key to the apartment I owned.

Sonuvabitch, I thought.

Her guest was brown–skinned, short and stocky. He stood 5'6" and had a muscular body frame, attractive and clean cut. Noki got anxious and started stuttering.

"Eddie . . . this . . . this . . . is a friend of mine. Her name is Nikki," she stammered.

"Whadup," he said.

"What up," I returned and did a head nod.

Noki made it clear that no one was to know we were sisters. All of her friends thought she was *Japanese* and she liked it like that. Her apartment was decorated in Japanese furnishing. She had a Japanese kotatsu table with a goza mat underneath it. Washi kimono coasters decorated her coffee table. A Japanese chochin lantern with dim lighting stood in her corner. When you walked in her doorway she had a gong and stand. In Asian culture if you are touched by a gong it brings happiness and strength. For protection she had two large marble peking foo dogs. The peking foo dog with the open mouth sucks in all evil spirits while the peking foo dog with the closed mouth keeps the spirits contained. Even though I too was half Japanese and respected my culture, I didn't decorate my home to reflect it. I chose to live my life as a black woman and Noki resented me for that too.

"What happened to your face?" he inquired.

Noki spun around to see what he was talking about.

Being so self-absorbed, she never would have noticed that I'd been smacked around.

"She was in a car accident," she nervously blurted out. Her olive skin turned red from embarrassment.

"That's right," I concurred.

I'd left my sister's apartment feeling really down. We weren't as close as we should have been. I kept trying to figure out what went wrong from my end. I thought I did everything for Noki that was within my reach.

When she turned 16, she finished high school with honors. I purchased her that condominium in Soho and a Tahoe Jeep to get around in. She was adamant that she didn't want to live with me anymore, so I obliged. When she turned seventeen, I bought her first motorcycle, the BMW 800. When I'd gotten my bike, Noki pouted until I bought her one. I was a little skeptical about buying her such an expensive toy because she didn't ride as well as me. And, of course, she resented me for that.

It was very easy for Noki to find reasons to resent me. I usually found myself walking on eggshells in her presence. Always trying to please her. Always trying to crack a joke to make her smile. Always trying to give her money to show how much I loved her. Plain and simple, I was always trying to please Noki. I spent my days and night catering to her every whim, trying to express my love and adoration for her. And the only regret I had was that she didn't reciprocate.

EIGHTEEN

NIKKI LING

It was no secret that Brian and I loved to role play. We'd been everything from strangers on a train where we made love inside a dirty subway car, to teacher and student where we actually snuck inside a local public school and made love on an elementary desk. Today Brian called and said, "Come over now. Put your hair up in a tight bun. Wear a pair of cat-rimmed glasses, business skirt suit, no panties, and heels."

Click.

I rushed over.

When I arrived at Brian's plush New York apartment, he quickly led me in. I thought he'd be in a character but he wasn't. He was wearing a sweat shirt, jeans and eating a bowl of cereal.

"Hi lover," I said and smiled. I was a little disappointed but not for long. Brian gave me a wet, juicy kiss and slapped me on my ass.

"Nice . . . you know I like it rough," I seductively said.

"Don't have me put a hurtin' on that ass," he bragged.

"Please. You can't handle this," I teased and got lost in his expressive, round eyes.

"Oh really?" he said and put down his cereal bowl. Brian walked over to me and looked me from head to toe.

"Another bitch-ass "John" had a problem with keeping

his hands to himself?"

Brian said after getting a closer look at my face.

"He was a real asshole," I retorted but didn't go into details. Brian hated listening to me complain about my dates.

"You still look sexy," he said.

"Tell me something I don't know," I said and put my hands on my hips.

"Come here," he commanded and I did as I was told. "Open your legs."

I went and stood before Brian and opened my legs. He sat down on the edge of his sofa, took his right hand and slowly went up my leg until he felt my bush. When he stuck his finger in my pussy, I trembled.

"Take your skirt off," he commanded. I gently unbuttoned my skirt and let it fall to the floor. "Nice . . . stay put. I'll be back."

Brian went inside his bathroom and came out with an electric razor. "Hold still."

As Brian took his electric razor and began to shave off my pussy hair I felt an indescribable sensation. The intimacy of having my man shave my pussy was so overwhelming. I purposely let my pussy hair go neglected for this very reason. I could afford the Brazilian bikini wax but I opted for the "Brian Carter Special" any day.

After Brian trimmed my box, he gently kissed my navel. "Perfect," he said.

"Come here," I breathed. I was so excited. Brian's massive dick had gotten hard as he clipped my pussy. I could tell he was excited as well. I led Brian into his room and crawled on his bed. I kept on my heels, cat-rimmed glasses, and discarded everything else. Brian took down my hair and it hung low, underneath my ass. Then he reached inside his dresser drawer and pulled out a silk scarf.

"I see you want to play dirty. You still can't handle me even while I'm tied down," I teased.

"Put your hands over your head," he commanded. As I reached up Brian wrapped the silk scarf around my wrists and bound me to his bed post.

Once he had me tied, he entwined my hair in his strong hands and mounted me. His cold, moist lips gently kissed my ears while his tongue tasted my lobes. I moaned in pleasure. Brian began sucking aggressively around my neck and then moved to my large breasts.

"You have the most beautiful breasts I've even seen," he breathed. Men loved that I had large nipples and large, perky breasts. "I could stare at your sexy areolas forever."

As Brian hungrily sucked my breast, I gently parted my legs. As he sucked and kissed each inch of my body, he stopped only momentarily to kiss *around* my pussy. Then he began to kiss and suck each toe. At this point I was in ecstasy.

"Fuck me . . ." I murmured. "Fuck me now."

Brian got more aggressive. He entered me roughly and I screamed in pleasure. As he rode me, his strong hands were entwined in my hair. As his ass pumped in and out I wrapped my long legs around his muscular backside. We made love in sync as if we were riding the same wave in an ocean. I could feel that he was about to take me to a climax and I didn't want to cum yet. I tugged at the silk scarf until I was freed. Then, I flipped Brian over and rode him feverishly. His strong hands gripped my ass and guided me with precision.

"I'm . . . going . . . to . . . cum," he breathed.

"Is it good . . . ah-h-h-h-h, it's so-o-o-o good," I crooned and tightened my kegal muscle and felt Brian explode inside me.

As we both climaxed my whole body shuttered. I collapsed on Brian's strong chest.

We were both sweating freely and breathing rapidly.

After two bowls of ice-cream and a cold pizza, I looked directly in Brian's eyes and said, "Brian, do you love me?"

With a mouthful of pizza, he replied, "Nik, you know how I feel about you."

"Good. Then let's make it official."

"Make what official?" he said and stopped chewing.

"Our relationship. I've been thinking that we should get married. You know . . . make an honest woman out of me," I said jokingly.

"Come on now I'm eating!" he stated.

"And I'm what? Making you lose your appetite?"

"I don't want to talk about this right now."

"You don't ever want to talk about it. I'm starting to think we don't have a future. Maybe you don't love me. If that's true, I'm a big girl. Just tell me!" As soon as I said it, I was immediately frightened. There was no way I'd be able to handle rejection from Brian.

"You're always thinking and talking negatively and going off on tangents. How did we end up here? We were just making love."

"Were we? I'm starting to think all we do is fuck! Why didn't you eat my pussy!" I screamed.

"I've never eaten your pussy and it's never been a problem."

"Well it is now."

"I don't have to eat your pussy to express how I feel about you," he said and jumped off the bed. I was right on his heels.

"I beg to differ!"

"Frankly, I don't give a fuck! I already told you that I don't eat pussy! Not yours or the next bitch!"

"So now I'm a bitch?"

"Stop being a melodramatic brat. You know I'd never call you such a thing. You're just trying to start an argument."

"So what other *bitch* pussy aren't you eating? I thought we were in a monogamous relationship," I asked.

"You've got to be kidding me. You take ten appointments a week to fuck other men and we're in a monogamous relationship?" he spat.

"That's different. That's work! And you know that I'd stop once you marry me."

"Look, I don't like this conversation. You're starting to piss me off. There are certain things that I don't do in relationships just as there are certain things that you don't do."

"I don't swallow but at least I've sucked your little dick!" I yelled.

"My dick ain't little," he said and grinned as he touched his dick. Instantly he grew hard.

"Come here girl," he said and grabbed me.

"Get off of me. I hate you," I said all baby-like.

"Come give daddy some sugar."

And I did. I gave my daddy all the *sugar* he wanted.

NINETEEN

NIKKI LING

After Brian and I made love for hours, I ran home and showered, ate a bagel, and had a cappuccino. Then I relaxed for an hour. I had two appointments tonight, Jack was coming at seven, and Lawrence was coming at nine. They were both regulars.

Then I got up and started decorating the room the way Jack liked it. It had to be all white: linen, flowers, lingerie, and vanilla-scented candles.

Jack arrived promptly with a warm smile. He was much older than me. If I had to guess, I'd say he was 55. But let Jack tell it, he's 30.

Jack was 5'10" and in poor physical shape. His protruding gut hung low, and he was always out of breath. He had a caramel complexion, a goatee, and sleepy eyes. His salt-and-pepper hair added mystique to his dull character.

"Hello, Jack, good evening," I said.

"Nikkisi, darling, how are you?"

"Very well, please come in," I said and nodded to his two bodyguards. Jack always had his bodyguards accompany him wherever he went. He was most paranoid about being kidnapped.

While his bodyguards remained stationed outside my apartment door, I led Jack into my bathroom, where he watched me strip down naked to bathe. Jack would time my baths, and they were to last thirty minutes. The tub was filled with water and white roses, which was really quite romantic. Only Jack didn't role-play. He stood sternly in the doorway and gave strict instructions on where he wanted me to scrub. He was a fanatic about cleanliness. I assumed this was some sort of obsessive-compulsive behavior. In my work, I've seen and experienced almost everything.

Next, we both walked into my bedroom and sat on a bed of white roses that had been delivered by Le Sha Florist only moments earlier. The white candles illuminated the room, and set the perfect ambiance. My guests pay lots of money for my services and expect nothing less than perfection.

Soon, we lay down side by side–not touching–and began our discussion.

"What are your plans for your future?"

"I'm thinking about getting into modeling."

"At your age?"

"Well, I think my looks speak for themselves."

"Don't be ridiculous, Nikkisi. It takes more than a pretty face to make it in the modeling industry."

"Like what? And please don't say brains."

"Why don't you go back to school?"

"Dude, that's too intense for me right now. It's not my cup of tea."

"Are you going to tell me who smacked you around?"

"I don't discuss my other clients."

"I've been wanting to make you this offer for a while and now seems appropriate. I'd like to purchase you exclusively. You know, you'd only see me, no other clients. Would you like that?"

"I get $5,000 a date, plus extra for different requests. I make anywhere from $20,000 to $40,000 a week. You couldn't afford that . . . could you?"

"I'll give you $60,000 a month and pay your housing expenses. That is a great offer. If I find out you have cut any side deals—it's over. I would request a key and be able to come and go as I please. I will call you one hour in advance so you can prepare for my arrival whether you are in the middle of something urgent, whether some ailment has befallen you, or whether a member of your immediate family has met a tragic fate, you are expected to drop everything for my well-being. Is this proposition something that will meet your needs?"

"No," I stated.

"Why?" he asked.

"Because I want more. Not just for me but mainly for my sister."

"Money?"

"Not the way you think."

"Please elaborate, Nikkisi. Our time is almost up for the evening."

"Make an honest woman out of me."

"You mean marriage?"

"Precisely. My sister hates me because I do this. She doesn't respect me, Jack. No one does."

"Surely, people's perception of you shouldn't influence your decisions. That's a sign of weakness. Once a person knows your weakness, they can use it against you. Always remember that, Nikkisi."

"Stop talking to me as if I'm a fucking child! Now, you started this damn conversation, Jack. I can see that you have a weakness for me. I'm going to exploit that to get what I want. And what I want is to be married. Married to a rich, well-respected, intelligent man. Is that too much to ask?"

"Why are you so combative? It doesn't become you," he said. Jack was so calm as he spoke. So eloquent. I admired that about him. As he lay on the bed, I wondered briefly if I could fall in love with him. He wasn't a bad-looking man. His caramel skin was smooth; he had a broad nose, full lips, and a chiseled jaw line. His salt-and-pepper hair indicated that he was a seasoned person of knowledge and wisdom.

"Of course there would be a prenuptial agreement," he continued after a long pause.

"It would have to be tolerable. You know I don't have it bad and I'm not complaining. I have steady, wealthy customers who adore me. I make lots of money and I have freedom. Can you offer me something better or equally stimulating?

"Ah, yes, the insatiable Nikkisi Ling."

"Precisely. Also, I would want you to adopt Noki, give her a respectable last name."

"I'm hardly father material. That's why I've never had any children of my own."

"She would only get your last name, Jack. Noki is hardly the sheltered 17-year-old. She will continue to live on her own."

"This sounds reasonable."

"I'll have to think about your offer though, Jack. I'll have an answer for you next time we meet. But before you go, tell me why you want to shake things up when they're going well already?"

"I'm a lonely man Nikkisi who doesn't have much to give. A beautiful, young woman will want more than I can offer. She will pretend that it's more the relationship than it is the money. And that will infuriate me. With you, I know it's the money.

"And with you, I know it's about the looks. A powerful businessman like yourself needs a beautiful young woman on your arm."

"Someone that's a professional. If I tell you to go sit, you sit. If I say lie down, you lie down. I don't need the other rhetoric. I don't have to participate in the romantic fantasies, mental stimulation, or the occasional compliments. It will be exactly the way it is now. So, our date is concluded. Please let me know whether you accept my proposal on our next evening. Goodnight, darling."

As soon as Jack left, I ran to the telephone and called Brian. He had just come from an important business meeting.

"Brian, do you have a moment?"

"Sure, Nik what's up?"

"Let's get married," I asked.

"How many times we gotta go through this?" he roared and startled me.

"We've been together forever! You've got millions, while I'm out here selling ass! Why can't you make an honest woman out of me?"

"I think it's a little too late for that," he said. His voice was icy and insensitive.

"Really? Well that's not what Jack thinks," I stated, trying to get him jealous.

"How you gonna try and play me throwing some trick-ass nigga in my face to make me jealous."

"He ain't a trick. I met him in a supermarket two months ago. He's rich and powerful and wants to marry me."

"You fucked him?"

"Not yet," I said, which wasn't a lie. Jack has been a client for the past three years, and he's never wanted sex. We just talk. That's it.

"You didn't fuck him, and he wants to marry you? Some rich dude?"

"Yes."

"Well what do you want, my blessing. I say go for yours."

"What?" I asked incredulously.

"If you got some rich cat asking to marry you, you better run to the altar. You ain't getting no younger."

"I want to run to the altar with you, Brian," I said, my voice barely a whisper.

"Here we go again. Look, I gotta go. I'll hit you back later." Click. Brian hung up.

I held onto the telephone for a while before ultimately letting it go. In my heart, I knew I had to let Brian go as well. He'd showed me in too many blatant ways that I didn't mean anything to him. He was always nonchalant when I wanted to talk about getting serious. I hated to believe that it had to do with my profession, but the reality of it is he didn't respect me. No one did.

My mother didn't raise a crybaby, so I didn't cry. My heart felt heavy though, I must admit. Sometimes, I think about the day my mother committed suicide. How all her problems disappeared when she made her fateful decision. And I wonder, could I ever get enough courage to check-out when I'm tired? That was always a thought.

I collected myself and took my next appointment. Brian never did call back like he said he would.

TWENTY

LACEY DEVANEY

2001

They say what doesn't kill you should only make you stronger. If there was just a hint of truth in that statement, I'd find solace. Admittedly, my life has surpassed any expectations I may have had. I went from living in a small town, flipping burgers at the local fast food restaurant, to inheriting my sister's fortune from her estate. Of course, I had to forge her Last Will and Testament but being a Devaney, deceit had come easily.

Not a day goes by that I don't despise my sister. My hate for her grows like a fungus eroding my body and sucking up any ounce of goodness I thought lived within me. When she died, I thought, "Good. She deserves it! Now I can finally start living happily ever after like I've always deserved."

Except that my life is shrouded in darkness. Every time I take two steps ahead, some sort of tragedy strikes, and I'm pulled three steps back. Being an educated black woman doesn't always ensure you'll make educated decisions. My decision to meet and fall in love with the ex-boyfriend of my sister was one of my more regrettable mistakes. Not only am I now dependent on cocaine and alcohol, I also have a man in jail to support.

When Joshua was busted for buying cocaine, I felt like I had played an integral role in getting him in trouble. That feeling lasted two full days. After he was processed and the whole scene sunk in, I started to feel like Joshua had quickly become a burden. He was much too heavy for my weakening arms to carry.

As I walked through my mansion in New Jersey, I felt depressed. The place needed life breathed back into it. Instead of sulking around the house, constantly dwelling in my woes, I needed to liven things up. I decided that I'd start inviting my friends over more. Have a few parties and become a social butterfly. I'm a great hostess. It's noticeable that I'm not getting any younger, and I'd hate to end up like my mother– old and bitter. But for now I had to put my plans on hold because I was going on yet another visit to the Rikers Island correctional facility to see Joshua. They had his scary ass in protective custody. I knew they had to because he was responsible for putting a lot of guys in jail. But he could have at least resisted and been a man about the situation.

Inside the marble bathroom of my New Jersey mansion, I did a few lines of coke just to pep me up for the miserable day ahead of me. As I inhaled each line, the coke tingled my nostrils. I felt a calming sensation come over me, and it was only then that I felt like I could handle today's event. While walking around in my Casabella thong panties, I felt sexy. I wanted to fuck but again to my dismay it wasn't about to happen. I needed a life makeover and fast.

When I reached Rikers Island, the whole process was laborious. I had my driver take me as far as he could, then

I was expected to board a bus that would take me and the other visitors the rest of the way. I was annoyed. I clearly wasn't cut out for this.

On this particular fall morning I wore a dyed pink mink jacket with a provocative, clingy, pink Roberto Cavalli dress. Gucci heels adorned my feet, and a pink diamond tennis bracelet graced my wrist. I looked sensational. My chestnut brown eyes exerted confidence as I strutted through each security check gate.

When I finally reached the visiting room, I had to sit and wait for Joshua. When he was led in, his appearance shocked me; he had changed so much since the last time I'd visited. He'd lost a lot of weight and his body was bony. His face looked gaunt and almost frightening, to say the very least. His blond hair was disheveled and his blue eyes looked despondent. I stood up so he could admire my outfit, but he ignored me and just sat down.

"The least you could have done was shave," I said dryly.

"That's the least of my worries," he snapped.

"How can you stand to be in here with no amenities? I'd go crazy," I announced as I took a quick look around.

"Good question. Why haven't you posted my bail yet? I've been in here five weeks, Lacey. I have to come home so I can fight this case. I don't think I can stand another night in here," he pleaded.

"I think we should wait until you go in front of the judge again. I'm sure he'll lower your bail."

"Jesus, Mary and Joseph! That's not for another four weeks. I know you have the money."

"Well $300,000 is more than I can part with right

now. Neither one of us are working. We can't live off my inheritance forever," I reasoned.

"Are you kidding me? Let's not forget that I'm in here because of you," he whispered and looked around to make sure no one heard him.

"Don't fucking lay that bullshit on me. You're in here because of Lyric! If you weren't out trying to play fucking Columbo and capture her murderer, no one would have cared about an assistant district attorney buying coke in the 'hood."

"She was your twin sister for God's sake. Don't you have an ounce of remorse?" he asked.

"Lighten the fuck up! My sister had a penchant for danger and put herself in a compromising situation," I huffed.

"Your sister had an affair. Period. You don't go around killing people because they're unfaithful."

"Well, I guess Estelle Cardinale didn't get the memo ..."

"Why do you have this undying hate for your sister? I will never understand it," he said, shaking his head as if to say I'm pathetic.

"And your boundless love for her memory is starting to become boring. Don't look for me on your next visit. I may have something really important to do . . . like wash my hair," I stated and started to get up to leave when Joshua grabbed my arm. I yanked it away and the guards glanced over.

"Lacey . . . please . . . don't do this to me. I really need your strength. I promise you that I'll make everything all right. Just believe in me and don't abandon me when I need you most," he pleaded.

I was already tired of this tumultuous affair. I didn't love Joshua, and he didn't love me. We were together because of his love for my sister and my hate for her. How long could we expect that to hold us together?

Besides, his being in jail was cramping my style. I was 39 years old and Joshua was making me feel every bit my age.

"Listen, you're going down. They have a treasure-trove of evidence against you and I feel that if you loved me, you wouldn't want to put me through this."

"Lacey, please just bail me out. That's all I ask from you, and I'll leave you alone," he begged.

"I'll think about it Josh," I said and sauntered out.

TWENTY·ONE

IVANKA ZAMORA

2001

When the news about my aunt's arrest for murder hit the tabloids, I was livid. The video replayed constantly on every media outlet nationally and internationally. The humiliation came not from the murder, but from the mere fact that she'd been caught.

She was immediately arraigned and set free on $1 million bail. The public was outraged. The media had already tried and convicted her while the black community protested and rallied over the preferential treatment my aunt was shown by the judge setting bail.

As I watched the despicable scene on television, anger swelled inside me. The niggers had the audacity to crawl up the Supreme Court steps in lower Manhattan with a clergyman leading the pact, screaming, "No justice—no peace." They looked like little ants migrating to their motherland. Situations like these leave me perplexed. If there is "no justice or peace" for them here in America, why don't they get their oppressed asses back on a boat and go the fuck back home to Africa?

Once everything settled down, I went to visit my aunt to give her support. We needed to show a united front to the media and public. Also, I needed her wisdom on a matter that had been troubling me for some time.

"Aunt Estelle," I greeted her as I was led into her study. She was sitting facing the window in a pale blue Ellen Tracy two-piece pantsuit. Her blond hair had grown since the last time I'd seen her and was hanging near her shoulders. She looked peaceful as if she didn't have a care in the world.

"Ivanka, what on earth are you doing here? It's such a wonderful surprise . . ."

"Where is Uncle Richard? I expected him to be here," I asked looking around for him.

"He is here...he's hiding upstairs in the den. He hasn't come out since the incident made the front page of the *New York Times*."

"So, do you want to talk?"

"About why I murdered that slut, Lyric Devaney?"

"Well, I know why, Aunt Estelle. But I don't know how you were caught. You've always been the brains behind this family. I would have assumed you would have executed your plan only after double-checking even the most minute detail to ultimately commit the perfect murder."

"Even the perfect murder can have a flaw . . .," she said and looked away.

"Do you have any regrets," I said and hoped her answer lived up to my expectation.

"No!" she replied without hesitation.

My heart sighed relief. I needed to talk with my aunt and hoped she would guide me on the right path.

"Aunt Estelle, when my mother died, she was worth $1

billion. As you know, at the reading of her will, she wrote me out of her estate."

"Yes, dear. I also know that was a grave mistake."

"Pardon."

"Not leaving you all of her estate. Your father isn't worth a penny of my sister's money. He's never loved my sister. He married her for the love of her money. He was nothing but a handsome con-artist," she spat.

"Aunt Estelle," I interjected. I so hated that she didn't like my father, whom I loved.

"My sister was nothing like me or you for that matter. She didn't have a backbone. She was weak and feeble, characteristics I loathe."

"Isn't it ironic that I was her child, especially when you and I have so much in common? I always loathed mother as well," I chimed in.

"Well, she's gone . . . " Aunt Estelle stated, as if we should celebrate that fact.

"Yes. That's what I want to talk about. My father has inherited her estate and her company."

"Which will go to you when he passes away . . ."

"Well, not exactly."

"Please, Ivanka, get to the point. I don't have all day."

"Yes, ma'am. Well, my father is engaged . . . to be married . . . to a black woman."

All the color drained from Aunt Estelle's face; she turned stark white. Her mouth had become dry and she signaled me to get her a drink of vodka. I immediately poured her one and rushed it over to her. She drank quickly from her Lenox crystal and regained her composure.

"This is the ultimate betrayal!" she accused. "How dare he remarry so soon after my sister's death! And to disgrace this family and soil our bloodline by marrying a nigger . . . I will not hear of it. Get your father on the line now!" she commanded.

"Aunt Estelle, it's not that simple. You know how much I love my father. Ever since he inherited my mother's money, he's turned his back on me. He doesn't accept my telephone calls. He doesn't come to see me. I think she has him brainwashed, probably doing that black voodoo. It's strange that he treats me as though I'm not his child . . ." I was hurt just simply speaking about it.

"Why, you were the apple in his eye."

"I used to be," I said sourly.

"Well, you only have one solution to your problem."

"That's precisely why I'm here. I need your guidance."

"You know what you have to do. You have the same bloodline as me . . ." Her voice was eerily cold.

"I've tried to pay her off already. She won't go. She said she's going to have lots of babies. That I will have half-black brothers and sisters spending all of my mother's money."

"Your mother will roll over in her grave! If she weren't dead—I'd kill her myself. This embarrassment will fall on me. She always left it up to me to clean up her mess. She brought your low-life father into our family and this is how he repays us?"

"What can I do to help?"

"Kill her! With no flaws . . ." she stated unemotionally.

"Aunt Estelle I can't . . ."

"Scared?" she challenged.

"Never! But I've reviewed the situation a million times over in my head, and I can't pull it off without ending up in your situation. My background . . . my medical records . . . will all be held against me. She's already stated to anyone within earshot that, if something awful should befall her, that I'm to blame."

"Smart darkie."

"They all get clever when money is at stake."

"Well, then maybe the problem doesn't lie with the girl. They're not married yet, correct?"

"Correct. What are you implying?"

"Maybe the problem isn't the girl. Maybe the problem can be taken care of by dealing with your father . . ." She purposely let her words trail off again and dismissed me before I could try to reason with her.

As I exited her study, she called out and said one last thing to me, "Remember . . . no flaws."

TWENTY·TWO

LACEY DEVANEY

After the disturbing incident with Joshua, I decided it was time to let my hair down. A new friend had invited me to a social gathering at the home of an Emmy award-winning actress in the Hamptons on Long Island. There were going to be many celebrities there and quite possibly my future husband. I realized that I wasn't getting any younger, and my fortune was diminishing by the day. I shuttered to think how little money I had left from the nearly $8 million I had embezzled from my dead sister's estate.

I realized that money attracts money. If I wanted to marry rich, it would be slightly easier to reinvent myself as a young heiress. Instead of 39-yearold Lacey Devaney, the thought of being 26-year-old heiress or something, appealed to me.

For this party, I decided to pull out the good stuff. I wore a couture $3000 pale colored Chloe one-piece jumper, $1700 Manolo Blahnik heels and a Chanel clutch pocketbook. Then I walked over to my jewelry box and pulled out my $100,000 Piaget watch, with 310 diamonds, and my platinum-and-diamond hoop earrings. That was enough. I didn't need anything else. I looked stunning. My light brown hair was newly cut into layers that fell just below my shoulders and my chestnut brown eyes were sparkling.

My chauffeur, Charles, drove my silver Bentley to the

estate in record time. It was a beautiful evening. I sat hiding behind my Chanel navy blue shades that faded to black. These were my favorite sunglasses. They made me feel important.

Once I got there, a host of vehicles were being valet parked. This was a party fit only for elite socialites, and I was one of them. This exclusive event had been kept secret right up to the last moment. First we were given a CD letting us know that there would be a party in the very near future and we were invited. This was followed by a telegram telling us the dress code for the night and the party's theme. Finally, we received a DVD Fed Exed to our doors. The DVD had the party's location and doubled as a pass.

It seems celebrities have a little too much time and money on their hands if it took such extraordinary measures just to have a fun.

As I entered the beautifully decorated extravaganza, I wasn't paying attention to décor. I was sizing up every male in the place. From looks to bank account—I wanted in.

I was there no more than three minutes when I noticed HIM. He had a chiseled body, dark chocolate skin, and a thin scar on his cheek that gave him character. Not to mention he'd also made the latest edition of Forbes "Top 40 Millionaires Under 30" list. I had thoroughly read the magazine and committed each face to my memory.

I had to have him.

TWENTY·THREE

JOSHUA TUNE

Every night I'd hear, "Lock down!" and the cell block doors slam shut, and another part of me would die. I'd just about given up on everything and everyone. I had been incarcerated for five months now. Even though I was in protective custody, I still had to watch my back. Criminals were clever enough to get someone on the inside as they masterminded your murder. I never got any sleep in this place for fear it would be my last night alive. The only thing that kept me going was wanting to fight my case. I couldn't imagine spending the next twenty years in a correctional facility.

We were woken up at dawn every day. I got a job in the kitchen preparing breakfast for the inmates. Jesus, Mary and Joseph! The things some inmates do to the food are unconscionable. At dinner they would mix feces in stews or urinate in sauces. They behaved like animals and were treated accordingly by the correction officers.

Luckily for me, I had a legal background, so I was an asset. The inmates all wanted to protect me and do favors for me, so I could review their cases and give them legal advice. This was difficult because I was working on my case. The judge had assigned me a legal aid lawyer named Brad Beckingsel. He was a real asshole and had a reputation for making deals whether you were innocent or not. Two weeks of his representing me, I made a motion to the court to represent myself and it was granted. I couldn't put my life in his hands. At first encounter he said, "Joshua, I could get a sweet deal for you. I'm talking five years maximum. You'll be out in three for good behavior."

From there, it only went downhill. He didn't want to do his job, which was to defend his client. My ex-wife, Parker offered to retain an attorney for me, but I wouldn't hear of it. I noticed that her marriage had become a little turbulent with her dedicating so much attention to me and my case. Her husband is a good man, but a man can only take so much and be only so understanding. So I backed off and tried to depend on Lacey. Only Lacey hadn't been making herself available to me lately. After breakfast, I went up to shower. Parker was coming to visit me this morning to bring me a dark blue suit and tie for court. She promised that she'd be there front and center every day of my trial to show support. I asked her to reach out to as many of my friends as possible to ask them to be in the courtroom. It was extremely important to let the jury see that you had support.

Before my visit, I called Lacey. After the operator announced that she had a collect call from a correctional facility I heard her sulk and suck her teeth.

"Yes," she snapped in the phone.

"Hi . . . Lacey," I hesitated.

"What, Joshua? I have a million things to do this morning."

"Well, I'm not calling about bail anymore. I just wanted to know if you were going to be in court for me this week."

"What's happening this week?" she snapped.

"Trial. I start trial this week."

"Wow, time sure does fly. Has it been that long?"

"Lacey, time isn't flying for me. I notice every second in this place. I take solace in knowing that I have a shot at beating this case. Will you be there? Can you make it for me?"

"No," she stated without explanation.

"Lacey, I feel like we've grown apart to say the least. But I promise you when I get home I'll make it up to you. I won't be in here forever. I'm a fighter Lacey. I just need you by my side. I can't keep depending on Parker. I want to depend on you. My girl . . ." my voice trailed off because I heard the faint male voice in the background.

"Joshua, I guess now's a good time to tell you that I'm seeing someone else. And he'd appreciate it if you didn't call here collect anymore. In fact, he asked me to change my telephone number and I told him I would. This time tomorrow you won't be able to get through nor will I be making any courtroom guest appearances or sending you any money orders. You're on your own." Click. She hung up the telephone.

For the first time since I'd been incarcerated, I cried. I felt so helpless and alone. I did a lot of reflecting on my life and how cruel love could be. I had been cruel to the only person who truly loved me; therefore, karma had to reciprocate.

A few hours later I was called down to the visiting room. Parker was sitting there waiting for me. She looked great. Her long, naturally red dredlocks were pulled nicely back in a pony-tail. She wore a pair of jeans and a button-down shirt. The only jewelry she wore was her wedding ring.

We embraced and she smiled politely.

"How are you?" she questioned.

"I'm doing great," I lied. I didn't want her knowing my circumstances with Lacey and feeling even more sorry for me.

"Good . . . good. I left you a dark blue suit, tie, shoes and dress socks. I have all the confidence that you will put on a strong defense, Josh."

"You have more confidence than I do," I said.

"Well, I've seen you in action. You're brilliant!" she said trying to boost my morale.

"Thanks, Parker," I said, my voice barely a whisper. Truthfully, I was terrified. This was my life on the line.

"Hey, look what I brought," she said pulling out photographs of baby Mia at her fourth birthday party. I took one look and my eyes welled up with tears. She was gorgeous.

Parker did manage to cheer me up during the visit. It felt nice to smell nice perfume and be in the presence of someone soft. I returned back to the law library and continued to prepare for my defense. The prosecution's whole case was going to hinge on the audio tape with me stating I was purchasing narcotics, the detective's statement, and the statement of a snitch, Bee-For-Real.

I was shepardizing cases and researching case law to see if there were any cases to support my getting the audio evidence thrown out. The jury didn't need to hear that. I had to win this motion!

TWENTY·FOUR

KAPRI HENDERSON

2001

I woke up feelin' nice this mornin' 'cause I was gettin' a visit from my cousin, Portia. That bitch deserves a beatdown for not comin' to check me sooner . . . but I'll let her slide since we fam. Last night I had Keisha braid my hair all back and I had her clean my sneakers. She was my steady bitch now. Anything I asked her to do—she jumped to get it done. Lately she been ridin' me too. I can't breathe in this mutherfucker without her askin' me if I need air. She's all over me. After her man left her for another girl out on the street, she directed all her attention to me. It was cool in the beginnin', but now I need room to get my fuck on wit this other chick. Her name is Hattie. She came in a few weeks ago for stabbin' a bitch to death over her baby-daddy. Hattie said she blacked out. The coroner said she'd hit every major artery in that girl's body. The girl never had a chance. Serves bitches right for fuckin' wit your man. All I know is I woulda killed a bitch too over Knowledge and dat's my word.

I think Keisha knows that I'm fuckin' wit the new chick that just came through. But her scared ass ain't gonna say shit. Hattie got bitches in here shook, except me! I still run this mutherfucker.

"Kapri Henderson . . . visit," Bob, the correction officer yelled.

Bob was an asshole. He always be doin' his best to keep drugs off our ward. He was always doin' surprise shakedowns. Tossin' our cells lookin' for weapons and drugs. I done got hit three times already at the Parole Board because of his mutherfuckin' cell searches. I always got caught wit a shank. That's a homemade knife. I had to protect myself. I never got caught wit drugs. I let my flunkies hold my shit. They hit you wit too much time for that and considering I'm already in here for a drug charge, I'd never see the street again if I got caught wit that shit.

I walked over to Bob and entered the elevator wit the other inmates who had visits. Once we were on the lower level, we were all subjected to body searchers.

"Pull down your pants . . . squat . . . open your butt-cheeks . . . cough . . . open your mouth . . . lift your tongue . . . left . . . right . . . up."

Once we all passed inspection, we were led into the visitin' room. It took a moment for me to recognize Portia. She was sittin' at a table lookin' all fat 'n shit. Some dude had obviously knocked my baby cousin up. For some reason, this didn't sit well wit me.

Her long black hair was pulled back in a tight ponytail, and she had on a dark-blue sweat suit. Portia's thin nose had spread and her slanted eyes were even more chinese-lookin'.

"Whaddup yo," I greeted my cousin and gave her a big hug.

"Hello, sweetie," she responded.

"Sweetie?" I asked, but she ignored me.

"I wanted to come and see you so you could see I'm having a baby. It would have been a shame for you to come home and find out that way."

"So who's the mutherfucker that got you knocked up? Who he down wit? Where he hustlin'? In New York or O.T.? He better be makin' paper. Babies ain't cheap…"

"Kapri –"

"Call me Kapone," I corrected.

"Kapri, he doesn't sell drugs in New York or out-of-town. He works for the New York City Transit Authority and I'm a registered nurse. We're about to get married," she squealed.

Something was different about her. This wasn't the spunky, tough cousin I remembered. What the fuck happened to her?

"Word," I said dryly. Her visit was quickly turning to a waste of my mutherfuckin' time.

"Yes. But enough about me. It's good to see you."

"You don't look happy," I observed. Her eyes looked sad.

She shrugged her shoulders and said, "I'm still haunted by the death of my best friend, Lyric. I just recently found out that she didn't commit suicide … she was murdered."

"Did I ever meet her?" I asked. The visit started to pick-up since she started talkin' 'bout murder.

"Maybe … when we were in high school. I'm not sure though…"

"So who killed da bitch? You want me to take care of them when I git out?"

"Don't refer to her as a bitch Kapri. And I don't want you to take care of anything criminal when you come home. Anyway, this situation is way over your head. Over my head. It's just too much. It's all over the news. Did you read about the actress who was allegedly murdered by the senator's wife."

"Allegedly? What the fuck does that mean. Was she killed or not?"

"Yes, she was murdered. Listen, this is a little too depressing for me," she continued, "I really need to change the subject before I break down crying. So, how have you been? Please accept my apology for not coming to see you earlier."

"Accept your apology? Nah, it ain't that mutherfuckin' easy," I said and rolled my eyes.

"Look, I'm sorry. I can't imagine being in here without my family. I understand why you may be upset."

"A bitch been locked down for over a decade and all you can mutherfuckin' say is sorry? Fuck dat! I heard 'bout you ridin' 'round in jeeps 'n shit while I'm up in here starvin'."

"I was much younger back then and immature."

"I should beat ya ass for disrespectin' me," I threatened.

"Beat who ass?" she asked.

"I ain't the same chick that came up in dis piece. My mutherfuckin' name is Kapone. And if you disrespect me again and call me Kapri, I'll beat the shit outta you. I don't give a fuck if you pregnant . . ." I exploded. She had gotten on my last nerve wit her 'I'm better than you' routine.

Portia had the look of pure shock on her face, but she quickly shook that shit off and said, "Bitch, who the fuck you threatening? I don't give a fuck what they call you up in this piece. Pregnant and all, I will whip your motherfucking ass in here! Don't make me catch a case. You dumb, ignorant, silly bitch. Doing time for a no-good motherfucker, and you're trying to flip on me! I don't think so . . ." she screamed so loud her belly moved with every syllable. I didn't expect it to go this far.

The guards immediately came rushin' over to shut down our situation. Portia saw them but still she didn't let up. She started takin' off her earrings, challengin' me to a fight. All her proper talk and self-awareness had died.

I jumped up to handle the situation. "Chill-out Portia . . . they gonna lock you up!" I warned.

"I don't give a fuck!" she continued. She was furious wit me. The whole room stopped their visits and watched the commotion. Eventually, Portia was escorted out and my visit was over. I fucked that up. I didn't even get to tell her that I was comin' home soon.

TWENTY·FIVE

JOSHUA TUNE

Clearly, I now have a low tolerance for asinine antics at this stage in my life. Nor am I prone to sit and wallow in guilt. I fucked up. That's it. No long analogies or formal apologies to those who feel I let them down. Every day I sit in this torturous cage and build my mind up. I think of creative ways to legally gain my freedom. I write motions, research case law, and shepardize. All these things used to be mundane for any hotshot lawyer, but not me. My last motion requesting that the audio tape be thrown out as evidence was 106 pages. It may have been a little repetitive, but every line was necessary. This isn't a joke.

I used to brag that my heart has never been snubbed in any relationship. I was usually the one in control. I called the shots. I had a plethora of women at my beck and call and I relished every moment of it. Women made me feel virile and needed. That was until I met Monique. Sweet Monique . . . who ultimately left me with a sour taste in my mouth. From her I moved on to Lacey. Her beauty left me speechless, but I was first to admit I wasn't in love.

In all my years of being a man's man, independent and strong willed, I got lost in my own cockiness and fell tenfold harder than the average man. When I think about the insensibility of Lacey's actions, absconding when I needed her most, I think that was the ultimate betrayal. Thus my heart aches at night. Not for love but for commitment. Loyalty. How hypocritical am I?

This morning was my first day of trial. I opted to have a bench trial. That's where there is no jury, and the judge rules on the case from his legal expertise. I look at it like this, if I wanted to rely on emotions, then I'd use a jury trial. But I needed to rely on the law to exonerate me; therefore, I preferred to have a bench trial.

Most jurors saw my face splashed across every news channel for the past year, and they've already convicted me. The pressure of trying to win over twelve jurors would have been overwhelming.

We had to meet at 9:00 a.m. for Judge Herkowitz to rule on the motion to suppress the audio tape. Then we'd recess and come back after lunch and start trial. Judge Merrill would be presiding over my case.

The trial is expected to last two days. There are only a total of five witnesses from the prosecution, and I'm not expected to take the stand in my own defense. It could open the door for too many inconsistencies. My main focal point was to cast doubt on Detective Holmes. I need to establish that he had a motive to set me up. The thought of cross-examining him was daunting, not because I thought he had an ounce of intelligence. (He's street smart but he's no Einstein). Instead, sheer embarrassment is my Achilles heel. Detective Holmes knew about my cocaine addiction. I could just picture the smug look he'd have plastered on his face during the trial.

I walked into the courtroom dressed as the quintessential prep school boy. My blond hair was slicked back and I was clean-shaven. Parker had picked out a nice dark blue Ralph Lauren suit and a pair of Salvatore Ferragamo shoes. She knew he was my favorite designer. She was truly a gem . . .

The correction officers at Rikers Island loaded twelve inmates onto the bus at 4:00 a.m.. Most were going to court for bail hearings, or they'd gotten hit with another charge. I was the only one going to trial.

"So you're the white mutherfucker who tried to push coke through my 'hood!" one inmate stated.

"Excuse me?"

"You heard me, you blond mutherfucker. I'm from the East . . . I heard about you," he grunted.

"Likewise," I stated and turned away. I wasn't about to let him get under my skin this goddamn early in the morning. I felt like I was in a scene from the HBO series, "Oz." I was Beecher, the timid white attorney about to be fucked up the ass by Adebisi. This disturbed me.

The morning started off the wrong way, and I couldn't help but wonder if there'd be hope for me inside the courtroom.

As I was ushered into the courtroom my heart started to palpitate. The assistant district attorney was the latest hotshot attorney. His name is Jonathan Spitzer. They'd pulled out the best to nail me at my own goddamn office. Jesus, Mary and Joseph! I guess there really is no loyalty among thieves. Those bastards could have at least thrown me a bone. I'd been reading about this guy's victories for the past year. He played hardball.

Then I realized that I'm Joshua Tune. The best goddamn attorney in New York City. He was no match for my legal skills. I'm too experienced. My ego just needed a boost. Being incarcerated can affect your self-esteem.

I stood stone-faced before Judge Herkowitz.

"Your honor, I would like to make a motion to suppress the audio tape evidence in this case. The prosecution has lost the original audio tape and produced a copy," I said with my voice wavering. I was a little rusty.

"Your honor, Mr. Tune has a baseless motion," said Mr. Spitzer. "Although the original has been misplaced… somewhere in the precinct…we still are in possession of a perfectly good audio."

"Judge, it's fair to say that if this is not the original, the audio could have been doctored. Words could have been omitted—" "I object!" the prosecutor yelled. "Overruled," Judge Herkowitz said and I realized that I may have a shot.

"Your honor, without the original, this tape could have been doctored, and I can't possibly controvert the evidence. If the original was lost, then we can't even establish the chain of custody. If we can't establish where it's been, then I am requesting that the evidence be suppressed. Thank you your honor," I said and gracefully took my seat.

"Your honor, although the original was misplaced, the copy was vouched immediately thereafter into evidence. I will have the officers testify that this is the exact replica of the original tape that was in their custody. I request that Your Honor admit the tape into evidence. Thank you."

"We'll take a thirty-minute recess, and I'll come back and render my decision," the judge said. He hit his gavel and court was over. I glanced over at the DA, and he had a grim look on his face. That felt good.

TWENTY·SIX

NIKKI LING

SPRING 2002

Traffic on the FDR North was moving at a snails pace. I let my Yamaha XVZ-1300 motorcycle glide in and out of traffic with ease. When I saw my exit approaching, I shifted gears, leaned back, and did a one leg pop wheelie for about half a mile. As I came down, my heart fluttered from the adrenaline rush. Today was a good day. I turned back to see if my sister was close behind. She just shook her head at my antics. We exited the ramp at 34th Street in New York City. Once on the street, I cut a car off and experienced first hand road rage. A Jaguar was right on my ass! He chased me several blocks before he decided to give up. I pulled over to park.

"Why here?" Noki asked.

"Why not? I feel the vibe."

"There's no money out here," she whined. I snubbed her last remark, dug into my Hermes Burkin bag, and pulled out my Christian Dior shades. "Let's work," I demanded.

I spotted my mark immediately. We were standing in front of Macy's 34th Street. All the shoppers had tunnel vision. Everyone seemed to be in a shopping frenzy. "A sale must be going on," I thought. My mark fiddled inside her oversized Gucci pocketbook and pulled out a broach she wanted to show her friend. It had to be worth $2,000 dollars. The friend admired it for a moment, and then it was placed back inside the bag. The woman looked to be in her mid–sixties, a wealthy, tourist.

I walked over to the frankfurter stand. I ordered a hot dog and then gave my sister an eye signal. She was on–point. With my hot dog in my right hand, I used my two left fingers to lift the latch on the mark's Gucci pocketbook. In less than thirty seconds, I had her wallet and broach in my possession. Never did I stop chewing my hot dog or lose sight of my surroundings. I swiftly gave the mark my back while passing off the merchandise to my sister–who kept it moving. We split up immediately just in case undercover detectives had made me. Ten minutes later, I met her back at our meeting place. A small diner on 33rd and 5th Avenue.

"That shit was sweet!" I whispered when I arrived and slid in the booth. Once the waiter took our usual orders, Noki gave me the wallet. I opened it and all I saw were big faces. I counted over $4,000.

"Didn't I tell you!" I bragged. "I could just feel that shit."

"How did you know? I mean she looked ragged."

"Her clothes were old, but they were once stylish in her day. Her hands were manicured and her jewels told a story of their own. Give me the broach."

"What?"

"The broach Noki. I bagged the broach as well." Noki stared at me for a brief second, challenging me to doubt my abilities in my craft. I hated the fact that she was this petty. I let my eyes hood over and she realized I was not in the mood. She reluctantly pulled it out. I snatched it and began divvying up the money. I shelled out a little over $2,500 to Noki and kept the remaining $1,500 and the broach.

"Why do you even do this? You don't even need the money," Noki replied.

"It's the thrill, baby. The thrill!"

TWENTY·SEVEN

NIKKI LING

I laid back in my chaise longue on the balcony overlooking Manhattan. My husband Jack owned a four-story penthouse apartment on Central Park West, not too far from where Madonna lives with her husband Guy Ritchie. Now Guy Ritchie is fine! The apartment was complete with four bedrooms, five marble bathrooms, one elevator, a gymnasium, a spa, a roof-top swimming pool and a terrace with a panoramic view of the city.

I languorously puffed on my Newport cigarette wishing it were the chronic weed, I had just last night. Life for me had become mundane. The temperature was oddly fifty degrees yet all I was wearing was a "Fuck–U White Trash" T-shirt and a pair of low–rider Diesel jeans.

I jumped up spontaneously, went inside to the bar, popped open a bottle of Cristal champagne and mixed it with orange juice for a morning mimosa. As I clicked on the television set, I heard housekeeping open the front door. I had visitors. It was my best friend Kayla and her friend Veronica. Although I disliked Veronica, Noki *hated* her. They clashed a year ago over a guy Veronica was sleeping with who ultimately ended up in Noki's bed.

"Hey my yute. Wa' ah gwan?" Veronica said in her thick Jamaican dialect, softly tapping me on my shoulder. I barely acknowledged her presence. I sipped on my drink a few more times, then said, "Who invited you over this morning?"

"Mi just dropin pon yu. Bumboclot Yankee gal. Yu waan tess mi?"

Veronica said, sucking her teeth in a grotesque way. I cut my eyes at her immediately. I hated that she always had to tag along to my home when she knew I didn't care for her.

Finally, Kayla said, "Girrl, I'm leaving that son-of-a-bitch!" I laughed because sonuvabitch was my favorite terminology, and Kayla was always getting on me for that.

Kayla now worked for Soulful-Soul Records as a receptionist. She kept me apprised of the latest gossip the rap artists had to dish out. She was also fucking platinum rap artist, ex-drug–hustler, movie mogul Jay Kapone. The very infamous Jay Kapone who had dated the slain actress, Lyric Devaney. He was putting my poor friend through hell. He kept running from Kayla to his long-time girlfriend Marisol. He just couldn't seem to make up his mind. Actually, I tried to tell Kayla that he wasn't leaving Marisol for her because Kayla didn't give him reason to. If you can have the milk free, why buy the cow? My dad used to say that all the time when we were little. Nevertheless, Kayla loved drama.

"Kayla, it's not over until Jay Kapone says it's over. You take anything his ugly ass got to dish out," I said teasingly.

"I do not! He's the one who keeps running back to me. 'Oh baby, baby, I can't live without you!'" Kayla said imitating him.

"Shut up!" I said, dismissing her. Didn't she know that's what men do? Beg and cry when they've fucked up? But, you're not supposed to take them seriously.

Just then, the morning news came on. We all scrambled to turn the volume up. The latest trial had become the next soap opera since the O.J. Simpson trial. It was the trial of former Senator Richard Cardinale's wife Estelle. Estelle Cardinale was arrested last summer for the murder of actress Lyric Devaney. Lyric was having an affair with Estelle's husband, and the murder had been caught on videotape. We watched as the senator's wife stood stone–faced in the courtroom as the defense put in a motion to suppress evidence.

The former senator was nowhere around. He had since resigned from his position, filed for divorce, taken the children and moved out to Los Angeles. The tabloids reported that he was dating a 20-year–old *Sports Illustrated* model.

"That dike–looking chick is gangster!" I teased after observing the courtroom drama for a while.

"I know she has to be hurting right now. That shit wasn't even worth it. And that cheating husband of hers is sitting in the shade drinking lemonade," Kayla stated.

"Did you see the movie "Silk" with Lyric Devaney?" I asked.

"Oh, you trying to be funny?" she questioned.

"What the hell are you talking about?"

"Why you asking about Lyric? You know how I felt about her and now you trying to throw her up in my face."

"Are you crazy or just plain stupid? What do you mean, 'I know how you felt about her?' You didn't even know her. You let that creep play with your mind and bring out your insecurities. The worst thing you can do is let a person know your weaknesses," I retorted.

Kayla thought for a moment and then said, "Yeah, I saw the movie. Do you think she was as gorgeous in person as the tabloids say?"

"Why should I care about how a dead actress looked? Unless I was fucking her man, and even then she wouldn't be a second thought."

"You're right. I was just asking your opinion because Jay Kapone is always going off on tangents about how beautiful she was. And when I look at her photos, I mean she's cute, but you look way better than her," Kayla said, fidgeting in her short hair cut. Her unusually light skin was a shade darker from the sun.

"Well I'm a tall glass to fill. The glass is always half empty when it's sitting next to me."

"You are so pompous gal. Mi tink you ride pon your ego too much. You not special. You Jane just like we mon," Veronica stated.

"Mi not like we gal. Mi don't need a green card mon. Mi legal mon. Mi married millions mon. Mi no Jane Bitch! I'm LING. Nikki Ling. And bitches better get it right!"

I had no idea why Kayla always brought her around to aggravate me. Soon our talk went back to the slain actress, Lyric Devaney.

"Did you see the videotape?" I asked Kayla. "They were selling the uncut version up in Harlem on 125th for $20 bucks." But Veronica answered, "No mon. Mi only saw it pon the news."

"Well, girlie, she played herself swallowing those pills and killing herself. She didn't even know if the gun was loaded. I would have had to test that bitch. Bitch shoot me in the toe, so I can see where your mind is at," I laughed.

"You're a sick chick, Nik. Always willing to push the envelope," Kayla said in amazement.

"There's no other way!" I responded truthfully.

As we sat there talking about what we would have done in the same situation, Jack came in early from work.

"Greetings, Kayla, Veronica," he said as he loosened his shirt and tie. Veronica jumped to attention. Her large grin consumed her face. "Hey monn-n-n," she said with a seductive drawl. I just shook my head, went over, and gave my husband a perky kiss. He barely acknowledged me and headed into his study. No doubt, he would be in there all night.

"Let's get out of here," I said.

"Go where? Where ya gwan go? Go, go, go run dem streets."

"Run dem streets mon—meet and greet mon," I said emulating Veronica. I thought for a moment, and then said, "I want to go where the rich players go!"

Then we all said in unison, "The Upper East Side gym!"

I called out to my husband and let him know I'd be stepping out for a few hours.

"Take Bobby and Rick with you," he called out to me.

"I'll be fine," I responded back and left quickly before he could give me a lecture.

Bobby and Rick were our bodyguards simply because Jack was a rich and paranoid man. He was always talking about the lingering threat that I could be kidnapped for ransom money. He said that kidnapping of high– profile people wasn't as widely done in America as it was in his native continent Africa, but we couldn't be too careful. So, he always warned me that I had to use my discretion. When we were first married, Bobby and Rick escorted me everywhere. I was still intimidated by Jack and his lifestyle. Years later, I've settled back into my own and disregard our bodyguards and Jack's constant bickering about safety. Noki never allowed Jack or me to tell her what she could do and wasn't about to let two stiff bodyguards tag along with her and her friends. We both felt that we were street-savvy and could take care of ourselves. Unbeknownst to me at the time, I wasn't as street-savvy as I thought I was.

TWENTY·EIGHT

NIKKI LING

Kayla called me that night to apologize for bringing Veronica over.

"I apologize, Nikki. But once I mentioned I was dropping by your house, she wanted to tag along," she explained.

"No problem. But next time, I wont be so forgiving," I warned.

"I'm sorry," she said again.

"Kayla, I'm joking." Changing the subject I said, "Your 24th birthday is coming soon. What are your plans?"

"I don't have any yet. I hope Jay Kapone is planning something special for me," she said with hope.

"He's such a loser," I said. "You're too good for him."

"Tell that to my heart," she replied honestly.

"So did he hint around to what he may be getting you? He knows you need a car. There's no reason why you should still be riding the train when you're involved with a high-profile celebrity."

"A car!" she yelled. "He's not going to buy me a car. Besides, I've been saving money to purchase my own car. I want to do this by myself."

"Why would you want to do that?"

"To show him that I'm independent. That I can hold my own up against his other girlfriend . . . the infamous Marisol," she joked.

"You have nothing to prove to them. Besides, independence is hard work. I hate being independent. That's why I got married so I can put my independent heels in storage. But I do understand your point. How much do you have saved?"

"$1500."

"$1500! What are you trying to buy? A Neon?" I teased.

"Girrl, you know I can't come through driving a Neon."

"Exactly! You need a car to make Jay Kapone wonder where you got the cash. You need a car that will say, 'I may have another man checking for me.'"

"Yes! Like a Maximum!" she squealed.

"A Maximum is for kids graduating from high school. You need a Mercedes."

"I can't afford that."

"You can't afford much, but I can," I said.

"Oh-h-h-h, Nikki. No-o-o-o, you can't. You're the most generous person I know."

"Tell me something I don't know," I boasted.

"I love you."

"I know that."

"I really, really love you. I wish I were your sister instead of Noki."

"I wish you were my sister as well as Noki," I said truthfully.

"She doesn't appreciate you. All you've done for her and she has the nerve to not want people to know you're sisters. She should be dropping rose petals at your feet when you walk. Instead she's running around saying, 'I'm Japanese.' Like who cares? No one believes her anyway. All that junk in her trunk–it's obvious he's half black!"

"Noki is young and misunderstood. She'll eventually grow out of denying her heritage. Until then all I can do is support her."

"That's all she wants you to do. She's a freeloader. A fat, lazy, ungrateful–"

"Hey, hey. Calm down. That's my sister you're demeaning."

"I apologize. Listen, we'll talk later."

When Kayla's birthday came as promised, I rode her on my motorcycle to the Mercedes dealer on the East Side in Manhattan. Kayla was a scarety-cat when it came to bikes. She said that when she was younger she dated a guy who had a bike. One day he picked her up for a ride and they had gotten into a minor accident. Of course her love for me helped her overcome her fear, and she reluctantly got on my bike.

When we got inside the dealership, Kayla's face beamed with the enthusiasm of a young child on Christmas day.

"I can't believe you're doing this for me," she said shaking her head in disbelief.

"Kayla you've been here for me on more than one occasion. I honestly don't know what my life would be like if you weren't in it. Besides, I'm spending Jack's money on your gift."

"Jack?"

"Yes. He gives me an allowance and up until today, I've only used it on Noki."

I went to Charles. He's Jack's agent. As he filled out the paperwork for the convertible E 430, midnight blue exterior, with black leather interior, fully loaded and equipped, Kayla planted a fat, wet kiss on my cheek.

"I love you," she grinned.

"You luv my money," I joked.

"How will you be paying for this Mrs. Okayo," Charles asked.

I pulled out my black Centurion American Express and said, "Charge."

"Great. Just another few moments and you're all done."

Charles excused himself for a moment and I took this opportunity to confide in Kayla.

"Kayla, I'm not happy with Jack."

"I know."

"But I've never spoke about this before."

"You didn't have to. I know money doesn't buy love. You're not that kind of girl. I know you wish you could be with Brian."

"I do. I love him so much Kayla it hurts my heart," I whispered.

"Nikki, you're beautiful. There are a lot of men out here that will love you. Listen to me giving out advice. My man has another woman."

"You can take him from her. Work those hips girl," I laughed.

"Now it's time for me to confide something . . ."

"What?"

"I don't like sex . . . and I don't think I'm very good in bed."

"What!"

"It's true. Jay Kapone and I don't have sex very often. We just hang out and enjoy each other's company."

"Well, when was the last time you two made love?"

"About four months ago."

"Does he try to make love and you refuse?" I asked trying to assess the situation before commenting.

"No. Not really. He's stopped trying. I just ... I've never ... had an orgasm."

"What!" I yelled again. When everyone stopped and looked around at me, I whispered, "Why didn't you ever tell me?"

"What was I supposed to say?"

"What you just said."

"It's not like you can help. I think something is wrong with me."

"Not at all. It happens to most women because these men don't know what they're doing. It takes at least 20 minutes of foreplay and another 20 minutes of intercourse for a woman to have an orgasm. Did you know that?"

"No but Jay Kapone is a great lover. He's just ... a little ..."

"A little what?"

"A little," she said flatly.

"Oh, I get it. But size really doesn't matter. Just ride on top," I said trying to coach my friend into having an active sex life.

"I'm too self-conscience to ride on top. It embarrasses me."

"You're too sexy to be self-conscience. You better ride on top."

"How does that help *me*?"

"It gives you control in the bedroom with large or small penises. And try watching a porno movie and smoking some weed to loosen you up," I joked even though I was serious. Sex without an orgasm is like fame without the fortune. There's just no point. Then something spontaneously popped in my head.

"Kayla, I got a great idea."

"What's up?"

"Let's do something wild and crazy."

"Wild and crazy? On my birthday? I'm down."

"You better be. I want to get a tattoo with Brian's name on it."

"Nikki, you've haven't been with Brian in years. This is stupid."

I hadn't heard from him in years, a fact that had virtually left me devastated. Last time we spoke, I told him that I was going to go through with the marriage to Jack. I so desperately wanted him to stop me, but he didn't. Oddly Brian grew to resent me and felt that I'd betrayed him. I knew of Brian's adulation for me, but was it love? That question has haunted me like the spirit of my mother.

"So then I'm stupid. Listen, he's been calling me lately. He misses me. I think I hurt him marrying Jack. I want to do this gesture to prove to him once and for all that I love him and not Jack."

"Does a tattoo represent all of that?"

"A tattoo is more permanent than a marriage certificate. You can't divorce a tattoo, Kayla. But I can divorce Jack," I lamented.

"Would you?"

"Only for Brian. Now are you down?"

"To go with you? Sure."

"No. Are you down to get Jay Kapone's name? What do you say? It'll be fun."

Kayla thought for a moment, then said, "Hey, I only live once. Let's do it."

TWENTY·NINE

NIKKI LING

Kayla drove her new, shiny, Mercedes Benz off the lot and followed me on my motorcycle to West 4th Street. There on the corner of 8th Street was a small body piercing shop and tattoo artist. As we walked inside the place, I thought briefly about changing my mind. How could I conceal it from Jack? And could this small gesture finally convince Brian that I loved him?

Although it was my idea, Kayla seemed a little more excited than I was. She jumped out her new car with a huge grin plastered to her face. I'd never seen her look happier.

The shop was clean and smelled like a sterile doctor's office. A male with numerous body-piercing greeted us warmly.

"My name's Richard. What can I do for you ladies?" he asked.

"We're here to get a tattoo," I said.

"Well, you're in the right place. Take a look at our designs."

"Um-m-m, we kinda know what we want. We both want names. Our man name's."

He smiled and said, "Nice. I got my man's name on me too."

We all burst out into laughter.

"Come with me," he said and led us upstairs to a

tiny room. There you heard the drilling of a needle and someone grunting in pain.

"So, who's first?" he said as he pointed to an empty seat.

"I'll go," Kayla said before I had a chance to. "His name is Jay Kapone."

"Is he some sort of mafia figure?" Richard asked.

"Palezze," Kayla stated. "He wish. Where should I put it?"

"I don't know. Where do you want to put it?" I asked.

"Maybe on my forearm. So everyone can see it."

"Girlfriend, you do not want to put it there. That is so Rikers Island," Richard warned and I agreed.

"Well, I'm thinking about putting it on my ass. That way it will be concealed at all times. And the only person that will see it is my man. God knows my husband doesn't venture back there."

"Husband *and* boyfriend. Cute. I like your style," Richard commented.

Kayla agreed and put Jay Kapone's name on her butt. She screamed during the whole process and scared me to death. But after she had gotten the first one she said, "I want another one."

"After what you've been through?" I asked.

"Yes. I want another name."

"So you have a husband and boyfriend too?" Richard questioned.

"Not a boyfriend. I got a girlfriend though!" she exclaimed. "Nikki I want to put your name on me. You're my best friend."

"Kayla, you don't have to do this. Really. Does this have anything to do with the car?"

"Not at all. It's sort of like becoming blood sisters. But since that's so juvenile, this will have to do."

Kayla and I hugged and gave each other friendly kisses.

"Where do you want this one?" Richard asked.

"On the back of my neck. Could you right her name in Japanese lettering?" she questioned.

"Not a problem."

When it was my turn I decided to get Kayla's name written in Japanese on the back of my neck as well. Then I had Richard write *"Brian's Brat"* on my ass.

"Why brat?" Kayla asked.

"You know how Brian is always calling me a Melodrama Brat. I think he'll get a kick out of it."

"He'd better or else," Kayla warned.

We left out feeling really high off of life, and I was determined not to let anyone spoil that for me.

THIRTY

NIKKI LING

I was sleeping peacefully in our king-sized bed when someone came in and abruptly woke me. I was startled for a moment because I couldn't make out the silhouette in the dark. Briefly, I thought it was a kidnapping. Finally, my eyes adjusted and I could make out my husband.

"Get up!" he demanded. I quickly hustled out of the bed and did as I was told. I was then dragged into the shower to scrub. Jack turned the water on hot, and threw me in. I felt like lobsters being thrown into a scolding pot of water as I tried to fight my way back out. The water felt like fire as my skin was singed; I screamed in agony.

"Shut up you little whore and scrub!"

I grabbed the soap as I had done on so many occasions and complied. Jack soon assisted me with a hard-bristle brush that ripped my skin apart. I stayed mute from fear of what he would do if I protested. With my skin pink and raw, I was finally allowed to emerge from the shower. From there, I was led back into our bedroom. I was nude and dripping wet. If Jack had noticed my new tattoo, he never said a word.

"Fuck me!" Jack said in a perverse tone. I gently laid myself down on the bed, careful not to voice my discomfort and spread my legs wide open. Jack stood back in the corner and lit a flashlight on me and I began.

I started to massage my breast sensually until my nipples were erect. Then I inserted my left nipple in my mouth and began to suck passionately. I softly let out a moan. With my right hand, I started to massage my clitoris until my pussy was pulsating. I then inserted my index finger and started to grind my hips until I was breathing heavily and moaning softly just as Jack liked me to do. Suddenly he thrust a vibrator on the bed. "Fuck me, bitch!" he snickered. I reached for it and began to masturbate. I turned it on and thrust the vibrator in my pussy with force. Jack would have it no other way. With both hands guiding the vibrator, I hit my G-spot and climaxed all over our $5,000 Queen Helene silk sheets. I knew I had satisfied him. I lay still until Jack left to take a shower. He had to scrub himself clean after each "lovemaking" session. Jack and I had never consummated our marriage. On our wedding night, I was given a hot shower and an artificial dick. Instantly, I realized I had been bamboozled.

I lay there looking up at the ceiling until tiny tears of frustration escaped my eyes. I was nothing but a dirty little whore.

When morning came, I awoke to a brand new Mercedes Benz G-500 truck. A gift from Jack. I smiled politely and accepted his peace offering. Jack's generosity paled in comparison to his misogynistic character.

I threw the keys to my new G-5 truck in the bureau. I knew I'd never drive that vehicle.

THIRTY·ONE

KAPRI HENDERSON

2002

Bitches better stay the fuck outta my face and dat's my word!" I screamed and slammed my front door in that trifling whore's face.

I was talkin' to my landlord. She keeps tryin' to play me. E'er since my aunt left me this crib, which is rent-stabilized, my landlord keeps comin' fo me. She wants my black ass out so she kin hike up da rent. But no–can–do. I keep tellin' her a bitch did 13 years upstate–I am not the one. Word.

I kicked off my brand new pair of Timberland boots (a bitch keep a fresh pair) and walked barefoot through my crib. I was about to relax in front my large screen TV, when someone knocked on the door. I sucked my teeth and yelled, "Who?" No one answered. It better not be my son, Kareem, saying he lost his keys.

When I opened the door, it was one of my customers, Gigit.

"Wassup Kapri. I got this here fo' you," she said and smiled a toothless grin. I looked and it was a practically new DVD player.

"This shit is phat!" I said and invited her in. "Where you git this from?"

She looked over her shoulders—'cause a bitch was paranoid and said, "I boosted it from my aunt. She don't need it no way. You want it?"

"How much?"

"Fifty dollars."

"Fifty dollars," I said, already jewin' her down in my mind.

"Yeah. How much you got? I can take some now and den come back later fo' da rest."

"Stay right here," I said. "And you better not move Gigit. If I come back and if'n it looks like you tried to steal from me, I'ma whip your ass! A bitch did 13 years upstate."

I ran in my bedroom into my stash and pulled out 5 nickels of crack vials. I went back into the living room and Gigit was still standin' there in the same spot. Pacin' and lookin' around.

"Here. It's all I got."

"$25. You ain't got two more? Come on K—"

"I said this all I mutherfuckin' got! Do you want it or not?"

Gigit stuffed the cocaine–crack viles in her pocket and scurried out my front door. I was mad happy! I needed a DVD player to hook-up on my big–ass TV. I already had the X–Box and VCR. All the little gadgets to keep a man happy 'cause I ain't down wit that gay shit no more.

Shortly after I had took off my jeans to relax, my son Kareem came home. It was nearly ten o'clock at night.

"Kareem, git your ass in here now boy!" I yelled. He dropped something on the floor (it sounded like his coat and books) and came to the back where my bedroom was.

"Yes ma'am."

"Don't fuckin' ma'am me, smart-ass. I dun tole your fool–ass I ain't no ol' lady. Call me Kapri. I dun had your ass back for a year now from your foster home, and you keep fuckin' up. You as dumb as a day is long!" I yelled at his stupid–ass.

"Yes, Kapri," he said and put his head down. He looked just like his no–good father, whoever he was, 'cause a bitch didn't know. But I knew he didn't look like me.

"Look in my top drawer and take out fifty–jumbos and go up on Parkside Avenue and sell my shit. It's too hot downstairs to sell my crack. 5-O been bustin' niggas right and left."

"Now?"

"Boy git your ass over there and git my crack and make my money. Shit! I gotta pay rent up in here."

"Kapri, it's late. I have to go to school tomorrow," he sulked.

I jumped up immediately. This boy was workin' my nerves.

"Out! Get the fuck out and make my mutherfuckin' money!" I yelled and punched him in his chest.

Kareem snatched the crack, and mumbled underneath his breath, "If I get killed, don't say nothing!"

"Boy pa-leeze," I said and dismissed him.

THIRTY·TWO

KAPRI HENDERSON

I had been thinkin' 'bout my drug operation fo some time now and wanted to expand. I needed more paper so I could buy more coke and make a bigger profit. I wanted to buy me a phat ride. I gotz to get the Cadillac Escalade. I want it white and chromed out, sittin' on dubs with the Spreewells that keep on spinnin'. That shit is so hot right now.

And I didn't splurge my money on stupid shit, like platinum jewelry and bottles of Moet in the club. I was saving for my future. A bitch deserved to get up out da 'hood soon. The only luxury I'ma allow myself is a jeep. Drop thirty, forty grand on it. Cash. That's how I want it to go down. Yeah, I'ma go to the dealer this week and price my shit.

Today, I was knocked out sleepin' until damn near five o'clock in the afternoon. I got up to an empty apartment. Kareem wasn't around. I didn't have shit to do, so I decided to walk to McDonald's up on Parkside Avenue. Give me somethin' to do. Now the only thing I hadda do was find somethin' to wear: I got an image to keep up wit.

I went to my closet, which was filled wit nothin' but clothes wit tags on them. I pulled out a blue velour Rockawear sweat suit, a pair of black Diesel sneakers, and a blue Gucci bag. I was tight. I had went up on Flatbush

Avenue to Maribel's Hair Salon and got a wash and set, so my shoulder length hair was silky.

Once I was dressed, I looked in the mirror at my ass. I loved the way the velour made my ass look. I'ma go and git me a few more of these sweat suits in ev'ry color. Then I went to my stash that I kept hidden in shoe boxes in the bottom of my closet, and pulled out a wad of cash. I didn't count it. I just put a rubber band around it and broke out.

As I was walkin' across Ocean Avenue, a black Range Rover came cruisin' by and slowed down as I passed. I peeped in the back and saw it was a 4.0, instead of a 4.6, so I wasn't impressed.

"Yo, shorty, hold up," the passenger said.

Why is it always the passenger tryin' to get ya number? All they fuckin' do is hang out the car window and holla at girls. And we don't want their 'no car having' asses.

I just kept walkin' towards McDonald's, but he wouldn't let up. The car was drivin' slowly, parallel from where I was walkin'.

"You lookin' good, sexy. Could I git ya digits?" he begged.

I looked at him; he was cute too. But I wanted the driver, although he wasn't as cute as his friend. But he had the ride, which meant he had the paper. So, I slowed down, then stopped.

"Whadup," I said with a smile. I was lookin' directly at the driver.

"Hey, shorty, whadup?" the passenger said.

"Shit. Whadup wit you and your mans 'n them?" I asked. The passenger got the hint.

"She talkin' 'bout you kid," the passenger said to his friend.

"Oh word," the driver said.

"Word. What's really good?" I asked.

"You tell me, Ma," the driver said.

"Well, I'm what's really good," I said flirting.

"Shorty, what's your name," the passenger said tryin' to git back in my conversation.

"Kapri."

"Kapri. That's very cute. My name is Keith and this is Eddie," the passenger said.

"So, Eddie, what's up with the 4.0. Didn't you hear Jay–Z say true players drive 'round in 4.6."

"Yo, fuck that nigga, yo. You like him?"

"I like how he came up. I'm from the gutter just like Jay. I wanna come up too, ya heard."

"Yeah, that's what's up," he remarked. "Could I git your number. You got a man?" Eddie asked.

"Naw, I ain't got no man. I got friends though," I flirted as I wrote down my digits and passed it to him.

"I hear that. We 'bout to bounce, though. I'ma hit you up later," Eddie said.

As I turned to walk away, Keith called my name, "Kapri."

When I turned around, he threw an empty plastic bottle at me and said, "Skeezer!"

As Eddie pulled off, I could hear Keith burstin' into laughter.

Stupid mutherfucker, I thought, as I looked around to make sure no one had seen what happened.

THIRTY·THREE

NIKKI LING

Noki, pick up the phone." I was talking to my sister's answering machine. She always screened her calls.

"Kon'nichi wa," she responded as she picked up the telephone.

"You ready? I want to work today." I was in a bad mood from last night and wanted to go out hustling.

"What's wrong? You sound a little edgy . . . not that I really care," she tried to say it as a joke but deep down I knew she was telling the truth. She didn't care.

"Nothing's wrong. My fingers are tingling. I want to be paid today! I want to hit the LIRR, this afternoon. You down?" I asked.

"Nikki, I am always down to get paid. Noki needs a new pair of Manolos." We both laughed and met an hour later.

I wore my usual black ensemble. That was the rule. Never wear bright colors. You had to blend into the crowd. I always tried to be as nondescript as possible.

We had been in the LIRR station nearly an hour before I spotted my mark. He wore an overcoat and carried a briefcase. He was clean–shaven, his fingers were manicured, and his upper-left side pocket was bulging. I immediately pepped up. Until now, I had been down.

I gave Noki the signal, and we both boarded the train with my mark. It was approximately three minutes between station stops–so I had to be precise in my maneuvering.

The mark was engrossed in a *New York Times* article about the former senator's wife, Estelle Cardinale. He grunted a little in disgust. "Waste of intelligence," I heard him mumble, while I was lifting his wallet from his overcoat. He never suspected a thing. I was good at my shit!

I immediately passed off the mark's wallet to Noki, and we both exited the train with the rest of the passengers in anonymity. Noki met me back at our diner on 33rd and 5th thirty minutes later. We always said that if something went wrong, we would meet under the Brooklyn Bridge.

I divvied up the $6,000 dollars and we ordered lunch.

"Not bad for a couple hours work!" I bragged.

After lunch, I left Noki, headed over to Chase Manhattan Bank on Lexington Avenue, and stashed my money in my safety deposit box. I had opened up my account seven years earlier. I never counted my money because it was an old taboo belief that if I did, the money would stop rolling in. So, I just let it pile up for a rainy day. At 25, life was—for the most part—splendid. I did what I wanted to do. Bought what I wanted to buy. In addition, fucked whomever I wanted to fuck. Could I ask for more? Sure! But, can't everyone?

THIRTY·FOUR

NIKKI LING

Next, I headed over to Celina's Day Spa at 59th and Park Avenue. This was an exclusive day spa and gym and the membership fee was $34,000 a year, which I charged to my black Centurion American Express card. I went every Friday at noon. I walked in with mucho bravado. Head held high, chest out, and attitude intact. My 5' 10", statuesque figure usually intimidates people.

After my luxurious massage, I went into the steam room. My body needed hydration because this weather chaps the skin. I was in there alone for maybe ten minutes when this attractive, petite, white woman joined me. We made eye contact. I didn't recognize her, but she smiled familiarly anyway. Fearing she may want to engage in "small talk," I rolled my eyes and shifted my body away from her. She sat quietly for a moment. Then looked around and whispered, "Your name is Nikki Ling-Okayo. Correct?"

Taken aback, I said, "That's my sister. I'm Noki. Pardon, have we met?"

"Nikki we've never met before, but we will get to know each other soon," she responded.

I wondered briefly if she was a cop. Upon close examination, I knew she wasn't. Too pampered.

"Really?" I said and my forehead creased in bewilderment.

"Yes. I've been watching you for a while . . . ."

"*Watching* me?"

"Intently," she said.

"And . . .?"

"And I think we should make each other's acquaintance."

"Sorry, you're not my type," I said and rolled my Japanese eyes.

"Don't flatter yourself, bitch! Let's just say I'm the bearer of bad news, the grim reaper," she coldly stated.

"What the fuck are you talking about? And be specific because I hate riddles. They're for kids."

"The news I have is for adults only."

"Is this news going to cost me?"

"That depends on whether you're a person who makes things happen, or a person who sits back and watches things happen."

"Cut the trivia, cunt, and spill it," I snapped.

She looked me in my eyes intently then said, "Your name is Nikkisi Ling. You're 25 years old and married to one of the richest, most powerful men in South Africa, Jack Okayo. Your mother was a prostitute, killed herself when you were young. You and your sister went to different foster homes until you were fourteen. From there, you took your sibling, four years your junior and supported her and yourself by picking pockets and turning tricks. You were arrested quite a few times but never did any hard time. You soon perfected your craft, which allowed you to live an opulent lifestyle. Soon you were hooked up with the rich and famous, mingling, fucking, while lying to acquaintances about your identity. Three years ago, you married Jack Okayo and things seemed brighter. I'm here to tell you that your ice castle is slowly melting."

"Humor me," I said nonchalantly, showing no sign of fear.

"Jack is going to file for an annulment approximately one month before your five-year anniversary. You will be removed from your home, bank accounts will be frozen, and no one will return your calls. His friends will alienate themselves from you. Two months later, you will be a memory. In the blink of an eye your plush lifestyle will be ripped from your grasp!"

"Who are you? Are you his attorney? Why are you telling me this?"

"Because I have a proposition for you. A way you can keep your title as Jack Okayo's wife and his money. All of it!"

"But my prenuptial agreement specifies that if we are married for five years I get $10 million. After ten years, I get $15 million. If I have children, I get $2 million per child. I haven't met any of these requirements."

"And you won't. Jack never intended for you or any other woman to ever get their hands on his money. Moreover, he's sterile. Therefore, you will bear him no child. It's part of his sick, twisted personality. It's all a game, Nikki, but you can get the last laugh!"

I sat there almost trembling at the fact that I could lose my multi-million-dollar status and the prestige of being Mrs. Okayo. But I wondered for a moment how this stranger knew so much. What did she want?

"Are you trying to get rid of me so you can fill my shoes?"

"Nikki, I've already been there. I, too, am an ex-wife of Jack's. He nearly ruined my life. He filed for an annulment, and I was left penniless. Out of desperation, I slit my wrist. Luckily, someone found me and God gave me my life back. A year after my divorce from Jack, I remarried a wealthy banker who died in a tragic plane crash. I was the sole heir to his estate. At 27, I am worth millions."

"Dude, I have no time for this. I've heard enough of this charade." I tried to get up and leave when she grabbed my wrist and held me down tightly. For a petite woman she had a strong grip. I shook myself loose, but didn't move. She continued, "I have to protect my assets. I'm in a peculiar situation with a cheating husband. I've been married to my current husband for a few years and he has the goods on me. He has pictures of me . . . with . . . other women. He's threatened to go to the tabloids. . ."

"What does that have to do with me?"

"I need you to kill him."

Her eyes were icy gray. She sent a chill down my spine as she casually said "kill" as though it was as widely accepted as the word "love." I exhaled, then said, "Your problems are your problems. I think you're the one with the sick, twisted mind."

"Nikki, don't take me for a fool or insult my intelligence. It makes me angry. I want you to kill my husband, so I can keep my fortune. In return, I'll kill your husband, and you'll get to keep all *his* fortune."

"Murder has never been my thing."

"Who are you fooling? You're a thief."

"And I'm good with my shit, but I am no murderer."

"Nikki this is the perfect plan. We'll swap murders just like in the Alfred Hitchcock film *Strangers on a Train*. No one will connect me to your murder and no one will connect you to mine. We are perfect strangers.

We'll just *criss cross*."

"What type of asinine plan is that? They'd have my black ass strapped to the electric chair before the guilty verdict was rendered! Just in case you didn't do enough research on me, Nikki Ling can take care of herself. Maybe I'll even take that soon-to-be ex-husband of yours. How much did you say he's worth?"

Suddenly, I had become bored with this psycho chick. Jack wasn't going anywhere. I consistently gave him what he wanted. What man on earth could leave me behind? I got up to leave this time, and I gave her a look to let her know that if she even looked like she was going to reach for me, I'd karate-chop her ass. As I strolled out, she yelled after me, "You have eight weeks, Nikki, then it'll be too late."

THIRTY·FIVE

NIKKI LING

As I rode the West Side Highway on my motorcycle, I thought about my encounter with the stranger. *"You have eight weeks, then it'll be too late,"* she'd said. Curiously, I wondered if there was any merit to her assumption that Jack was going to divorce me. Feeling slightly anxious, I decided I needed a drink.

I was driving aimlessly around because I didn't feel like going home. When I found myself on Chambers Street near the Brooklyn Bridge, I parked my bike and randomly chose a local bar. As I entered Joey's Tavern, I heard the jukebox playing old Jimi Hendrix tunes and immediately wanted to do an about face. But, for some strange reason, I entered anyway.

The bar was downstairs, but many people were standing outside and smoking cigarettes. I made my way to the bartender and ordered a Heineken. As soon as my beer came, a patron walked over and struck up a conversation.

"May I pay for that?" he announced grandly.

"Dude, I can drop three bucks on a beer. If you want to impress me, disappear," I stated. Startled, he backed off.

As I surveyed the room, I noticed most of the men were checking me out; all but one, a scruffy guy who looked drunk. He had blond hair, blue eyes, and was sitting alone with several empty beer bottles cluttering his table. He was now gobbling up hot wings from the kitchen, no doubt trying to absorb the liquor in his body. I approached him with caution and, to my surprise, I immediately recognized him.

"May I join you?" I asked.

Startled, he looked up at me with a blank expression. His eyes were searching for a clue as to where he knew me. Once he realized I was a stranger, he said, "Not tonight slim."

"Thank you," I said and sat down anyway.

He stopped eating for a brief second, clearly agitated at my blatant disregard for his order and yelled, "Jesus, Mary and Joseph! If you're a hooker, I'm broke! And I'm not partial to any freebies."

"Dude, you couldn't afford me . . ."

"What?" he asked, perplexed.

"You're the lawyer from television, aren't you? The dope dealer that got busted?" I asked.

"This is where I get the fuck up and leave," he announced. He tried to get up, wobbled, then sat back down. Slowly, he lifted his hands and cradled his head as if he were rocking the pain away. He looked a mess.

"Take it easy pops . . . I ain't judging you. If you want to snort Peru— that's your bag. I've got my own issues."

"I'm innocent," he whispered and looked nervously around. "Don't you read the papers? My conviction was overturned. And I wasn't arrested for snorting Peru, the charge was for buying with the intent to distribute narcotics, Ms. Know-it-all!"

"Dude, I have a real keen sense of my environment, and I know you weren't pushing coke through it. I know that because you have tell-tale signs of a user. You've left one addiction for another one," I accused.

Whether or not I was accurate in my analysis wasn't relevant. All I wanted to do was get a reaction and have a little fun. He didn't remember me, but when I was 15 years old I was busted for prostituting. He was the D.A. at the time and wanted me to do some real jail time. But the judge was a little more sympathetic, and I got a slap on the wrist. Funny how our lives had criss crossed.

"Je-sus! What's wrong with you? I'm an innocent man. The court of appeals overturned my conviction. I was framed."

"I don't know about all of that . . . ," I said still badgering him.

"Did someone send you here? Are you some sort of *snitch* the D.A. has

planted? They want you to lure me into saying something incriminating?"

"You are the paranoid one, aren't you?" I accused.

"Paranoid? No. Let's just say that I have a real keen sense of my environment and I know that out of all the seats you could have taken in this joint, you took the one next to me. Now either my unshaven, inebriated appearance is attractive to you. Or . . . you've been planted."

"I love smelly, old men," I joked–only he didn't laugh. There was something extremely *sexy* about this white guy. Even though he was having a bad day, he looked every bit as scrumptious as Brad Pitt on a good day. I was instantly turned on.

"Tell the truth. Detective Holmes sent you, didn't he?

You coming in here with your long hair weave, long legs and—"he slurred.

"Hair weave?" I asked and he looked at me in the most peculiar fashion.

"Listen Slim, I'm in a rush to go nowhere. Will you excuse me?" he said. This time when he stood up, he didn't wobble. He marched right out of the bar, and I watched him go. My fun was over for the night.

THIRTY·SIX

NOKI LING

2002

As I sat nibbling on my fingernails, I suddenly had an epiphany. If I started stashing money *before* Nikki and I met at the diner, how would she know? She doesn't handle the money until I pass it to her. So why not cut myself a side deal before her arrival. I smiled to myself at my newfound plan. It was brilliant! Anyway, it's not like Nikki *needs* the money. She's fucking loaded. She lucked out marrying that prick. I was getting a little impatient waiting for someone of his caliber with money to marry me.

I honestly was left baffled as to how a prostitute could land a multimillionaire, while I was left out in the cold. I mean, sure Nikki is attractive, but she's dumb. And I guess men like long legs, but she's too skinny. And, what's most important, is that I bet she can't even count how many men she's been with. Now I, too, have had my share of men. But, at least I never sold my body. I'm clearly the better choice here. So, why was everyone blinded by Nikki?

I can't stand it. I have to lie to her about everything just to get a few extra bucks. My most recent lie is that I'm still in Barnard. I dropped out a while ago, but I still collected a hefty check from Nikki to pay college tuition.

As I already stated, Nikki's not the sharpest knife in the drawer. She's just plain stupid.

After sulking for a while, I realized my morning had been uneventful. I decided to get dressed and run down to Bergdorf Goodman on 5th Avenue to go shopping.

With a garment bag draping my arm, I strolled, head held high, into the store. I took the escalator directly to the third floor and headed to the John Galliano section. The floor was virtually empty since it was midday. I immediately saw the most divine, three-piece pantsuit. Once I located my size, a solid fourteen, I looked around briefly to see if anyone was watching me. No one. Then I bent down and quickly bit on the plastic sensomatic alarm. Click-clack. It popped off with ease. I proceeded to remove the rest of the alarms. Click-clack. Click-clack.

Once the items were clean, I moved further into a corner and put two sets of the outfit inside my garment bag. Just as I zipped up my bag, I realized the store had a camera in the section. "These old cameras don't work," I thought. Next, I looked around to find a place to stash the alarms I had removed. I walked around with them concealed until I found a spot that held folded cashmere sweaters. I just casually placed them underneath a sweater and continued to look for more clothing to steal.

Two other black women were also browsing in this section. We greeted each other with smiles. They didn't suspect a thing. Then I spotted this gorgeous brown cashmere sweater trimmed in mink. The price tag was a ridiculous $4200. With the other two women in the section, I quickly bent down and snapped the alarm. Click-clack. Everyone froze. A nosy sales representative, who must have heard the familiar sound of thievery, came over quickly. Her eyes met mine first, then they went to my garment bag.

"May I help you with something?" she asked. I immediately felt nervous. "Not at this moment," I said in Japanese, pretending not to know any English. I smiled grandly and flashed my presidential Rolex in her face. Although she had no idea what I'd said, she immediately backed down and diverted her attention to the two black women who had up until now gone unnoticed.

She walked over to them and asked the same question. They both politely refused her assistance, but she didn't leave them alone. She stayed on their backs like black to night. While she was focused on the black women, this helped me to take the gorgeous sweater I wanted. As I slipped it inside my garment bag, the sales representative found the alarms I had left behind and went ballistic. "Security! Security!" she screamed.

The well-dressed black women were startled. As they tried to exit and get away from this overzealous woman, she grabbed the handles of both of their shopping bags so they couldn't leave. As security came running down the hall, I passed them on the walkway and slowly exited the store, garments in tow. In fact, the door attendant actually held the door open for my departure.

As the afternoon air hit my face, I let out a healthy laugh. It felt good. I felt wonderful, but my day wasn't over yet. I ran back to my car and dumped the clothes into my trunk. Then I went right back into the store to the John Galliano section. Once there, I called for assistance. You could still hear the commotion over on the other side. I'm sure those two women were outraged at the way they were treated.

The sales representative came over immediately. I picked up the same suit I had just stolen and purchased it, careful to purchase the same size I had in the trunk—so the SKU could match the receipt of the items I had stolen. The sales representative rang up my items, which totaled $6000. I paid cash.

"May I have a gift receipt in addition to my receipt," I asked. Then added, "Just in case they would like to return it for something else."

"Sure, I understand. Not a problem. Would you like this gift wrapped," he smiled.

"No, thank you," I politely replied. "Are you here all day?"

"I get off at three. Will you be needing anything else?"

"No, thank you."

"Have a good day."

"Thank you. You do the same."

When I got out of Bergdorf's for the second time, I hit a couple more stores. Saks, Hermes, Henry Bendell. By the time I was done, my trunk was full of luxurious items. I had well over $30,000 worth of merchandise I had shoplifted. I wasn't just the average "booster" as they say in the streets. I was a businesswoman. A good businesswoman deals in currency. So at approximately four o'clock, I marched right back to Bergdorf Goodman's John Galliano section. Just as the sales representative had said, he was gone. This time a red-haired, refined, forty-ish-looking woman was on duty. She smiled politely at me.

"May I help you with something?" she asked. I immediately thrust the stolen three-piece suit in her face.

"My sister just purchased this for me today as a consolation gift for fucking my husband. And, in true *bitch* fashion, she got me a much larger size than I really need. Now look at me," I said and stood back so she could admire my figure. Then continued, "Do I look like a size fourteen?"

I could tell she was perplexed from my use of profanity as well as my most uppity tone. Her eyes glanced at the price tags, then over to me. She then lifted her right eyebrow in skepticism and said, "You want to return this?"

"Oh, heavens no. The garments are lovely. I just would like my size, darling."

"Do you have a receipt?"

"To exchange? Do I really need one?"

"Yes. If you do not have one, perhaps you could go back to your sister and return with the receipt, in which case we will be happy to do an exchange."

I fumbled inside my yellow Samantha Thavasa handbag, pulled out my recently received gift receipt, and presented it to the cautious sales representative. Once this was done, everything changed. The earlier skepticism turned into kind smiles and kind words. I was led over to the rack of garments, where she picked out a size twelve for me, took me back to the register and rang-up my items, thus giving me a new original receipt. Once again, Bergdorf Goodman let me walk out with my merchandise.

Yet, my hustle still wasn't over. In the next week, I returned both suits, receiving my original $6,000, and another $6,000, in addition to a luxurious $6000, John Galliano suit to sport out on a hot date. Life was so sweet.

THIRTY·SEVEN

NOKI LING

You da bomb Ling," Eddie drawled. He called me Ling instead of Noki. He was infatuated with the fact that I was Japanese. He had no idea I was half-black. No one knew . . . except Nikki. Eddie and I have been dating for years, but I don't take him seriously. He never takes me out anywhere and we spend most of our time in my apartment. Fucking. When I ask him personal questions, he's evasive. Recently I've been missing expensive garments out of my closet. I've questioned Eddie but he denied any knowledge of the missing items. I've given up trying to get to know Eddie. The most he's told me, is that he has a daughter by a girl named Trisha and, although he said they aren't together, I suspected otherwise.

We were in my Soho duplex listening to the new Tweet CD. *"Oops, there goes my skirt . . ."* I had on Vicky Secret's best silk lingerie, and my man appreciated every inch of me.

He was laying across my queen-size mahogany bed with no shirt, blue jeans, and Timberland boots on. He was such a thug! His brown skin, muscular frame and sneaky eyes had me mesmerized. He always kept his mustache and beard shaved and had his wavy-hair cut really low. He always looked neat.

I walked over to my stereo and put on a mixed tape to get my private party started. *"Don't stop, get it, get it, pop that pussy . . . do-do brown,"* blared from the system.

"Come on, Ma, make your booty clap. Back dat thang up," he cheered as I wobbled around gyrating my hips like I see the girls in the music videos do. I opened my legs, squatted down, and thrust my hips in and out. After a few minutes, I was out of breath. I started to perspire and I smelled a pungent odor coming from in between my legs. I slowly came up and danced off beat in my stilettos over to where Eddie was.

Eddie grabbed me roughly, threw me upon the bed, and began to rip my $200 silk lingerie off. I squealed with delight. Eddie knew me well. I loved rough sex. Once he had ripped off my clothing, he turned me over and slapped my ass. Smack! It jiggled like Jell-o. Smack . . . smack . . . smack. My once olive skin was now red and bruised. Eddie then grabbed out his rock–hard penis through his jeans and roughly rammed it into my ass. I was crouched over holding my bedpost for support. Eddie grabbed my jet-black hair and twisted my soft locks around his fingers and pulled like it were reigns on a horse while he had me mounted.

"This shit is s-o-o-o-o good. Damn Ling you got a nigga whipped!" he crooned.

As he pumped in and out, he damn near ripped my hair from my head. Experienced enough to keep fucking on beat, I simultaneously reached up and grabbed Eddie's hands and removed them from my hair. He was getting a little carried away.

Eddie then focused on my ass cheeks and began to massage them. As he slowed down, he gently pulled his penis out and inserted his tongue in my anus. My eyes popped open in surprise. He'd never done *this* before. As his tongue darted in and out, he took his index finger and played with my pussy. At first, he inserted it gently; my warm juices ran down his finger. Next, he inserted two fingers at one time and moved them in a circular motion all while his tongue licked and sucked my anal passage.

"How does it feel, mommy?" Eddie panted in between licks.

"Yes . . . yes . . . keep doing it like that . . . right there . . . it feels so-o-o-o-o good," I crooned.

"Say dat shit in Japanese, ma. Say it for daddy in dat fly shit you be kickin."

"Ren'aich . . . neru . . . neru . . . oh . . . neru . . . koibito . . . ooh," I moaned little sentiments of love in his ear.

"I want you to have my kids, Ling. I want a baby girl wit dat good hair you got," he breathed heavily.

"I want you to cum in me daddy. I want . . . ahhh . . . ooh . . ." my words trailed off because the pleasure was too intense for talking.

I flipped over and pushed Eddie back so he could admire all one hundred and sixty pounds of sexiness. Then I laid back on the bed and spread my legs open.

"Come to big-momma," I commanded.

Eddie came at me with the force of a gladiator swinging his cock like an expert swordsman. He mounted me and we moved in harmony. We were both sweating copiously as we both reached our peaks. I could feel Eddie tense up and arch his back. I contracted my pussy as we both exploded into each other. It felt like it lasted for hours, as we lay there exhausted.

I jumped up spontaneously, ran naked through the house to the kitchen, and came back with some Haagen–Dazs vanilla ice cream. Eddie was immediately furious. His thick eyebrows merged together. He lashed out, "Can't your fat-ass stop fuckin' eatin' everythin' in sight? Damn, yo—you really know how to turn a nigga off!"

Eddie immediately jumped off the bed and began getting dressed. I was in shock. I still had the spoon in between my lips and ice cream dripping out the corner of my mouth as he was lacing up his Timberland boots. I could not figure out what had just happened. We were just making love.

"And take your silly-ass back to school and get your degree. You 21— ya ass gettin' old. I can't have no lazy, dumb broad raisin' my kids," he yelled.

What kids? I thought but said nothing.

Eddie pushed past me and slammed the door downstairs leaving just the echo of his harsh words behind.

THIRTY·EIGHT

NIKKI LING

I stood in the mirror admiring my chocolate–shaded statuesque figure. I was completely naked. My firm 36 D–cup breasts were just as perky now as when I was fifteen years old. Only now, my body had matured. My waist was an extraordinary 19-inches and my hips were 36-inches. I was *Playboy* material. No bitch could fuck with me!

Instead of honing my talent as the world's greatest jostler, I should have been modeling all through Europe. I sure as hell look better than most of them model broads. Naomi has nothing on Nikki. Often I get mistaken for Naomi Campbell until they realize that I have Asian eyes and hair. I'd be just as fierce on the catwalk.

Just then, a rap song came on over the radio, *"Move bitch, get out the way."* I just laughed outwardly and decided to get dressed, although I had nowhere to go. I grabbed a pair of vintage Levi boot-cut jeans, a T-shirt that said, "Melodramatic Brat" and a pair of crocodile cowboy boots. I pulled my hair back in a tight ponytail and put on a pair of dangling sterling silver earrings. Marriage had afforded me the platinum jewelry if I wanted it–the pink diamonds, Rolex watches, Cartier trinkets–but that just wasn't my style. I like simple things. I must admit that I love designer pocketbooks and nice shoes and boots, but that's my limit. My sister, on the other hand, is a name–

brand whore. She's a little pretentious, but I know it has a lot to do with our upbringing, not having much of anything; now, thanks to me, she has enough money to afford a decent lifestyle.

I decided to take a walk in Central Park, when my cell phone rang. I answered on the third ring, "This me–this you?" I said, not knowing of who was on the other end.

"Why you give my pussy away?" the caller questioned. I could tell from the voice it was Brian, Brian Carter.

"Dude, it's still yours. Say the word and let's make it happen."

My heart was pounding faster from the sound of his voice.

"Are you wearing panties?" he quizzed. He already knew the answer to that question.

"Do I ever?"

"That's a good look for you," he said, while laughing.

"Always," I retorted.

"Come to my office," he breathed. Without hesitation, I said, "I'll be there in ten minutes." We both hung up and I felt elated. I grabbed a taxi to Wall Street where he was located.

I took the elevator up to the 43rd floor. His whole staff knew me well. I walked through like I was royalty. His secretary, an ordinary-looking black woman with a bad hair weave, didn't particularly care for my presence. As soon as I came through the large cherry wood doors, she made a lemon-sucking face, then rolled her blue contact lenses. I had long ago suspected that Brian had fucked his secretary and may be still fucking her.

"Tell Brian I've arrived," I demanded.

"Your name?" she sarcastically replied.

"Ling. Nikki LING. And bitches better get it right!" I snapped. She stared at me firmly, then said into the intercom, "Mrs. Okayo is here."

Not wanting to be outdone, I grabbed a memo pad off her desk and signed my name then gave it to her.

"What's this for?" she asked.

"Sweetie, it's my autograph to a fan. Maybe you can sell it on E-bay to get enough coins to tighten up your weave. Ciao." Having said that I sauntered into Brian's office knowing she was watching each leg extend beyond the other.

Once inside, I quickly locked his door, so we wouldn't be disturbed. We embraced and he smelled wonderful. I couldn't make out the scent, but it was worth every penny he'd paid. It was driving me crazy.

I looked directly into his eyes and smiled. He'd done so well for himself at such a young age. Sadly, instead of us building an empire together, he built his alone with me peeking over his shoulders.

"You know, you really have to do something about that miserable bitch out there."

"Who Joy?" he asked innocently.

"You fucked her, didn't you?"

"Is that a question?"

"Whatever," I said, dismissing the subject and walked over to his windows to admire the view. I suddenly felt sad. I was feeling somewhat nostalgic, and I didn't like it one bit. Also, the encounter I had at the day-spa was haunting me. What if this mysterious stranger was correct? What if Jack really planned on annulling our marriage and leaving me penniless? What would I do? What *could* I do? Go back to prostituting? Noticing my mood had shifted, he walked over and embraced me.

"Let's get out of here," I said.

"You want to go to lunch?"

"No. Not like that. Let's leave here. Let's go to Egypt and see the pyramids. Or Paris and see the Eiffel Tower. Let's just go . . . together . . . we can do it. We can do anything we want. There's nothing stopping us, Brian."

"Really? What about a marriage decree," he mockingly replied. Then continued, "Yeah, how 'bout that!"

"You know how much I love you, Brian. Don't do this to me. I never loved Jack. It was never about Jack."

"Just his money."

"Exactly," I replied. Then said, "I am my mother's child. I needed stability for Noki and me. You know you could have stopped me . . . if you truly loved me, you could have stopped me."

"Don't blame our break-up on me! You made all the choices. I was just a pawn in your chess game."

"You don't really believe that, do you? That I ran around looking for a victim. Any old dude would do."

The room fell silent as we both studied each other.

"I have a gift for you," I said, turned around, pulled down my jeans and let him see my tattoo.

"Brian's Brat, huh?" he chuckled. "How long you had that?"

"Long enough."

"You fuck your husband with my name on your ass?" he said seductively getting turned on.

We embraced again and synchronously started to softly kiss each other. My tongue playfully teased his until he cupped my face and made each kiss long and sensual. I started to feel faint as he kissed and gently bit my neck. His hands methodically groped my breasts until I was ripping off his shirt and pulling off my jeans.

He threw me up against the wall and I straddled him with my long legs. With his legs as strong as pillars, he held all my weight and entered me feverishly. I moaned in pleasure trying to take in every inch of his enormous dick. Each time he would push a little harder trying to open my deep cave to its full capacity. Finally, my body welcomed all of him. I was so warm and wet and extremely horny. I wanted to take him in my mouth like old times.

"Let me suck your dick, daddy," I whispered in his ear.

"I fuck you better than that motherfucker don't I, Nikki? I fuck you better than your husband?" he asked, ignoring my request.

"Yes, daddy . . . oh yes."

"You miss this dick don't you, Nikki?"

"Oh yes, I miss your dick."

"Say it. Say I fuck you better than your husband," he demanded.

He was pumping aggressively, with a hatred that was so sinister and sexy, it turned me on. We were both sweating freely. He was giving me every ounce of emotion he could muster up.

"Say it!" he demanded.

"You fuck me better than my husband," I breathed.

"Are you getting ready to cum?"

"Yes, daddy, I'm getting ready to cum," I panted.

"Good. Me too," he said. Then he forcefully pulled out of me, pushing me back as I came crashing down to the floor with a loud thud. Only to be met by squirts of cum as he jerked off in my hair and face. I sat body and ego bruised on his imported European rug.

"That's how I treat whores who fuck on their husbands. Now get the fuck out, bitch!"

Brian had devastated me. I thought he understood me. I thought we had something special.

"Joy, confirm my tickets to the Mike Tyson fight and send Lacey a dozen roses with a note attached that reads: *To the woman of my dreams,*" he said then hung up his intercom.

That was my cue to get myself together.

THIRTY·NINE

IVANKA ZAMORA

2002

I was pacing around my New York condominium when the doorbell finally rang. I had bitten my fingernails down so low they had begun to bleed. This unbreakable childhood habit infuriated me.

As my housekeeper went for the door, I cut her off—nearly knocking her to her elderly knees.

"I'LL GET IT!" I yelled as I darted to open the door for Jimmy.

"What's up, baby?" he casually replied as if he weren't three hours late.

"Where the *fuck* have you been?" I discretely replied.

Before Jimmy had a chance to answer, his eyes looked over my shoulders. I turned around slightly, and there was my housekeeper, Maria, peering over my shoulder with her hands akimbo and her lips tightly pursed together.

"Don't make me call INS and have your ass deported!" I screamed. Maria quickly scurried out of sight. At any moment, I was about to really lose it. Ten years in therapy, and I still cracked under pressure.

Jimmy followed me inside to my living room and produced a large baggy of goodies.

"Where's the rest of it?"

"Calm down, Ms. Lady. Papa's got a brand new bag," he replied and pulled out another baggy of goodies. I snatched both baggies from him and then threw him $3,000 in a tight rubber band.

Jimmy was a highly recommended drug dealer. He only sells to the elite and you have to go to him with three solid references from other socialites to ensure you're not an undercover cop. He was very cautious. I thought of Jimmy as being analogous to a pharmacy. Only, instead of handing him a prescription, you handed him cash. And lots of it.

As I sat down and indulged in my new "goodie bag" of pure cocaine, Special K, ecstasy, lithium and Quaaludes— Jimmy just sat down, grabbed the remote and clicked on MTV. He didn't indulge in drugs. He was a smart kid. Rich daddy and mommy. Good looks. Ivy League school. Actually, he really didn't have a reason to sell drugs, other than to rebel against his upbringing.

Once I pushed back a couple of pills and rolled me a cocaine cigarette, I was ready to socialize.

"Stoic resignation in the face of hunger," I said, then inhaled on my coke cigarette.

"Ah, the words of the great John F. Kennedy."

"Naturally. He was a babe. I would have loved to fuck his son's brains out."

"Why would you want to do that? That guy was such a loser!" Jimmy angrily snapped. He looked a little uptight as he ran his hands through his thick jet–black hair.

"Darling, do not confuse American royalty with the average boy–toy. He was more than just a pretty face. He was the son of an icon. For God's sake, his mother was–"

"Don't lecture me about the accomplishments of his parents and their legacy. We are talking about some dumb fuck that tried everything but achieved nothing. He couldn't even fly the fucking plane without fucking that up too!"

"Did I ever tell you, you look like John junior?"

"Fuck–you," he smiled.

"Then let's fuck."

I stood up and took off my sweatpants, T-shirt, and panties. I was completely naked. The foul odor of my coke cigarette permeated the room. I was high and horny and looking for a good time.

Occasionally, I would fuck Jimmy–though he was nothing to whistle Dixie over. He was usually my last resort. His problem was he was a little uptight. He didn't explore all the possibilities life had to offer. He didn't know how to live hard. He didn't know how to fuck hard.

As a melody came from the television, still on the MTV channel, I immediately chimed in. "It's murda," I said and threw up fictitious gang signs. Then I hopped up on my marble coffee table and started emulating a rapper named Ja Rule in his music video. I rapped every line verbatim, while Jimmy sat back amused.

When the video was over, he clapped. "Amazing. Not bad, for a *white* girl," he said. I thought quickly of what my staff would think if they saw me in rare form. Or should I say, "true" form.

I jumped down from the table and fell to the sofa and laughed so hard tears streaked my porcelain skin. My legs were cocked open, which instantly turned Jimmy on. He took his index finger and inserted it into my pussy. I stopped laughing abruptly.

"Are you ready?" I questioned.

"Yeah, baby, I'm ready," he panted, while ripping off his blazer and loosening his tie.

"No, I mean are you *really* ready?" I asked, staring directly into his eyes. Jimmy stopped fidgeting and shook his head "yes." I stood up and led the way to one of the six bedrooms in my apartment. This door was always kept locked. Jimmy had no idea what to expect, but I felt his eagerness to explore the unknown.

The room was dark and you couldn't make out a thing. Jimmy was frozen. I stood behind him, then pushed him inside. He stumbled for a moment, until I grabbed his hands and guided him in the darkness. Once we reached the bed, I climbed on top and Jimmy followed. His hands searched for my face to kiss me, but I pulled back. I was the aggressor in the "black room."

I clicked on my light switch. A blue, florescent light illuminated the black-painted walls, which had 1980's era graffiti on them. The words read: SEX, SLAVE, DIE, KILL, FUCK, HARD, BITCH and other words that tried to describe my insatiable appetite.

"Lie down!" I commanded. Jimmy relaxed on my silk sheets while I took off his clothing. I could feel his legs quaking with fear. He was such a pussy! But, he allowed me to tie his legs and arms to each bedpost, rendering him helpless. Once I felt that he was secure and I was in control, I lit my scented candles. Naked, I got up briefly to turn on my CD player. My favorite rock band, Psycho, blared out *"burn, burn, burn in my hell. Turn in your grave, I'm gonna kill your spirit."*

I sang along, ignoring Jimmy's request for me to cut it down. "Shut up pussy!" I scolded and slapped his face. He was shocked as the impact startled him. I grabbed his hair roughly and bent over and kissed him passionately. He was a little apprehensive at first, then quickly started to respond to my skillful tongue. I playfully bit his lips and sucked hard on his neck, then nipples. When his nipples were erect, I bit down hard on one drawing blood. "Ouch, bitch!" he screamed in agony, interrupting the mood. As his body squirmed and tried to wiggle free from his captive state, I began to caress his penis. Within seconds, it was rock solid.

I sat on top of him and began to gyrate my hips over his penis, then crawled up to his mouth and without warning, I sat on his face smothering him. "Eat me!" I demanded. He tried to squirm free, but I had his head clamped between my strong thighs.

Soon he gave up and made a weak attempt at eating my pussy. This turned me on, because Jimmy was an advocate for men who don't "go down" on women. Next, I "69" positioned myself and engulfed his penis. I let my saliva slide down his shaft and my small hands massaged his balls. My jaws sucked aggressively until I saw a vein bulging in his penis. He was ready to burst at any second.

Over my head, I had a "hangman" sex gadget installed. I stopped briefly to get the hood, which I put over his head. He was now in complete darkness again. Then I slid the rope around his throat and fastened my hands through the reins. Then I mounted him like a horse and rode him home. The faster I pumped on his dick, the harder I would pull the reins cutting off his oxygen supply. Then I would ease up and go slowly . . . softer, letting him catch his breath . . . then I'd started fucking him harder . . . and harder . . . and harder.

After almost an hour of skillfully pleasuring Jimmy with my "hangman" sex gadget, he started gagging and gasping for air. His body was squirming and jerking involuntarily as I tightened the reins around his throat.

"Relax!" I commanded. "Stop being such a killjoy."

My pussy was so wet as I felt him explode inside of me. I arched my back as I climaxed and shuddered as I had multiple orgasms. I collapsed on top of Jimmy because I was out of breath. My breathing was fast and short. Then I realized I couldn't feel Jimmy breathing. "Jimmy," I said. He never responded. I started to shake him frantically, but his body felt like dead weight. I jumped up and clicked on the bright light switch. When I snatched the hood off, his face was blue. He wasn't breathing.

I screamed, "MARIA! MARIA! MARIA!"

The coroner stated that Jimmy had died from a heart attack. I had pleasured him thoroughly before he checked out. Although I wasn't responsible for his death, I still planted my signature purple lipstick on his cheek. My trademark.

FORTY

NIKKI LING

MIKE TYSON FIGHT JUNE 8,2002
MEMPHIS TENNESSEE

After the embarrassing episode I had with Brian in his office, I sank into a mild depression. And it wasn't until Kayla suggested that we follow him out to Memphis for the Mike Tyson fight that I saw an opportunity to mend what I had broken. This anticipated encounter gave me hope.

I said good-bye to my husband and Noki (she declined my invitation) and boarded our private Concord jet to Tennessee. Kayla joined me for moral support. Once we got to the adjoining presidential suites in the Four Seasons hotel, I was eager to get the party started. My once sullen mood came full circle. I was cheerful, laughing and having a great time.

Kayla and I went shopping, mingled with ball–players, actors, drug– hustlers and record producers. You name it. We were socializing with them.

The night of the fight, I still hadn't run into Brian. I started to think he had changed his mind and hadn't come.

"What are you wearing to the fight?" Kayla asked. I walked over to my suitcase and pulled out a pair of jeans and a T-shirt that read: "Psycho Bitch."

"Nikki, you are beautiful. Yes. But you cannot wear a pair of *jeans* to a Mike Tyson fight. Chicks are going to be in the best designer clothing money can buy."

"Good for them," I said, dismissing the insinuation. Kayla just stared at me for a moment.

"Well, since you asked," Kayla said sarcastically, then continued, "I'm wearing this blue Dolce & Gabbana outfit. And I bought the pocketbook to match. Do you think anyone else will have this outfit on?"

"How should I know?"

"Well, humor me. I paid a fortune for this bitch. I better not see some ho in it!"

Kayla still didn't get it. Or shall I say, get *me*. I didn't concentrate on other women.

We both showered and got dressed. I decided to wear my hair loose and apply a little lip-gloss. I turned around and Kayla said, "You look gorgeous."

"Hey, thanks," I retorted and grabbed the Lincoln Navigator rent-a-car keys so we could begin our night.

The Lennox Lewis vs. Mike Tyson fight was a blast. The crowd was cheering, yelling, and screaming obscenities as Tyson was dropped in the eighth round. That man got his ass beat. Lennox put a whipping on Mike.

Kayla and I had ringside seats, courtesy of Jack. Suddenly, I glanced over and saw Brian. He was sitting next to a couple of men, and they were enjoying the camaraderie. "Good," I thought. No female in sight. He must have flown down with just his boys. No need to bring sand to the beach, I figured.

The after–party was hell to get into until this stranger grabbed me by my hand and led me to the front of the line. I looked back and Kayla was right behind me. Once we got to the front, the bouncer opened the rope and we walked in V.I.P style. Kayla and I were very grateful. I assumed that this handsome stranger would want to hang around me all night, but he fooled me. He nodded his head and disappeared into the crowd.

"He was a cutie," Kayla remarked.

"You are right about that," I said.

"He is definitely from this town. You see how the bouncer gave him mad respect?"

"Listen, I'm here for Brian. So we have to casually cruise through the crowd until we spot him."

After an hour or so, Brian was still not there. I started to think that if he were in town, maybe he wasn't coming to this after party. There were so many parties going on, although this was THE one to be in.

Kayla and I were on the dance floor bumping and grinding when I spotted Brian. He was slow grooving off a fast song with some chick. They were tongue kissing and he was feeling her ass. I was fuming. My heart started pounding with fury—but I still held my head high.

When Nelly's, *"It's gettin' hot in herre"* came on, the crowd went wild. Even Brian pushed the girl back and started to dance. This was my cue. I danced over to Brian and gave him my million–dollar smile. I must have caught him off guard, because he smiled back. Ignoring the girl, he pulled me close.

"Whatcha doing here?" he inquired.

"I came to see you," I responded.

"I thought we settled our business already?"

"You settled *your* business. My business has just begun."

"Really?"

"Really!"

Brian pulled me in real close and whispered in my ear, "I'm glad you're here. I'm sorry about the other day. I was just tripping. I want you to come to my room with Candi and me later and participate in a threesome. You down for that?"

I stopped dancing and looked in his eyes. "Candi," who had never left, came in closer and Brian wrapped his arms around her. Rather than dignify his remark with a response, I just walked away with my head held high.

"Bye be-och!" he heckled after me.

FORTY·ONE

NIKKI LING

I walked away from Brian humiliated. He'd changed so much from the guy I had fallen in love with. Instead of trying to decipher his recent behavior, I decided to confront him. I marched right back over to where he was dancing with Candi and tapped him on his shoulder.

"Dude, let me holla at you for a moment," I said real gangster-style to let him know I was serious.

He looked me from head to toe and said, "Nik, I'm not in the mood for your melodrama. I'm busy."

"Cancel your plans," I said through clenched teeth.

Reluctantly Brian followed me to a secluded corner in the VIP section of the club. It was located on the second floor. The club had small, private rooms and we chose one so we could talk. I needed to get to the bottom of his behavior.

As soon as we sat down I said, "What's wrong with you lately? How can you treat me the way you do? I thought we had a future."

"How you gonna talk about a future with me? You're married."

"Sonuvabitch! I didn't want to marry Jack," I yelled. "How many times do I need to say this?"

"But you did. You violated our relationship when you made that move."

"Me? What about you. How long did you want me to wait on you? I believed you when you told me you'd take care of me one day."

"Nik, I was too young to get married. I was still on a paper chase. But you were always my number one girl."

"Liar! If you wanted to commit you'd at least bought a ring . . . or something. You never wanted to even discuss the subject. And when I told you about Jack, if you really loved me, you would have intervened. I should *not* be Mrs. Okayo!"

"Look, if you're miserable with the choices you've made, that's your fault. I don't have the patience to entertain this right now. I'm in Memphis on vacation. I don't have time to be catching headaches from some broad I used to date."

"Some broad?" I asked incredulously.

"Look," he replied sternly, "I am not the same kid you met almost a decade ago. I've changed."

"That's what I've been trying to tell you. All I want to know is the truth. Where do I stand in your life? Be honest . . . you owe me that much," I pleaded.

Brian took a deep breath, looked me intently in my eyes and said, "It was never going to work. Nik, you know how I feel about you, but I stopped respecting you a long time ago. Once I started making money, a plethora of beautiful women entered my life. Just as or even more beautiful than you. Women with college degrees and respectable careers. Women who've traveled the world and speak several different languages. I was left in awe. Speechless. Basically, I could never marry . . .

a . . . prostitute."

His words felt like daggers piercing my heart, but I couldn't give him up without a fight.

"Brian, I hustled because I had to. I was a little girl without choices."

"You could have stopped a long time ago," he accused.

"I stopped as soon as I could. Better yet, you could have stopped me sooner. You got rich and turned into a cliché. A black man not knowing how to act with money!"

"What do you want from me!" he yelled. "I'm a man. I'm only a man."

"I want you to love me!" I yelled back. Tears were streaming down my cheeks. "I want you to love me, Brian. I want to be your wife and have your kids. It's what I've always wanted. A normal life with you in it. Can't you see our future? Together we're unstoppable."

"It's too late, Nik. It's too late . . . I'm sorry."

Brian slowly got up and left me sitting alone in the room.

"I don't love him," I called after Brian. He didn't respond. I didn't know it at the time, but that would be the last time I'd ever see or speak to Brian again.

FORTY·TWO

NIKKI LING

I sat in the VIP room for thirty minutes before I regained my composure. As I walked downstairs to the bar, it took all my strength not to burst into tears. Inwardly, I was crying. But, not one person in that club would ever know it except Kayla who met me at the bar. Just as I was about to order myself a drink to help ease my pain, the handsome stranger who led us into the party came back.

"You're the best looking female up in this piece," he said.

"Tell me something I don't know," I said sourly.

"Steven."

"Pardon me."

"My name's Steven."

I smiled faintly, "Oh, I get it. Well, Steven, my name's Ling. Nikki Ling."

"Well, Miss Nikki, what are you drinking?"

"Krug Rose."

Steven called the bartender over and ordered a chilled bottle of Krug Rose. When the champagne arrived, he poured Kayla and me a glass. I downed my glass in seconds. I smiled. He smiled and poured me a second glass. Kayla sauntered back on the dance floor and left us alone.

"Don't you drink?"

"No."

"Sexy."

I looked in his round eyes and got lost. He was very attractive. He had caramel smooth skin, curly black hair with a mustache and goatee and a body to die for. He was very doable.

"What do you do for a living?" he asked.

"I'm a model."

"I should have known that. You're gorgeous. You have that model air. Only a model can walk in a party like this with a pair of jeans and a T-shirt. Cute shirt by the way."

"And what do you do?"

"I'm a record producer."

"Really. Do you know Brian Carter?" I asked to make sure I wasn't about to push up on one of Brian's friends.

"No, I don't know that brother. Why?"

"No reason. Well I just thought that you would know him since you're in the same business. I thought the business was so small."

"So, are you single? Married. Indifferent," he asked, changing the subject.

"Married," I casually responded. His eyes immediately darted to my ring less ring finger. He smiled, then said, "Girl, you had me going for a minute. I thought I was going to have to say goodbye to you for the night."

"Dude, marriage is a speed bump that may slow me down a little. But, it's hardly a stop sign."

I could tell Steven enjoyed my remark. He filled my glass again, then came in real close and said, "Do you want to get outta here?"

"Let's roll."

I found Kayla on the dance floor and told her I'd see her back at the hotel tomorrow. I was definitely going to make this an all–night event with this one.

FORTY·THREE

NIKKI LING

Steven had a black Bentley awaiting him outside. I jumped in the passenger seat and we were off. The champagne had me feeling a little better. I tried leaving all negative vibes back at the club.

"So, where we headed?"

"Well, I was thinking that we could go back to my place and watch a movie, or just talk. Whatever you like."

"Dude if I go back to your place, I don't want to watch a movie, nor do I want to talk. Well not much anyway," I joked.

Steven reached his hand over and squeezed my thigh. I looked at his sexy pink lips, and my pussy started throbbing. I was determined to make the most of this trip.

Steven had a house up on a hill. He was obviously doing very well for himself in the music industry. It's a very lucrative career for some.

I got out of the car and walked over to Steven and gave him a soft kiss. He led the way to his front door as we smooched. We were laughing and having a nice time.

All of a sudden from behind my back a gruff voice said, "Don't move muthafucker!"

And everything started to move in slow motion. There was a masked man with a gun pointed at Steven's head. Steven put his hands in the air and stood frozen. Then another man came out of the bushes and grabbed me roughly by my arm.

"Get the fuck off me!" I yelled and yanked my arm free from his grasp. My entire body was trembling with fear and I burst into tears as my eyes focused on the assailant's handgun. I had an awful premonition that if I entered that house with these assailants, I would not come out alive.

As the assailant tried to restrain me, I screamed, "Help-p-p-p!" and was silenced by a firm slap. I started fighting for my life just as I learned when I was younger. I was kicking, punching, and biting my attacker but he remained unaffected.

The same masked man entwined my hair in his hands and pulled with a stern grip until my knees were buckling and my lips were mouthing the word, 'ouch.'

They forced us inside Steven's house and made us lie face–down on the floor.

"Where's the safe?" they kept asking Steven.

"I don't keep any money here," he replied. And each time he'd deny keeping money in his home, he'd be struck in the face with the butt of the gun.

I was screaming and crying with my head buried in the floor.

"Bitch, shut up before I shut you up!" someone yelled.

They were throwing furniture around, turning dresser draws upside down trying to locate a safe.

"Steven, what's going on?" I asked.

"Nikki, just be quiet okay. I'm so, so sorry I got you into this. Just be easy, so they can take what they want and leave."

One of the intruders overheard Steven and interjected,

"Oh, you think shit is *sweet* muthafucker. Huh? You pretty muthafucker. I should cap a bullet in ya ass right now!"

Steven's remark had infuriated the assailants. They began kicking him in his head, back and stomach mercilessly. There was a large gash in Steven's head where you could see bone and flesh. One of the assailants had on Timberland boots and when he kicked Steven in his eye, it split open and blood squirted out like a water balloon with a hole. He looked awful. After each punch, they'd again asked Steven where the money was. One perpetrator in particular seemed to get increasingly aggravated with him after each denial.

He was a tall, burly guy with a big head and a deep, baritone voice. I noticed that he was doing the worst damage. They both were attacking Steven, but this guy seemed to take pleasure in fucking Steven up. Like it was personal.

In fact, the burly guy seemed to be in charge of torturing Steven and keeping an eye on me.

The other guy was slender, but muscular, with extremely large hands and feet. He would take long periods in the other rooms searching for the money.

When he came back, he pulled the burly assailant to the side and they began a secret conversation. Then the burly guy walked back over to Steven while pulling out a pocketknife. The other assailant turned on the stereo loud. The burly guy then stabbed Steven in his upper leg, and twisted the knife around until he screamed in agony.

"Don't hurt him!" I screamed again. By this time, I had realized Steven was no record producer. I had gone home with a drug-hustler.

"This is it," I thought. I'm going to die. I'm going to die at 25 years of age. As I lay there, I kept trying to imagine how it would feel to have a bullet pierce my skull. How much pain would I feel? Would I go to heaven? Would I see my mother and father? How would Noki survive? Who would take care of her?

Just then, I realized I could not be a victim. I can't let them just kill me without a fight. I sprang to my feet and attacked one intruder with all my might. With one swift movement, the assailant punched me in my eye, I landed on my ass. I was then dragged back by my hair to where Steven lay.

"Please . . . please don't do this. I don't want to die," I protested all the way.

"Shut that silly bitch up for good!" someone said.

"No-o-o, please. Please don't kill me!" I begged for my life. I was trembling and crying hysterically. Snot was oozing out of my nose as they placed duct tape over my mouth and hog-tied my hands and legs. I was immobile.

After the assailants had me under control they began to torture Steven again. The burly guy grabbed Steven in a tight bear-hug while the other assailant spread Steven's right hand on his coffee table.

"Come on now man, that ain't necessary," Steven protested vehemently but to no avail. The assailant took the pocket knife and began slicing off Steven's index finger.

"Ah-h-h-h-h!" Steven screamed in agony as I watched in horror. The assailant had a little trouble cutting through the bone but eventually it came off. The slender assailant then tossed Steven's finger to the burly assailant. They tossed it back and forth for a minute taunting Steven. The burly assailant went into the kitchen and came out with a can of salt. He stood over Steven and poured the salt in every open wound on his body. I looked at his face and he looked deformed. He was unrecognizable. His eyes were so swollen they were almost closed. His skin looked like he'd been painted red because he was saturated in his own blood. They continued to torture Steven for what seemed like hours. He was actually begging for death.

"Do whatchu gotta do son," Steven challenged.

"Soon muthafucker. Soon!" one assailant sneered.

"Do whatchu gotta do son," Steven pleaded. "I can't take the pain . . . I can't take the pain anymore."

"You ready to talk? Where the fuck is the money and jewels?"

"I'll show you . . . I'll show you," Steven breathed.

They grabbed Steven so he could walk them around the house. Soon they returned with laundry bags filled with cash and jewelry. I was furious. All this time he had money hidden in his home and he didn't want to give it up!

Was money worth dying over?

Once they had the money, they took Steven and began tying him up with duct–tape just like they had me.

Before they put the duct tape on his mouth, Steven uttered, in a barely audible tone, "I'ma see you two. This ain't over until I say it's over!"

"Word?" one of the assailants replied to Steven's threat as he put the duct tape over Steven's mouth so he couldn't respond.

Steven was just inches away from me. Our eyes met and

spoke what we couldn't say to each other. I knew Steven was truly sorry. And it wasn't *totally* his fault.

Right before my eyes, one assailant put a silver plated gun to Steven's head and pulled the trigger! Steven's head exploded and his body involuntarily jerked one last time. He was dead.

I peed on myself. As the hot liquid left my body, I wished I could escape just as easily.

"What about the bitch?" The other assailant asked. I closed my eyes and anticipated death, but I never heard a response. They gathered their "bloodmoney" and discretely left.

I looked over at Steven who had just gotten his brains blown out. Blood was everywhere. Brain parts were in my hair and on my clothing.

Was money worth killing over?

I lay still for hours, afraid they'd come back. When the sun came through the windows, I planned my escape. I pulled and tugged until I was free from bondage. I was so nervous trying to get out of Steven's home, that I tripped over his dining room chair and scraped my knee. I never even felt the pain. I ran so hard and fast until I was miles from his home. When I finally did stop, I vomited, then fell to my knees. My heart was sick.

Soon, I got myself together and started to run with a slow jog. Then I picked up the pace. I never looked back. I wanted to just run . . . forever.

FORTY·FOUR

ESTELLE CARDINALE

2002

I was out of *jail* for almost a year on a $1 million–dollar bond. The judge who was presiding over my case was the ex–husband of an old college friend of mine. He had an ethical duty to recuse himself but did not. I'm sure he assumed no one would connect our past. And thus far, no one has. They're all such idiots. Meager–waged imbeciles with police badges and law degrees. Much to my chagrin, I would be tried by these assholes and my life depended on them.

The prosecution had the audacity to seek the death penalty. Naturally, I pleaded "not guilty" to the charge of premeditated murder of that whore, Lyric Devaney, or should I say that "calculating" whore. A calculating whore who videotaped her own murder. Thanks to her, I'd left a smoking gun at the crime scene.

Since my arrest, my husband Richard has divorced me and taken the children to Los Angeles. We don't have any contact with each other. He has committed the ultimate betrayal, and I swear on my very soul he will pay dearly.

This afternoon my attorneys were bringing in some hotshot lawyer from Miami to meet me. He's supposed to be brilliant.

This past year has been a travesty of justice. Day in and out, I dally around my home. I couldn't even entertain the possibility of going off my estate. Reporters were everywhere, ramming their cameras in my face, trying to provoke me into saying something that could incriminate me. But, I was far too clever to fall for such a childish ploy. So, I now live a reclusive lifestyle. That is until I have my day in court.

My housekeeper showed my two attorneys into my study. I came downstairs to greet them, fashionably late. They were less than pleased at being delayed for nearly an hour.

I smiled cordially at Michael and Kenneth and extended a warm handshake. Then my eyes diverted to the "hotshot" attorney from Miami and my heart stopped for a brief moment. I openly gasped, "You're black," I said.

"Quite perceptive. And you're white," he replied with bravado, then offered a soft chuckle.

I looked to Michael and Kenneth for answers. Michael spoke first, "Estelle, this is Robert Maximilian."

"Call me Bobby," he said and extended his hand. I disregarded his gesture and walked directly to my large storm windows.

"My rose garden is growing beautifully this season. What do you think Kenneth?" I said.

"Um...well, yes, but Estelle, we are here on important business. Your case. We want you to consider hiring Robert to take over."

"Never!" I spat. Then continued, "I will never let a nigger represent me. How dare you come in here parading him like he is *Jesus* himself. Like he is some sort of savior for me. I am *not* my ex–husband! I am no nigger lover! He's nothing but a Cochran knock-off. If justice granted O.J. freedom, then I will have it too."

I was appalled. Michael and Kenneth were obviously shaken by my outburst.

"Ms. Cardinale, I am no nigger. I am a proud black man who has never lost a case in six years. Who can get away with charging $5 million for retainer fees. If you disrespect me again, I will walk straight out that door and I will not represent you."

"$5 million!"

"It just went up to six!"

"Is he serious?"

"Do you want to go to seven?"

The room was pin–drop quiet. This man had certainly gotten my attention. He had the heart of a bull. I decided to listen to what he had to say.

"Tell me why I should pay you $5 million?" I asked.

"You're going to pay me $6 million because I am the only attorney that can get you acquitted of this murder charge."

"Nonsense. Michael and Kenneth are doing a great job."

"Estelle, we can't beat them. We're good. But, Robert Maximilian is the best. We will still sit second and third chair, but he needs to take over your case. You are looking at the death penalty. And with the overwhelming evidence . . ." Kenneth trailed off.

"The whore was sleeping with my husband!" I said, just

in case someone had missed my motivation.

"Adultery is not a defense for murder Estelle. Must I remind you that you are facing serious jail time if convicted. And if that doesn't make you shiver, the thought of the death penalty should," Kenneth offered.

I extended my right arm in the air and held it there, unwavering. I did this to prove a point to these men. I, too, had the heart of a bull.

Robert looked impatiently at his watch, then said, "Listen, I am going to make this as short and simple as possible. Your attorneys have stated you don't have an alibi for the night in question. Without that, you are going to jail."

"It's their job to keep me from that fate. I plan to take the stand and tell those jurors exactly why I killed the whore."

"You will do no such thing. In fact, you will only do what I tell you to do," Robert commanded.

"He can't be serious," I said and looked to Kenneth to intervene.

"I'm more serious than an eight-figure retainer fee. Your temporary insanity plea won't work. Insanity pleas hardly ever end in victory. The jury will think if they find you not guilty by reason of temporary insanity that you won't receive any punishment. That fear usually forces them to convict. I've been working on a strategy that I think will work. We're going to fight this tooth and nail. Get gritty and street!"

"Gritty? Street? Do you intend on smearing my good name?" I objected.

"Your name won't be worth a dollar food stamp in the 'hood if you're convicted. Now I'm looking into securing you an alibi."

"That's ridiculous. Who will perjure themselves for me?"

"Well, I have a host of upstanding citizens that are willing to do just that. Doctors, lawyers, teachers are all willing to testify. Yet, at this point, I'm still pondering whether they'll be needed."

"Isn't that unethical?"

"It's the American way."

We stared at each other for a long moment.

"I play for keeps Ms. Cardinale. My invoice will be in the mail. I have to go."

And with that, he was gone.

FORTY·FIVE

JOSHUA TUNE

awoke around noon and felt like shit. My head was throbbing from an all–night drinking binge. My small apartment, excuse me–room, I was renting was a mess. I had dirty clothes decorating my floor and furniture. Jesus! At this pace, my future seemed dismal. Naked, I stumbled to the kitchen and put on a pot of coffee.

Lately, I've had an inkling that things were going to get better. I mean, I have already hit rock bottom. There's nowhere to go but up. The sobering reality was I'd probably have to do it alone. I've been thinking about practicing law again. Since my conviction was overturned, I had petitioned the court for my license and won.

My best friend Dominick had distanced himself from me ever since I made the front pages of every newspaper nationally. What a prick. I mean, that guy used to idolize me. Now, it seems like a lifetime ago.

Just as I took a sip of my coffee, the telephone rang.

"Joshua, pick-up the telephone. It's me, Parker," she said into my answering machine.

I ignored Parker's call because I didn't want to be lectured. I didn't want to hear baby Mia giggling in the background, nor did I want to hear pots and pans clinking and clanking in her kitchen. Bottom line, I didn't want to hear happiness. Although I did owe Parker for sending in the videotape of Estelle murdering Lyric to every local news station and for being supportive during my trial and incarceration, I couldn't find it in me to allow her into my life as a friend.

Parker's calling had changed my mood. Instead of wanting to clear my head, I decided to keep it foggy. I tossed my coffee in the sink and walked to my refrigerator and pulled out an ice-cold Corona beer and took a swig.

"Ahhh," I said after I swallowed. Then I looked around and saw the empty beer cans decorating my floors and instantly felt upset. A few years ago, I was damn near a perfectionist. Now my life was quite pathetic. I had no will power because I didn't have a will to live.

A few more swigs and I'd downed my beer. Just as I was about to reach for another one, the telephone rang again. This time I picked up on the first ring.

"Hel-lo," I screamed in the telephone.

"Mr. Tune," an unfamiliar voice said.

"Yes. Who is this?"

"My name is Rosanne Levy, and I'm a reporter for the *New York Chronicle*. I'm interested in doing an exclusive story on your case. It will be an hour-long taping, live on Prime Time. This could be your only chance to tell your side of the story about the alleged set-up."

"I'm not interested," I sourly stated.

"But people want to know about your part in the Estelle Cardinale fiasco. And also how an assistant district attorney thought he could get away with buying and distributing cocaine…"

"Lady, I just said I'm not interested. And your response

is just the reason why. The public had already convicted me before my trial. All my speaking out will do is perpetuate more gossip. I need the press to go away and respect that I was vindicated."

"You're making a big mistake," she warned.

"Well, it won't be the first time now will it?" I said and hung up the telephone.

After I'd finished three more beers, my mind wandered to the sexy dark-chocolate girl I'd met at the bar. I'd been rude to her purposely. After I'd left, I couldn't help thinking about her. Thinking about her beauty. Her long legs. Her silky hair. Her sexy breasts. She was truly a looker. If I could rewind the clock a few years, I'd have had her. I'd have to have her.

FORTY·SIX

NIKKI LING

As my flight left Tennessee, I faced a grim realization. Life can transition into death in a nanosecond. I felt helpless as I came to grips with the fact that *people* can control your destiny. One second Steven was looking into my eyes trying to console me, the next second he was dead. I'll never understand why God had let our paths criss cross . . .

In the post–murder hours, I was silent. I never did tell Kayla what had happened the night before, no matter how much she pleaded. I was alive and that was all that mattered. I can truly say that I left a part of me back at Steven's house. I left part of my soul back there on his floor–staring into his eyes. I left optimism back in Tennessee.

As my car service drove into the City on the West Side Highway, all I could think about was Noki. My adorable, plump, baby sister. The thought of leaving her alone in this world . . .

With my Jackie Onassis signature bumblebee sunglasses adorning my face, Louis Vuitton luggage in tow, I entered my home. I knew Jack would be at the office, and I was fine with that. I needed time alone to figure out what story I'd tell him about my eye being bruised.

After settling in, soaking in a warm bath in our

whirlpool, I took a sedative and went to sleep.

I was abruptly startled by the ringing telephone. I was having a nightmare. I was at Steven's house and, this time, the intruders were going to kill *me* next. They panicked and just started shooting me.

I woke up covered in sweat. My soft hair was pasted to my forehead. I looked at the clock. It was six–thirty in the evening. Jack still wasn't home.

"This me–this you?" I said.

"Is this Nikki?" the caller said. The voice was somewhat distorted.

"Who is this?" I inquired, a bit annoyed at the bad connection.

"Listen carefully. We have your sister Noki–"

"Sonuvabitch! What precinct is she at?" I said jumping out of bed. If Noki had tried to go jostling alone, I was going to kill her!

"Shut up bitch! We have your sister Noki and if you want her back *alive*, you're going to get $1 million of unmarked money, untraceable $100 bills. You'll wait for further instructions. If you go to the police—she will die!" the caller hung–up the line.

I was visibly shaken. All the color drained from my face. My sister had been kidnapped!

FORTY·SEVEN

NIKKI LING

J ACK!" I screamed into the telephone.

"My darling are you all right?" he anxiously replied.

"Jack, you must come home right away," I breathed helplessly into his cellular phone.

"I'll be home within the hour. What's the urgency? How was your vacation?"

"I can't talk over the telephone. But please, hurry!"

"Nikkisi, I'm taking care of business. What on earth could be so important that you need to tell me in person?"

I was reluctant to discuss the kidnapping over the phone. What if the kidnappers had tapped our phone? Realizing I didn't have a choice, I said, "Noki's been kidnapped."

Jack was deadpan silent.

"Jack?" I said.

"Call Bobby and Rick and have them stationed outside our door. You are not to leave without taking them with you. Do not open the door for anyone. No deliveries, no repairman. No one. Do you understand me?"

"Yes."

Jack and I ended on that note.

"God, please, don't let Noki meet the same fate as Steven," I prayed.

After I hung up the phone with Jack, I called Kayla on her cellular phone. She picked up on the second ring, "Hello."

"Kayla," I cried.

"Nikki? Is that you? I can't hear you too clearly. The connection is bad."

"Yes, Kayla, it's me. I need to speak to you."

"What's up?" she said not detecting the anguish in my voice.

"Something bad has gone down with Noki."

"What has she done to you now?" she accused.

"It's not like that. She's needs us. I really don't want to talk over the phone. Do you think you could come over? What I have to say needs to be said in person."

"I'm a little tied up right now in New Jersey. I'm at the movies with Jay Kapone. But I'll come over as soon as we're done. Okay?" I knew once I mentioned Noki, Kayla had lost interest in the situation.

"Kayla, walk away from Jay Kapone. Go someplace you can hear me better."

Kayla did as I asked. When it got quieter I said, "Kayla, Noki's been kidnapped. I just got the ransom call a moment ago. They're demanding $1 million. Jack's on his way home."

"Omigod! I'm on my way," she screamed and hung up.

After I called our bodyguards, Bobby and Rick, I sat watching the telephone just in case the kidnappers called back again. Then it dawned on me—that this could be some sort of insensitive joke. I never did call Noki to see if she were home.

What had I become?

Just then, I tried to summon a glimmer of optimism. As I dialed her number, my fingers trembled. No answer.

I then called her cellular phone. No answer. Last, I paged her beeper every ten seconds. She never answered my pages. Finally, I started to panic all over again. I sat on the edge of my bed trembling. My thoughts were scrambled and my vision started to get blurry.

"Jack will make all of this go away," I said out loud. "He'll fix it," I reassured myself. I was rocking back and forth and wringing my hands together to stop them from shaking. Thirty minutes later, Jack still hadn't come home.

Where the hell was Jack?

It was close to an hour before Jack glided in.

"Jack, I'm terrified. They are demanding I pay them $1 million."

"Surely, they should know you don't have that sort of money."

"Well, of course I don't," I said and stopped crying as the reality of his words instantly hit me.

"This is nonsense dear–heart. I've been thinking we will call the authorities."

"Jack, we will do no such thing. They will kill her. First thing in the morning, we will go to the bank and get the money!"

"Nikkisi, I have no intention of entertaining your dilemma. Let's just say for argument's sake that I do believe you. Why on earth would I be persuaded to give away $1 million of my money to a few thieves?"

"Your conscience should *persuade* you! They have my sister!"

"And how do I know that you and your sister aren't trying to swindle me? I am *old* Nikkisi, but I am no fool.

After giving the situation more thought, I realized that I can't entertain your dilemma."

"Sonuvabitch! How dare you make such an insinuation. To think I would stoop so low as to try to con you out of money! Have I ever asked you for anything? Answer me!" I screamed incredulously.

"Don't portray the good little housewife, Nikki. It doesn't become you," he sarcastically replied.

Jack excused himself and walked over to his study with me right on his heels. Casually he strolled over to a locked file drawer and unlocked it. He came back holding a few files and tossed them at me. They hit the floor. Photos flew out showing me hand in hand with other men. Men I had slept with while being married to Jack. Police records of my previous arrests for pick–pocketing. Every skeleton in my walk–in closet came crashing to the floor. I stood dumbfounded.

"Now don't panic Nikkisi. I've known all along."

"How dare you?" I whispered.

"I always investigate my investments. Now this latest scam with you and your sister, I must admit, has taken me by surprise. I'm quite amused. The tears, involuntary shaking, I didn't think you were *that* good at deceit. I can truly say I underestimated you."

"Jack, please, I'm desperate. No matter what my past says, or how this may look, I would never *lie* about something this drastic. This is a ransom kidnapping and I have nothing to do with it. I need that–"

"SILENCE!" he belted out. His face turned beet red and his veins in his neck bulged out. I shut up immediately. Then he continued, "Go scrub. I'll be inside in a moment. And I better not hear another word about this kidnapping farce."

"FUCK YOU!" I cried. "Fuck you . . . you little . . . fucking . . . perverted, freak! I hate you! I hope you fucking die," I screamed and lunged at Jack.

Jack caught both my hands and tossed me across the room like a rag doll. I fell into our coffee table and tumbled over. I hurt my ankle. I jumped back up to my feet despite the pain and charged at him once again. He slapped my face, then got more aggressive. He grabbed my hair tightly and punched my already bruised face several times. I could instantly feel the swelling of my eyes and I was outraged. I swung a few punches that hit the air when Jack swung a right uppercut to my left jaw. My mouth snapped shut and my teeth cut the inside of my mouth. I tasted blood. I reached up and dug my fingernails deep into his face and left deep, long, scratch marks. He looked as if he'd just gotten scratched by an angry cat. Next, I extended my long leg and kicked Jack in his balls. "Oh-h-h-h-h," he screamed in agony and released me from his grip. I fell to the floor in pain.

"Bitch," Jack yelled and proceeded to kick me while I was down. He kicked me in my neck and ribs as I used my arms to shield me from each blow.

Jack's age soon got the best of him, and he had to sit down to regain his strength. I took this opportunity to strike. I picked up a $125,000 rare Rhododendron vase and slammed it up against his head. It broke into pieces.

"Goddammit!" he moaned as blood gush from his head.

He made a weak attempt to fight back, but he was totally winded. I jumped upon Jack like a wild monkey and started pounding my fist up against his head, face, and back. I was screaming obscenities at him, unleashing all the fury I had bottled up inside of me from Tennessee. When I leaned over and bit down into Jack's forearm, he had had enough.

"Ouc-c-c-c-h" he yelled in agony and flung me off him. Once again, I landed on my ass.

"You're insane," Jack huffed. "Crazy. You've simply lost your mind," he continued.

"You had better call the bank tomorrow Jack for the ransom money or else," I warned.

"Or else what?" he challenged.

"Or else I will become a very desperate woman!" I threatened.

Jack backed out of the room in defeat. When I heard the door to our bedroom lock, I knew I had won that battle.

I knew I'd have to sleep in the guest room that night.

Moments later Kayla was knocking at our front door. When she saw my face, she panicked.

"Did they try to kidnap you too?" she screamed as I led her into our living room.

"No, this is compliments of Jack," I sourly stated.

"Jack?"

"Yes. He seems to think that this is some sort of hoax. That somehow Noki and I are coconspirators in her kidnapping."

"What? That's ridiculous," she said shaking her head. "You would never do anything like that."

"I tried to tell him that we wouldn't try to swindle him, but he won't listen to reason. He said he's not going to pay the ransom."

"Well, I can certainly vouch for you. But I'm not too sure about Noki. Jack may have a point."

"Kayla, I don't believe I'm hearing this from you."

"Nikki, I can only keep it real with you. I'm not saying that Noki is behind this. I'm just saying that I wouldn't be surprised if she were."

"Just because Noki is spoiled–"

"And selfish."

"And selfish. But that doesn't mean that she would concoct her own kidnapping. You guys are forgetting one important detail. Noki has money."

"Not $1 million," Kayla pointed out.

Although Kayla was *like* a sister to me. The fact is she wasn't. Noki's safe return was my only concern. I couldn't get distracted by Jack or Kayla's cynicism. Kayla wanted to stay the night with me but I sent her home. There wasn't anything that she could do.

FORTY·EIGHT

NIKKI LING

I lay in bed tossing and turning all night. I kept envisioning Noki shot in the head. Her eyes were open and blood was oozing out from her wound. Just like Steven.

What I didn't understand was why the kidnappers had taken Noki and not me? I was Jack's wife. Were they under the assumption that I was the multi–millionaire? Then it dawned on me that maybe they took Noki because they couldn't wait for my arrival. Maybe my leaving for Tennessee had somehow altered their plan. Was Tennessee my fate? Some people believe that our lives are pre-planned. Had fate put me in a crisis to avoid one?

Soon, I decided that trying to get inside the head of criminals was not helpful. For once, nepotism was overrated. Noki always received preferential treatment as my sister. This time, it may have cost her her life.

When I awoke, it was a little after seven. I limped into our master bedroom. Jack was gone. I immediately ran around as best as I could, checking every room. He had left without me I realized. I tried him on his cellular phone and he picked up on the second ring.

"Jack, where are you?" I anxiously questioned.

"Nikki, I will not entertain this. I am on my way to the office."

"THE OFFICE!"

"Correct, the office."

"Jack, I need that mon—" click.

I showered and dressed in twenty minutes, threw on a pair of Jackie O signature sunglasses to cover my bruised eyes, a little lipstick to cover my bruised lips, and a tight T-shirt to distract from everything else. I looked quickly at my reflection in the mirror, concluded I looked great and headed straight over to National Republic Federal Bank where Jack had his accounts. I waited until the bank opened and asked to speak to the bank's manager.

A distinguished, older gentleman approached with caution.

"May I help you with something, madam?"

"Yes. My name is Nikkisi Ling—Okayo."

"Why, Mrs. Okayo, it's a pleasure to meet you," he replied with a broad grin, then continued, "Your husband is one of our valued customers. What can I do for you today?"

I wondered how much longer his fake grin would be plastered on his face once he heard my news.

"I need to make a withdrawal," I said unflinchingly. Then continued, "$1 million. I need that this morning."

"Are you authorized to withdraw from your husband's accounts?" he questioned. If he were suspicious of anything, he didn't waver in any way. He remained professional.

"Yes."

"Good. Just fill out this withdrawal slip, while I go in the back and check for your signature on file. Have a seat, it will only take a moment. But once this is done, it will take the bank a few hours to gather such an amount of money."

"Of course, it will. Just don't let it take longer than that," I boldly replied. We both smiled graciously at each other. Then his eyes glanced down at my T-shirt that read: I fucked Osama! He pursed his thin lips together and left me alone for a brief moment.

I sat fidgeting in my seat. My heart was thumping and each beat rang in my ears. I needed a cigarette badly. Just as I was about to ignore the "No Smoking" sign, the bank's manager returned with a grim expression. He must have telephoned Jack.

"Mrs. Okayo, I'm afraid that you cannot withdraw $1 million at one time on this account unless it has both yours and Mr. Okayo's signature."

"Bullshit!" I bellowed and all heads turned in the bank. The bank's manager kept talking despite my outburst.

"The maximum amount you can withdraw is $100,000 per day, everyday until the account is depleted if you wish. Or, you can make it easier on yourself and have your husband authorize the withdrawal."

"I, umm . . . he's . . . outta the country. And I *need* that money now. He won't be back for several weeks. Is there any other way?" I pleaded.

"No, unfortunately not. Maybe you should contact your husband," he said again, then dismissed me with a handshake.

Once outside, I broke down in tears. My baby sister was out there somewhere fighting for her life. And it was all my fault. And my husband didn't seem to care.

I knew only one other man who could help me, one other man that had that kind of money. Brian. Brian

Carter. But would he be there for me? I decided I'd soon find out.

I drove down the West-Side Highway on my motorcycle doing 100 miles per hour. My mother's words kept coming back to haunt me. "You are too defiant, Nikkisi."

I guess I kept crying because I knew what I had to do. I couldn't bow my head to my husband as my mother would have liked me to do, not when my sister's life was at stake. And Noki came first. We're blood after all.

Once I got to Brian's office, my nerves seemed to subside. I thought rationally and realized that Brian would help me. Despite what happened in Tennessee, I felt that Brian loved me. I hope his loved extended to Noki. He's known her since she was a kid. And he could certainly afford $1 million. He was worth a whopping $300 million.

As soon as I arrived, his secretary announced that he was not in. Not believing her, I barged into his office and much to my amazement, she was actually telling the truth.

I turned around slightly embarrassed by my display, and attempted an apology when she announced grandly, "As I said, Mr. Carter will be out of the office for two weeks. He's on his honeymoon."

Her words broke my heart into tiny little pieces. Did she say "honeymoon?" Brian had gotten married? But why? There must be some mistake.

I ran out of there and when I reached outside, I immediately dialed him on his cellular telephone. I heard a recording—*"The number you have reached has been disconnected."*

My head started spinning, and I suddenly felt ill. I hadn't felt this alone since Noki and I were living in separate foster homes.

I took baby steps back to my motorcycle. On my way, I passed a newsstand, and there, on the front page of every newspaper, was Brian and his new bride. The headlines read: "Mogul Marries Model."

I stared at her photo for long moments. She was very attractive. Cinnamon skin and chestnut brown eyes. Shoulder length hair, and a pearly white smile. There was something very familiar about this girl, but I couldn't put my finger on it. Brian had a large, stupid grin on his face.

The article read that the wedding had been spontaneous. They had flown to Las Vegas and had gotten married. It also reported he'd bought her a $2 million, 10 karat, blue-diamond wedding ring, set in platinum from Harry Winston. *You never said you loved me,* I thought. Brian had never actually *said* those words to me. I was such a naive, gullible fool.

Tears streamed down my cheeks. Then anger. "You spent $2 million on that bitch, when I need $1 million for my sister's life!" I screamed openly, desperately like a lunatic at the newsstand.

"Hey, lady, pay money for paper, or go," the Arabic newsstand owner said.

"Fuck you!" I screamed.

"No fuck you … you … you … crazy bitch!" he countered.

I threw the newspaper at him, and ran. I ran like I was

being chased by the police and hopped on my motorcycle. I rode for a while then pulled over to call Kayla at work.

"Soulful Soul records," she said.

"Kayla, I hate to bother you at work but I got more bad news."

"Nikki, I was just about to call you. I heard about the marriage. Everyone's talking about it around the office. How did you find out?"

"I read it in the newspaper," I said and my bottom lip trembled.

"I'm sorry. I didn't want you to find out about it that way. He's such a low-life. I will never speak to his tired-ass again."

"He never loved me-e-e-e-e," I said and burst out into tears.

"Nikki, don't cry. Of course he loved you. I saw you two together. I saw the love. He's just confused. I think you hurt him when you married Jack," she said truthfully.

"Sonuvabitch!" I exploded from stress. "All you ever do is fucking blame shit on me. I don't need this right now. I'm in the middle of a fucking crisis!" I screamed and hung-up the line.

Next I drove over to the Celina's Day Spa and hoped the offer with the mysterious stranger about the criss cross was still on the table. A broken heart was the least of my worries. I had to get my sister back.

FORTY·NINE

NIKKI LING

THE CRISS CROSS

I skipped my usual massage and headed straight for the steam room. I sat in there for three hours. My long-silky hair was plastered to my forehead and I was noticeably drained. I had been through too much in the past 48 hours. Just as I had given up, a short blond came strutting in. Her piercing gray eyes made contact with mine.

The room began to move in slow motion for me. I gently stood up and took my two index fingers together and let them *criss cross*. She gently nodded then directed her attention elsewhere. That was my cue to leave. But had I gotten my message across? Where were we to meet to discuss criss crossing our murders? I needed to speak to her to let her know the urgency of my situation.

I wondered if this woman actually had what it took to murder somebody. Although she seemed cold and aloof, was that enough? I ultimately had to decide if I had what it took to reciprocate the action. I decided not to think about it until I needed to follow through with it. I also decided not to think about Jack. It was either Jack's life or Noki's. And to me there was no debate. Besides, Jack had chosen his own fate. Just as Steven had chosen his. Such is life.

It had been sixteen hours since I had gotten the first of what would be a slew of telephone calls from the kidnappers. The gruff voice on the telephone was always barely audible, but there was always an undertone of aggression. I couldn't tell whether the voice was from a black or white assailant but the voice sounded like that of a mature individual.

After I came back from the Spa, I'd locked myself in our master bedroom. I didn't want to be disturbed. Jack was at the office, but our housekeeper was here. She was new. Apparently, our regular housekeeper had called in sick today, and Jack hadn't informed me. I gave her strict instructions *not* to answer the telephone.

As I sat back, reflecting on the week's recent events. I concluded that I was not acting within reason. The decision I had made with this stranger wasn't made with a sound mind. Even if I had Jack murdered, it would take weeks before I'd be able to get my hands on all his money. There would be the reading of his Last Will and Testament, and maybe even litigation. Possibly fearing a set-up, the kidnappers would surely kill Noki. Perhaps dispose of her body like she was a piece of trash.

I must admit I don't find myself crying often because it gives me an overwhelming feeling of helplessness, but my heart was so heavy with guilt. Noki, wouldn't be in this position if it weren't for me. If I had only chosen another path in life. Something simple. Maybe if I had moved Noki to a small town . . .

As the sun started to set, I resolved to get the money any way possible. But not at the expense of Jack's life. I didn't know how many more sunsets Noki would be afforded, so I had to think fast. I realized that there might be a decent amount of money, enough to persuade the kidnappers to release Noki, in my safety deposit boxes.

So, with a new outlook on the situation, I decided to take a shower to release some of my tension before Jack got home when I realized I needed to call off the hit! Then I wondered if I'd even agreed to the hit. I know I made the criss crossing gesture but what did that really mean?

"Nikki, are you resting darling?" Jack said, softly tapping on our bedroom door, interrupting my thoughts.

"Go away!" I shouted. I was still furious with him.

"Darling we need to talk," he replied as he used his key to open the door. As he stood before me, I noticed a briefcase in his hands.

"Jack, is that what I think—"

"Yes," he answered and walked further into our bedroom and sat down on our chaise longue.

"I'm sorry Nikki . . . for last night. The fighting and vituperative remarks. My behavior was irrational and disrespectful. So I have decided to give you the $1 million," he said.

I was elated. It felt like a heavy weight had been lifted from my shoulders.

"Jack, I can't thank you enough," I said and ran to embrace him when he stopped me.

"Nikki, I still have reservations about the kidnapping. Although, at first, I was skeptical that you may be involved in plotting to swindle me, on further thought, I realized that you didn't have that handicap dependency. You are used to getting what you want on your own merit. Noki, on the other hand . . ."

"No!" I screamed. "Noki couldn't be behind this. She wouldn't do this to me."

"Nikki Ling. Always putting Noki before common sense. Your sister is nothing but a parasite that despises you. You'll learn the hard way," Jack said.

He then left the money on the side of the bed and headed back to his office.

FIFTY

MADISON MICHAELS

CREEDMORE MENTAL INSTITUTION 2002

Madison, chile, it's time for your medicine," the nurse said. She had a little white medicine cup with two Haldol pills in it. I've been on Haldol, a psychotropic medication, for a few years. Last week, I decided to stop taking them. So, I pretend to swallow the pills and when she leaves, I spit them back out.

See, for some reason, they think I'm crazy, that somewhere down the line I lost my mind. When I tell the psychiatrist that I'm in this hospital because of Lyric Devaney and that she's sabotaged my life, they pull out their pads and start taking notes.

The whole scene provokes me, especially when they start speaking to me in a condescending voice as if I have a GED, as opposed to my law degree.

I looked up into the nurse's eyes, and started to bark like a dog. "Ruff, ruff, ruff," I said. I knew I wasn't a dog, but I was just having a little fun.

"Madison, stop barking like you're a dog. You know you ain't a dog. God, please help this poor chile to get her mind back. Chile, you a mess. You makin' my nerves bad. Now, here, take this medicine," she said.

I shook my head "no," and kept my mouth clamped

shut. Then the nurse looked around, and when she didn't see anyone coming, she pinched me!

"You bitch!" I screamed.

"Your mother," she whispered. So, I spit at her and she took my hand and twisted my fingers until I thought they would break.

"Ouch-h-h," I cried and immediately decided to behave. I had had enough. She was much too vicious . . . this one was.

Reluctantly, I opened my mouth and took the medicine. She smiled when I opened wide to show her I had swallowed them. She patted me on the head and scurried out. As I went to spit out the pills, someone else walked in.

"Well, well, if it isn't poor, pathetic Madison," the familiar voice said.

I swung around immediately because I knew the voice well. And there stood Lyric Maria Devaney.

"What are you doing here?" I asked in disbelief.

"I just stopped by to see you for a moment before I head over to Bergdorf's to go shoe shopping."

"I thought you . . . I thought they said . . . I thought you were dead?" I stammered.

"Ha! You thought you left me for dead. I'm like a twenty-year-old penis–I can't stay down," she laughed crudely.

"What was I supposed to do? They would have hurt me if I tried to help you. So, I . . . ummm . . . decided to go into hiding. This place is only temporary for me."

"Hiding! Temporary! Ha! I guess you're the one that flew over the cuckoo's nest," she sarcastically replied.

"Shut—up, Lyric! I know what you're trying to do. You're not real. You're dead."

"Do I look dead?"

"But, I went to your funeral. I saw you in your casket."

"You saw my twin sister in that casket."

"Lacey?"

"Yes."

"I don't believe it."

"Well, you're not actually of sound mind and body now, are you?" she teased.

"But I saw you!" I screamed.

"Negative! Do you know how easy it is for people to alter your perception of reality? Five years ago, I was getting ready to go to my premiere. I called my twin sister Lacey and invited her to come along. Since none of my friends were speaking to me, I needed to have someone by my side doting on me every second."

"Why would she show up? You two hadn't spoken in years. In fact, no one even knew you had a twin sister."

"Darling, she showed up because I'm Lyric Devaney. Who could ever resist when I came calling?"

"So, you killed her?" I asked. I was confused at this point.

"Don't you get the news channel in here?" she said. Not waiting for a response, she continued, "Of course I didn't kill her. I had gotten two telephone calls seconds behind each other. The first from Lacey, the second from Estelle Cardinale. They both told me they were on their way over. When the doorbell rang the first time, I thought it was Estelle, so I cut on my video camera. When I got to the door, it was Lacey. We greeted each other coldly, and then I excused myself to run some last-minute errands before my premiere. I had decided that I didn't want to see Estelle Cardinale after all, and told Lacey to get rid of her when she came. When I returned, Lacey was being wheeled out by the EMS. Baffled, I went into hiding until I found out what happened. I switched places and started living life as Lacey Devaney."

"But why didn't you tell anyone?"

"I just told you, didn't I?"

"You know what I mean."

"So you went from fat and ugly, to bald and anorexic, to just plain stupid and crazy."

"Shut up Lyric, before I–"

"Before you do what?"

"Get-out!" I screamed.

"Darling, you don't have to ask me twice."

She sauntered out, with her mink and chinchilla fur coat dangling from her shoulders. I nearly passed out on the spot.

FIFTY·ONE

NIKKI LING

The next few hours alone had an eerie effect on me. I thought about our childhood, my life of crime, Noki, Brian, Jack and, most surprisingly, Joshua. The sexy white guy I'd met at the bar.

After chain smoking my Newport cigarettes, I decided that I needed an afternoon cocktail and made my way to the kitchen where the new housekeeper was cleaning.

"Madam, it is good to see you up. I need to clean the gun cabinet before I leave, but it's not open," she said. She had a very weird accent. It didn't seem authentic. She sounded as if she were trying to put on a Spanish accent. I looked at her, she was small, with a black wig on. Very nondescript.

"Where's Jennifer?" I inquired.

"She called in sick. The agency had me fill in," she said with her imitated accent.

"Very well. Could you fix me a glass of champagne and bring it to my bedroom."

"Of course, Madam. But first, could you please unlock the gun cabinet?"

"Leave it. Jennifer will clean the cabinet when she returns," I said dismissing her. I glanced at the clock, hoping she would be leaving shortly.

"Madam—"

"It's Ling. Nikki Ling. Please don't call me madam. My husband is the old fart. I just reached my 25th birthday."

"Mrs. Ling, your husband gave me specific instructions to clean out his gun cabinet. I would hate for him to come in and think I overlooked it and call the agency."

She was working my nerves. I stormed into the living room quarters and opened the damn gun cabinet so she could clean it. She was one step behind me. As soon as I opened the case, she reached in and tried to start cleaning a gun when she dropped it on the floor, which hit my foot. I screamed in pain, while picking it up from the floor and placing it back in the case.

"I'm so sorry, Mrs. Ling," she said.

"You have thirty minutes to finish up your work and to leave. Do you understand me clearly?"

"Yes, Mrs. Nikki. Do you want me to lock the case back up?"

"Please do," I said and left her alone. I grabbed my own chilled bottle of champagne and returned to seclusion in my room.

Something about this stranger didn't sit well with me. I decided to call the agency to investigate whether she was an employee when I received a call.

"Hello," I said. My heart palpitating fast.

"Do you have the money?"

"Yes. Is my sister all right?"

"Take a cab to the Sunlight Cinema on 12th Street. Purchase a ticket to see the 7:00 p.m. showing of "The Bourne Identity." Sit one row from the back. Place the bag of money directly behind you and stare straight ahead.

Don't turn around. Stay until the movie is over, by the time you reach home, your sister will be released. Don't try any heroic shit. I will have several people in the theatre. If you turn around, or if anything looks suspicious, your sister will die!" Click. The caller hung up.

I ran downstairs in a frenzy, hopped on my bike, and headed to the cinema. In less than three hours, I should have my sister back.

FIFTY·TWO

JOSHUA TUNE

The weather was extremely calm on this Monday morning. I had rented out a small office space in downtown Brooklyn and hung my name plate on my door: *Joshua Tune, Attorney-at-Law.* I stood back and admired my new life. One morning I had an epiphany. I saw myself back in rare form. The old Joshua Tune. I cut out the booze and drugs and decided to remain high off life. Not too many people get second chances, so I was going to appreciate mine. There was absolutely no reason to wallow in self-pity, and that was exactly what I had been doing.

After I stayed at the office a full eight hours with not one telephone call, I walked around aimlessly for a while and then decided to catch the new movie with Matt Damon, "The Bourne Identity."

I rather fancied myself clever enough to be some sort of secret agent assassin. I uess it was a male thing.

The line to the movie was surprisingly short for the seven o'clock showing. As I approached the ticket counter, I saw a familiar face running into the theatre. She was alone. The beautiful girl with hot-chocolate skin from the bar. I purchased my ticket and immediately ran in after her.

The theatre was dark and, at first, I couldn't make her out. Once my eyes adjusted to the dim light, I saw her sitting in the next to the last row in the theatre. She placed a large briefcase behind her, looked around nervously, then sat down, and stared straight ahead.

I analyzed the situation before approaching with caution. She may be holding that seat she put the briefcase on for someone. A male friend perhaps. Soon the movie started and no one showed up. So, I proceeded over and sat directly behind her.

"Does this belong to you, miss?" I said picking up the heavy briefcase and handing it to her. Startled, she turned around and just stared at me. So, I extended my hand for a shake. She didn't respond.

"Joshua . . . from the bar the other night."

"It's a bad time. I need you to leave me alone."

"Sure. Is your boyfriend joining you?" I persisted. I was extremely attracted to her.

"Dude, it's not like that. I just need you to go watch the movie in another seat and leave me alone right now," she said. Her voice was stern.

She looked very sad. Her Asian eyes were red and puffy. Her lips were trembling, and I knew she was in some sort of trouble. I also knew when to back off. I gently placed the heavy briefcase back on the seat and went to watch the movie in another one. Occasionally, I glanced to see if she were still in the theatre. She was. I also noticed that no one had joined her.

Somewhere in the middle of the movie, I got up to get some popcorn and a soda. In the distance, a shadowy figure emerged from the darkness, dressed in all black, holding that same briefcase that was left upon the seat. From the distance, it looked like a husky male. The figure scurried out of the theatre. I tried to catch up to get a good look at the person, but when I got outside the movie, the person was gone. I shrugged off my suspicion, got my treats, and returned. As I passed, I noticed that the gorgeous girl was still there but the briefcase was gone.

When the movie was over, she rushed out of the theatre. I ran behind her and grabbed her arm. I knew something was very wrong.

"Are you all right?" I said.

"You again," she said and leaned in really close to me. "I thought I said that I needed to be left alone. You're ruining everything! I have to go," she yelled. She ran over and hopped on a large motorcycle and sped off into the night.

I had a bad feeling about this one. She may be trouble or *in* trouble. Either way I needed to back off.

FIFTY·THREE

MADISON MICHAELS

CREEDMORE MENTAL INSTITUTION

Although, it was sunny outside, it was very chilly inside my ward. I had to put on my winter white sweater over my hospital gown. Maurice told me he was coming to see me, but he hadn't arrived yet.

I did my hair really nice and put on make–up so I could look pretty for him. He likes me to look nice. I had my chair pulled in front of the window so I could see him coming up the walkway. He has such a nice walk.

"Madison?" a familiar voice said, but it wasn't Maurice. I knew Maurice's voice. As I turned around hesitantly, I was shocked to see Joshua.

"Hello," I said.

"Hi kid. Long time no talk, huh?" he replied.

"Really? Has it been long. I haven't noticed. Why have you come? Am I late for work?" I asked.

"Work?" he repeated.

"Yes, work. I must be late for you to come. I have good reason," I said.

Joshua looked like he was going to cry. I wondered what made him so sad. I was going to ask him just that when I got distracted. I saw movement outside the window and ran to it.

"Maurice . . . Maurice," I called, then spun around and continued, "Joshua, it was nice of you to come, but could you please leave now. Maurice is on his way up, and I want to be alone with him."

"Jesus, Mary and Joseph!" he declared, then said, "How long has Maurice been coming to visit you?"

I didn't like the way Joshua asked me that question. He sounded like the doctors. The very same doctors who wanted to keep me medicated. The very same doctors that wanted to keep Maurice and me, apart. The very same doctors that keep letting Lyric inside. So, I said, "Gotcha! I was just joking. I gotcha."

"Jesus, Madison. Don't play around like that. You almost made my heart stop right here and now. Listen kid, your actions are unpredictable and you're starting to make me a very nervous man."

"Sorry," I said, still watching the door for Maurice to enter.

"You do realize that Maurice is dead? He killed himself because he didn't want to face going to trial for your attempted murder. Remember…he tried to poison you to death with arsenic."

His words made me flinch. "Joshua, let's not relive the past," I said dismissing the subject.

Joshua shook his head in agreement, then said, "I know I haven't been here in a while kid, but I was dealing with some heavy shit. I don't know how much of this you know, but I was arrested last year for something really bad, but I fought my case and ultimately I prevailed. The court of appeals overturned my conviction . . ." his voice trailed off.

"Nice," I said only half listening. I really wished he would leave, but he decided to get comfortable.

"So now the state has to decide on whether they want to re-try my case. Meanwhile, I was able to get my law license back and I've opened my own practice. I want you to come and work for me, Madison, but first you need to stop fucking around in this loony bin and sign yourself out."

Inside, I burst into laughter! Ha! I could smell a rat. But I said nothing.

"Madi, you've been in here for a very long time, kid. It's time for you to reclaim your life. You're an intelligent woman. Don't waste away in here. I need you," he said.

"All right, Joshua. I will think about this. But please go now," I said hurrying him out.

Lyric was standing in the shadows waiting to come in. She was hiding from Joshua. She was always sneaky, but now being devious and underhanded with Joshua was unacceptable. As soon as Joshua left, I tore into her.

"What do you call yourself doing?"

"I couldn't stand to listen to another moment of Joshua's whining like a little girl. I'm so glad you kicked his ass out," she said.

"Why didn't you let him see you?"

"Why didn't you tell him I was here?" she countered.

"I'm not going to play your mind games, Lyric. I want you to leave," I demanded.

"You're so pathetic. Any sign of a challenge and you fold like a cheap chair from K-Mart. Look at you . . . hiding in seclusion, while your heart still flutters for that motherfucker that tried to poison you. How lame is that?"

"Liar!"

"He tried to kill you!"

"Stop it!" I screamed.

"You would be dead if it weren't for me. And look at the thanks I got. You thought you left me for dead soaking in a bathtub of my own blood."

"You are dead!"

"Do I look dead? Sweetheart, I'm luxuriating in my new identity."

"Liar. You are not Lacey. You're Lyric and Lyric is dead!"

"You're just crazy enough to believe that, aren't you?"

"I'm not crazy, Lyric . . . I'll admit I have a few issues . . ." I said trying to explain my recent behavior.

"Madison, who are you talking to?" Nurse Johnson said. Startled, I looked around for Lyric, but she was gone. She vanished instantaneously. She was always doing that.

FIFTY·FOUR

NIKKI LING

I had been ordered to go home after the movie, but I just couldn't. I rushed over to Noki's apartment to await her arrival. If she didn't show up soon, I'd decided to involve the police. The next hour would be critical as to whether my sister lived or died.

I parked my bike and ran up each flight of steps. I was frantically screaming, "Noki! Noki!" When I reached her floor, to my surprise, I heard someone unlocking the door. I slowed my pace with caution. Then Noki's face appeared. She had her security chain on and the door was slightly ajar. "They must still be inside," I thought.

"Noki, is everything all right?" I asked. Then mouthed the words, "Are they in there?"

"Nikki, this isn't some James Bond movie. No, they're not still here!" she spat. Startled, I kept approaching the door.

"Then let me in," I challenged.

"Not anymore," she said.

"What?" I asked. I was perplexed by her behavior.

"I'm not 'letting you in' my life anymore. You've done nothing but expose me to your seedy lifestyle. Your whoring and picking pockets. Look at what you've subjected me to. You were supposed to be some sort of role model for me, but instead I had to hide my face in shame because my sister was selling ass on the very sofa I went to sleep on every night! You were supposed to lead by example. But your attitude was 'do as I say not as I do!' You're pathetic. Always have been and always will be. And making matters worse is that I had a good life that I left behind to come and be with you!" she lied.

"At a time like this you have the audacity to look in my face and lie!" I challenged. "I know all about you getting caught sleeping with your foster father, Noki. I've known all along. I spoke with Mrs. Tanaka years ago. You didn't leave. You were thrown out."

"Whether I walked out or was thrown out is inconsequential. It was your responsibility to do better by me!"

"You little ungrateful bitch!" I yelled. I was finally fed up with Noki's abuse. "I did what I could for you. You're a grown ass woman and I'm still taking care of you. If it weren't for one of my tricks, your ass would still be held hostage. Jack paid $1 million to get you home safely. And by the way, how the fuck did you get out? Huh?"

"What do you mean? You expected them to *kill* me?"

"Of course not. I just have a slew of questions I need to know. Did you see anyone's face? Where were you abducted from? How many kidnappers were there? I need to know all of this because we still may be in danger." The questions tumbled out of my mouth so quickly.

"Do you know what they did to me? Do you? Instead of trying to console me in my time of grief, you're coming here and speaking skeptically," she screamed.

"Noki please let me in. I can't help you standing outside your door." I screamed. Then I physically broke down in front of her door.

"I hate you!" Noki yelled and shut the door in my face.

I must have pleaded with Noki to let me in for nearly an hour. My eyes were puffy from crying, and my heart was heavy at the thought of strangers hurting my sister.

Then I heard heavy footsteps approaching and a walkie-talkie device. Two police officers approached with caution. One was short and stocky, the other was slender.

"Ma'am, we got a telephone call of someone disturbing the peace and trespassing," the slender officer stated.

"Excuse me," I said.

"Do you have identification, ma'am? We may have to run you in."

"For what!" I yelled.

"Disorderly conduct and trespassing. This is private property," the short officer said. Meanwhile, he had his hand resting cautiously on his gun. I was outraged at my sister's cruelty.

"Trespassing? I own the place you're talking about! My name is Nikkisi Ling-Okayo," I stated while pulling out my license. "My sister and I are going through some problems that's all."

"Still, ma'am you cannot be in the hallway, yelling and screaming. That's the complaint we got. Either go inside your apartment and keep the noise down, or take a walk to cool off," he commanded.

I knew Noki wasn't letting me inside, so I decided to leave. I pushed past the officers, ran off into the calm night air and called Kayla.

"Kayla," I cried. "I need to see you now. Can I come over?"

"Nikki, I'm not always going to be at your beck and call. Nor am I your punching bag. I know you're going through a lot and I want to be there for you but I have feelings too. So unless you're physically hurt I need some time for myself."

"Of course you do," I said. I'd hurt Kayla's feelings and that was very hard to do. She was always so strong. "I just called to say that Noki's home safe."

"Surprise, surprise. Listen, I have company. Jay Kapone's here."

"Of course. Not a problem. I'll speak to you some other time."

Disappointed I hung up and dialed Jack. He was still in his office.

"Jack, darling, we've got Noki back," I said trying to hold in my frustration.

"I'd bet ten million without a scratch on her," he sarcastically replied.

"Jack you're wrong about this. You should have seen her. She's furious with me . . ."

"That's hardly convincing. She's always furious with you. Listen, darling, I'm glad your sister is home safe. This discussion isn't debate-worthy."

"But–"

"Click." Jack hung up the telephone. I wanted to call him back. I wanted to tell him all the mean things Noki said to me. I wanted to cry on his shoulder. I wanted to feel loved . . .

FIFTY·FIVE

JOSHUA TUNE

It was late and I was watching Howard Stern on cable. He had three ladies asking to be evaluated for *Playboy*. They all stripped naked while a room full of men gave them extremely low ratings on their physiques. As I watched, I pondered the reasons a person could possibly have to stoop to such a low level. I quickly lost interest and turned to CNN.

As I dozed off, someone knocked at my door. Startled, I jumped up and looked at the clock. It was almost midnight.

Annoyed, I yelled, "Who is it?"

No one answered. They just knocked again. Aggravated, I walked to the door and peered through the peephole. Much to my amazement, it was the beautiful girl from the bar. What was she doing here? How did she know where I lived? This one was definitely trouble. I wanted to turn back around and ignore her . . . but I couldn't. Slowly I opened the door and she said, "Hello."

"What are you doing here?"

"I needed someone to talk to. Since you seemed so concerned earlier, I came over."

"How did you find me?"

"I lifted your wallet. Bad habit of mine . . ."

"You what?" I asked incredulously and started patting the back pocket of my jeans.

"May I come in?" she asked.

She was wearing a T-shirt that read: "Brooklyn Bombshell," and a pair of tight fitting jeans. Her eyes were red and puffy, and her beautiful hair was pulled back into a tight ponytail. She was extremely sexy.

"Jesus! This is way over my head. A beautiful stranger shows up at my door, says she's stolen my wallet and wants to be invited in? How can I trust you?"

"Listen, I don't work for the police. This isn't about setting you up to take a fall. I . . . I . . . just need someone to talk to . . ." her eyes welled up with tears.

"Please come in," I said and moved to the side to allow her entry.

I escorted her into my cramped studio apartment and immediately felt embarrassed. Dirty clothes were on every piece of furniture. Old pizza boxes littered the floor. I started gathering the junk and removing it from the sofa so she could have a place to sit. She briefly looked around then gently sat down.

"I used to live in an apartment just like this…it seems like only yesterday," she said staring off into space. "This place is a dump," she concluded.

"Gee, thanks for the kind words," I said dryly.

She walked over to a few loose photos I had lying on my coffee table and picked up the bundle.

"So you really dated the slain actress?"

"Yes," I said as she studied the photo of Lyric.

"Who is this lady here with the red dreadlocks?"

"My ex-wife Parker."

"She's pretty. Who is . . .?"

I snatched my personal photos from her hand. She was beginning to irritate me.

"I'm the same way—afraid to let people in—secretive" she confessed.

"Listen, opening up to you is like trying to kick a cloud. Pointless. I would want to move forward with a beautiful young lady. Not bore her by telling her all the seedy details of my past," I reasoned.

"You think I'm beautiful?"

"Don't most men?"

"Yes."

"Well, I used to be quite a catch myself," I lamented and my guts twisted up.

"I see you like getting 'caught' by black women. Why is a blond haired, blue eyed, white guy dating black women? I bet you have blondes knocking your door down."

"I've always had a bigger attraction to sexy, black women. But don't worry, you guys have steadily worn me down," I joked.

"Coming out of a bad relationship, are we?" she inquired.

"As all great empires come to an end, so did my relationship. I didn't even know I was on the Titantic. I thought I was in for the whole trip but got cut out midway."

"Did you love her?"

"Let's just let sleeping dogs lie. I don't want to revisit my past relationships."

"Let's play a game tonight. Truth or dare. I'll ask you

a question, you'll tell the truth or take the dare," she said and flopped down on my sofa. I had no idea what was going on. I felt like I was in an episode of "Twilight Zone." I stood emotionless.

"Take me back to the night when your life fell apart. What was going through your mind?"

"Get out!" I roared. I sensed this could be some sort of set-up trying to get me to talk about my past.

"Dude, I'm not in the mood for any hostility. Can't you see that I'm hurting? Surely, you're good at reading people. Can't you see that my life is in shambles and that I must be in dire need of a shoulder to cry on if I picked a perfect stranger to spill my guts to?"

"Well, you better start talking fast and you can start off with your name."

"My name is Nikkisi Ling-Okayo. When I was eleven years old, my mother committed suicide . . . "

We talked until the sun rose. She told me all about her past. Jostling people and selling her body. Her foster father raping her and taking her virginity. She never told me about the event that led her to my doorstep. As she spoke, I listened intently. Nodding my head every so often to let her know she had my full attention.

"My sister hates me . . . " she whispered.

"She doesn't hate you," I soothed. "You two have had it rough. She is frustrated about the way her life is progressing and people usually lash out, unfortunately, against those who most love them. Don't worry . . . she'll come around."

"You think so?"

"Sure," I said and yawned. I was beat.

"I should be getting home," she worried.

"Stay a little while longer," I said.

Instantly we both fell into a deep, peaceful sleep.

FIFTY·SIX

NIKKI LING

In the early morning hours, I quietly left Joshua's apartment. He was sleeping peacefully on his sofa pullout bed. He looked like a 12-year-old boy. His blond hair was messy and his pink lips were curled almost in a smile. His pale skin was now tanned to a bronze complexion. He looked adorable. A turnaround from our last encounter at the bar. As I left, I hesitated in his doorway for a while and exhaled. A part of me wanted to remain cuddled in this stranger's arms while the sensible side knew I'd better go home. I'd have a lot of explaining to do to Jack regarding my whereabouts. As I approached my bike, I looked at my watch and realized that Jack would be leaving for the office soon. I decided to call home before he left. Our housekeeper picked up on the first ring.

"Okayo residence..." she said, her voice wavering.

"Jennifer, this is Nikki. Please put Jack on the telephone."

"Mrs. Nikki...oh God...Where are you? Do you know?"

"Know what?" I asked.

"Mrs. Nikki...Mr. Okayo...he was...he...was *killed* last night in his office. The polic–"

I hung up the telephone and screamed. What had I done? This was all my fault. I jumped on my bike and headed to Jack's office in the embassy. I was doing 140 mph. As I darted in and out of traffic, ran numerous red lights and nearly caused two collisions, I realized that I had gotten myself in trouble that was way over my head.

I'd driven from Brooklyn to Midtown in 15 minutes. Police cars were everywhere. As I parked my bike and ran to Jack's office, I was greeted by a uniformed police officer.

"Ma'am, you can't go inside there."

"That's my husband in there," I cried.

"You're Mrs. Okayo?"

"Yes."

"There are two detectives that want to have a word with you."

"Okay...not a problem. But I must see my husband . . ." I said as my voice trailed off. I was visibly weak. The afternoon my mother committed suicide flashed in my mind, her lifeless body floating in a tub of water.

The police officers had already started processing the crime scene. Yellow tape was put up to form a barrier so that no one could contaminate it. The officer asked me to wait in the outside vestibule while he went to get the detectives. There were numerous people there, all processing the crime scene. The coroner, forensic scientist, fingerprint analyst, detectives. All with one agenda: to find the person who murdered Jack Okayo, the wealthy, South African diplomat.

I felt uneasy just standing there. I managed to slip past several police officers and walked into Jack's office. The crime scene stopped me in my tracks and snatched my breath. There, Jack was sitting back in his brown leather chair. He was decapitated. His head was on the other side of the room on one of his African spears. His naked body was propped on his leather chair. His nipples were sliced off and there was a deep gash from his collar bone to his pelvis. He had been shot in both kneecaps. Last, there was a remnant of something even more peculiar than what I had already witnessed. Closer observation of his face indicated that there was a faint lip impression on his face. The stranger had kissed him and had left a pair of purple lips on his face. She'd kissed him after she'd killed him. Rigor mortis had already started. His eyes were open and his face had a look of fright plastered on it. Blood had dripped down onto his sleeve and his hand. His neck appeared to be slashed from left to right but there wasn't any blood oozing from the wound. I gathered that he was already dead when this wound was inflicted. The scene was horrible. You smelled death as you entered. And even though I wasn't in love with Jack, I felt a great deal of remorse and guilt that I had been put in this position that ultimately lead to his death.

"Mrs. Okayo," a middle-aged looking gentleman said, startling me.

"Yes," I said as my voice quivered. I hadn't even noticed that I'd been crying until the gentleman reached in his pocket and handed me his handkerchief.

"My name is Detective Oldham. You really shouldn't be in here," he said and looked sternly in my eyes. I could tell he was trying to read me.

"Detective . . . who would do such a thing to Jack . . .?"

"Well, I was hoping you could tell me just that," he retorted as he led me away from the crime scene.

"Excuse me?" I defensively asked.

"Perhaps you could be of some assistance in helping us with a motive . . . or suspect . . . in your husband's murder. Do you know of anyone who would want to see this *millionaire* murdered?"

The way he said "millionaire" confirmed that I may be on the top of his suspect list. He'd already started taking out his pad and pen to write down any statement that I was willing to give.

"Detective Oldham I feel terribly ill right now. I need to get home and make some telephone calls to his friends and family. They need to hear the news from me and not the media."

"Sure . . . sure. Here's my card if you decide you can assist us in this investigation today."

"Not a problem," I said as I tried to exit the scene of the crime.

"Oh, Mrs. Okayo," he called out to me. I turned back around.

"Yes."

"Don't take any sudden trips."

FIFTY·SEVEN

MADISON MICHAELS

CREEDMORE MENTAL INSTITUTION

On this particular morning, I decided to go into the television room and watch the news. I liked to keep current on events.

Everyone was in there acting crazy. Some were talking to themselves or seeing people that weren't there. This type of behavior really made me sick. Crazy people! Couldn't they just get it together. The only reason I'm still visiting in this here place is because I lost my apartment, but I'm supposed to be getting another one soon. Real soon and I won't have to be in here with these nutty people.

The news channel wasn't showing anything of interest so I decided to leave, when something caught my attention. The news reporter showed a couple and said:

This is Gilt Mcgronner, WLTV News reporting on the recent celebrity marriage of Brian Carter, the Renaissance man of the new millennium, and his beautiful bride, Lacey Devaney, sister of slain actress Lyric Devaney. The couple was married in Las Vegas."

"No!" I screamed. "His name is not Brian! It's Maurice! She can't marry Maurice," I screamed at the television until the nurses came to sedate me.

"Why is he lying?" I yelled. I wanted someone to answer me on why they said Maurice's name was Brian. And why did everyone think Lyric was Lacey. Didn't they know? Couldn't they see that she was fooling them?

As the medication started to slow me down, I decided that I knew what I had to do. I had to stop Lyric Devaney for the last time!

FIFTY·EIGHT

DETECTIVE OLDHAM

I sat around the noisy precinct trying to go over the evidence that was collected from the Okayo murder. I was more than certain his beautiful, young wife had something to do with it. The savage way he was murdered had given me nightmares. I literally woke up from a nightmare drenched in sweat. My wife had to calm me down. I've been on the force for close to twenty years, and I've never seen anything this hideous. His wife did her best to make it look like a ritual killing. Maybe have us think that someone from his native continent Africa had something to do with it. But I'm no rookie! I'm one of the best goddamn detectives around, and I'm not letting this case go cold.

I had been examining evidence for hours when my partner Ripton came in with a frail-looking white male trailing behind. He looked well-educated and rich. He had a massive amount of silver hair and a black mustache. His odd appearance was accentuated by his accent when he spoke.

"Detective, my name is Doctor Cohen. I've traveled all the way from Waco, Texas, to have a word with you," he said and extended his hand. I looked over to my partner who nodded. I shook the doctor's hand and stopped what I was doing.

"Oldham, I just had a lengthy interview with the doctor. I think you need to listen to what he has to say," Detective Ripton stated.

"I'm all ears," I said.

"I've been following several murders that have been in the papers for the past three years. They all have the same elements, but thus far no one has connected them. Recently, a South African diplomat was savagely murdered in his office. Unfortunately, I think I know who killed him."

His words piqued my interest.

"If you know something, you gotta tell us," I coached.

"In the past three years, there have been five murders. All have gone cold and no one has been arrested. Each murder consists of the victim's body being mutilated. The head is decapitated and positioned on the opposite end of the crime scene."

The doctor had described our crime scene down to the last detail. I was skeptical because usually when someone involves himself in a murder investigation, he is usually the killer. They want to get on the inside so they can find out what we know. I sat back and listened intently and wondered what part the doctor played in the murder.

"You've just described our crime scene doc. What do you know?" I asked impatiently.

"I treated a young lady named Ivanka Zamora. I diagnosed her with Psychotic Schizophrenia. Theoretically, everyone diagnosed with schizophrenia isn't a murderer unless psychosis is involved. I'm more than certain Ms. Ivanka Zamora is responsible for the slew of murders being committed from state to state. Ivanka is just as notorious as the infamous serial killer, Eileen Waronos. She needs to be captured and convicted!" he said and his eyes exuded fear.

"We don't know anything about other murders committed in the same fashion," Ripton stated.

"There was one murder in Seattle, Washington. A young, wealthy investment banker. I checked, and she was there around the time of his murder. Then, there was Chicago, Texas and now New York. She was in all of those states the time these murders happened. I tell you this woman is evil . . . pure evil. She has even killed her own mother," he said.

"Is there any evidence that supports her killing these people? Or her mother for that matter?"

"It's your job to collect the evidence. I'm only the messenger. And I want to clarify something. She didn't kill her mother in the way she's killed the rest of her victims. She drove her mother to an early death. She tormented her for years. Her mother's heart just gave out..." he said and put his head down.

"You and her mother were close?" I asked.

"She was a great lady."

"And she raised a monster. That's peculiar."

"Not really. Look at Jeffrey Dahmer's father. He can't understand how he could have raised a serial killer. Psychiatrists have been studying the dynamics of a serial killer. They are not raised, Detective Oldham. They're born."

I took a moment to take in everything he had to say.

"Well thanks for coming by. We'll look into this matter."

As he rose to leave he said, "You can't let this go. The longer she's out on the street, the more victims she'll have."

"I understand. We're taking everything you've told us seriously," I stated.

"And I know it wasn't written in the papers, but she has a signature trademark that she likes to leave. She kisses each victim with purple lipstick and removes one of their items. See if the victim is missing anything. Once she's apprehended, she'll have a host of articles in her collection. Serial killers like to keep something from each victim so they can relive the crime."

After he left, I just shook my head.

"What?" Ripton asked.

"What a quack."

"You have to admit that he was on the right track. I think we need to look into this Zamora lady. No one knew about the lipstick, Oldham."

"No one but Nikki Ling-Okayo. How much do you think she paid the good doctor to come and steer us in another direction?" I said.

"We should at least see if what he says pans out. Nothing else can be gleaned from the crime scene. Do you want me to investigate and see if there's any connection between her and the doctor?"

"No. I don't care about any connection. I want all our efforts to be put into nailing Nikkisi Ling. I now have a hard-on for charging her with murder."

FIFTY·NINE

NIKKI LING

I walked out of my dead husband's office in a state of delirium. My cell phone was ringing, but I thought the sound was inside my head. I was virtually numb from shock. Someone had left a message, and my phone vibrated to alert me, but I was too weak to talk. As I walked past each police officer, they all seemed to be laughing at me. Hideous smirks were plastered on their faces. They know. They know it's my fault Jack was murdered.

Once I got outside, I quickened my steps to get to my motorcycle, all the while looking over my shoulders. Looking for her. The mysterious stranger who'd gotten me into this mess. It was all her fault, I thought. Or was it?

When I got home, the house was eerily quiet. I immediately turned on every television and stereo in the house, then called Noki; she didn't pick up. Then I called Kayla; she wasn't home either. I realized that shortly they'd see the news and would be calling or coming over to console me. Could I tell them what I'd done? Could I trust either one of them to take my secret to their graves?

I walked into the kitchen to the refrigerator and pulled out an ice-cold bottle of Cristal champagne. As the refrigerator door closed shut, the noise startled me. I was practically afraid of my own shadow. And so I should be. Anyone capable of conspiring to kill their husband is certainly someone to reckon with. No matter how desperate my situation seemed, I should have never agreed to the criss cross. *Then my sister would be dead*, I thought. But I quickly realized that was untrue because Jack eventually gave me the money . . . .

One part of me keeps saying that I had no choice. My sister's life depended on me and me alone. I couldn't factor in the probability that Jack "might" give me the money. I had to act and act quickly, I reassured myself.

As the champagne bubbles tickled my throat, I walked to our elevator and took it to the fourth floor—our bedroom. Well, my bedroom . . . As I stepped into the room I looked at all of Jack's belongings. His slippers neatly left approximately 3 feet from the bed. His bathrobe folded neatly on the chaise. He was a stickler for such things. Oddly, I think I'm going to miss his psychotic antics. And if my suspicions turn out to be true, then I'm most likely just as sick as I thought Jack was.

I decided to turn on the television to see if the news had any leads on the murder. At this point I had consumed nearly the whole bottle of champagne. As I flipped through each channel, the telephone rang. It was one of our bodyguards. He'd just heard the news and wanted to know if he should come over. I told him I needed to be alone tonight but would call him tomorrow. He cautioned me to not leave the house without him and vowed to help the police as much as he could to find out who murdered Jack.

As soon as I hung up, the phone rang again. I thought it was our bodyguard calling back.

"This me—this you?"

"What a fabulous greeting . . ." the caller stated.

"Who is this?" I cautioned.

"Someone calling to collect on a debt."

"What do you want?" I asked, fearing the answer.

"It's time for you to kill my husband. Meet me tomorrow morning and I'll give you the itinerary. It has to be done tomorrow . . . there's no other time. I will call you to give you a location."

"I . . . I . . . can't go through with this. I never wanted you to kill him. I wanted to call it off! You didn't give me enough time," I babbled.

"You will go through with it and it will be done tomorrow!" she snapped.

"I can't do it!" I screamed back.

"So now the criss cross becomes the double cross?"

"Look, it's not safe to talk on this phone."

"Your phone isn't tapped . . . yet. You have 24 hours to complete our business arrangement. Otherwise . . ."

She purposely let her voice trail off to scare me. And it worked but I refused to give in. Briefly Jack's mutilated body flashed before my eyes and my stomach turned.

"I'll go to the police," I warned.

"And Santa Claus will deliver the smoking gun with your fingerprints on it!"

"What?" I asked incredulously.

"Hola Miss Nikki . . ." she said with a phony Hispanic accent, and I realized that she was the lady who filled in for my housekeeper. Her dropping the gun on my foot . . . me picking it up . . . it all flashed before my eyes.

"You bitch," I replied coldly.

"Precisely. Now quit fucking around and grow some balls. First thing tomorrow morning, I will call you to meet me at the Starbucks on the corner of 60th and Broadway," and she hung up. I had no choice. I had to do it.

SIXTY

KAPRI HENDERSON

It took that nigga Eddie like two weeks to hit a sistah back. It's not like I was sittin' bitin' my nails or anything, but I did wanna see what he was all about. I gave him my digits so he could holla at me and that bastard took forever to call. The day he called I had just copped a half kilo of cocaine. This was my largest score yet. If I got this off, I'd be able to move off this block for good. Maybe buy me a nice lil' house out on Long Island. I'd paid $16,500 for it, but the street value was close to eighty.

I was in my kitchen with a pot of boilin' water. The coke was mixed up with bakin' soda and ready to be dumped in. This was my second batch. With a razor blade, Kareem and I had already cut up the first batch into nickel vials of crack-cocaine for him to sell. It took hours and I still had a while to go. I paused a moment to answer my cell phone.

"Whadup?"

"Yo, can I speak to Candy?"

"To who?" I asked.

"I think her name is Candy . . . I met her up on Ocean Avenue a few days back," the male caller said.

"Oh whadup, this Kapri," I said and a large smile hit me.

"Hey girl, this Eddie," he said then paused, "Whatchu doin'?"

"Um-m-m-m, I'm…workin'."

CRYSTAL LACEY WINSLOW 271

"At home? What kinda work you do?"

"I mean I'm workin' 'round the house. Cleanin' shit up," I lied.

"Good, then shit should be lookin' right when I come through. Give me your address so I can holla at you for a minute."

I gave Eddie my address, and he said he'd be here in an hour. As my heart was racin' I ran 'round the house tryin' to get ready. I sent Kareem out on the block to move some of the crack we'd just bagged up. I gave him $2,000 street value of crack and told him not to come back until each vial was sold. I knew that'd take all night. I wanted to be alone with this new kid Eddie. Then I shut off the boilin' water and hid my coke in my hidin' spot. I climbed way up high on my kitchen table, lifted one of the boards in the ceilin' and stored my bundle.

Next, I quickly washed away any evidence of narcotics. With only minutes left before his was due to come through, I jumped in a fast shower. I quickly grabbed a Massengil Douch, just in case we get busy, and a bitch came out feelin' like a virgin. So fresh and clean.

In my closet, I couldn't decide what to wear. I mean all my gear was fly. Finally, I put on a black and gold J-Lo sweat suit and the latest high-top Adidas sneakers. I pulled my hair down that was wrapped in bobby pins from the Dominican hair stylist and waited. I waited for three mutherfuckin' hours. A bitch was hot by the time that bastard knocked on my door.

I hate that shit. A nigga tell you they on their way then take their time 'bout gettin' there. When my doorbell finally rang I yelled out, "Who!"

"It's Eddie," he casually replied.

I stomped over to my door and flung it open. Eddie was leaning against the doorframe lookin' delicious. He licked his lips and said, "Wassup sexy?"

I smiled and invited him into my living room.

Eddie had on a pair of white, Nike Air sneakers, and a dark-blue Rockawear sweat suit. His hair had recently been cut and he smelled like money. "Yea, this gonna be my man," I thought.

"You want somethin' to drink? I got Henny," I said referring to the large bottle of Hennessy I had stashed in my kitchen. Men love that shit.

"That's what's up," he said as he flopped down on my leather sofa. "Yo, you gotta fly crib."

"True . . . true," I called out from the kitchen. I was mad happy at the compliment.

As I walked back into the living room with our drinks, he said, "So tell the truth, you got a man takin' care of you? Buyin' you all this fly shit. And don't lie . . . I don't mind doin' shit on the down-low."

"Naw, I ain't got no man takin' care of me. I'm solo. For self. What about you? You gotta a girl? And don't lie . . ." I laughed.

"I got a baby momma. But we ain't together. She got my daughter though. That's it."

I shook my head to let him know I understood. Then said, "Yo, what took you so long? I was 'bout to call it a night and go to bed."

"Word? Well I was waitin' for my man to drop me off

with his ride. Remember, the kid that was wit me when I met you? That was his shit. He was actin' funny about takin' me over here."

"So that ain't your ride?" I asked realizin' I played myself.

"Naw…that's his shit," he said.

"So do you own a ride?" I hammered. My facial expression was distorted because I don't want no broke-ass nigga up in my crib. I can do bad by my damn self.

"Of course I got a ride," he stated.

"Whatchu got?" I challenged.

"I got the Mercedes CL600. I crashed it the day before I met you and now I have to depend on mutherfuckers to get me around until I get my shit out the shop."

I exhaled. This guy was a baller. A Mercedes CL600 was the shit!

"You got tinted windows on ya shit?" I questioned.

"And the Spreewell Chrome rims that keep on spinnin'."

"Say word!"

"Word."

After Eddie opened up about his car, the night went smoothly. He told me all about his business and all the money his no-good baby momma was tryin' to get from him. I knew at that moment me and his bitch was gonna have problems.

SIXTY·ONE

MADISON MICHAELS

CREEDMORE MENTAL INSTITUTION

After my outburst in the television room, Nurse Betty came to restrain me. She was an obese woman who was always complaining about her asthma. She came wobbling down the hallway as best as she could on her swollen ankles. She had a small medicine tray in her fat hands. She wanted to sedate me, but I was prepared. As she approached, I continued to scream like I was crazy, but I wasn't crazy. I was waiting for opportunity.

"Madison, stop making that noise," she yelled, then clutched her chest like she was having an attack. Any movement was overexertion for her.

"Ahhhhhhhh! I'll kill you," I continued.

"Didn't I tell–"

I gave her a swift uppercut to her right cheek. The medicine tray flew up over her head; and she went flying backwards, nearly losing her balance. Her fingers went up to shield her from further blows. She immediately called for back up, "Help!"

"Shut-up bitch!" I yelled and pounced on her. I dug my nails in her face and bit down into her porcelain skin. Then I started choking her to stop her from screaming. Everyone in my ward was giggling and laughing hysterically. Some of them started banging their heads on the walls and throwing tantrums.

The ward was short staffed so only two other employees came. They each grabbed one of my arms and forcibly put me inside a straitjacket. I protested the whole time. I tried to fight as best as I could, but I was no match for two at one time. Once they had me restrained, they gave me 1000 cc's of chlorohydrate and 10 mg Ativan. Within seconds, I felt lazy, tranquil. Then I nestled into my own zone. I would continue tomorrow.

A few hours later, I heard Joshua's voice. He stopped at the nurse's desk before he entered my room to get an update on my condition. I crept to the doorway so I could hear what they were saying. They told him all about my outburst.

"I think her condition is worsening," Nurse Betty stated.

"She's been in here for a long time. She should be getting better, not worsening. What does her doctor have to say about this?" Joshua retorted.

"He's thinking about giving her electric shock treatments. She's hallucinating and experiencing long periods of psychosis. She's detrimental to her own health and the welfare of our other patients," Nurse Betty lied.

"Jesus, Mary and Joseph! That girl has been through enough. Why can't therapy combined with Haldol curb her psychotic outbreaks. It helps everyone else," he stated. "Tell her doctor to give me a call. I need to have a word with him!" Joshua was livid.

Joshua angrily walked away from the nurse's station and came into my room. I loved how he stood up for me.

Joshua understood me. I took this opportunity to confide in him.

"Hi, gorgeous," he said and kissed me on my cheek. "Kid, you need to eat a hamburger or something. You've lost an awful lot of weight since the last time I saw you."

Ignoring his comment, and trying to prepare him for my news, I said, "Joshua, you'll never believe what I'm about to tell you."

"Try me."

"Lyric Maria Devaney isn't dead."

Joshua blinked a few times, twisted up his mouth, then said, "Listen, kid, you can't keep living in denial. Lyric is dead. She's been dead for quite some time. I know what happened Madison . . . you at Lyric's the night of her murder . . . with the two other girls. I know you could have saved her, but you didn't. I know you may be feeling guilty . . ."

"I didn't kill her! How dare you," I exclaimed.

"I know you didn't," Joshua said, patronizing me. He was such a dumb-ass. No wonder Lyric dumped him. I started to loathe Joshua just as she had.

"If you could just listen, you might learn something," I said and put my hands on my hips just as Lyric had done on so many occasions. "Lyric came to visit me a few weeks back. She said that she wasn't dead like everyone thought. She said that it was actually Lacey who'd been murdered."

"Lacey?" Joshua asked incredulously.

"Yes. She said that she had contacted Lacey weeks before her premiere and invited her to come. When Lacey arrived she told her that she had to run a quick errand.

When she came back, Lacey was being wheeled out by paramedics. From that night on, her and Lacey's life criss crossed."

I could tell that Joshua was considering the story.

"I didn't believe it either. I called her a liar and told her to leave. That was until I saw her on television. The press was announcing her marriage to millionaire Brian Carter."

"You saw her on television?"

"Marrying a millionaire. That is such typical Lyric behavior," I said.

"Or Lacey," Joshua lamented. "Listen, Madi, the woman you saw was Lacey not Lyric."

"Joshua, I of all people can recognize Lyric. I know her. I know her smile . . . her eyes. It was her!"

"Madison, let us not forget that Lyric and Lacey are identical twins."

"Could you just look into the matter?"

"Why do you care so much?"

"Because the guy she married isn't Brian Carter . . . he's Maurice Mungin!" I stated and looked him directly in his eyes.

"You know what—that's it! Snap out of it. I can admit you had me going. Madi, you can't seriously want me to believe that tall tale. Listen kid, I'm sorry but I'm not going to entertain this. I'll be back once you make an effort to take your medication so you can get better. I can't stand to see you like this. It's tearing me apart."

I could tell that I had upset Joshua. He got up and walked out. I decided that I had to prove to him and the world that Lyric Maria Devaney wasn't dead . . . yet!

SIXTY·TWO

KAPRI HENDERSON

I didn't fuck Eddie on our first date 'cause he didn't push up. We sat around bullshittin', gettin' to know each other.

Eddie came to my crib late e'ry night for a week. Never askin' to take me out or anythin'. He just made himself comfy, drinkin' up my liquor and watchin' my DVD player. Sometimes he wanted me to cook! It was cool though 'cause I liked his comp'ny.

Tonight Eddie came through my crib with some cheap ass roses. I know he copped them from a local bodega. It was cool though. I'll let him slide 'cause I know he had enough papah to git me the good shit. He must have been rushin'. He also had a shoppin' bag from Gucci. I was hyped thinkin' what he'd gotten me.

This night Eddie didn't want to sit, talk and bullshit. He wanted to fuck. I threw the roses in water and he grabbed me from behind and started to lick my neck. I felt a bulge in his jeans. A large bulge that he pressed up against me and made my pussy wet.

His lips were so soft on my skin that I got lost. My pussy started pulsating, so I reached for his massive penis and nearly choked. For a little guy—he was packing somethin' big. After feelin' his package, I realized I had had enough foreplay. I wanted to get busy, and led him into my room. There we both stripped naked rather quickly. There was no

romance. No dim lights. No seducin'. Just straight fuckin'.
Raw dog and sweaty.

Eddie ran up in me hard. I wrapped my legs around his
waist and we both pumped away. As we had sex, I couldn't
help but think of Knowledge. The love of my life. Eddie
sort of reminded me of Knowledge. I couldn't understand
why . . . but he did.

As Eddie's tight ass moved in and out, I lost it and
started to growl. "Graaaa-a-a-a-a-," I said and he paused
for a moment. I took this opportunity to flip him over and
mount him. My athletic hips pumped in and out. Now
we were both growlin' from the intense sensation we were
both feelin'. Sweat was pourin' off my body and drippin'
on Eddie. He was lickin' every inch of my body and his
strong hands groped my breast. I was in ecstasy until I
heard Kareem's key hit the lock.

"Who's dat?" Eddie panicked.

"My son," I whispered.

"Why the fuck you didn't tell me you had a son?"

"Nigga keep fuckin'," I said dissing him.

Eddie did as I said. When the fuckin' got too loud for
Kareem, he started actin' childish by slammin' his room
door and turnin' up the radio.

After our third round, we were both exhausted. We
both breathed heavily in and out until we could get our
breathin' to a normal pace. Then Eddie jumped out the
bed and went towards the living room butt-ass naked.

"Where ya goin'?" I yelled. He ignored me, but soon
came back carryin' that Gucci shoppin' bag. He tossed
it on the bed at me. Excited I clicked on the light and

reached inside the bag. I pulled out a lady's black, size 14, Gucci shirt. The price tag read $1200.

"Oh dip!" I squealed with delight.

"You like that, sexy?"

"Word up! It's a little too big though. Why did you pick up such a big size?"

"I dunno how to shop for ladies' shit. I thought you'd be happy," he said and his eyes hooded over. I could tell I had him pissed.

"I am happy. I'm mad happy. I know guys don't know how to pick out women shit. For future purchasin'," I smiled, "I wear a size 10."

"For future fucks . . . my dick's a size 12!" he said and crawled back into bed wit me. We fucked 'til the early mornin'.

SIXTY·THREE

ESTELLE CARDINALE

The morning of the trial I came to court in my chauffeur-driven Phantom, Rolls Royce. I was besieged by the press. I emerged in front of Supreme Court, 60 Centre Street, looking fabulous. I had on a pale beige Yves Saint Laurent three-piece skirt suit. My hair was newly cut and highlighted. For a woman facing 25-to-life behind bars, I looked undaunted.

I waltzed into court ten minutes late to the dismay of my attorneys. Robert Maximilian was the first one to pull me aside and try to scold me.

"Why on earth are you showboating? Most of these jurors are making less than $30,000 a year and you're carrying a $9,000 Hermes pocketbook. Jurors hate rich people flaunting their wealth! They think you assume you can buy freedom."

"I will not represent myself in anything less than the best. Jurors are no fools. If I come in here looking like a church choir girl they will surely see through the facade."

"When did you get a law degree," he spat. "I'll tell you how this trial will be run, down to your clothing. Now I already told you what you should be wearing. Tomorrow, don't make the same mistake. I won't tolerate it!" He walked away.

When court convened, it was packed. Every journalist and radio personality was in the audience. I looked around to see only a handful of the victim's family and friends. They were perched behind the prosecution. The only recognizable face was Joshua Tune. I despised him! Didn't he get enough of showing support for his dead friend? It cost him his career and freedom. If I had a million years to ponder it, I would never understand what Lyric Devaney had over these men.

The courtroom drama actually bored me. During each break, I would pull out my cellular telephone and make calls. I spoke to my broker about stocks, my housekeeper regarding dinner and even my niece, Ivanka. I wanted to know how her situation with her loathsome father was progressing. When I wasn't using the phone, I would touch up my make-up in a mirror or openly yawn at the rants of the prosecution.

The prosecution is allowed the opening statement and closing argument first. Robert explained that's because they have the burden of proof.

On about the third day of trial, I started to pay attention. I started taking notes and listening intently to the prosecution's witnesses. Something about the zealousness of the prosecution in wanting to secure a conviction against me made me snap out of the wonderland I was in. My life was on the line. I told Robert that I was going to testify and he agreed.

Robert fortunately hired Kaitlyn Boswell; a publicist. Together they worked on damage control. They leaked information about the numerous charities I was involved with and my pristine reputation as a pillar in my community. They wanted to counter the allegations the press had developed regarding my apathy in the trial. The press surreptitiously splashed my face across every newspaper and tabloid as I exited my Rolls Royce. They drew charts listing each item I wore and the cost. They made me out to be a fashion monger. As I read each article, I realized that Robert had been right. My antics could ultimately cost me my freedom.

SIXTY·FOUR

NIKKI LING

The call from the mysterious stranger had disturbed me. I needed a realistic way out, but a solution kept failing me. *You're a hustler, Nikki*, I thought. I can do this. I can outsmart this chick. I've gotten myself out of tight situations before and I'll do it again. There was absolutely no way I was going down for this. Nor was I going to *murder* her husband.

I tossed and turned all night. I woke up several times with visions of Jack's mutilated body haunting me. I was drenched in sweat. I quickly jumped up and turned on the lights. I couldn't sleep in the dark. I was too spooked. I didn't want anything to drink either. I needed to be sober while I weighed my options. If I went to the police and told them about the criss cross, I would be incriminating myself in a conspiracy to commit murder. I was the only person with something to gain after Jack's murder. That, coupled with the fact that I had a rap sheet longer than my right arm...things seemed grim.

In the light of morning I had finally come up with a solution. I decided that I'd get the stranger to admit on tape that she had killed Jack and wanted me to kill her husband. With that tape as evidence I could use it as leverage against her. I'd tell her that if she sent the gun to the police, I would turn over the tape. We'd both go down!

I so desperately needed Brian's street smarts and wit in this matter ...

Then I decided as a precautionary measure to report Jack's gun stolen. I'll say someone stole it before Jack was murdered to give myself an alibi. I knew I was slicing the situation thin but at least I had a plan.

I dressed in a black T-shirt that read "Bitch" and a pair of Filthmore jeans, pulled my hair tightly back and covered my puffy eyes with bumblebee Jackie Onassis shades. Then I hopped on my bike and headed over to the 6th precinct just two miles away. As the wind hit my face, I took solace in the fact that although I lost Jack, I still had my sister Noki.

As I approached, police officers were standing outside talking and smoking cigarettes. I quickly ran up the steps, avoiding eye contact and went to their front desk.

"May I help you, ma'am?" the sergeant asked.

"Yes ... I ... would like to report a gun missing," I hesitated.

"Do you have a license for it?" he raised his eyebrow skeptically.

"Yes, sir," I said fumbling through my oversized Hermes bag until I pulled out my husband's paperwork.

"Was there a break in?"

"Not to my knowledge. But we have people in and out all the time. Someone must have stolen it. It's a very valuable gun. 19th-century, nickle-plated. It's alleged to have been the same gun that killed Lincoln."

"Well, I hope that's the only person who's fallen victim to that gun. Have a seat, I'll have one of our officers take your statement."

"Thanks."

I walked over to a wooden bench and stared at the criminals being processed. I had sat so many times in different precincts that the thought sent chills down my spine. I can't go through this again. That's why I married Jack ... to escape my past.

Soon Officer Jones walked over and told me to follow him upstairs to process my report. He asked a litany of questions and then gave me a telephone number to call for my complaint number. Everything seemed to go well.

"I'll walk you out," Officer Jones said. I could tell that he found me appealing. He wasn't the least bit attractive but he seemed pleasant enough. I quickly glanced at my watch and decided that I'd go over to Staples and purchase a small recording device and then sit around and wait for the stranger to call. I was about two steps away from the door when I heard someone say, "Mrs. Okayo."

I turned around and was met by the Detective Oldham on Jack's case. Why was he here? This wasn't his precinct.

"Hello . . . detective . . . what are you doing here?" I stammered.

"I was just about to ask you the same thing. Did you get any leads on your husband's murder?" he asked suspiciously.

"No ... I um ... I had to make a report. Now I have to run ... but if I think of anything, I'll certainly call you."

I tried to leave when he grabbed a hold of my arm. It wasn't a friendly grasp. It was territorial and I felt frightened.

"What type of report?" he asked, then released my arm. He looked to the officer to answer.

"Well, Mrs. Okayo just filled out a report for a missing gun. A real expensive collector's item was stolen from her apartment."

"Really?" he said with a tight lip, then continued, "When was the item stolen?"

"The last time I saw it was weeks ago. Jack was going to make the report . . . but . . ." I purposely let my voice trail off. My eyes welled up with tears. I clutched my breast like I was going to faint. Officer Jones quickly passed me a tissue, but it was Detective Oldham that looked unfazed by my display of melodrama.

"I'm sorry, but it's difficult for me," I said, then continued, "I really need to get home before dark. I'm afraid to walk the street alone."

"Of course you are," Detective Oldham said, "but since I have you here I'd like to make a formal request for you to come down to the station tomorrow morning. Eleven sharp. I need you to assist in this investigation. Also, if you want me to put an officer at your door, I'd be glad to. For your safety, of course."

"That won't be necessary. I have two wonderful bodyguards. I'll see you tomorrow. Eleven. Sharp. Good day," I said and practically ran out of the precinct. Although I never turned around, I could feel his eyes on me. Watching.

SIXTY·FIVE

KAPRI HENDERSON

The afternoon sun was beamin' down on the ghetto and givin' our already brown skin an even darker glow. I was sittin' outside my buildin' wit a few of my neighbors, gossipin' and talkin' shit. We had a half dozen forty ounce bottles of Colt 45 malt liquor. That combined wit the heat, we were fucked up.

I had a stash of crack hidden in my socks so I wasn't just chillin' but I was workin' too. Countin' paper on Crooke Avenue. The name fittin' for the bunch of crooks we were.

"So, Kapri, who dat fine mutherfucker I see creepin' in ya crib at night when you think ain't nobody 'round," Ms. Joy said. She was my next-door neighbor and nosy as hell. She was around 60 years old. Her whole head was covered wit nappy, gray hair. She could hang out just like she was twenty, but the doctors said she ain't got much longer to live. Her liver all fucked up from drinkin'.

"He's my mutherfuckin' business," I teased and took another gulp of my beer.

"Mi know you not hide cock from mi gal. You got man?" Veronica asked. She lived on the first floor and often let the building know if the cops were out shakin' someone down. She's cool. I like her. She's always hangin' in Manhattan wit her high-class friends and then comes back on the block to talk about them.

"Yea, it's this new kid that I met. A trick. That mutherfucker bring me somethin' new e'ry night. Gucci, Prada, Christian Dior . . . he's really feelin' me."

"'Im ya bumbs . . . ya sugar daddy? Ya suck a mean cock mon," Veronica heckled.

"Till the vein bulge," I added.

"'Im a grindsman?" Veronica asked.

"What dat mean?" I said.

"A grindsman. 'Im good in bed."

"No doubt," I cheered.

"Why he buyin' you fancy-smancy clothes. That Gucci and Prada mess. Can't he see he just wastin' his money," Ms. Joy stated. "He's foolish chile. That's like tryin' to eat caviar and pork chops. It just don't mix."

"My man eats me very well. Fuck-you-very-much," I said.

What did Ms. Joy know anyway? I had enough class to get away with wearin' Prada and Gucci.

We were listenin' to my boom-box that I had brought outside when the radio played an old school joint. "La-de-dottie," by Dougie Fresh and Slick Rick. I jumped out my seat and started doin' a dance called the whop. This song reminded me of before I got locked up. I was dancin' around when I saw my son Kareem come runnin' down the block with two of his friends behind him. When he reached me, I could tell he'd just gotten in a fight. His right eye was swollen and his lip was busted.

"Boy, what the fuck happened to you!" I bellowed.

Before he could open his mouth, he burst out into tears. "I . . .just . . . had a fight."

"I know you ain't standin' in my fuckin' face cryin'," I said and punched him in his pathetic chest. "Shut up!"

He put his head down real low and tried to stop his tears. I looked over to his two friends who looked nervous.

"What happened?" I asked Kareem.

"I was up on Parkside Avenue movin' your product—"

"They took my shit?"

"No, ma'am . . . I mean Kapri."

"Oh, go ahead."

"Well, as I said, I was up on Parkside when this boy named Jamel walked past me and bumped me. So I told him that he could at least say excuse me—"

"Excuse me? Boy we in the mutherfuckin' 'hood. Don't nobody say excuse me. Serves you right for bein' such a smart-ass. He should have whipped your ass. What ya friends do? They didn't jump in?" I asked rollin' my eyes at the two losers.

"No Kapri. They just let us fight."

"Well, by the look on your face, you ain't do much fightin'. It look like that Jamel did all the fightin'."

"Kapri, why don't you let up on the boy," Ms. Joy said.

"Let up? Don't tell me how to raise my son. In fact, show me where this Jamel live. You gonna fight his ass again. And you better not lose or else you gotta deal wit me."

"Kapri, I don't want to fight him again," he whined.

"I don't give a fuck what you want. I pay the bills 'round here. If your father Knowledge-Born was here, he'd make you do the same thing. His father didn't take no shit from nobody."

"I don't even know my father!" he yelled at me.

In all this commotion, I didn't realize that Jamel was walkin' down our block wit three guys 'n a ol' lady.

"Ka-pri, I tink you got visitors gal," Veronica said and hipped me to the situation. When I turned 'round, I was greeted by a loud mouth.

"This here the mutherfucker that bit you Jamel," the older broad said. She looked around 35 years old, husky, wit a long cut from her right eye to the tip of her top lip. She had pointed her index finger in Kareem's face.

"Yea, that's him."

"Hold the fuck up," I screamed. "Who da fuck is you?"

"This my son," she said.

"And this my son!"

"Well your mutherfuckin' son is a bitch. He gonna fuckin' bit my son in his arm, now he gotta go and get a tetanus shot!"

"Too mutherfuckin' bad! I know you ain't runnin' up on my block poppin' shit. A bitch did thirteen years upstate! I am not the one to fuck wit."

"Bitch, I don't give a fuck if you did jail time . . ." she said and started to reach in her back pocket for a razorblade. Thinkin' quickly, I looked around for a weapon.

"Ka-pri, da bokkle! Da bokkle!" Veronica coaxed.

When I spotted a beer bottle, I lunged for it. I picked up an empty forty-ounce bottle and bashed her upside her head. Her head split open like a cantaloupe. Swiftly I grabbed hold of her arm and twisted it back with one hand. I wanted to break dat shit. Wit my free hand I landed several punches in her face. Then I flipped her over my back, and she landed on the ground wit a hard thud. I took this opportunity to stomp her head into the concrete. When the blood squirted everywhere, the bystanders all moved back and let us fight. I handled the husky broad like I was back in cellblock D. I whipped her ass quickly and said, "I mutherfuckin' dare somebody to jump in!"

When the police sirens came on the block, everyone scattered. Kareem and I ran into Veronica's apartment for fear dat someone would snitch me out. I sat in Veronica's crib all night drenched in that bitch's blood. I kept thinkin' that 5-0 was gonna bust my apartment. But they didn't. I guess dat bitch knew the code of the street: Don't snitch.

SIXTY·SIX

NIKKI LING

When I reached home, I had several messages from Noki and Kayla. I called Noki first. "Noki, pick up...it's me."

"Why didn't you call me and tell me about Jack!"she accused.

"I tried calling you, Noki, but I couldn't get you on the phone," I said and didn't realize that tears were streaming down my face.

"I had to hear about my legal guardian being murdered from the local news channel?"

"Noki, please don't make this about you. Jack is dead. I need your support," I pleaded.

"Well, what can I do?"

"Good-bye, Noki," I said and hung up the phone. I had a headache.

I rode the elevator down to the second floor and decided to work out in the gym. I was nervous that the stranger hadn't called yet as she had promised. What about the criss cross? Had she reneged?

As I aggressively walked the treadmill, the telephone rang. I jumped off the treadmill and answered it on the fourth ring.

"This me—this you?" I was barely able to catch my breath.

"I'm on my way over!" Kayla said and hung up. The concern and urgency in her voice brought me to tears. I just stood there and let out a blood curdling scream. My knees went weak, and I collapsed to the floor. I was still cradling the receiver.

"My life is over! My life is over!" I screamed. A tremendous cloud of guilt loomed over me. I knew that I was responsible for Jack's murder. I was the reason he was dead. I pulled myself up from the floor and headed straight to Jack's bathroom.

His dark brown decor matched my mood. I ran a warm bath, stripped naked, grabbed a shiny razorblade and decided to let history repeat itself.

The despair and angst I was feeling was overwhelming. My head felt heavy and my stomach upset.

As the sharp blade glided over my skin, I felt a basic sense of relief. "I can do this," I said.

Just as I was about to apply more pressure, the doorbell rang and bolted me out of the trance-like state I was in. "Kayla?" I said.

"Kayla!" I screamed and jumped out the tub. I dropped the razorblade and grabbed Jack's terrycloth bathrobe.

Kayla was ringing the bell and banging on the door, screaming my name. I opened it quickly. We hugged so tight I absorbed some of her strength. I could tell she'd been crying.

"I came as quickly as I heard. Nikki it's all over the news . . . the press are downstairs camping out."

She walked me over to our large storm windows. I looked out and saw numerous news vans parked all over Central Park West. I collapsed on my sofa and cried.

"Nikki what happened? Are you in danger? Why

didn't you call me?"she questioned.

I couldn't look at Kayla. I was ashamed. I just shook my head in bewilderment. She cradled my head in her arms and tried to console me.

"Nikki, why would anyone want to kill Jack?"

"I don't know," I lied.

"Jack has always been concerned about his safety as well as yours. Nikki, where are your bodyguards? They need to be here."

"I'm all right," I stated.

"Huh?" she said in astonishment. She couldn't understand how I could be tough in the face of danger.

"I don't want anyone feeling sorry for me. Jack is the true victim here. Someone beat, mutilated and mangled his body," I cried.

"How could someone do something so evil and cruel?"

"People are sick!" I lamented.

"Where's Noki?" Kayla said, looking around as if Noki was hidden in a crevice of the apartment.

"She's very upset and needed time alone to grieve. You know how she adored Jack," I lied.

"You're his wife. She should be here consoling you in your grief," Kayla stated. She was one of many who didn't particularly care for Noki.

Before I could respond, the telephone rang. Without hesitation, Kayla picked up the telephone and I panicked. Could it be the stranger?

"Hello," she said, and I snatched the telephone from her hands, nearly knocking her to the floor.

"Hello," I screamed into the phone.

"This is Jennifer Garth from Channel 8 News. I wanted to know . . .." I slammed down the phone.

"Who was that?"

"Sonuvabitch! A reporter," I screamed.

Kayla shook her head, "Don't they have any compassion. You just lost your husband, and they want the next hot headline."

"They don't care about me . . . no one does," I said, feeling sorry for myself.

"I care about you . . . I love you. You're my sister," Kayla soothed. "Listen it's late. You need your rest. I'll put you to bed."

SIXTY·SEVEN

ESTELLE CARDINALE

As court recessed, Robert and I had a short chat. "Everything is going to hinge on your testimony. The jury will not expect you to testify. They want you to make it easy for them to convict. I need you to get up there and make them feel compassion for you," he coached.

"Me? I don't think I've ever been able to exude compassion," I stated.

Robert gave me a stern look, then said, "I don't want to hear what you can't do. You had enough gumption in you to murder a human being. I'm sure you are clever enough to convey a particular emotion. You will have approximately 60 minutes to convince 12 jurors of your innocence."

I thought about what he said, and he was absolutely right. I almost got away with the *perfect* murder. Surely I can fool a litany of fools. The night before I took the stand, I hired a private masseuse to remove any tension that I had bottled up. My shoulders were extremely tight. After the massage, I concentrated on Robert's words. I had to make 12 people feel compassion for me and not that whore bitch, Lyric! I could do it. I can actually do anything I set my mind to.

The next morning I wore a soft-pink Tahari pantsuit. I had my hair pulled back tight in a bun. I didn't have on even one piece of jewelry.

When it came time to take the stand, I sat down and was sworn in. Robert calmly approached the stand and began his questioning.

"Could you state your name for the record?"

"Estelle Marilyn Cardinale."

"Now, Mrs. Cardinale, could you please tell the court how you first came to know about Ms. Lyric Devaney."

"My husband came in and told me he was having an affair."

"Did you suspect him?"

"My husband and I had been married for 25 years. I'd speculated he'd had numerous affairs."

"Speculated? Did he ever admit to any of them?"

"No."

"Did he ever waltz in before and admit to an affair he wasn't accused of having?"

"No, sir."

"So what was going through your mind when he told you about Ms. Devaney?"

"I'll admit that I was disappointed. But the hurt had long since disappeared. I'd grown numb to my husband's infidelities."

"After your husband's sudden burst of honesty, what happened next?"

"One night, he came home and told me that he'd ended his affair with Ms. Devaney."

"Did you ask him to end his affair?"

"No, sir."

"You were his wife and never asked him to end his affair?"

"Correct. My husband wasn't partial to being told what to do. I learned that a long time ago. My only concern was raising our children."

"After he told you he ended the affair, what happened next?"

"He would constantly complain about Ms. Devaney stalking him. Then he alleged that she was blackmailing him. He said that she was relentless in trying to ruin his political career."

"What else did he say?"

"He said he'd never allow that to happen . . . ."

"Objection!" the prosecution roared. The judge hit his gavel a few times and said, "Overruled."

"Please continue," Robert said.

"My husband would come home and divulge information about Ms. Devaney that I never inquired about."

"Like what?"

"Like where she lived, noting that she lived alone. And her schedule. He'd always say she never left the house until nightfall."

"Why do you think he was dropping all these tidbits of information?"

"He wanted me to take the fall for her murder...."

"Objection, Your Honor. The witness cannot access the thoughts of someone else. She's not qualified."

"Judge, Mrs. Cardinale is qualified to access the intentions of her husband. They were married 25 years."

"Overruled."

"Mrs. Cardinale, when your husband would come in and tell you details about Ms. Devaney, did you want her dead?"

"No, sir."

Then Robert went and pulled out Exhibit 45. It was a photo of a woman Richard had had an affair with.

"Mrs. Cardinale, do you recognize this woman?"

"Yes."

"Could you please tell the court who she is."

"She was my children's nanny?"

"Is she still your children's nanny."

"No, sir."

"Please tell the court why."

"I caught her and Richard having sex in our bedroom," I said and started sobbing. The courtroom erupted.

"Is she still alive?" Robert asked when everything calmed down.

"Of course she is . . . I ran into her just last week."

From that point on Robert pulled out photo after photo of beautiful women Richard had had affairs with throughout our marriage. They all had the same common denomination: they had all had an affair with my husband, yet they were all still alive. I looked over at the jury and could tell that they got the point Robert was making.

"Mrs. Cardinale, was there a time when you and your husband had an argument?"

"Yes. Richard came in complaining that his political career would be over if Ms. Devaney went to the press. It was at that moment I told him I planned to divorce him. I told him that I wanted to pursue my career in politics and his recent behavior could cost me the election. I was going to run for mayor of New York. I wanted to succeed him in the next election."

"How did he take your news?"

"He was appalled!"

"How much longer after that incident were you arrested for the murder of Ms. Devaney?"

"Exactly one week . . ."

Again, the courtroom had to be silenced by the judge's gavel.

"Mrs. Cardinale, did you kill Ms. Devaney?"

"No, sir."

"Where were you on the night of her murder?"

"My sister was dying. I was at her bedside."

"Is your sister alive to verify your alibi?"

"No, sir, but my niece was there the whole time," I said and looked to Ivanka. She was ready to take the stand any day now on my behalf.

"Your honor, I'd like to play the tape once again for the jury," Robert said.

As the jury watched the murder tape for the second time, Robert would pause the tape, then ask me a question. He pointed out that the tape was somewhat distorted. The quality was grainy. Not to mention the lighting inside Lyric's apartment was dim. She had a seductive theme going on when I entered her apartment. The dim lighting should ultimately benefit me. Since the video camera was mounted in one spot, only one angle was videotaped. So, for during most of the tape, my back was towards the camera.

"Mrs. Cardinale, I have a few more questions. The woman you see in this tape, murdering Mrs. Lyric Devaney . . . is that you?"

"No, sir," I said and the courtroom ignited.

"Who do you think that is in this videotape?"

"Why it looks like Richard dressing up like me once again."

"Objection!" the prosecution stated trying to salvage his case.

"Your Honor, we'd like to submit for evidence some recent photos uncovered by our private detective of Mr. Richard Cardinale dressed in ladies lingerie and clothing," Robert stated.

"Sidebar, Your Honor," the prosecution said. Both attorneys walked over to the judge's desk and began to whisper.

Then the judge looked over the photos and shook his head. "I'll admit them into evidence," Judge Hatchett stated. "Of course you will," I thought.

SIXTY-EIGHT

KAPRI HENDERSON

For the next couplea days, I decided to lay low in my crib til the heat died down. Jamel and his moms never came back, and Kareem's scary ass was still too shook to go off da block. I had him sellin' my drugs from in front da buildin' where I could keep an eye on him.

I was in the kitchen makin' Eddie's favorite dish, baked macaroni 'n cheese 'n fried chicken wings, when he came over a lil' early.

"Whadup boo," he said and kissed my full lips.

"Shit," I said and started fixin' his plate. When we sat down to eat, it felt nice, like family. Like I'd imagined life wit Knowledge. I realized that I was really feelin' Eddie. The sex was da bomb. He was a lil' cutie. And he had dough. He was perfect. The only thing dat was missin' was that I didn't really know much about him other than what he had told me. He never took a chick to his crib or 'round his peoples. We always just met up here.

"You lookin' fly as usual boo," he said commentin' on my brand new Gucci sweat suit. I didn't git it from da Gucci store. I went up on 125th Street in Harlem and let this kid put Gucci bag material on my jean suit. It was so dope.

"I try to look good for my man."

"So where you get the paper to stay fly? You don't work," he asked, and I was at a loss for words.

"I'm still livin' off my paychecks from when I was workin' in the city. I told you 'bout dat job, didn't I?"

"No," he said, and I was saved by his cell phone ringin'. It never dawned on me to tell Eddie what I did for a livin'. I just assumed he knew I was out hustlin'. It felt weird to come out and say it.

As he yapped on da phone, I could hear a chick's voice on the other line.

"Well, how did that happen?" he said into the phone. His voice was different. Soft. Soothin'. Baby-like. A way you talk to your bitch. Immediately I was pissed off. I know this boy ain't tryin' to play me.

"Yo—" I tried to speak up but he silenced me wit his hand.

After he finished his phone conversation, I started breakin'.

"Who the fuck was dat!"

"That was Trisha. My baby momma," he said casually.

"I don't give a fuck who she is. Why the fuck I gotta be quiet. This my motherfuckin' crib. I thought you said you two ain't together."

"We not. But we give each other that respect. See, my baby mom's ain't like most these chicks out here. She real smart. She a doctor. She got all these degrees on her wall 'n shit. Sometimes she be talkin' 'bout shit I can't even understand."

"What dat gotta do wit you makin' me shut da fuck up?"

"If she think that I'm runnin' with rough girls like you . . . she won't let me see my daughter."

"Rough? Since when I'm rough, yo."

He laughed and said, "You've got to be jokin'."

"Ha. Ha. No I'm not jokin'. Tell me how the fuck I'm rough!"

"My daughter's mother is classy. She has expensive taste. Drives the Mercedes S-600. Goes to dinner with lawyers and senators. She pays for my daughter's private school . . . she even bought me the Benz I got now even though we're not together. She's real generous like that. Now you . . . if you weren't so cute, I'd think you were a dude. You have this rough edge . . . like a dike would have."

I was heated. I could not believe he was talkin' to me like that. Sittin' in my mutherfuckin' crib praisin' the next bitch. And he didn't stop there, he continued, "Trisha is from a wealthy family. My daughter is gonna get paid when she turns eighteen. My daughter looks just like her mother, too. She has long pretty hair. She doesn't need a relaxer to straighten her hair. You got a relaxer in your hair?" he asked.

"Umm . . . no. I just go to the Dominican's to get it set. Dis my natural hair texture too," I lied. My voice was mad low. No wonder he had dat expensive taste. Comin' over here wit bags from Prada and Gucci. His baby momma was sophisticated.

We ate the rest of our dinner in silence. Then I decided dat I couldn't let a bitch get one up on me.

"Eddie, what are you doin' tomorrow afternoon?"

"I don't know yet. Why?"

"'Cause I wanted to go to the dealer and git me a jeep . A bitch tired of takin' cabs."

"Word, what you wanna get?" he asked uninterested.

"I'm thinkin''bout gettin' the Cadillac Escalade jeep . . ."

"Say word!" he stated wit a huge grin on his face. I grinned, too.

"Yea, so you down to go wit me?"

"No doubt."

SIXTY·NINE

MADISON MICHAELS

CREEDMORE MENTAL INSTITUTION

On this particular night I put my plan into motion. I was going back to the Pink Houses project in East New York, Brooklyn to find Sweepy and Redbone. I needed them to help me stop Lyric for good! When they came around with meds, I didn't put up a fight. I opened my mouth and pretended to swallow. When the ward was quiet and most of the nurses were sleeping at their post, I made my move. Just as I suspected, they were all asleep except for one. She was in the kitchen heating up her food in the microwave. As the microwave ticked, I sneaked into their locker room and stole a nurse's overcoats. In a last-minute decision I stuck my hands through everyone's coat pocket and collected over $100. Next, I dashed to the elevator, then made my way out of the facility undetected.

Once outside in the night air, I felt free. Well, I was free. I would no longer have those mean nurses telling me when to go to bed. Holding back privileges if they felt like I had done something wrong. That was so juvenile, yet the State gave them total control over me. Not anymore.

I wandered aimlessly for hours until I found the Pink Houses. This was the last place I remembered. It was nearly 3:00 a.m., but it was crowded outside. I heard loud music blaring. People were dancing, drinking and smoking marijuana. I just eased into the crowd and sat on the bench and listened. I knew Portia had lived out here. I wondered if she was still here, so I decided to go to her house.

I rode the elevator to her floor and knocked on her door. I knocked for a long time until I heard someone yell, "Who's dat?"

"It's me, Madison," I cheered. I felt so happy.

The door swung open, and I was greeted by an old lady. Her face was mean.

"Chile, whatchu doin' here bangin' on my door. Who you want?"

"Is Portia here?" I asked, already peering through her apartment.

"Portia don't live here no more!" she said and slammed the door in my face. I stood there for a moment, then left.

As I made my way back to the elevator, she opened her door again, "Chile, you got a witch ridin' your back. Don't come 'round here wit no foolishness. That dead girl in here protectin' me from you. She said you evil!"

Once again she slammed her door.

"Crazy lady!" I yelled and my voice echoed in the narrow hallway. And they had *me* locked up for years . . .

SEVENTY

NIKKI LING

I waited all night for the stranger to contact me. She didn't. The next morning I left Kayla and rode my motorcycle over to the 11th precinct for my eleven o'clock meeting. I walked over to the sergeant who seemed to recognize me when I walked in. He looked like he had a sour taste in his mouth. He was a burly white guy with a mane of thick, black hair. He directed me up the station steps to the second floor, Homicide Unit. There Detective Oldham sat brooding.

"Mrs. Okayo, please have a seat," he said and smiled grandly. He seemed much gentler today.

"Hello, detective."

"I think you'll be pleased to know that I've been working non-stop on your husband's case. I've been interviewing witnesses and following leads. Strangely, not one person that I've interviewed has a motive..."

I shook my head, "I don't know who would want to kill Jack. And the vicious way he was slaughtered."

"Did Jack have any enemies? Any recent disputes in the days before he was killed?"

"No . . . no, everyone loved Jack. He was such a giving man."

"Correct. That's exactly what his records show. He just withdrew one million dollars the day before he was murdered," he stated.

"You've reviewed our bank records?"

"And I even spoke with the bank's manager. He said you were looking to withdraw the same amount one day previously. Could you explain why?"

"I . . . um . . . was trying to withdraw that money at Jack's request. He didn't tell me why." As soon as I said it, I knew it was a mistake. I'm sure the bank manager must have already told the Detective that I tried to get the money without Jack's signature. Even if he had caught me in a lie, he didn't say a word.

"Maybe you could help me with this case. Give me a little insight. If you were a killer, how would you plan to get away with this crime? How would you commit the perfect murder?"

"I don't think I'm qualified to answer that question," I stated. I felt uneasy.

"Of course not," he said with a smirk, almost mocking my answer. He seemed amused as if it was his duty to patronize me.

"I've been up all night trying to think of something . . . anything that could help with the investigation, but I'm clueless."

"I understand. Do you think your husband was having an affair? Maybe his mistress was blackmailing him. Do you think that could be the case?" he quizzed.

"They say the wife's always the last to know. But that's a thought. Jack loved pretty women," I said hoping he'd go on a wild goose chase.

"My question is what are *your* thoughts on another woman involved. Did you two ever fight over his infidelities? Or yours perhaps ..."

My stomach sank. What did he know?

"Mine?"

"Correct. Have you ever been unfaithful to your husband, Mrs. Okayo?"

"I think I may need to speak with an attorney before I answer any more questions," I blurted out. I could easily incriminate myself if I said anything further. If I opted to tell the truth about my affairs, I'd surely become a suspect. "Am I free to leave or am I under arrest?"

"You're free to walk right out that front door," he said and smiled. His phony smile was intimidating. "Before you go, would you mind telling me where you were on the night your husband was killed?"

"The movies," I stated and concluded our interview.

Once outside, I decided I couldn't confide in anyone. I couldn't tell Kayla or Noki. I know the games police officers play, and they could easily trick either one of them into saying something that could incriminate me.

As an afterthought, I rode over to the bank and my safety deposit box. I needed to tally up how much money I had just in case an impromptu situation arose. I know I'd always stated that I didn't count my money, an old taboo belief, but I needed to push those superstitions aside. After I had safely buried my husband, I was going to skip town. Go underground and live off my savings until I felt it was safe to resurface. Then I'd have Jack's money to ensure my future.

I ran into the bank and was escorted to a private room with my safety deposit box. Once alone, I unlocked my box and sat down for six hours counting out my money. I had exactly $785,000! That was a lot of cash. I had no idea I had anywhere near that amount. A decade worth of crime.

It was close to closing time at the bank. I returned my cash back to the safety of my box and went home to start to work on my husband's funeral arrangements. I think I still didn't quite believe he was gone. It all felt surreal.

SEVENTY·ONE

KAPRI HENDERSON

Eddie and I went to the Cadillac dealer up on Flatbush Avenue near Kings Plaza. We were in and out in thirty minutes. When I opened up my duffle bag and paid for my jeep in cash, Eddie took notice. I could see he was feelin' the way I was movin' shit.

When they drove my jeep off da lot and handed me the keys, Eddie snatched them and jumped in the driver's seat. Briefly, I thought 'bout the first time we met. He was in someone else's driver seat. That was some time ago and Eddie still hasn't come 'round wit his Benz yet.

As we drove down Flatbush Avenue, I enjoyed the smooth ride. We had the six-disc CD changer bumpin' Foxy Brown, *"Lemme tell you where I grew up at . . . BK . . . threw up at . . . Brooklyn. . ."*

We were chillin'. When Eddie pulled up on da block, all heads turned towards us.

"So, I'm gonna show everyone on the block my new shit . . . but I don't wanna stay here. I wanna hang out. Where can we go?" I asked Eddie. I thought now would be a good time for him to take me out to dinner or a movie.

"Kapri, I gotta make a quick stop. I need to do this alone. I'm workin' on somethin' big. A huge business deal is about to be wrapped up. I'm about to get paid. So I'ma drop you off and come right back and pick you up," he said.

Before I could think, he'd kissed me on my lips and kicked me out of my own jeep . All I saw as he sped off were the break lights on the jeep when he reached the corner.

I went upstairs tryin' to figure out if this nigga just played me? Then I shook those feelings off. "That's my man," I thought. Bitches gotta ride or die fo their nigga. Just as that thought came in my head, I felt stupid. Knowledge used to always say that shit to me. And look how I ended up . . .

I grabbed a Pepsi from out my refrigerator and clicked on the huge-screen television in my living room. I kicked off my brand new Nike sneakers and started to flip through channels when somethin' caught my attention. It was the murder trial wit that crazy white bitch who killed dat black actress. As I watched, my stomach sank and I felt nauseous. Three lawyers were on television talkin'''bout their client's innocence.

"I am confident today that at trial, our client will be vindicated in a court of law," one said.

I scrambled to turn the television up louder. Then I moved in so close to the television set that I felt blind—my vision was so blurry. I sat there and just shook my head. I was buggin'. That mutherfuckin' lawyer who said his name is Robert Maximilian, was bitch **ass** Knowledge Born from the Marcy projects! After all these years, I finally know how his life turned out.

"I thought you were dead . . .," I said and tears slowly streamed down my cheeks.

I was filled wit anger and rage. He'd reinvented himself

on the sweat, time and tears I done locked up in an upstate correctional facility. I ran to the window and called, "Kareem, git up here boy!"

"Yes ma'am," his stupid ass said.

Once he came in the house I had already put my sneakers back on.

"Kareem, where's the nearest library?"

"On Beverly Road."

"Good, go and call a cab. I need you to help me wit somethin'."

"Why we gotta catch a cab when you just bought a jeep? Why you let that guy take our ride?"

You would think that this boy would know when to push my mutherfuckin' buttons. Couldn't he see I wasn't in the mood for his smart-ass mouth? I gave him a stern look 'cause if I raised my hands to him, I'd kill him in this crib.

"Lord, please don't let me catch another case," I prayed.

Kareem got the hint and called us a cab. When we got inside the library, I told him exactly what I wanted him to do.

"Kareem, I need you to find out as much as you can on these here computers in dis library on a man named Robert Maximilian."

"Why?"

"Because he's your father!" I screamed and everyone looked at me.

"I thought Knowledge was my father," he said tryin' to win the "I'm smart" award.

"Robert is Knowledge. Fuck! I'll explain it later. Just do it."

Kareem first got online and did a Google search. He punched in Robert Maximilian and mad shit came up. He had found the address and telephone number to Knowledge Born's law firm and the most recent newspaper articles involvin' the trial. He printed them all out. After he was done, I learned that Robert Maximilian graduated from New York Law School wit honors in 1995. Then he moved to Miami and became some hotshot attorney, winnin' all his cases. He was worth millions. It appeared that he didn't have any children and wasn't married. For some reason, that information gave me comfort. Was Knowledge waitin' on me all this time? I didn't know the answer, but soon I'd find out!

SEVENTY·TWO

NIKKI LING

Nothing was spared at my husband's funeral. I selected a lavish chrome coffin with a plush white interior. Jack's name was engraved on the side. Jack had requested that he wanted to be buried in South Africa, his native home next to his parents. So I arranged to have a small memorial service here in America, then I'd fly to Africa with Jack's body.

The service was held at Laurelton & Sons on Long Island, a quaint funeral home that Jack's friend owned. Jack's staff, attorney, Kayla, Noki and I attended. When the service was over, Jack's attorney Sam Stakel and I arranged to hear the reading of his Last Will and Testament.

"The reading will begin tomorrow morning in my office at ten o'clock. Try to get some rest, Nikkisi," Sam said.

"I will, Sam," I replied and we quickly embraced.

I greeted everyone at the funeral home and looked forward to going home and getting some rest. I continually looked around, over my shoulders, looking for her. The stranger. But I didn't see her.

In the distance, I heard a faint noise drawing closer. The noise became more distinct as the sirens came nearer. As three cop cars with sirens blaring came disrupting the silence of the moment, I froze. My heart started fluttering and the hair on the back on my neck started tingling. I had an inkling that something awful was about to happen.

Detective Oldham came rushing towards the funeral home with his gun drawn. Then several news camera crews all descended on the property like a flock of seagulls over a rind of bread.

"Nikkisi Ling-Okayo," Detective Oldham stated.

"Yes?"

"You're under arrest for the murder of Jack Okayo," he said and put cold, metal handcuffs over my wrists.

"What's going on?" Kayla screamed, coming to my defense. Noki hovered in the background.

Then the camera crews, all stations, thrust their microphones in my face as I was being led to the police car.

"Mrs. Okayo, why'd you do it?" Channel 6 asked.

"Mrs. Okayo, was this about money?" Channel 9 queried.

"Mrs. Okayo, where were you when you found out that police had recovered the gun used to kill your husband?"

I fainted. My life was over.

SEVENTY·THREE

NIKKI LING

At the precinct, I was processed and fingerprinted. I wasn't allowed any visits from Noki or Kayla but I heard the commotion downstairs. Kayla was flipping out when they refused her request to see me. I kept hoping that she'd stop. I didn't want her getting in any trouble because of me. A few hours later I was allowed a telephone call. I quickly called Jack's attorney, Sam.

"Sam," I cried. "I need . . . you . . . to get me out of this mess. I need you to hire me a top defense attorney and post bail tomorrow at my arraignment," I cried. I'd cried more in a week than I'd done my whole life.

"Nikkisi, I'm your husband's attorney–not yours. New York law states that you cannot inherit money from the estate of a victim when you've been implicated in their murder," he stated. His voice was icy.

"But I'm innocent!" I screamed out of anguish.

"Until you're exonerated, Jack's estate will be put in escrow. You cannot receive a dime. Not for bail nor for your defense. I'm afraid you're on your own . . ."

"Sam, I've known you for years. You know I'm not capable of doing such a disgusting thing. I loved Jack."

"The old adage goes that only two things are certain: Death and taxes."

He was being facetious. But I continued to plead, "Sam,

I can't survive in jail. I'm not cut out for that. I can't stay another moment in this hell hole."

"Nikki," he said, no longer calling me by my full name, "Jack and I have had a business relationship for twenty years. We've been friends for thirty. I know everything about you. Everything. So don't pretend to be someone you're not."

"What do you want me to do, beg? Okay Sam, I'm begging. I'm begging for my freedom. Please . . . please don't leave me in here. I'll do anything," I pleaded.

"That won't be necessary," he spat. "Your services may have tempted Jack—"

"Sam, I didn't mean it like that," I said.

"Good-bye Nikkisi." Click.

I was taken back to a holding cell and handcuffed to a wall. I wasn't allowed to sit down, and there I remained for hours. My legs were weak, my arm was stiff and my throat was dry. They were trying to break me.

"Could I have some water!" I yelled out after several hours in custody.

"Shut-up bitch!" one police officer stated.

"Fuck you!" I yelled back. "FUCK YOU-U-U-U."

I was trying to be brave but I was terrified. I was so scared . . .

Their tactics were inhumane, but it was an everyday occurrence when trying to secure a confession. When my eyes started stinging from fatigue and my stomach growled from hunger, Detective Oldham came and brought me to an interrogation room.

"Have a seat," he commanded.

There was another detective in the room. He said his name was Detective Ripton. They started in with the "good cop–bad cop" routine.

"So tell us what happened, Nikki," Detective Ripton said in a soothing voice. "I'm sure it wasn't your fault. Did he hit you? Was that it? Did he put his hands on you and you lost it?"

"As I've already stated, I didn't kill my husband. I know you're only doing your job but you have to believe me. I'm innocent," I said and my bottom lip trembled. "I could never do such a thing."

"Listen save your tears and quit fuckin' around here. You murdered your husband, you ruthless bitch! We got your fingerprints on the murder weapon that you dumped in a trash can in back of your residence. Ballistics have already confirmed that the gun matches the slugs you put in your husband's kneecaps."

"I had no reason to kill my husband!" I screamed. I was tired and angry.

"You had $400 million reasons to kill your husband!" Detective Oldham shot back. Then he threw a slew of papers at me, the same papers that Jack had also assaulted me with. I glanced down and saw the photos of me with other men. My criminal records. And something I didn't see before. It was an old, tattered article about my mother's suicide. *"Prostitute and Mother of Two Commits Suicide,"* the article read. I'd never seen this article, and it made me cry.

"Nikki, it's okay. I understand. Why don't you make this easier on yourself and tell the truth? Did Jack find out about the other men and your mother? Did he threaten to divorce you? I'll help you, Nikki, if you let me," Detective Ripton said.

"Dude, you're wasting your fucking time! I ain't confessing to a murder. You see my rap sheet. I'm a veteran in this interrogation bullshit. I ain't talking!"

Detective Ripton then hoisted me up by my neck and slammed me up against the wall. With his hands tightly gripped around my neck, I struggled to breathe. I tried to kick him but knocked over the chair instead, it went crashing to the floor. Detective Oldham waited right before I was about to pass out before he pulled Detective Ripton off me. I collapsed to the floor gasping for air. Detective Ripton then pulled me up by my hair and threw me back in a seat.

"You think I'm fucking around! I'll slam your fucking head in this steel desk and break your fucking nose! Now you better start talking or else . . ."

This type of abuse went on for hours until the bus loading the inmates to court arrived. I was shipped to Central Booking in Lower Manhattan shortly after midnight. I knew the routine well. I'd go before the judge possibly tomorrow evening for arraignment, where the judge would set bail. I had about two hours to make bail before I'd be shipped to Rikers Island Correctional Facility. I couldn't let that happen. I'd already been through hell.

SEVENTY·FOUR

MADISON MICHAELS

After I'd left Portia's apartment, I made my way back downstairs and decided to have fun. I sat back on the bench and watched the late-night festivities. Finally someone noticed I was an outsider.

"Yo, whadup?" a guy said and did a head nod.

"What up," I said and gave the same gesture.

"What's your name, shorty," he said and took a swig from his beer.

I thought for a moment then said, "Lyric."

"Word, that's cute. My name's True. Who you out here wit?" he continued.

"I'm looking for my cousin, Sweepy."

"Word. Sweepy ya cousin. You ain't heard 'bout what happened to her?" he stated.

"Nah."

"She got merked."

"What?" I said. I had no idea what that meant.

"Yeah, she got killed. I'm sorry yo."

I didn't care, but I pretended to be angry. I fell into the lingo and used the situation to my advantage. "Let me holla at you for a moment," I said to the guy.

"No doubt," he said, and we walked into the building.

"Yo, I need a burner. I got a situation I gotta handle with this chick. I would have got it from my cousin . . . but . . ."

"If Sweepy ya cousin why you didn't know she got merked?" he asked suspiciously.

Thinking quickly I said, "I've . . . been away. Locked down for a while."

"Word? No doubt. I just came from up North. I gotchu. Come wit me to my crib," he said and looked around. "Sweepy was my home girl."

"Word."

I followed him to his roach-infested apartment. As soon as we walked in, I nearly choked on the smell of urine. Disgusting. We walked in the back to his bedroom. There were two twin beds with several people asleep. The hot summer air was stifling. He clicked on the light so he could locate his gun. As soon as he put on the light, someone said, "Come on yo."

"Chill!" True said.

He reached on top of his closet and pulled out a sneaker box. Then he motioned for me to follow him into his bathroom. I went quietly. Once inside, he opened the shoe box, revealing three guns. There was a shiny chrome gun, a large black gun and a revolver. My eyes quickly focused on the shiny chrome gun.

"I want this one," I said.

"Ah-h-h-h, you got good taste. How much money you got 'cause this ain't cheap."

"I don't want to buy it. I just want to borrow it."

"Huh? We don't do that in my 'hood. I mean if you my mans, then I'll slide you a burner if you got beef. But you ain't my man. No doubt you Sweepy's blood, but I don't operate like that. I need papah," he said and looked a little agitated.

I caught a quick flashback from years back. I was in an uncompromising position with Sweepy and Redbone. Thinking quickly, I pulled out my money and said, "All I got is this."

He stared at my money for a moment. "How much is that?"

"One hundred dollars," I said and hid the remaining $10 dollars.

"I can't do nothin' wit dat," he spat.

"Well that's all I got. I guess I'll take my money elsewhere," I said and tried to walk out his bathroom when he stopped me.

"Hold up, shorty. You can't get this one, but for that money I'll give you this one," he said and gave me the revolver. I was upset because I really wanted the shiny one, but I took the revolver anyway. As I held the gun, I felt powerful. I was now in control of my destiny as well as many other people's. I was no longer timid, crazy Madison. I was now someone to be reckoned with.

We parted ways. I wandered in the night air with my gun snug in my waist. I had some unfinished business to attend to.

SEVENTY·FIVE

NIKKI LING

In Central Booking I was placed on a hard bench with several other offenders. The piss-smelling cell was a nightmare. I positioned myself far in the corner and tried to get some sleep when the soap opera began.

"Whatchu in here fo shorty?" a petite girl asked. She had light skin, blue contact lenses and a full blond hair weave. I could see she was the lonely type.

"I'm not in the mood for small talk," I said dismissing her.

"Bitch, don't act tough!" she yelled.

Before she could show out further, I gave her a long hard stare, a stare that epitomized that I was someone to reckon with. She backed off quickly. She walked over to the commode and used the bathroom. I cringed.

When they brought around thick boloney sandwiches and warm milk, I passed. I couldn't wait to see the judge.

The long, arduous process was finally reaching its climax. I sat in the back of the holding pen of the courtroom. Initially, the state gives you an attorney if you don't have one present. If you have income, you're responsible for hiring your own attorney; but if you can't afford one then the initial attorney will represent you. At this point I couldn't afford one, but as soon as I got out and got my hands on my money, I would hire the best.

I waited patiently for my legal aide to show up. They

usually prep you an hour before you go in front of the judge. Mine was definitely late. Finally, I saw a well-dressed, white male approaching. He had blond hair cut low, a dark blue suit and a briefcase. There was a familiarity in his frame. The closer he got, I realized exactly who he was and my heart sank. It was Joshua Tune.

Joshua walked up, reading my file. For some reason, he was oblivious to my identity until he sat down and took a closer look at me. I was disheveled and withdrawn. He took one look at me, and his mouth dropped open.

"Jesus, Mary and Joseph!" he exclaimed. "What type of trouble have you gotten into?" He sat down next to me and began to whisper, "Listen, we go before the judge in a few minutes. I'm going to ask that you be released on your own recognizance. That means without a bail. Most likely the judge will set a bail. How are your finances?"

"What are you doing here? How...when...how are you able to practice law?" I stammered.

"My conviction was overturned, remember? I went before the board and petitioned to get my license back. I didn't want to go back to the D.A.'s office so I opened my own practice. And to no surprise, I can't get one client to represent. Since I'm on the 18-B panel, they assign lawyers cases. It pays the bills. You're my first client."

"No disrespect, but I don't want you either. Your face is tainted with guilt. I can't associate myself with you. Dude, they'll surely think I'm guilty . . . As soon as I get out of here, I'm going to hire a top defense attorney."

Joshua looked sad at what I'd said. He put his head down and looked defeated. "Well until you get new counsel, I'm your lawyer. I'll do my best to get you out of here. How much bail can you make?"

"My sister will most likely post my bail. She should have something stashed. I have some money tucked away that I can't get my hands on right now."

"Try Gary Scheck," he stated.

"What?"

"Gary Scheck. He's the best defense attorney your money can buy . . . besides me," he said and smiled. He was a good dude.

SEVENTY·SIX

KAPRI HENDERSON

Eddie didn't come back with my jeep until the next mornin'. A bitch pressure was up! He came in smellin' like Henny. He'd been drinkin' and drivin' in MY shit. I was furious.

"Eddie, where the fuck you been? I been callin' your punk ass all night!" I yelled. Eddie just pushed past me and collapsed on my bed and instantly fell asleep. I will deal wit him later, I thought. I had important shit to take care of.

When I jumped in my jeep, it was filthy. He had Burger King food wrappers, empty soda cans, and ashes from smokin' weed. And to top it off that nigga got a $55 ticket on my new shit! Who the fuck he think gonna pay for it?

I grabbed the ticket and opened my glove compartment and a pair of black G-string panties fell out. I gasped. Shit like this is enough to make a bitch commit a double-homicide. I sat and started breathin'. I needed to focus on Knowledge Born.

As I crossed the Brooklyn Bridge, I wondered what I would do or say to Knowledge. It had been so long. Would he still be down? Would he try to play me wit his newfound smartness? I didn't have long to wonder 'cause before I knew it I was parked in front of One Park Plaza. His office was located on the twenty-first floor.

I hopped out my ride and was about to enter the buildin' when a police officer came walkin' quickly towards me, wavin' his arms. I looked around 'cause I thought he couldn't be tryin' to get my attention. But he was.

"Ma'am, you can't leave your vehicle there. It'll be towed," the handsome black police officer said.

"Word?" I said. I was flirtin' wit my eyes.

"Yes," he said and smiled.

"So what am I supposed to do, yo," I said and licked my lips.

"Well, there's a parking lot directly across the street. You can park in there."

"True," I said and glanced across the street.

"So who are you going to see in One Park Plaza?"

I looked at his name tag and it read "Santiago."

"Why is your name, Santiago. Ain't that a Puerto Rican name?"

"My mother is Dominican and my father is black. So what brings you to Midtown?" he asked again. Now *he* was flirting.

The thought of confrontin' Knowledge made me angry again.

"I'm heated, yo. This mutherfucker got my pressure up! I'm here to see my baby-daddy. You heard of him? Robert Maximilian. He some big shot lawyer," I said. I was shoutin' and usin' hand gestures to make the point that I was upset. Somehow my outburst changed the mood of the police officer. He was no longer flirtin'.

"Ma'am, you got 10 seconds to move your car before I give you a ticket," he said and walked away.

What happened? I thought as I jumped in the driver's seat and paid for parkin'. Parkin' in New York City was damn near rent money.

I entered the ritzy buildin' and felt a twang of jealousy in my gut. Immediately I felt self conscious. I looked at my clothin'. I had on a brand new J-Lo sweat suit and that was fly in my 'hood, but it couldn't compare to the expensive clothin' these professional people had on.

The women all wore three-piece skirt suits and carried Louis Vuitton briefcases. Their hair was pulled back in tight buns, and they all had French manicures. When I got off the elevator, I walked toward two large oak doors. The sign on them said Shapiro & Shapiro. This is where Knowledge was workin' while in New York. I buzzed the intercom and was immediately let in.

A pretty white girl had a headset on while speakin' on the telephone and entering data on the computer. She was multi-tasking. I had heard about that on the news.

"May I help you?" she asked. She had nice teeth.

"I'm here to see . . . Robert Maximilian," I stammered. I almost called him Knowledge.

"Do you have an appointment?"

"No."

"I'm sorry. He's in a meeting right now. Perhaps you can leave your name and telephone number, and he'll surely get back to you," she said. She sounded like a recordin' as she tried to dismiss me.

"I'm not leavin' here till I see Max! Now make yourself useful and tell him that Kapri is here," I yelled.

Startled she asked, "Your last name."

"I don't need one."

We stared at each other for a moment. Then she did as she was told. She had to say my name twice before he told her to show me in. I was directed toward the back. As I walked down the marble hallway, my stomach became squeamish. What would I say? Why was I here?

I stood in front of his door and took a deep breath. I decided to be the "angry bitch", so I banged on the door.

"Please come in," he said.

As I pushed the door open, my heart sank. There standin' before me was Knowledge Born. My nigga was still fine. I could still see the outline of his bow legs through his tailored business suit. His hair was cut low, no longer sportin' the high top fade. His mustache was trimmed nice and it was met by a goatee. He looked like a million bucks.

"Kapri, please have a seat."

I inched in further.

"Knowledge Born! So this is what you've been doin' since you got me locked up. Playin' a fuckin' smartass!" I said lookin' at the law degree displayed on the wall.

"I didn't get you locked up. You could have easily said no. It was your choice," he said. "And secondly I earned that degree. Your arrest was a wake-up call. I decided that drugs wasn't the answer. If I wanted to make money, I'd have to do it legitimately if I didn't want the same fate as you."

"You played me. You manipulated my mind, and I took the fall."

"I'm a changed man, Kapri."

"People don't change. How the fuck you make it through

law school? That degree probably fake!" I challenged. I was jealous that he was a hotshot lawyer.

"I assure you that it's the real McCoy. I was always an intelligent man. I just used my intellect for the streets."

"What intellect? You Knowledge Born from the 'hood. Who you foolin'?"

"You look beautiful, Kapri," he said, changing the subject.

"I got a man," I said, just in case he thought he could hit it.

"I'm not looking for a date. I'm seeing someone myself . . ."

His words stung. I wanted to forgive him for leavin' me. I wanted to walk off into the sunset. But I had to stand my ground. This piece of shit didn't give a fuck about me. All those years I was locked up, he didn't come to check on me once.

"I'm just here to let you know that I need some paper. If you don't hit me off, I'm goin' to the cops and tell them that you helped me conspire to sell drugs!"

"I know you're angry with me. You have every right to be. But I couldn't see you locked down like that. I can't explain it, but . . ." he truly looked hurt.

"You couldn't see me locked down. Nigga, I *was* locked down. I want $50,000 or else!"

"Don't threaten me, I don't like it," he said, and I finally saw a glimpse of Knowledge.

"Well, what about your son? You makin' all this money, and you ain't even paid child support! You can go to jail for not payin' child support!" I warned.

"What son? Please don't say you were pregnant when you got arrested. Do I have a child out here all these years?"

"Kareem!"

"What are you talking about. Kareem was already two years old when I met you! He's not my son," he said. Now he was furious.

"You're the only father he knows!" I challenged.

"Listen, Kapri, blackmail is against the law, so I'll pretend that we never had this conversation. Secondly, the statute of limitation has already run out on the drug conspiracy. But I'm glad you came," he said and walked over to me.

"Why?" I said.

"Because I've been wanting to see you for a long time. What I did was a horrible thing. I've put some money to the side for you. So you can get yourself together. Come by next Monday and I'll have $250,000 for you. Is that all right with you?"

I was dumbfounded. I'd never seen that amount of money at one time. "I want double that. You think that you can make me go away wit pennies?" I said. "I'm not going to continue this conversation. Be here 2:00 p.m. sharp next Monday. Good day, Kapri." I ran out of Knowledge's office mad happy! I was 'bout to be paid.

SEVENTY·SEVEN

NIKKI LING

I was led into the courtroom and looked out at the audience. I saw Kayla. She waved when she saw me. She was worried and looked petrified. I searched the courtroom for Noki but didn't see her.

"Where's Noki," I mouthed to Kayla. She shrugged her shoulders. My heart dropped from disappointment.

As I stood before the judge, I listened to the prosecution make me out to be a monster.

"Judge, this defendant is charged with murder in the first degree. She's accused of murdering her husband for his fortune. She shot, mutilated and tortured the deceased and tried to make it look like a robbery. Ballistics confirm her fingerprints on the murder weapon. The state is requesting that you deny bail. She's a flight risk. She has family in Japan and may flee there to escape prosecution," the assistant DA said. She was a tough-talking, Hispanic woman with a mane of jet-black hair. She was barely five feet tall but she had a presence.

"How does your client plead?" the judge asked Joshua.

"Judge, my client pleads not guilty. She's prepared to turnover her passport. She has strong ties in her community and is not a flight risk. Her only immediate family is here. She wants to stay and prove her innocence. I am requesting that she be released on her own recognizance. She cannot possibly make any bail. All her assets are frozen."

The judge looked me over for a moment. His eyes rested on my breasts momentarily. Then he announced, "Bail set at $300,000 cash or bond!" he said and hit his gavel on the desk.

I turned around and looked at Kayla. She couldn't afford that. "I'll get you out!" she yelled and was ordered to be quiet. Meanwhile, I was whisked back to jail.

I was on Rikers Island for 24 hours before I had my first visit. Kayla came with a look of despair. We embraced and sat down.

"Still no Noki?" I asked.

"Nikki, she won't return my phone calls or answer her door. I don't know why she's doing this," Kayla said.

"She thinks I killed Jack."

"Why would she think that? She knows you're not capable of doing such a thing."

"I'm a whore Kayla. Whores are capable of doing anything."

"Now you sound like Noki. Nikki, I'm sorry I can't do more for you. I asked Jay Kapone to bail you out, but he said he didn't want to be involved. I tried getting in touch with Brian, but he hasn't returned my calls either. I don't know where else to go."

"Don't worry Kayla. You've done everything possible. I have a solution," I said and looked around. "I'm going to give you my safety deposit box key. Go and get my bike. There's a compartment over the wheel that I had put in. The code is 188. The month and year my mother committed suicide. The compartment will open and there you'll find the extra key to my box. There's close to $800,000 in there."

"My God, Nikki, where did you get so much money?" she questioned.

"A lifetime of crime Kayla," I said and put my head down. Hot tears streamed down my cheeks.

"Don't cry, Nikki. We'll beat this thing. I got your back!"

"I know you do," I said through tears.

"Once I get the key, how will I be able to open your box? Aren't banks strict about such things?"

"I put you and Noki as additional signers on my account. For emergencies. Now, once you get the money, be very careful that no one is following you. Take $30,000 to a bail-bondsman and get me bonded out of jail–"

"But you have enough cash to bail yourself out."

Kayla was so adorable. She just didn't understand the politics of being a criminal. So I explained, "Kayla, if you waltz in and drop three-hundred grand on the table, the DA will want to investigate where the money came from. Neither one of us can account for that kind of cash. Besides, I need to keep as much money at my disposal as possible. I need to hire an attorney."

"What about the attorney you have?"

"You didn't recognize him?"

"From where?"

"He's the attorney who was busted making a drug buy in East New York."

"Lyric Devaney's friend?"

"Precisely . . ."

I watched Kayla eyes grow dark. She still couldn't get over Lyric.

I couldn't wait to get out of this place. I needed to talk to Noki and explain I had nothing to do with Jack's murder. I couldn't lose Jack *and* my sister. We concluded our visit, and Kayla promised to get me out before nightfall.

SEVENTY EIGHT

MADISON MICHAELS

As the morning sun rose, I realized I had made it to Midtown Manhattan. There was a Marriott Hotel directly in front of me. I walked in and rode the elevator up to the 9th floor. It was busy in the hotel. Housekeeping was cleaning rooms and business people were rushing out for early-morning meetings.

I looked at the floor. There were several open room doors, and I quietly slipped into one. I went and hid in the closet. I watched as the housekeeper came in, put mints on the pillow and rushed out. When she closed the door, I emerged. Once alone, I took a look around. There were several personal items in the room. I rummaged through some things in a drawer and noticed there was a wallet. I opened it and saw the name of a woman, Jacqueline Petterson. I couldn't tell from the name whether she was black or white. Then I went and opened a suitcase that was inside the closet. Her luggage set was Louis Vuitton. Classy. I unzipped the garment bag and there was an array of beautiful clothing. I squealed with delight.

She had a peach-colored Roberto Cavalli halter-top and long skirt. It was new. The price tag was a whooping $2,000. I looked at the tag and it was a size 6. Perfect. Considering that I had been steadily losing weight, this would fit just right. Then I searched further and pulled out a pair of shoes. They were peach as well. No doubt she'd purchased them to match the outfit. They were a size 8. That was a little too small for my size 9 feet, but luckily they were slip-ons.

After selecting my outfit, I went into the bathroom to shower. I finally took off the trenchcoat that I had been using to conceal my hospital garments. I cut off my name tag and tossed it in the garbage along with my pajamas. Then I gently laid my gun down on the desk next to the telephone book. Next, I stepped into a steaming hot shower. I let the water massage my neck and back while contemplating my next move.

I emerged feeling wonderful. Although I really didn't have a plan, I knew that I had to confront Lyric and make her tell Maurice the truth. Tell him that she's the lying whore I always told him she was.

After I came out of the shower, I felt exhausted. I realized I hadn't slept. I called room service and ordered salmon and rice with asparagus spears, fresh-squeezed orange juice mixed with Cristal champagne and strawberries.

"Shall I charge this to your room, Ms. Petterson?" room service asked.

"Please do," I stated.

A half hour later I received a knock on the door. It was room service. I walked to the door wearing only a terrycloth bathrobe. My naked body peaked out seductively.

"Hello, ma'am, where would you like this?" the waiter asked.

"Please put it by the bed," I said as I gave him a quick peek. He stared for a moment then lowered his eyes. As he rolled the cart into my room, I walked directly behind him.

"Will that be all, ma'am?"

"Negative! I haven't been fucked in years. I'll show you a good time if you can handle it," I said seductively.

The waiter was in shock. His mouth fell open and he just stared. Men. I decided I'd have to handle this and take the lead. I took my right hand and grabbed his dick. I caressed it as I stuck my tongue in his ears. Within seconds his dick was rock solid. Then I forcibly pushed him back on the bed. He still had the stupidest look on his face. I climbed on top of him and loosened his pants. When I ripped open his shirt, he finally objected.

"Hey, I still have to go back to work . . ." he whined.

"Shut the fuck up!" I demanded and grinded my hips into his groin. When I let my bathrobe fall off my shoulders and my size 34-D cups came tumbling out, he couldn't resist. His hands immediately went up and started to grope my breasts. I looked at his cinnamon skin, full pink lips and broad nose and wondered if he loved me. I could love him, a man that looked as good as he did.

He entered me feverishly and I nearly lost my breath. His large dick filled every inch of my vagina, and it still pushed looking for more. I had my legs wrapped tightly around his waist as his ass pumped in and out. As we moved in unison I asked, "Do you love me?"

"Oh, yes, baby . . . I love you."

"Is it good?"

"Damn…it's so-o-o-o-o good. Your pussy is so tight," he sang.

"You feel good too," I said.

As he was about to climax he asked, "What's . . . what's . . . your name?"

"Lyric," I said as we both exploded. Hot juices filled up inside me, and I screamed as I climaxed.

We lay there for a few moments breathing hard. Once I caught my breath I stated, "Now get the fuck out!"

Once I got rid of the waiter, I took a quick nap. Then I happily got dressed, packed a small bag of Jacqueline's clothing, took her wallet, and left.

I went downstairs and the doorman hailed me a cab. He walked me over, opened the door and waited for a tip. I looked him up and down like he was dirt underneath my shoe and he quickly got the message.

"Where to, ma'am."

"Don't fucking 'ma'am' me. My name is Lyric Maria Devaney and people better start recognizing!"

"Recognize what?" the cab driver stated in a patronizing tone.

"I'm a renowned actress. Forget it. Just take me to 55 Park Avenue and 56th Street."

"That large building on the corner? The ritzy apartment building?" he asked.

"Precisely. I need to make a quick stop. I'll need you to wait for me. I have to go into Brooklyn," I lied because I didn't have any money to pay the fare. Frankly, there were no other stops. This is where Maurice and Lyric were shacking up. I knew that piece of information from the newscast. The night they broadcast the event about the wedding, they were standing in front of the building where they lived. As a celebrity, you have absolutely no privacy. This was unfortunate ... for them!

SEVENTY·NINE

KAPRI HENDERSON

When I got home, my mood soured. Eddie was still asleep, and I wanted to see what was up wit those panties in my shit. Then I decided to do a little snoopin'. Eddie must have gotten up while I was gone 'cause he had stripped naked. All his clothin' was thrown on my bedroom floor. Sneakily I dug in his jeans pocket and pulled out his wallet and cell phone. Then I went inside the bathroom to do my investigation.

I closed the door and locked it. My heart was beatin' fast. First I looked through his wallet. I didn't see much but a bunch of receipts for sneakers 'n shit. Then I stumbled on a photo. It was an Asian girl. A fat bitch! She was cheesin' for the camera. Could this be his baby-momma? Eddie never said she was Asian. Thinkin' like a smart-ass, I went to Eddie's phonebook in his cell phone. I scrolled down until I stopped at a name that seemed Asian. Noki. Immediately I called and the answerin' machine picked up.

So I said, "My name's Kapri. I'm lookin' for the bitch dat's fuckin' my man." Immediately someone picked up.

"Who's your man?" she said. She had an Asian accent. I knew she was the girl in the photo.

"Eddie, bitch!" I screamed. I was heated. I hated her, and I didn't know why.

"Yes, I'm fucking Eddie. That's my man and he loves me. Who's this? His daughter's mother?" she asked. Then I knew what was up. She was a new ho Eddie was fuckin'.

"No, bitch. My name's Kapri!"

"You sound like an angry black girl. Don't call my phone no more. I have no time," she said and hung the telephone up in my ear.

I called back non-stop but she never picked it up. I chilled for ten minutes then called again. She picked up on the first ring.

"Eddie's in my bed. We just fucked," I said, tryin' to make her angry.

"Silly girl, I doubt Eddie is capable of fucking anyone anytime soon. Not after last night . . . we fucked from my apartment to his jeep."

As soon as I heard the word "jeep" I lost it.

"Bitch i'ma kill you!"

"I have a better idea, kill yourself. You sound miserable," she said.

"When I catch you, i'ma put my foot up your ass!"

"Get a life." Click.

She hung up. I was furious. I ran right in the room and threw his cell phone and wallet at his head.

"Eddie! Wake the fuck up. Who the fuck is Noki?" I screamed. Eddie was still groggy as he struggled to wake up.

"You heard me, mutherfucker! Who you been fuckin' in my jeep?"

"Come on now," he said.

"I just spoke to Noki, Eddie. She told me everythin'!"

Once he heard me say "Noki," he immediately jumped up and studied the situation. He got angry.

"Why the fuck you goin' through my shit?"

"She said you her man."

"Why are you goin' through my personal shit? Whatever she said is good for you. If your feelings are hurt, too bad. That's what happens when you go lookin' for shit."

"What about you fuckin' in *my* personal shit! How 'bout that," I yelled.

"Kapri, I'm so tired of your ghetto ass!" he yelled and I felt my pressure go up.

"Who you callin' ghetto? That's why your momma buy groceries from the 99 cent store!" I said and put my hands on my hips.

For a moment I thought I was back in Marcy projects on the bench rankin'. When Eddie laced up his Timberland boots and walked out the front door, I got a reality check. I watched him jump in a cab from my window. Then I raced downstairs and got the address off the ticket Eddie had gotten on my jeep . I jumped in my jeep and headed to the address. I was sure this was her address. When I got there, I saw a fly buildin'. That bitch must be rich. At first I was jealous, then I realized that in three days, I too would be rich. Then Eddie would be all on my shit.

I wanted to leave, but my street instinct told me to stay. I wanted to confront Eddie wit this bitch. I wanted him to choose right there who he wanted to be wit. I wasn't gonna sit back and let him run from her to me whenever he felt like it. Wakin' me up at all times of the night and makin' me fix breakfast. I only do that for my man.

I walked over to her buildin' but I didn't feel good about it. I walked in and looked on the mailboxes. I saw Noki Ling, Apt. 3. Hesitantly, I walked up two flights. When I approached her door, I could hear talkin' and laughter. I banged, "Boom, boom." I could hear footsteps approachin,' then someone looked through the peephole. Seconds later, the door flung open. There stood a Japanese girl. She had her hands on her fat hips. Her face was pretty, but everythin' else was jacked up.

"What you want?" she inquired. Then Eddie approached and stood behind her. As soon as he saw my face, his eyes grew angry and hooded over. I pushed my way into her crib, lookin' around to see how she was livin'. Takin' in the scenery.

"I'm Kapri . . . Eddie's girl. No more games, Eddie. Who's it gonna be? Me or fatso?" I said and put my hands on *my* hips.

"You so stupid, girl. Coming here trying to go up against me. You're a little funky mess . . . and you look like a man," she said, and walked away in her stiletto heels. "Eddie get rid of that trash. Dump her outside on the sidewalk."

I was speechless.

"Come on, Kapri, you gotta break out," Eddie said and tried to grab my arm. I looked him sternly in his face. How easy it was for him to disrespect me! The second man in my life who wasn't there for me when I needed him. I pushed past Eddie and grabbed Noki by her soft hair and flipped her heavy ass over my back. She came crashin' to the floor wit a loud thud. Then I began whippin' her Asian ass black-girl style. She screamed for her life as Eddie grabbed a hold of me. He flung me across the room, and I hit the wall. I came out swingin'. Eddie and I went head-up. He fought me like I was a nigga. He started boxin', swingin' uppercuts, left and right jabs–the whole nine yards. But I handled him.

I fought hard, but I was no match for Eddie. The last punch to my left jaw was so powerful my tooth loosened. My jaw snapped shut and cut the inside of my mouth. I spit out blood. Dizzy, I fell to my knees and was dragged out by my hair. Eddie opened the door and tossed me out. Just like Noki told him to do. Before he slammed the door, I threatened, "I'ma see you."

"Fuck you, bitch!" he said and slammed the door in my face. I'll never forget how they both laughed hysterically.

EIGHTY

NIKKI LING

Three days later, I was still at Rikers Island. Every night, I called Kayla's apartment but she never picked up. In desperation I tried calling Noki, but she always let her answering machine pick up. She was screening her calls. It took a few days for me to believe that Kayla had taken my money and run. I guess the old adage that you never really know a person was really true. In a million years I never would have guessed that Kayla could betray me this way. I loved her. I thought she loved me too. I thought realistically. Kayla probably wouldn't ever see that much money in her whole lifetime. I had given it to her on a silver platter.

On my fourth day of incarceration, Joshua Tune came. He looked a little annoyed that he was still assigned to my case. My pompous attitude that I had originally displayed was gone. I swallowed my pride and was eager to talk to him.

"Why are you still here?" he asked.

"I couldn't make bail."

"Obviously. I did a little research on your background. You're penniless. Your husband was your care giver. And since you're charged with his murder, you can't use his money to fund your defense. Thus, I still have your case. But what about your sister and your stash?"

"I thought I explained that my sister hates me . . . and my stash ran off with my best friend."

"Jesus! I thought I had it bad with relationships. Truthfully, I was a little hesitant about taking your case. But now, since I have no choice, I need to know everything. Explain to me exactly what happened to your husband."

"I don't know. Someone killed him and framed me . . ." I said and put my head down. He stared at me for a moment then said, "Listen, if you want me to get you out of this mess, you're going to have to start being truthful with me. I'm your attorney. Our discussions are privileged information. It can't be used against you. I'm an officer of the law . . . who's been in a tight situation just like yours. I'm not a prick, Nikki. I want to help."

He sounded so confident that he could actually get me out of this situation. I needed to believe him. I wanted to believe him. I sighed and began my story.

"Everything was going great in my life until one day–about a month ago–I was in a steam room when this mysterious stranger appeared. She came and sat close to me and just stared for a moment. Then she said that she knew all about my past–"

"Prostituting and jostling?" he interjected.

"Yes," I said and felt an overwhelming feeling of embarrassment. "She said that Jack planned on divorcing me and leaving me penniless."

"How did she know that?"

"I asked that same question. She said he'd done the same thing to her, nearly ruining her life."

"So what does that have to do with you?"

"Precisely. Now get this," I said and exhaled, "She suggested that we swop murders just like the old Alfred Hitchcock film "Strangers on a Train." She wanted to criss cross . . ."

"What!" he asked incredulously.

"She said no one would connect her to my murder and vice versa."

"So you agreed?" he said, and I heard the disappointment in his voice.

"Not exactly."

"Well, your husband is dead," he retorted.

"Dude are you judging me before I've told you the whole story?"

"Maybe . . . this doesn't look good, Nikki."

"I didn't want to do it. I told her no! But then . . ."

"What?"

"Then my sister got kidnapped. I went to Jack for the $1 million ransom money but he refused. Desperate I went back to the day spa and waited for her. The stranger. When she came, I agreed to the criss cross. The biggest mistake in my life!" I said and burst out into tears. He took a moment to respond then said, "You've been played."

"Huh?" I managed to say through sobbing.

"I don't know all the particulars yet, but I'll bet that your sister is behind this. Your chance meeting with that stranger wasn't chance at all. It was pre-planned. You were set-up to take this fall. I just don't know why yet."

"Joshua, everyone is always dogging my sister because they don't know her–"

"Are you sure *you* know her?"

"I know she loves me and would never want to see me in this predicament."

"Well, let me do some investigating before I make my conclusion. One question."

"Yes?"

"Was the ransom paid?"

"Yes . . . the night at the movie theatre."

"I see. One more question—"

"Yes?"

"Do you still want me to represent you? Or are you looking for someone better?"

I looked him directly in the eyes and said, "I want you."

EIGHTY-ONE

KAPRI HENDERSON

I drove home like a maniac. It wasn't over. I jumped out the car barely, puttin' it in park. I ran upstairs and called Portia.

"Yo, I got beef," I said.

"What's going on?" she asked. Hearin' the panic in her voice broke me down. I just started sobbin'. I was cryin' uncontrollably into the phone. I had been through a lot in a matter of hours. Knowledge. Eddie. Noki.

"This kid just beat the shit outta me. He stomped me out for this bitch!" I screamed into the phone.

"Well call the cops and get him arrested. He shouldn't be putting his hands on you!" she yelled.

"I gotta handle this myself. I ain't callin' 5-0. I need you to be down wit me. I need you to have my back. I know we can whip his ass if we jump him."

"Kapri, I'm too old to be out here fighting and so are you. You're my cousin and I love you. I don't want to see you get into any more trouble, especially over another man," she scolded.

"I can't let this go, yo," I cried. "I gotta get his punk-ass fucked up!"

"Then what?"

"Then I'll feel better!" I screamed. Portia was actin' like she didn't understand. She done beat plenty a bitch or nigga ass in her day. But I decided to respect her for changin'. Portia continued to speak truth to me, but I wouldn't listen to reason.

"Put Aunt Pearl on the phone," I said. "Why do you want to speak to my mother?" "Because I just want to. I'm tired of talkin' to you. I need to speak to someone who understands."

Portia put the phone down and went and got my aunt.

Aunt Pearl picked up the phone and said, "Chile, when you come home?"

"Aunt Pearl, I been home for a while now. Listen, I need your help but you got to promise not to tell Portia," I said and hipped her to secrecy.

She immediately lowered her voice and said, "What's troublin' you?"

"I got a situation with my ex-man and his bitch! I just got beat down."

"He put his hands on you?"

"Yeah. And I don't wanna do nothin' drastic and end up gettin' locked up. Can you help me?" I pleaded.

"Now what type of help are you lookin' for?"

"The kind that gets results but doesn't leave any evidence."

"Come over this time tomorrow. I'll have somethin' for you."

EIGHTY·TWO

MADISON MICHAELS

I got out of the cab and waltzed into the building. As I entered, I noticed that there was a chiropractor renting space in the plush high-rise. As I breezed past the receptionist, I announced, "I'm going to see Dr. Steinman."

"Ma'am you need to sign in," she stated.

"My name's Lyric!" I snapped. "What's with the ma'am shit?"

I made my way inside the doctor's office and decided that I needed to compete for the Oscar.

"May I help you?" the male receptionist asked.

"I have an appointment today to see Dr. Steinman."

"Your name?"

"Lyric . . . um . . . Madison Michaels."

He looked at me peculiarly then shrugged it off. He glanced down at his appointment book and said, "Are you sure you have an appointment for today?"

"I'm supposed to. My girlfriend made it for me."

"I don't see you here . . . or for this whole month."

"Goddamn it!" I said. "I really needed this appointment. I have been having major back pain after my Pilates class, and she assured me that your doctor was the best."

"We can't take you without an appointment. Would you like to make one now? What type of insurance do you have?"

"I'm paying cash."

I saw how his interest piqued.

"Well, I could see if the doctor could fit you in. Do you want to hold on a moment?" he eagerly asked.

Before responding, I sighed deeply then said, "I asked Lacey to do me one favor and she couldn't even pull that off."

"Lacey?"

"Yes. She's the one I asked to make the appointment."

"Mrs. Carter is in here all the time. Why didn't you tell me that? Wait I'll call her so you can speak to her. I don't know if she's home though."

As he reached for the telephone, I noticed the four numbers he punched in, 4-4-6-7. I nervously waited as he called and much to my satisfaction no one answered.

"Just as I thought. No one is there. But I'm sure you can see the doctor. Have a seat."

"I'll be right back. I just forgot that I have a taxi waiting for me. It'll only take a second," I said and scurried out. I slipped into the elevator and saw that the last numbered floor was 43; then there was the penthouse. I assumed 4467 was on the 44th floor, which was the penthouse.

EIGHTY·THREE

KAPRI HENDERSON

That night I couldn't sleep. Every inch of my body was achin'. I couldn't open my mouth wide. My eyes were slightly bruised. My back was in pain. I was fucked up. The only relief I had was knowin' that I would be gettin' my revenge soon.

I woke up in the early afternoon to a loud television in my living room. I jumped up and Kareem was in there entertainin' a girl. They were watching a DVD. He had Pepsi and pizza on my coffee table. The mere site of him sent me into a fury.

"Boy, what the fuck you doin' up in here? Why aren't you workin'?" I screamed on him.

"Kapri, I wanted to take a break and watch a movie with my friend. Her name is Lisa," he said. He looked real nervous.

"I don't give a fuck what her name is. All I care about is you gettin' my mutherfuckin' paper!"

"What happened to your face?" he asked and I lost it. I picked up the Pepsi bottle and bust him upside his head. The top flew off and soda squirted all over him and his chick. Then I turned the soda bottle upside down over his head and let the soda drench him. When the bottle was empty, I threw it at him.

"Any more stupid questions?" I asked.

Kareem bawled up his fist as if he was gonna hit me. I stared him down.

"Boy, you lift up that fist and you won't be able to put it back down!" I warned.

"I'm tired of you! I hate you! I hope you go back to jail," he screamed. He was just showin' off for his chick. He ain't never raised his voice to me before. I was almost proud of him. I'd been tryin' to turn his pussy ass into a man since I got home.

"Shut the fuck up, pussy. The both of you can git the fuck out!"

I rolled into Pink Houses wit my music pumpin'. I parked then sat in my jeep. I was flossin' my jeep for the crowd. Once I was certain everyone saw me, I walked over to the small crowd that was sittin' on the bench. It was Big Monica, Lil' Monica, Troy, City, Cross, Bee-For-Real, Shine, Nita, Alisha, Sherry, Kisha, and Molisha. That crew stayed fly so I hadda represent.

"Whaddup," I greeted.

"Whaddup," the crowd said.

"That's ya jeep?" Troy asked.

"Yea, that's my shit."

"You see my jeep? It's the Range Rover parked in back of yours."

"Oh dip, that's what's up. You stay fly, Troy," I said and gave him a pound. I could see City eyein' me. We had a fight years ago before I went upstate over this kid named E-Zo. Back then neither one of us won the fight. We tied. I stared her down sternly. I knew I could whip her ass now but I had shit to do. I ran upstairs, and knocked on my aunt's door.

"Come in chile. Auntie will make it better," she said, and I followed her to her room.

EIGHTY·FOUR

NIKKI LING

Joshua came to visit me twice a week, each time with new developments about my case. He said we'd be going before the judge in two weeks for a bail hearing. Hopefully the judge would lower my bail, but it was unlikely he'd let me go on my own recognizance.

On this particular date he had some astonishing news. He had a friend in the telephone company and had her pull Noki's telephone records. Since Noki's apartment, telephone and everything else she owned was in my name, he was able to get a subpoena. He noticed a pattern. Noki had consistently called a particular telephone number, especially before, during and after the alleged kidnapping.

"I have a friend in the police department. She ran a check on the individual and got a hit," he said. I could tell he was excited.

"You sure do have a lot of friends willing to do you favors . . . and all women," I said and felt a slight twinge of jealousy.

He smiled a boyish grin and continued, "The person your sister is in constant contact with is Ivanka Zamora. Do you know her?" "Her name doesn't ring a bell."

"I didn't think so."

"But I don't know all of Noki's friends. She's secretive," I said, coming to her defense.

"Do you know her?" he said and pulled out a photo. I gasped.

"That's her! The stranger who proposed the criss cross."

"Precisely. Ivanka Zamora. She was supposed to be the heir to a billion-dollar estate when, at eighteen years old, her mother wrote her out of her Last Will and Testament, leaving the sole inheritance to her father. Her father has since treated her like a pauper, giving her a meager allowance, paying for her apartment and allowing her to run her mother's company— whose stock options have been declining steadily since she took over."

"But why would she or Noki want Jack dead?" I said. I was still perplexed at this elaborate scheme to kill Jack and frame me.

"Are you ready for this?"

"I don't think so . . . but, please go ahead."

"Money. The root of all evil. If Jack is dead, and you are incarcerated for his murder, Noki stands to inherit $400,000,000 dollars! All the money in Jack's estate rolls over to Noki Ling."

I nearly fainted. That spoiled, ungrateful bitch! All the years of giving her a plush lifestyle. Putting her needs before my own. And Jack . . . legally adopting her to give her dignity. This is how she repays us! I literally stood up and screamed. I was so damn mad.

"Why would she get his money? I was his wife. Wouldn't his money go to charity?"

"When Jack legally adopted Noki, he made her an heir to his fortune. He was a pretty decent guy. His Will stated that if he died before you, you'd inherit 80 percent of his fortune. The other 20 percent would go to Noki. He didn't have any family. But the law states that anyone convicted of murder cannot inherit the victim's fortune; thus, 100 percent of his fortune would go to Noki."

"Over my dead body!" I exclaimed.

"Well, hopefully, it won't get that far. I still have to build a case. The fact still remains you did agree to the criss cross."

Hot tears streamed down my high cheekbones. I never had a clue. "When Jack came with the ransom money, I wanted to call it off. I never had a chance . . ."

"They wouldn't have let you anyway. I honestly don't think they expected Jack to come through with the money. They probably wanted you two to bicker over the money for days, establishing your motive. Your sister knew you'd do everything in your power to get that money. I'm sure you left a trail of evidence. When you came up with the money—Jack's date of death came sooner than later. They had to do it before you'd have a chance to call it off."

"So there never was to be any criss cross?"

"I can't answer that. It's not likely."

"But the stranger called and said I had to kill her husband."

"She's not married."

"Of course not . . .," I said and wondered how I could have been such a fool. I looked over to Joshua and he had a gleam in his eyes. I could tell he was excited about the progress he was making.

"Joshua, there's still something missing," I said. "How did Noki and Ivanka meet?"

"I interviewed Ivanka's doorman the other day. When

I showed him Noki's picture he said he hadn't seen her in a while but she began visiting Ivanka last year. He said that Ivanka would have wild sex parties and the neighbors complained. Her father immediately put a stop to it."

"Sex parties?"

"Well that's alleged. Do you think Noki would participate in such behavior?"

"With a G-string and whip cream," I sourly said.

"And I thought you were the wild one," he joked. I had to laugh even though the joke was on me.

EIGHTY·FIVE

KAPRI HENDERSON

Even though Portia didn't live wit her anymore, Aunt Pearl still kept her room the same way. I remembered playin' with Portia in her room when we were little. Portia would call me over when she had beef and we'd fight the whole project. No one could fuck wit us on the hand tip. I miss those days.

My Aunt Pearl wanted to do a readin' first. She had her tarot cards out, candles lit and was ready. When we were younger neither Portia nor I believed in that voodoo mess. I'm not sure I believe in it now, but I wanted to be open minded. Eddie still hadn't called to apologize. For some reason, I thought he would swing by my apartment all apologetic. But he didn't. I woke up this mornin' wit an awful feelin' in the pit of my stomach. I can't explain it. I felt the same way when Knowledge never came to visit. I felt alone.

"Now what happened chile? Who hurt you?" she said.

"Aunt Pearl, I was datin' this guy named Eddie. I thought we were serious 'til I found out he was seein' this Asian bitch. I went to her house to confront them, and he nearly killed me! Look at my face . . ." I said and started to cry.

"He put his hands on you?"

"I already told you he did," I said, annoyed that she'd forgotten.

"What about the girl? She touch you?"

"No, auntie. But she laughed at me. They both laughed at me. I hate him, Aunt Pearl. You seen what happened to me wit Knowledge. How he left me. This nigga thinks he can do the same thing!"

"Don't worry, I got somethin' for both their asses," she said and handed me a deck of tarot cards. "Shuffle them, cut the deck and give them back to me."

I did as I was told.

"Do you love this guy?" she asked.

"I hate him. I want him to rot in hell!" I said and meant every word.

As my Aunt Pearl flipped seven cards, I waited patiently for her to tell me what she saw. As she read her seven card spread, her eyes grew dark. I immediately sensed tension.

"What do you see?" I asked.

"This here is the 8 of swords," she said pointin' to a card. "It means negative bondage. What you out in these streets doin' Kapri?"

"Nothin'. Just chillin'."

"You better not be out there sellin' that stuff. If you are, you better stop and quickly," she stated.

"I'm not, I swear," I said, which wasn't truly a lie. I had Kareem out in the street sellin' for me. I'll let him stop sellin' when I get the money from Knowledge, not one day before. "What does that mean? Negative bondage."

"Hush up for a minute," she said and continued to stare at the deck. I glanced further and noticed a card that looked horrible.

"What's that?" I asked and pointed to a card.

"That's the death card."

"What?" I screamed. I didn't like how this was goin' down.

"It means a radical change, it doesn't necessarily mean death. Your life is about to change in a drastic way. Now don't panic, chile. Whatever I read here doesn't mean it *must* happen. It means it *can* happen. Nothin' is written in stone. I'll give you a prayer to say before you leave. For protection."

"I'm no punk, but what you're sayin' is scarin' me."

"Don't be no fool, chile. Take heed to what I've said and you'll be ok."

"What do you see about Eddie and Noki?" I asked.

That's where my concentration was. I couldn't think about me. I'm not even sure I believed any of this witchcraft mess. My aunt had made voodoo her religion when she was just ten years old. My mother used to say Aunt Pearl was clairvoyant. That means she can see and feel spirits. They talk to her and tell her things. I hope they tell her how the fuck I can git my revenge!

EIGHTY·SIX

NIKKI LING

I woke up around three o'clock in the morning. I would have a visit from Joshua later today. He wasn't making much progress in my case. Yesterday we went before the judge and asked for a reduction in my bail. It was denied. I wasn't disappointed. I was getting used to being let down. I realized that I had to sit tight and fight my case. I was a fighter . . . I've always been.

The other day I got a new cell mate. Her name was Lisa. She pretended to be this down-ass-chick, someone I could confide in, someone that had my back. She kept asking me questions about my case, then divulging details about her case. I never said anything except how I was innocent. Sometimes the police will plant a snitch inside your cell. The snitch will get you to admit details about your crime that the police don't know and then testify against you. I was too hip for such tactics.

Lately I had started to look deeper into Joshua's blue eyes. I felt a strong attraction to him; it felt genuine. The last time I felt like this about a man was with Brian, the love of my life who'd abandoned me when I needed him most.

This morning I painted my nails a pale beige and washed my hair. I let it air dry and it curled up nicely. I ironed my shirt and correctional khaki pants and waited impatiently. When he arrived, he smelled wonderful.

"Hi," I said and smiled broadly.

"Well, you're in an exceptionally good mood today," he said and smiled his boyish grin.

"I really want to thank you for all the work you're doing on my behalf. I wish I could pay you for your services."

"I'm getting paid by the State to represent you. Otherwise I wouldn't be here," he stated.

His words seemed a little harsh. My smile faded, and I realized this wasn't about me. He was just doing a job.

"Well maybe I would be here," he continued and I perked up. "This is a high-profile case. Since I've been representing you, my practice has picked up. I think I'm going to be able to hire a paralegal and secretary soon," he said and I noticeably sulked.

"Good for you," I said sourly. Sensing my mood had changed he said, "So let's get back to the important things at hand."

We turned our attention back to my case. That night in my cell I realized that I was always reaching for the stars. Why would an intelligent attorney want to be serious with someone who was on trial for murdering her husband, not to mention a convicted prostitute?

EIGHTY·SEVEN

MADISON MICHAELS

I rode the elevator upstairs to the penthouse. Just as I thought, the number on the door was 4467. Now I only had to think of a way to get inside. Right next to the door was a staircase. I ducked into it and waited. To my amazement, I didn't have to wait long. Lyric and Maurice emerged from the elevator in a heated argument. I watched in disgust. Lyric wore an all-white outfit and stiletto heels. Maurice was wearing a track sweat suit and lots of platinum jewelry. He managed to do very well for himself as I rotted away in a psych ward. I grew angrier by the second.

"What do you mean 'it's no big deal'?" Maurice yelled.

"Just as I fucking said, my age shouldn't matter. I look 25."

"Well, it does matter. If it didn't, you wouldn't have ever lied."

"Look, women lie. Get over it. I'm your wife now."

"Not for long," he yelled. "I'm getting our marriage annulled!"

"What?" she asked and clutched invisible pearls.

"You heard me. You're in the shadow of forty. I'm a young, virile 27year-old man. I want to have kids. You're too old to have my kids. You could be somebody's grandmother!"

"Negative! You—"

The opening of the staircase door startled them. As it should. I had my revolver out and I was determined to use it. Lyric hovered behind Maurice for protection. I wanted to pull the trigger and let a bullet enter her chestnut-colored eye. But I didn't.

"What do you want," Maurice said, trying to sound tough.

"Shut up! Open the door, or I'll put three bullets in your pathetic gut," I warned.

Maurice stood still trying to decide how he could control the situation. I was close enough to shoot accurately but far enough away that he couldn't lunge for the gun. As he hesitated, Lyric said, "Do as she says."

"You better do as your whore says, Maurice."

"Who?" he asked.

"Look, quit fucking around. My patience is growing thin. You have your slut bride to thank for getting you in this mess," I stated.

"Me?" Lyric asked incredulously.

Maurice looked over at her with disdain. He started realizing he had made the worst mistake of his life hooking up with Lyric. Reluctantly he opened the door. By this time, I had come up behind him and had the gun nestled in his muscular back. Once we were all inside the apartment, I controlled the situation. I realized that Maurice could have overpowered me and taken the gun, but in the face of danger, people try to think rationally. Not everyone is a hero, especially in the face of danger.

"Maurice, didn't I tell you she was a whore?" I asked.

"Whose Maurice?" he asked, trying to confuse me.

"You ask that question one more time and I'll splatter your brains all over your marble floor. You got me?" I said. My voice was unwavering.

"Yeah, I got you," he said dryly.

"So Lyric—"

"Lyric?" she stated. I guess she didn't get the warning I'd just given to Maurice.

"Say another word and you're dead, bitch!" I said and inched towards her. She flinched and moved closer to Maurice.

"Lyric, you're still lying about your age? You dried up, old whore. It's over for you. At 41 you're nothing but a lying, scheming, manipulating bitch!" I yelled. The mere sight of her made me cringe.

"Forty one?" Maurice asked and looked at Lyric like he'd been bamboozled.

"Shut-up!" she snapped at him. She always hated to discuss her age. "Can't you see something isn't right with her? She thinks I'm my twin sister."

"What twin? Is your name even Lacey?" Maurice asked.

"Now's not the time."

As they bickered back and forth, I noticed a closet door half open. I saw something white and fury sticking out.

"Quiet!" I said. "Lyric, go over to the closet and bring me that white, furry object," I commanded.

"Huh?" she asked.

"If you can 'huh,' you can hear!" I yelled.

As I finished my sentence, she stopped and looked at me strangely. Then said, "Now I remember you. You were my sister's friend . . . Melissa . . . Mary . . . Madi . . . something like that. Yes, that's it. Why are you doing this?"

"Of course you remember me, bitch! You destroyed my life and took my man. Now I'm going to destroy your life and take my man back."

"This is over a man?" she asked in disbelief.

I pointed the gun directly at her forehead and said through clenched teeth, "Go to that motherfucking closet and bring me what the fuck I asked for!"

Lyric carefully walked over to the closet and pulled out what I thought I saw. Her white mink coat. It was the one she was going to wear to her premiere. "But I thought it had chinchilla on it," I thought, then realized that this was the original one. "But I thought Redbone and Sweepy had stolen it," I thought, then realized that they couldn't have because Lyric had it all along.

"Give it to me!" I commanded. I needed that coat. It was rightfully mine. I'd waited five years for this moment.

"Now Maurice . . . you, me, and this coat are going to walk out of here. I've exposed Lyric for who she truly is. I will tell the world about this horrible specimen of a woman."

"Can we talk about this for a moment?" Maurice asked, and I got angry again. He didn't want to leave with me. He wanted to stay here with the whore.

As I was about to respond, there was a loud bang on the door, "Police, open up!"

Lyric instantly lunged toward the door and tried to open it, so I had to stop her. I squeezed the trigger four times and each bullet landed in her back. She collapsed to the floor with a loud thud. Maurice then tried to wrestle me to the ground. We struggled for the gun and it accidently went off. The sound echoed in the spacious penthouse. At first I didn't know who was shot. Maurice or me. I looked in his eyes and they were popped open. He clutched his stomach and caved in. I was horrified.

"Look what you made me do!" I screamed. "You stupid ass! Get up!" I demanded but Maurice remained motionless.

As the police pounded on the door, breaking it down, I gently put down the gun. I put on my white mink coat just as the door flung open.

"Police, don't move!" someone yelled. Several police officers swarmed into the apartment. I was wrestled to the floor and handcuffed. They had guns pointed to my head. Maurice was lying on the floor and our eyes met.

"No-o-o-o-o," I screamed. "She killed Maurice. She did it! She's a whore," I cried.

One of the police put his finger to Lyric's neck, "She's dead."

They pulled me out the apartment before I could hear about the fate of Maurice.

As I walked out the building in my white mink coat, the hot summer heat hit my face. The press were all swarming around the building, and I spotted the cab driver I'd stiffed for his fare. Each news station was there with their cameras rolling. Cameras that captured me in my white mink coat. "Come to my premiere tonight," I stated as they put their microphones to my mouth. "Don't be late."

EIGHTY·EIGHT

JOSHUA TUNE

I had been so inundated lately with trying to free Nikki in the Jack Okayo murder case, I had been neglecting Madison. The last time I was at Creedmore, the nurses warned me that her condition was worsening, that she could be detrimental to herself or to the well-being of others.

As I watched the six o'clock news, Madison was being led out in handcuffs. As they named her victims, the blood drained from my face. The kid had finally lost it. I rushed to the police station as her lawyer and asked to see her. They had her handcuffed to a bench inside a holding cell. She had on a white mink coat and stylish clothing. The arresting officer stated that she refused to talk to anyone unless they called her "Lyric."

"Madi, it's me kid," I said and walked further in. She didn't say a word. "It seems you've gotten yourself into a lot of trouble."

I sat down next to her and tried to find a connection. Her eyes looked dilated and her mouth was dry. She stared past me, like she couldn't recognize me. I continued to try to communicate with her but to no avail. Then the police officer walked by and said, "Lyric, I loved you in your last movie." He then burst out into laughter.

Quickly, she responded, "Oh, thank you. I just adore my fans."

I was annoyed at the antics of the police. I refused to facilitate Madison's delusions by calling her Lyric, so I left. Next I went to identify Lacey's body. The coroner was an old friend of mine. His name was Mort. He pulled the cover back from Lacey's head, and I shook my head. As I began to walk away, I stopped dead in my tracks.

"Mort, I need to see one thing," I said. I walked over and lifted the cover up and to my amazement, Lacey had the exact replica of a tattoo Lyric had. A beautiful butterfly was tattooed in between her thighs. My stomach twisted up.

"What's wrong, Joshua?" Mort asked.

"Listen, I need a favor. I need you to perform DNA testing on Lacey. It's a strange request, I know. But I need to make sure she's not Lyric."

"Sorry, Joshua, it won't do no good. Identical twins have the same DNA."

"What?" I asked incredulously.

"It's true. Her DNA can't answer your question."

"Well, there must be something we can do to properly identify her."

"I'll check into getting dental records pulled. I'll keep you posted."

"Thanks, Mort. I need to go and tell her mother in person."

I left and headed over to Ms. Devaney's house to tell her the bad news. I wasn't sure she'd even consider it bad. It was no secret how she felt about Lacey. I thought briefly about discussing Madison's suspicion with her but ultimately decided against it. For now it would be a mystery whether Lyric was more recently murdered in 2002 or in 1997. Either way, she was gone . . .

EIGHTY·NINE

NIKKI LING

Correction Officer Black came and woke me at 5 o'clock in the morning.

"Get up Okayo, you've made bail," he said, standing in the doorway of my cell. "You heard me. Get up. I'm not going to tell you twice."

Quickly, I gathered my thoughts. "Who?" I asked.

"Dunno. Don't care."

I jumped in the shower and was ready to go. I wasn't taking anything with me. "Kayla," I thought. She must have finally come to bail me out.

Once outside, I didn't see Kayla. I waited around for a moment, then decided to leave. Kayla might be embarrassed and couldn't face me. As I walked down the steps, I slowed down my pace. Ivanka Zamora was waiting for me. She was the one who bailed me out! I was so damn mad, I ran up to her and slapped her face! Her head swung around and she was nearly knocked off balance.

"This is all your fault!" I screamed.

"If you ever raise your hand to me, I'll make sure you don't have it for long. Take that hint as a courtesy," she stated and her icy gray eyes became very small.

"You don't scare me," I countered.

"Really? Then why are you trembling?" she challenged.

"I'm not going to entertain you. You set me up."

"Before you set me up, I thought we had a deal. Then

you went to the police . . . very clever."

"I wanted to call it off."

"But you didn't! We had a deal and you haven't fulfilled your end yet."

"Sonuvabitch! I know all about the criss cross. Jack was going to be killed whether I agreed or not. You and Noki set me up to take the fall!" I said elatedly. I had her up against the ropes.

"Noki is just as much a pawn in my chess game. I played her and I played you. She has nothing to do with this," she retorted.

"Liar."

"Precisely. But not about this. Now you have a murder to commit. Tonight."

"What murder? There isn't supposed to be another murder to commit. You and Noki framed me for Jack's money. I've already done my part!"

"I guess you're really as dumb as Noki pegs you out to be. In order for this to work you have to kill somebody. I want you to kill my husband."

"First off, you're not married. Secondly, my attorney has discovered that you and Noki set me up. And third, let's just see how *dumb* I am when I outsmart you and Noki at your own game."

"Goddamn them for assigning you, Joshua Tune. That slick-maneuvering, coke-head is smarter than I thought."

"He doesn't do drugs!"

"Whatever. Now listen carefully. True, I'm not married. My ringless finger should have led you to that fact long ago. But I do need someone dead. My father. He has to go. Tonight!"

"Do you not remember that you don't have any leverage over me? You already turned over the gun with my fingerprints to the cops. I'm going down for your murder."

"I turned over the gun, yes. But I wiped it clean of your fingerprints first. A sign that I'm going to honor our original agreement."

"Do you ever stop lying? Ballistics already came back stating that the bullets match those taken out of Jack. And the police also lifted my prints from the murder weapon!"

"Did you hear that from your attorney or from the prosecution?"

"Does it matter?"

"If you want to be a free woman, it does. Have your attorney hire someone to run the test. The police and prosecution lied. Once they don't have your prints, and you can establish your alibi . . . you're free."

My head was spinning. I had no idea how much of what she said was true. So I challenged, "If the gun doesn't have my prints on it, you can't blackmail me anymore. I don't have to do anything you want, especially kill your father!"

"You will kill my father tonight as planned or I will kill your sister."

The cold, callous way she said that made my heart tremble. Then I realized that she was lying again. She and Noki were coconspirators.

"So be it . . ." I stated and walked away. She called after me but I kept on walking. Quickly.

NINETY

NIKKI LING

My first day of freedom, I headed straight over to Noki's apartment. It took me forever since I didn't have my ride or any money. Noki and I had some unfinished business to complete. When I got there, I pounded on her door, "Noki, open up!"

I was furious that not only did she want the guilt of Jack's murder on my conscience, but she wanted me to *kill* a perfect stranger.

I banged a few more times until Noki came to the door. She slowly opened the door and I pushed my way in.

"You little bitch," I said and smacked her. I was getting good at that. Noki's hand flew up to her face and she cried out.

"Me? This is all your fault!" she accused.

"How is murdering Jack to pay for your phony ransom so you could ultimately get your hands on Jack's fortune my fault!" I said, letting her know I knew everything.

"Nikki, you are so gullible."

"I used to be but not for you anymore!"

"Do you believe everything you're told? Don't you have one ounce of common sense in your hollow head?"

"Don't speak to me like that, Noki. I know everything!"

"Don't you know how easy it is for a person to distort reality? We've been played Nikki," she said. "Sit down," she commanded, and I did as I was told.

"I had a friend. Ivanka Zamora. We met a few years back in the East Village. She was smart, rich, and wild. I'd talk to her like you talk to Kayla. You know . . . about our past," she said and her voice trailed off. I knew what she meant.

"I thought she understood and really wanted to be my friend. She never judged me. She'd always ask questions about you, Jack, and my childhood. I guess I told her too much because she used it against me. Despite what you may think, I was really kidnapped. When I was released, I telephoned her. She turned me against you. Said it was all your fault. It was no secret between her and me about how much I resented you. She played upon that. And then Jack was murdered, and I thought it had something to do with your past. Some crazed john had probably wanted him dead. I distanced myself from you and your lifestyle. Then you were arrested for Jack's murder. And again I turned to her and she went psycho on me. She admitted that you two had conspired to murder each other's husbands. Now that you were arrested for Jack's murder, you couldn't fulfill your end of the deal. She said that I had to complete the criss cross. She said that I had to murder her husband or else she would murder me!"

My heart sank. What had I gotten Noki and myself into? *Was* Noki telling the truth? I knew that Ivanka was crazy but I was starting to realize that Noki may be a liar. I proceeded with caution.

"Noki, if there's anything I've learned these past few weeks is that I can't trust anyone. I may not even be able to trust you and that's hard for me to accept but I will. If what my attorney says is true, you are a coconspirator in this murder. You are after Jack's money. And I swear on my parent's grave I will not let that happen!"

"I may be a lot of things, Nikki, but I could never do such a thing! I loved Jack. I loved Jack more than I love . . ." she cried and her honesty stung my heart like a thorn. Not for what Noki said but for what she didn't say. It was then I realized that Noki could never harm Jack.

"Noki, I'm sorry that I got you into this," I said and tried to embrace Noki. She pulled away.

"I'm locked up in here day in and day out. I'm scared, Nikki . . . you have to do something."

"I don't know what to do," I sobbed.

"There's really no point in crying," she stated coldly. "You only have one option to get me and you out of this mess. You have to do what she says. You have to kill her husband. There's no other way."

"Noki, I can't kill someone!"

"Then why did you agree to it! Now she's going to kill me. I'm telling you, Nikki, she's crazy. She's on all types of medication. I'm afraid of her."

"We can go to the police."

"And say what? Admit to your part in the criss cross? You'll be convicted and all they will have on Ivanka is circumstantial evidence. Our word against hers."

"Then, let's run. Let's get out of here. Go to Europe."

"You're being selfish. Why should I give up my life for you? You're already in trouble. I will be too if I leave with you. You want me to just throw my life away?"

"I need to think," I finally said. I was exhausted. "I'll get some sleep and in the morning I'll think of something."

"You can't stay here!" she said.

"Why?"

"Nikki, I don't feel safe with you here. Look, I have a couple of dollars to give you. You should go to Kayla's apartment. Nobody knows about her. You'll be safe there," she said and went over to her chest and gave me $200. I didn't want to tell her about Kayla. I was too ashamed.

"That's all I got," she said and shoved the money in my hand. "You have to go now."

NINETY·ONE

NOKI LING

When I heard the closet door open, I turned around. "Do you think she suspects anything?"

"She so stupid, that black girl. She doesn't know anything," I stated.

"Well, she had better live up to her end of the deal!" Ivanka warned.

"There wasn't supposed to really be a deal, Ivanka. When we planned this, Nikki killing your father was never part of the deal. She was just supposed to be framed for Jack's murder until I got my hands on his money. Then we'd split my inheritance and forward the police the knife and gun with Eddie's fingerprints on it. He was supposed to take the fall—not Nikki."

"Things changed. I want my father dead. Your inheritance is only worth $400 million. My father is worth over $1 billion. And I'm not letting his black, housing project whore get one penny of it. So your sister better do the criss cross or else she won't live to see another day!"

"There is no criss cross!" I shouted. "A deal is a deal. We have to stick to the plan or things will get complicated. Nikki is not capable of killing anyone. You would have better luck asking me to do it."

"Don't flatter yourself, bitch! You're nothing but a weak, whiney, leech. You better convince your sister to kill my father or else . . ."

"Or else what?"

"You don't want to know!" she said and pushed me up against the wall. With her right hand gripped tightly around my throat she squeezed until I couldn't breathe. As I was gasping for air she pulled out a sharpened icepick and stuck it in my nostril. I was thinking she would puncture an artery as she applied pressure. As I twitched and kicked my legs for mercy she had a peculiar look on her face. She was enjoying watching me squirm. As my eyes pleaded for my life, I realized I was in over my head. What had I gotten myself in to? Suddenly she released me and I collapsed to the floor.

"If you don't want to make the front page of every newspaper, you better get your sister to follow through with the criss cross!" she said through clenched teeth and left.

I sat on the floor visibly trembling. The situation had gotten out of hand. That crazy girl was going to ruin everything and get us busted by the police! I didn't know who was more unstable: Nikki or Ivanka. I didn't like this one bit.

NINETY·TWO

KAPRI HENDERSON

Aunt Pearl took me back into the kitchen where she kept all her candles and oils.

"For Eddie, I'm gonna give you this black candle and damnation oil. I want you to light this candle at the stroke of midnight after you put two drops of the damnation oil on top of the candle. While the candle is burnin', I want you to say Psalm 109. Do this every night."

"What will happen?" I asked.

"He will pay with his life for hurtin' you," she said. The way she looked at me sent chills down my spine.

"What about the girl?"

"Well, since she didn't put her hands on you, I'm gonna give you the madness spell. Here take dis candle," she said and handed me a black candle wit a skull. "Light this too at midnight. The house has to be in complete darkness so that the evil night spirits will come. Say this chant I wrote out for you: 'Mother of darkness, father of death, for every ounce of my sadness make Noki lose her mind and drown in complete madness.'"

It all seemed silly.

"Aunt Pearl, you sure this gonna work? If not, I'll look into gettin' him fucked up. Maybe find some guys to do the job for me."

"I thought you said you wanted results that don't leave no evidence."

"I do."

"So how does bringin' in outsiders help ya situation?"

"Okay, I hear you."

"Don't doubt your aunt's abilities."

My aunt had believed in this for so long that once I left her apartment, I started to believe as well.

That night I did as I was told. I turned off all the lights and lit the candle with the skull first. Just as I was about to begin, someone banged on my door.

"Who?" I yelled, hoping it was Eddie.

"Ka-pri, it's mi. Veronica."

What she want?

"Whaddup?" I asked as I opened the door.

"Mi just drop in pon you," she said pushin' past me. I was vexed. I didn't want her to see my shit but she did. She took a good look at my candles and oil and knew what was up.

"Ka-pri, no-o-o. Don't mess wit Obeah. It wicked mon."

"I got problems, yo."

"A wa do yu?"

"That bitch ass Eddie left me for this Asia ho named Noki. Look what da fuck he did to my face."

"Noki?" she said.

"Yea, Noki. You know her?" I said as I shoved the photo of Noki in her hand.

"No, mon."

"She's a fat, stink, ugly, nasty lookin' chick. I woulda handled this another way but I don't wanna catch another case," I said then remembered that Veronica was Jamaican. "Don't you know how to do this shit? Help me out."

"Mi naa waan fi do it. Not Obeah. Mi see wah it wen do to mi mudda."

"So it does work. Good. My aunt gave me somethin' to make his bitch lose her mind. And for his punk ass, he gonna die!" I said and felt a chill go down my spine.

"No Ka-pri. Dis bad. Just box 'im face. Git a bokkle and box 'im face," she pleaded.

"Look, I got shit to do. Now either you down or you wastin' my time."

"Ease up. Mi gon," she said and left.

Then I said my chant, *"Mother of darkness, father of death, for every ounce of my sadness make Noki lose her mind and drown in complete madness."*

Next I lit the black candle for Eddie, poured two drops of damnation oil and read from the Bible Psalm 109: *"O God, whom I praise, do not remain silent, for wicked and deceitful men have opened their mouth against me; they have spoken against me with lying tongues, with words of hatred they surround me; they attack me without cause . . . they repay me evil for good, and hatred for my friendship. May his children be fatherless . . . May his children be wandering beggars; may they be driven from their ruined homes. May a creditor seize all he has; may strangers plunder the fruits of his labor. May no one extend kindness to him or take pity on his fatherless children . . ."*

I chanted theses words e'ry night and nothin' happened. I spied on that ho Noki and Eddie's bitch ass e'ry day. I was obsessin'. I would take a livery cab to her block and I'd just sit and watch those bastards. E'ry day I would pay $300 for two hours of watchin'. I would watch them comin' and goin'. Smilin' and laughin'. Meanwhile, I was fucked up inside. It took all my control not to jump out and whip her ass! The only thing that kept me from losin' it was the paper I was 'bout to git from Knowledge Born tomorrow. Wit that money, I'd start all over.

NINETY·THREE

NIKKI LING

With nowhere to go, I ended up at Joshua's apartment. I knocked and no one answered. I put my ear to his door and it was quiet. He wasn't home. I hung out downstairs until he came home. When he saw me, his face dropped.

"What on earth are you doing here?" he asked in astonishment.

"I was bailed out."

"Well, I hope so. I know you didn't break out."

"I need to talk. There have been some developments in my case."

Joshua led me to his apartment where he fixed me something to eat and I took a hot shower. Once I was relaxed, I began my story.

"Ivanka bailed me out."

"Jesus, Mary and Joseph! What does she want?"

"Me to go through with the criss cross. She wants me to kill her father."

"Why on earth would you honor the criss cross when she double crossed you?"

"She stated that the gun report that says my fingerprints are on the gun is a lie. She said for you to get the gun retested."

"So?"

"So with no prints and my alibi, I should be acquitted."

"But what if . . ."

"There are no what if's. She doesn't care. She wants me to kill her father or else she's going to kill Noki."

"This is a load of bullshit. You are smart enough to see the smoke screen."

"Fuck! Why is everyone always speaking like I'm a fucking idiot. Truthfully, I don't know what to believe. Or who to believe. I'm the one in trouble!"

"Calm down . . . I apologize." Joshua said and came over and wrapped his arms around me. I felt safe. "What else did you find out?"

"I went over to Noki's. She's scared out of her mind. She had nothing to do with this. Ivanka planned the whole thing. Now she's threatened to kill Noki if I don't go through with the murder. Joshua, you saw how she slaughtered Jack," I cried.

"I'm sure Noki will be fine."

"You don't believe her, do you?"

"I'm an attorney. I follow the evidence and it says she's involved."

"The evidence also says I shot and slaughtered my husband. We have to use logic. There was no point in Noki devising this elaborate plan. She was well-taken care of. And she stood to inherit $80 million at the time of Jack's death. That's more than enough money."

"For some people. Well let's not worry about that now. You have to lay low until your trial. Where are you staying?"

"I . . . um . . . I don't really have a place to lay low. I have somewhere I can go . . . but soon enough the press will be camped outside. I'm thinking I'll have to stay here."

"What?" he asked incredulously.

"I don't eat much and I clean up after myself," I joked.

"There's no room! And I'm your attorney . . . I can hardly see you in your pajamas. It's unethical. I won't stand for it."

"I'll see you in the morning," I said and collapsed on his sofabed.

NINETY·FOUR

ESTELLE CARDINALE

Robert Maximilian showed each juror the most embarrassing photos of Richard Cardinale dressed in woman's clothing. He had on lipstick and hideous wigs. He was posed in the most awkward positions you could possibly think of. His pale, hairy, chest had on expensive Victoria Secret bras, and he wore panties with stiletto heels adorning his huge feet. It was most embarrassing. And I appeared to be the humiliated wife, of course.

"Mrs. Cardinale, where is your husband now?"

"He's divorced me, taken my children, and is now living with a swimsuit model in Los Angeles."

I took this opportunity to break down. Tears streamed down my cheeks, and my lips quivered involuntarily. Robert handed me a tissue. This time I looked over to the women in the jury pool. They were hanging on to my every word.

"Your Honor, I think we should take a recess so Mrs. Cardinale can compose herself," the prosecution said. But I wasn't going to let that happen. Robert had already told me that if the judge asks whether I want to take a recess, I should decline. Just move forward with the testimony. If we recess, I could lose any juror.

"Mrs. Cardinale, would you like to take a ten-minute break?" the judge asked.

"No . . . no, I'm fine, Your Honor. I can continue," I said and dabbed my eyes.

"Please continue. What went through your mind when Mr. Cardinale asked you for a divorce?" Robert asked.

"I thought he'd just gotten away with the perfect murder," I said in a matter-of-fact manner. The look on each woman's face sitting on the jury was one of pure disgust. They despised Richard Cardinale.

Robert had done more than proven reasonable doubt. And I did my part, too. When the prosecutor got up to cross-examine me, he was livid. He badgered me to the best of his ability but I wouldn't budge. I left my stern, strong demeanor outside of the courtroom. I pretended to be timid and almost afraid of him and his ranting. He played right into my hands. The jury didn't like him at all.

When he stood up to give his closing argument, some of the jurors were asleep or picking at their fingernails. He couldn't hold anyone's attention.

Then Robert stood up.

"Ladies and gentleman of the jury, what you have here before you is an innocent woman on trial for her life. She's on trial because the very person who masterminded, plotted and killed Ms. Lyric Devaney has fled the state and is now shacking up with a swimsuit model. I contend that if you look carefully, you'll see smoke and mirrors. Magic. That's what the prosecution's case is made up of. Look at Mrs. Cardinale. Could she have actually picked up Ms. Devaney, and hoisted her up over her shoulders? At that point Mrs. Devaney was almost dead weight and seven months pregnant. But I contend that only an athletic, virile man like Mr. Cardinale could have done just that. Only Mr. Cardinale had knowledge that Lyric videotaped her sexual escapades. He knew this because he was in most of them. I contend that he called her and told her he was coming for quick sexual gratification. When the doorbell rang, as you saw on the tape, Ms. Devaney clicked on her video camera. She was ready for sex. She was dressed in lingerie . . . not the outfit you wear when you are about to confront the wife of your lover . . .

NINETY·FIVE

NIKKI LING

I got up early and decided to go home. Not to Jack's apartment, but to my Upper East-Side apartment. I hadn't been there in years. But I still paid the rent. When Jack and I got together, I'd go there occasionally to get away from him. As I adjusted to his quirky ways, my visits to my apartment grew less frequent.

I took a cab and arrived there in less than thirty minutes. My doorman greeted me warmly. I got the extra key I left at their station and went upstairs. I gathered a few items of clothing to take back to Joshua's apartment when someone banged on the front door. It must be the press, I thought. Then they banged again, "Police, open up!"

What did they want? Did something happen to Noki? I ran to open the door. Detectives Oldham and Ripton were standing there.

"Nikkisi Ling-Okayo, I'm placing you under arrest for the murder of Steven Jackson," he announced as he placed the cuffs on my wrists as he read me my Miranda rights. My mind rewound to that fateful day in Memphis, when the two assailants murdered Steven, the drug-hustler I had gone home with.

My throat was dry and my vision blurred. I couldn't go back to Rikers Island. I couldn't go back to jail.

At the precinct, they started with the interrogation.

"You just can't seem to get a break, huh Nikki?" Detective Ripton gloated.

"You're turning out to be a serial killer," Detective Oldham chimed in.

"I want to call my attorney," I stated.

"Soon honey. We're just talking among friends. Why you wanna mess that up?" Detective Ripton said.

"I know my rights!" I screamed.

"Did you know that you have a right to be extradited to Memphis to be officially charged with murdering your boyfriend, ransacking his house and stealing his drug money? Your fingerprints are all over the place and we found unknown DNA in his living room."

"I don't want to exercise that right," I stated as I remembered scrapping my knee as I tried to flee the murder scene back at Steven's house.

"Too bad. We're waiting for two detectives to fly in from Memphis. They are eager to read you your rights!"

As they hammered me mercilessly, I tried to focus. There was no way I was going to beat these two cases. No way at all.

"I need to use the bathroom," I finally asked. They'd been interrogating me for hours.

They were tired and needed a break as well. Detective Oldham asked a lady police officer to escort me. I used the bathroom and as she led me back up the stairs, I lifted her handcuff key. She took me back in the interrogation room where they told her that Detective Oldham and Ripton had gone out for a dinner break.

"Come on, you can wait for them in here," she led me in

a room that had a bench. She left the door ajar to keep an eye on me and handcuffed me to the wall. I sat anxiously waiting for the right opportunity. The room was four feet away from the staircase, but I realized I couldn't make it past all the cops downstairs. I'd surely get busted. Then I realized there was a window in the room. The window had bars on it but someone had already bent them to one side. I realized that there was just enough open for me to slide through.

When the pizza delivery came and everyone started eating and drinking Pepsi, I unlocked my handcuff and crept to the window. My heart was racing. I slowly pushed the window out, hoisted my body up and crawled out. I was two stories up. I climbed down a tree and escaped.

I made it over to Joshua's house without being spotted. I gently tapped on his door until he came to it.

"Who?" he called out. I didn't say a word. I looked nervously around to see if anyone was coming. Joshua looked through his peephole and when he saw me, he flung his door open. He smiled, "I just can't get rid of you, huh?"

I pushed into his apartment, shut off his lights and pulled down his curtains.

"What's going on?" he asked. I clicked on the television and just as I had suspected, my face was splashed across every news channel.

"Jesus, Mary and Joseph!" was the last thing he said before he turned stark white.

NINETY·SIX

NIKKI LING

You have to turn yourself in, Nikki," he demanded. We had the television up so no one could hear us. We were talking in his bathroom with the door closed.

"I can't do that. They are shipping me to Memphis to be arraigned on murder charges."

"I'm your attorney. Why didn't you tell me about Memphis?"

"I've been through hell, Joshua. Jack was my focus. I buried that situation with Steven in the back of my mind. I didn't think it necessary to bring it up. I didn't do it . . ."

"You didn't do anything yet you're in a whole lot of trouble. Now a trail of dead men are systematically piling up behind you," he whispered.

"Don't judge me, Joshua!"

"Listen, you cannot stay here!" he said and grabbed me by my arm. He started dragging me out of his bathroom. "I could lose my license and end up in a jail cell next to you. This is obstruction of justice and aiding and abetting a fugitive. I cannot ruin my life for another beautiful woman who will ultimately end up leaving me."

As he went to open his front door and throw me out, I kissed him. He pulled back. Then I kissed him again. This time he responded. My tongue explored the inside of his mouth. His pink lips were soft and inviting. I wanted more but he backed off.

"I need to go to the precinct and inquire on your whereabouts. Since it's on every news channel, they won't be suspicious. Did anyone see you come here?"

"No."

"Did you tell anyone? Noki? Anyone?"

"No."

"Don't use the telephone. Don't speak. Don't move. When I leave I will turn off the television. Don't turn it back on. I will operate like I'm here alone, until I can sort out this mess. But you will surrender as soon as I understand what's going on."

A moment later he was gone.

NINETY·SEVEN

ESTELLE CARDINALE

As the jury came in, none of them looked at me. All heads were faced down towards the floor. I sat up even straighter in my chair. I looked to Robert and he was stone-faced. I couldn't read him.

"Jury foreman, have you reached a verdict?"

"Yes, Your Honor."

"How do you find the defendant?"

"In the State of New York, we find the defendant not guilty on all counts," he exclaimed. The courtroom flared up. People were yelling and screaming "Injustice!" Journalists were snapping pictures. Radio personalities were scurrying out to report the news. Robert and I embraced momentarily. I cannot express the keen sense of respect I felt for him. He was a genius.

"Job well done," I said to Robert.

Whoever said the rich can buy freedom was absolutely correct. My money bought me the best lawyers. With their legal finagling, I escaped justice. People may say that I'll have to pay my Maker. I say, "Does he take cash or check?"

NINETY·EIGHT

NIKKI LING

Over the next few days, the sexual tension building up between Joshua and me was unbearable. I was used to sleeping with men on the first night–if that was what I wanted. And I wanted to make love to Joshua, but he wasn't giving in. He was protecting his heart from women like me. These past few nights he'd opened up about his ex-wife, Lyric, Monique and Lacey. He had a bad track record. I understood why he wouldn't want to take a chance on someone charged in connection with two homicides, and an ex-prostitute and renowned pick-pocket. Still I tried to seduce him every chance I got.

On this particular evening, I showered, washed my hair and came out with just a T-shirt on. I was still wet so the T-shirt stuck to my nipples (I wasn't wearing a bra) and you could see my areolas. I flopped on his sofa and exhaled. He was reading case law trying to save my ass.

I had a bottle of Victoria's Secret lotion that he'd picked up for me in my hands. As he read, I poured scented lotion in my hands and massaged it into my legs. With each circular motion he'd peek over, momentarily, and then return to reading.

"What are you reading?" I finally said distracting him. I still continued to put lotion all over my body.

"Extradition law in Memphis."

"Oh," I said and began to rub lotion on my thighs.

"Um . . . could you . . . can't you do that somewhere else?" he stuttered.

"You've got to be joking. You live in a closet. Here," I said and shoved the bottle in his hands, "could you rub some on my back."

I tried to lift up my shirt when he pulled it back down.

"I can't do this," he stated.

"Do what?" I said and leaned over and kissed him. I felt his hands trembling as he groped my large breasts. As his tongue explored my mouth, I tried to rip his shirt off because I was immensely turned on.

"Slow down," he murmured. "Let's take it slow. We have all night." With ease, he took off my T-shirt and stared at my naked body.

"You are the most alluring, amazing woman, I've ever met," he said and looked directly in my eyes. His sincerity had taken me off guard. I burst into tears and looked away.

"Sh-h-h-h-h," he soothed. He put his hand underneath my chin and made me look into his eyes. "Let's pretend . . . just for tonight that we're happy. No tears."

I smiled faintly, "No tears."

Then Joshua's wet tongue gently sucked my nipples with a synchronized rhythm. I moaned in pleasure. As he kissed and licked my neck, I gently nibbled on his ears. I was enjoying our foreplay. His wet tongue kissed every inch of my welcoming body, sending chills down my spine. As he kissed the inside of my thighs and made his way down to my feet, there was a casualness with his touch. A confident man was making love to me. Joshua aggressively sucked each toe and my pussy tingled in anticipation. I so desperately wanted him to enter me. When he went down and buried his head in my pussy, I fell in love. Skillfully his tongue flickered back and forth rapidly. Then he slowed down and began to lick and suck my pussy. He tasted me as if he was enjoying an exquisite delicacy. I had to bite down hard on my tongue to keep from screaming out.

"Turn over," he breathed. When I hesitated for a moment he said, "I want you to turn over."

Listening to my lover I turned over and lay on my stomach. I could feel his eyes staring at my ass.

"I love the small of your back," he murmured then he softly parted my butt cheeks with his masculine hands. When his moist tongue licked my anus, I moaned in pleasure. Joshua then inserted his index finger and twirled it around.

"I want to enter you," he asked. I shook my head unable to speak. He slowly climbed on top of me and entered me from the back. He was so gentle. As his ass pumped in and out, tiny tears escaped my eyes. He was making love to me like he *loved* me. It had been so long since someone had treated me so gently. The exquisite pain mixed with pleasure was gratifying as we both climaxed. As we lay on Joshua's small sofa bed, I didn't want to think about tomorrow. I was wallowing in today.

While I stroked Joshua's chest, his hands lightly played in my hair.

"You have soft hair," he said. He was still trying to catch his breath.

"So do you," I said and let my hand twirl his pubic hair. His dick immediately got hard. "I see someone likes compliments."

Joshua and I switched to the missionary position. When I went down to engulf his penis, he pulled me back up and kissed my mouth.

"But I want to," I protested.

"You think you *need* to," he retorted and entered me for the second time. We made love doggie and frog style. Just when I thought we were done, he got up naked and walked to his CD player.

"What are you doing?" I asked. I stretched my body and yawned from fatigue. Joshua didn't answer me. When I heard Luther Vandross's voice resonating, *"Let me hold you tight . . . if only for one night . . ."* I grinned.

"I thought we were done."

"We're just getting started."

That night, Joshua and I made love.

NINETY·NINE

KAPRI HENDERSON

I got home rather early this Sunday mornin'. I expected Kareem to be home doin' his homework for school tomorrow, but he wasn't around. I noticed that the house was spotless. Good. I had nothin' to beef about. Kareem had been holdin' me down lately. He's been out pushin' my shit without givin' me any lip. The embarrassin' incident wit the Pepsi bottle seemed to straighten his stupid ass out. He's been stayin' out my way lately.

My brain has been so stressed out I didn't get a chance to tell Kareem 'bout the paper I was 'bout to cop from his father. Once I get that shit, I'm outta here. I hate bein' in this crib–I think about Eddie.

I walked into the kitchen and decided to cook dinner for me and Kareem. I was gonna make spaghetti. As I put on a pot of boilin' water, I heard a large bang at my front door. The force was so strong the floor vibrated, and it sounded like a large explosion. Before I could realize what was happenin', the floor vibrated again and I heard the large explosion.

"What the fuck . . ." I said as I walked to the front door. It flung open and several police officers in combat gear came swarmin' in. They had their guns drawn.

"Police! Don't fucking move, asshole," someone said to me. I was thrown to the floor and handcuffed. Once they secured the premises, they calmed down. The detective in charge came over. He said his name was Detective Shue.

"Kapri Henderson . . . you've been up to no good."

"I don't know what you're talkin' 'bout," I said. My voice was mad shaky. I watched as the police officers searched my crib lookin' for drugs. They had my hands cuffed behind my back, and I was sittin' on the floor in the living room. The police officers ransacked my house for an hour. When one police officer took a little too long in the kitchen I knew somethin' was up.

"I got a hit," a police officer yelled and my heart sank. "It's over a kilogram of uncut cocaine!"

He came out smilin', holdin' a box of drugs. Then Detective Shue bent down and said, "Looks like you're going down for at least thirty years . . . Kapone!"

"Fuck you!" I snapped.

"Don't think so," he said and laughed. "By the way, someone out here doesn't like you very much. They called and snitched on your drug operation."

As they picked me up off the floor to take me to the station, I kept wonderin' who the fuck ratted me out. It had to be Knowledge Born! For the second time, he'd snaked me. I was so stupid thinkin' he was gonna compensate me for my years in prison. Instead he wanted to send me right back!

As I was brought out the buildin', there was a huge crowd. I spotted Kareem lingerin' in the crowd. It was a good thing he wasn't in the apartment. They would have locked him up too. When they stuffed me in the back of the car, I looked to Kareem and mouthed the words, "I'm sorry." And I truly was.

ONE HUNDRED

NIKKI LING

Joshua and I grew closer in the next few days. Everyday he would tell me that my time to turn myself in was coming near.

"You can't stay hiding in here forever," he said.

I knew he was right. I had to face my situation, but I was afraid. I couldn't go to jail. So when Joshua left for work, I decided that I needed some cash. I was going to run. Alone. I knew Noki would never follow, and I didn't want her to. Most likely I'd be waiting tables or serving drinks in a bar. But I was never, ever going to sell my body again. Once dressed, I slowly opened Joshua's door. No one. Then as I crept out, I was met by a neighbor.

"Good morning," someone said and startled me.

"Good morning," I blurted out and scurried out of the building. The neighbor looked at me strangely. Even though I had on a baseball cap and dark glasses, I felt like the nosy neighbor had recognized me. Then I brushed it off and stuck to my plan.

I went to my old stomping ground, 34th Street, because I needed some money if I was going to run. If I could just get my hands on a few thousand dollars, I could go.

I must have stood out there for eight hours without spotting my mark. I was too paranoid.

I kept thinking someone was going to recognize me. Then I kept thinking that I shouldn't be stealing from people anyway. If I got caught stealing someone's wallet, it would be only that much more difficult to prove my innocence.

When the sun went down, I decided to go back to Joshua's. When I arrived, there were cop cars everywhere. Joshua was being led out in handcuffs. The detectives had a white plastic bag with my things in them. I had fucked up.

I got out of there quickly. When I got to a safe, secluded area, I called Noki. I couldn't reach her at home but got her on her cell phone.

"Noki, I need your help!" I breathed into the phone.

"You're in a lot of trouble," she stated.

"I can't do this. I'm in deep shit. Jack, Steven, they're going to hang me. I need money to leave town. Can you help me, Noki?"

"I don't know," she retorted.

"Noki, the news channels have been suggesting the death penalty. They want me to die for murders I didn't commit. Noki, I love you. And no matter how much you deny we're sisters—you are my sister. You're my blood, Noki. Remember when we were little . . . how I would protect you, Noki. Remember . . . remember mommy and daddy, Noki. Please don't shut me out Noki. I would die for you!" I screamed out of sheer desperation.

"Okay. I'll help. It's not safe to talk on this line. Meet me at our resting spot in one hour. I'll have 100 K for you. Bye," she said and hung up the phone. There was a glimmer of hope.

It wasn't safe for me to go back to Jack's, but I realized that was the last place the police would be looking. I snuck into our parking garage and realized that my bike and my Mercedes G-500 truck were still there. I lifted up my secret compartment, hoping that my safety deposit key would still be there, but it wasn't. Of course it wasn't. Kayla had stolen my money and run. But the extra set of keys to my bike was there. I hopped on and raced over to our secret resting spot. In less than one hour, I'd be on my way to a new life.

ONE HUNDRED·ONE

NOKI LING

The telephone conversation with Nikki caused me to have a miserable day in the city, so I decided to go home earlier than I planned. I hated that I had to let go of some of my ransom money but everything had gone awry. Now Nikki needed to skip town or surely they'd give her the death penalty. Since that had never been my intention when I helped concoct the criss cross, I decided it was best Nikki got lost. Besides, I'd be getting my inheritance in the up coming weeks.

As I approached, I noticed Eddie walking into my apartment building with a dark-skinned black girl. He was carrying a black duffle bag. As they entered the building, I saw the girl's profile. It was the mother of Eddie's kid and I knew exactly what was about to happen!

I entered the building and crept upstairs. As I approached the door, I heard voices inside my apartment. They were far away, so I couldn't make out what they were saying. Carefully I opened the door. (Being a skilled thief affords you steadiness.) Once inside, I kneeled down in the kitchen behind a counter and listened to them bicker.

"Hurry up," Eddie said as they stuffed my million-dollar ransom inside his duffle bag. His hands were trembling.

"Why we gotta hurry up? I thought you said she wouldn't be back for hours," she asked.

"That girl is inconsistent. I don't want her to come back and find us here."

"Well, we can't just take the money and leave," Trisha stated.

"That's exactly what we're doing."

"Eddie, if we take this money she will call the cops. I can't go to jail."

"She ain't calling no cops. This money is stolen. She'll go to jail too."

"I don't feel comfortable leaving her alive, Eddie."

"What?" he asked. "What the hell you talkin' 'bout? I ain't killing her over no money."

As I listened, I started to panic. From where I was sitting I could see everything. Trisha ignored Eddie and went into my room. She took a long time and then emerged holding bags of my designer clothing and jewelry.

"Look, Eddie, this is too much to carry out of here at one time. Someone will surely be suspicious and report us to the cops. The only way to get away with this is to do it right. We're halfway there, Eddie. You gotta kill her. That way we will have all evening to slowly remove her things from her apartment. She has too much nice shit to leave behind."

"Why are you taking all that bullshit? We got a million dollars here. We can buy you anything you want!" he yelled. I could tell he was getting annoyed because his eyes hooded over.

"Why should we spend the money on what we can have for free? Besides, I want to wait until she comes home so I can take her Rolex watch from her. I always wanted a Rolex. You know that Eddie."

"Look, stop fuckin' whining. You know I hate that shit."

"You just don't want to confront her!" she challenged. "Now you taking her side over mine!"

"I don't give a fuck about that fat bitch! I was just using her for her money," he said. "If you want her dead, you kill her!" Eddie then removed a gun from his waist and handed it to her. She took it and said she'd do it. "Pussy," she called him.

"Whatever!" he retorted.

When Trisha decided to go and gather more of my things, she laid the gun down on the coffee table. Moments later she and Eddie were arguing again.

I took this opportunity to lunge for the gun. As I emerged from the kitchen, everything seemed to be moving in slow motion. Eddie spotted me from his peripheral vision, realized what I was reaching for, and lunged too. We both simultaneously grabbed the gun. I felt the cold steel of the handgun and my adrenaline started racing. As I tugged for the gun, I realized that Eddie was much stronger than I was. The gun started to slip from my grasp. As my fingers started to give in to his strength, I leaned in and bit Eddie's knuckles. His grip loosened but he didn't let go of the gun. We both fell up against my wall knocking over my Kanji clock. Eddie and I both clung to the gun because we knew what was at stake. When we both tripped and fell over my coffee table, my two large marble peking foo dogs came crashing down and broke into pieces. As we rolled around on the floor, the gun went off . . .

ONE HUNDRED·TWO

NIKKI LING

I safely made it to our resting spot underneath the Brooklyn Bridge. I shut off my bike and waited for Noki. It was close to ten o'clock. As I waited, I felt a tremendous amount of guilt for Joshua. All he wanted to do was help. Funny how I always thought Noki was selfish, and I ended up being just that. How could I have put Joshua in that peculiar situation? A situation that will cost him his license and freedom? After everything he went through to clear his name and get his life back on track, in a matter of days I had taken all of that from him.

I thought about his ex-wife Parker, who unmistakably still loved him. How disappointed she will be seeing his face flashed across the evening news in yet another daunting situation. The most frustrating thing was that I couldn't help him. Even if I turned myself in he'd still be in jail.

An hour later, I was still waiting for Noki. My cell phone battery was almost dead, but I didn't want to use it anyway. What if the police had a trace on it? They could detect my location from the tower the cell phone company uses to communicate and have a dozen cop cars out here to arrest me. All I could do was wait.

ONE HUNDRED·THREE

NOKI LING

I pushed Eddie's dead weight off of me and he came crashing to the floor with a loud thud. Trisha stood frozen like a deer blinded by headlights. I lifted up the gun and pulled the trigger. It hit her square in between her green eyes of envy.

"Tell me again how you want me dead, bitch!" I said and kicked her. Then, strangely enough, I emptied the clip inside her. For that split second, I had completely lost my mind. I wanted to stop myself but I couldn't. It was as if I was a third party, standing outside of my body watching the events unfold. When I realized that I had committed a double homicide, I fled the scene.

My predilection for money had left me in an uncompromising situation that I needed to get myself out of. I grabbed the same duffle bag that Eddie had packed with the $1 million, then packed another duffle bag with a few personal items and jewelry, and left the scene. The police would be here momentarily. I was most certain someone had called 911 after hearing numerous gunshots.

As soon as I got downstairs, I heard the police sirens blaring. Two detectives were sitting in an unmarked car. Had they been staking out my apartment building, most likely looking for Nikki? When they noticed I had spotted them, they both emerged from the car.

"Noki Ling? Could we have a moment to talk to you about your sister?" one said.

I didn't stay to answer their questions. In a few seconds, several police officers would be responding to a 911 call. I ran as fast as I could to my bike. The two detectives did a slow trollop towards me. Once on my bike, I revved up my engine and was off. Within seconds, I had several police cars chasing me. All that was going through my mind was that I had to get as far away from here as possible . . .

ONE HUNDRED·FOUR

NIKKI LING

When midnight approached, I realized there would be no meeting between Noki and me. She wasn't coming to assist me in my flight. She probably feels that I'm the murderer the media is making me out to be. After all I've done for her, this is the thanks I get. As I sulked, cried and ultimately gave up hope, I heard the faint sound of police sirens in the distance.

As the sound became more distinct, I jumped up and started my bike. They found me! They were coming. Did Noki send them? As I contemplated my escape, I heard the engine of a bike. Then in the distance I saw Noki on her bike flying down the highway. "Oh my God!" I screamed.

Noki was the target of a high-speed police chase. With sirens blaring, six police cars were chasing my baby sister. "You can make it, Noki," I cried. She had to . . .

When Noki got close enough, I revved up my bike and the chase was on. Noki stuck close to me, and we dipped in and out of traffic going 100 miles per hour. The police wouldn't fall back. Their sirens were blaring as they got so close to me I could reach out and touch one car. I felt the thrill of the chase as I skillfully maneuvered my bike. It was on! There was no way I was going to do time for murders I didn't commit. I was determined to do whatever I could to get away. And if that meant risking my life. So be it.

I would die on this very day trying to get away.

My adrenaline was pumping as we tried to perfect our escape. Noki, not being as skilled in riding as I, was having trouble keeping up with my pace. I kept slowing up so she could catch up. Twice she almost had a near fatal crash, but she made it.

We were riding side by side when Noki took from her shoulders a large duffle bag and handed it to me. I received the extremely heavy bag yet was able to still maneuver my bike. I thought that this transfer would help Noki to ride better, but it didn't. When it seemed like the police were closing in, Noki slowed down and waved me on. The ramp was approaching. I shook my head.

There was a ramp up ahead that was a shortcut to the highway. If we made the ramp, we'd have a better chance at escaping. Although Noki had never been able to make the jump, I felt confident that this time she could. Again, I tried to fall back so she could understand I didn't want to leave her, but she waved me on again. For the first time in our lives, Noki was thinking about my safety and it nearly broke my heart. My sister did love me! She loved me . . .

I kicked my bike into gear, sped up, and braced myself for the leap. As my bike accelerated, in mid-air I felt like I was on top of the world. My adrenaline was pumping. I hit the ground on both wheels and sped off into the night. I was a mile away when I heard a large explosion. I turned around and saw the aftermath. A large cloud of smoke loomed in the thin night air and flames were bursting into the sky.

What happened?

ONE HUNDRED·FIVE

ESTELLE CARDINALE

The next day I had to put on a disguise in order to get to my attorney's office. Last night the black community was so outraged at the verdict they started burning down their community. They broke storefront windows, set fire to commercial property and assaulted any white person in the vicinity of their riot. The press called it 'The Riot of 02.'

When I entered Robert's office, he was watching CNN. They were televising the commotion live.

"They're burning down their own communities," he said and shook his head.

"They're angry."

"They're misguided."

"This should all be over by nightfall," I stated, trying to show concern. Truthfully I had low tolerance for such idiotic behavior. But I pretended to sympathize with Robert.

"Listen, let's get down to business," he said. I could tell he was troubled by the events of his people. "Here's a check for the $1 million that you had in our escrow account."

I took the check, sighed deeply and said, "Keep it."

"What? For what? You've already paid my fee."

"Keep it as a retainer," I said.

"A retainer fee? You've been acquitted, Estelle. There's nothing further."

"Keep this as a retainer fee. I've booked a flight to Los Angeles. I have an ex-husband I need to deal with . . ."

ONE HUNDRED·SIX

NIKKI LING

I rode my bike until I reached Philadelphia and realized that I needed to get rid of my bike and change my identity. With my helmet still on, I walked into a 24-hour CVS. I purchased a pair of scissors, red hair dye, thick-framed glasses and duct tape. Then I rode until I found a Motel 6. The motel attendant was a scrawny, white fellow. He had oily hair, rotten teeth and body odor.

"How many hours do you want the room for?" he asked.

"Six hours should be fine," I said.

"Fine, I'll need a major credit card and license."

"I don't have either...I lost them," I stuttered.

The attendant took a long glance at me. Then he looked to his television set which he had on mute. The television wasn't facing me, but I was certain that I was on it. Then he confirmed my thoughts.

"It looks like you're in a bit of trouble," he stated.

"Precisely," I retorted and dug my hand into the duffle bag Noki had given me. I peeled off a stack of hundred dollar bills. "Let's keep my troubles between me and God."

He looked down at the stack of crisp hundred dollar bills and got excited.

"I make $6 dollars a hour, and I ain't partial to being comfy with no cops," he said and grabbed the money.

Then he noticed my bike. "A fellow like me could sure use a nice bike like yours . . ."

"That's a Yamaha XVZ-1300 with a Chrome gas tank. Only three in the world," I said.

"I know. I have a picture of that bike that I carry in my wallet," he said and pulled out a crinkled photo of the bike cut out of a magazine.

"If you want the bike, it's yours. But I'll need a vehicle."

"You can take mine. It's a piece of junk, but it has a decent engine. It'll get you away from here. Probably a few states. Anything more than that I don't know."

"Give me three days before you report your car stolen," I said and tossed him the keys to my bike. He gave me a room on the first floor facing the back, hid my bike and drove his car directly in front of my room door.

Once inside the room, I took the scissors and cut off all my hair. As my locks hit the sink, I couldn't comprehend how my life had changed so quickly. I decided that I couldn't dwell on how I got to where I was; I needed to focus on how to get out of my situation. After I dyed my naturally black hair red, I went to sleep for a few hours. I was exhausted.

I bolted up out of my sleep just before dawn and clicked on the television. I was sweating profusely. I clicked through each channel until I found a news channel. It would take only a moment before I saw my mug shot displayed on the television. I turned it up louder and heard:

This is Gilt McGronner with WLTV channel 10 News. The police are putting on a massive manhunt for alleged murderer Nikkisi Ling-Okayo. She's accused of plotting to kill her husband for his $400 million estate. Also it is alleged that she robbed and murdered a drug-dealer out in Memphis, Tennessee for his drug money. We have footage of the high speed chase she and her sister put authorities through last night. The sisters were on a killing spree. They are now being called a modern day Thelma and Louise. Her sister was wanted in connection with killing her boyfriend, Eddie Long, last night in her apartment. According to police, neighbors allege that there had been a lover's quarrel and Noki Ling killed Eddie Long and his wife, Trisha. The police chased Noki Ling to where she met up with her sister Nikki. The two had planned on fleeing together when Noki met an unforeseeable fate. She crashed her motorcycle into the pier, and died instantly. Forensic scientists are studying the scene and think this may have been suicide. There were no skid marks on the ground indicating she may have purposely tried to cause a distraction so her sister could get away. Two other people have fallen victim to Nikkisi Ling-Okayo, now being dubbed the 'Black Widow.' Joshua Tune was arrested yesterday for obstruction of justice and aiding and abetting a fugitive. He is being held on $100,000 bail. And Ling-Okayo's best friend, Kayla Shim, was arrested at Chase Manhattan Bank three weeks ago after authorities followed her. Apparently she was receiving close to $800,000 of what is suspected to be drug money in connection with the murder of Steven Jackson. Also authorities recovered a broach that was reported stolen by a British socialite. Kayla Shim hasn't been able to post bail either. Neither person is cooperating with authorities . . ."

"Oh, Kayla-a-a-a," I cried. "You didn't betray me. You didn't betray me . . ."

mother and try to mend our relationship but I refused. I was glad I had lost my mother, because I gained a father! He was someone I could look up to.

ONE HUNDRED·SEVEN

KAREEM HENDERSON

After my mother was arrested, I didn't have anywhere to go. That night I stayed at Veronica's house, and first thing in the morning I rode the D-train into the city. When I got off the train, I walked to One Park Plaza. My father's office. I took the elevator up to the 21st floor. I walked to the receptionist, a pretty white girl, and asked if I could see Robert Maximilian.

"Do you have an appointment?" she asked.

"No, ma'am. But please tell him that Kareem Henderson needs to speak to him. It's very urgent, ma'am," I replied.

She called him and told me to have a seat, that he'd be with me in a moment. I nervously looked down at my clothes. I had on dark blue jean shorts and a T-shirt. I wanted to dress especially nice to meet him, but I only had the clothes on my back. The police had sealed off our apartment and labeled it a crime scene, so I wasn't able to get any of my belongings.

"Mr. Henderson, he will see you right now," the receptionist said.

I walked down the long hallway and realized I was visibly trembling. I'd never seen my father but had heard only good things about him from my mother. I walked in and saw my dad. He looked at me.

"Hello, sir," I said.

"Hello, Kareem. It's a pleasure to meet you."

"Thank you, sir."

"Please call me Robert."

"Okay, sir."

"So, where's your mother?" he said, as he took a seat and motioned for me to take one. He had pulled out a checkbook and started writing.

"My mother's been arrested for possession, sir. She won't be coming home anytime soon," I said. He stopped writing.

He shook his head, "My God, this is so unfortunate. When did this happen?"

"Yesterday," I said.

"Where did they make the arrest?"

"Our apartment."

"It was a raid? Thank God you weren't there. You must be devastated," he said and looked to me to give a reaction, but I didn't.

"Sir, my mother said you're my father. I don't want to live in another foster home. Can I live with you?" I pleaded. Not waiting for a response, I said, "I get good grades in school, and I want to be a lawyer just like you. I don't need my own room, I can sleep on the floor or the sofa."

My father hesitated for a moment, sighed deeply, then said, "My life's a little hectic. I don't cook and I live life as a bachelor. I'm not a good father figure."

"But you're my father," I said. "You can't just send me away, not when I need you. You owe me that much. I've lived in a foster home all my life. All I want is to live a normal life with my father."

"Kareem."

"Yes?"

"I'm not . . . I'm not . . ."

"Yes?"

"I'm not . . . sure I can give you what you need," he

"Sure you can," I cheered. "I'm so proud of you. Y my hero and I don't even know you."

He just smiled. So I continued, "Besides, I look ju you."

"Indeed you do," he said and smiled. His sm inviting. "I think you need to know that I don't New York. I live in Miami now. Do you think yo like it there?"

"Sir, anywhere is better than where I've beer past sixteen years," I said and he came and embr When he wanted to let go, I held him tighte want him to see the tears in my eyes.

"Are you hungry?" he asked.

"Starving," I answered truthfully.

"Great, then we'll go and have breakfast," h called his secretary.

As we were leaving he said, "Kareem, one q

"Yes, sir."

"Did you take part in getting your mother said and looked me directly in the eyes.

I hesitated for a moment, then said, "Yes, s

That was the only time he'd ever ask m happened to my mother on that fateful Su he hired the best criminal defense lawyer hi buy to represent her. My dad encouraged n

ONE HUNDRED·EIGHT

IVANKA ZAMORA

I was summoned into my father's office this morning in what he called a private meeting. Only it wasn't private. As soon as I entered, I noticed a room full of people. Dr. Cohen, my father's bitch fiancée, Renee, and two other strong-looking men.

"What's this about?" I asked.

"Have a seat, Ivanka," he casually replied. He wasn't even looking me in the eyes. I noticed how distant we were. I loathed him and couldn't wait for his death. If we were alone, I felt confident that I would have ended his life. I reached my hand inside my red Louis Vuitton pocketbook and twirled my icepick.

"Fuck-you," I roared. I was livid. What type of gathering was this?

"You're a disgrace to our family, Ivanka. You've been nothing but trouble to your mother and now you've become a nuisance to me. Dr. Cohen and I have gone to court and received an order to commit. I'm invoking my guardianship over you and having you committed to a psychiatric facility back in Texas. Dr. Cohen will oversee your treatment. You will remain there until you're better. Not one day before. If you choose to resist treatment you will rot inside the facility. The choice is yours!"

Before I could object, the two burly men started placing

me inside a straitjacket. I screamed my disapproval. I glanced over and saw the satisfied look on that black bitch's face.

"Father," I whined, "She's manipulating you. She wants you to hate me because I know the truth about her. I hired a private investigator and he said she was raised in the ghetto. She's from a housing development in East New York, Brooklyn. The Pink Houses. Her family still lives there. You can't marry her father! You will disgrace our family name."

"He's knows all about my past Ivanka," Renee gloated. "He loves me unconditionally."

"This is your fault!" I yelled at his whore. "I'll kill you!"

"No, actually, this was my idea, Ivanka," Dr. Cohen spoke up. "I've been following you for a while. You've been leaving dead bodies in your path for quite some time. You needed to be stopped. I went to the police first and they've refused to help. I took my evidence to your father, and he's a reasonable man. He knows you need help . . . before you start hurting people closer to you. Your father . . . or his soon-to-be bride," Dr. Cohen lectured.

"Father, I could never hurt you. You know how I feel about you," I whimpered.

My father didn't even stay to see them take me away. He and his bitch exited. Once they were gone, Dr. Cohen came over and whispered in my ear, "I've won. You will never see the light of day again—not while I'm alive."

For the first time in my life, I was afraid.

ONE HUNDRED·NINE

NIKKI LING

I cried my eyes out. I was devastated at the death and destruction that had taken place. So many lives taken. So many lives destroyed from one chance encounter with a stranger. I decided that I had to keep on moving if I were going to have any chance at escaping. I used the duct tape to flatten my breast, put on my baseball cap, glasses and then looked in the mirror. I looked remarkably different. I didn't look like I was trying to disguise myself . . . I just looked different. Then I walked over to the duffle bag of money that Noki had insisted I take. When I opened it, I nearly fainted. There was $1 million of ransom money in it. Jack and Joshua were right. Noki did have something to do with the criss cross and the phony ransom. Jack paid with his life and Joshua paid with his freedom.

Tucked inside the bag neatly was the Kokeshi doll my mother had bought Noki when we were just kids. I can't believe she held on to it all these years. Noki had always expressed hatred towards our family. Maybe she just had a hard time expressing love. As I closed up the bag, a manila envelope caught my attention. I reached for it and pulled out what was left of a photo. The photo was taken years ago of my father, mother, me and Noki. Only this picture didn't reflect that. Noki had cut my father, my mother and me out of the picture. I collapsed. Noki didn't love us. She didn't love me. She never did. What I can't understand is why she'd decided to help me? If I lived into eternity, I'll still ponder over this very question.

ONE HUNDRED·TEN

VERONICA

CROOKE AVENUE

O h, Jah! Oh Jah! Mi tink she really gon' mad mon,"
mi scream affa di television.

"Whatchu talkin' 'bout?" Ms. Joy said.

"We look pon di hot steppers pon di news, Nikki and
Noki. The news seh dat Noki kill 'im dead. Eddie and
'im baby madda. Dem tek police pon a high speed chase
before she kill 'erself."

"'Im a dead! 'Im a dead. Ka-pri put Obeah pon 'im and
di ooman, Noki."

"Who dat?" Ms. Joy asked.

"Eddie. The grindsman who sneak over 'ere ah night
time fi see Kapri. 'Im ah rude bwoy."

"So who Noki?"

"Pussyclot. His girlfriend. Those gals on TV are the
high class friends mi go see in the city," I explained.

"So Kapri killed Eddie?"

"Yea, mon."

"I thought she was locked up for drugs."

"Rassclot," mi say and suck mi teet. "Mi tell you say Kapri was practicing voodoo. A fuckery dat. She fight 'gainst
mi. She say is no odda way. She say a powerful chant mon.
Psalm 109 . . ."

"Psalm 109? That can kill someone?"

"If it use pro-per-ly mon. Nuh mess wit no raggamuffin. Dem wicked. Mi dun seen death . . . destruction. Mi know di power ah voodoo."

"So dat voodoo made Noki lose her mind and caused Eddie's death?"

"Yea, mon. She shot 'im dead and 'im baby madda."

"Shit, were was dat voodoo shit 30 years ago? I coulda had my lyin', cheatin' ex-husband bumped off."

"It not too late, mon. If you believe . . ."

ONE

BOOK TWO

JUNE 2003 IBIZA, SPAIN

I had been living in a small hut on the beach in Spain since I fled from America. The scenery was tranquil and serene. I didn't have any visitors and remained virtually a recluse. I grew my own vegetables and washed my clothing by hand. I didn't have any amenities from the outside world. No telephone or television. It was common for people around here to mind their own business.

On this particular morning, I was sleeping peacefully when I heard a noise. Without hesitation, I jumped up and pulled out a butcher's knife that I kept underneath my pillow. As the footsteps grew closer I held my breath and expected the worst. "They found me," I thought. I swung the door open and was startled.

"Jesus, Nikki . . . are you going to use that?" he said and smiled his boyish grin. I immediately dropped the knife and jumped into his arms. He grabbed me in a bear hug and spun me around.

"Is it really you?" I squealed. "How did you find me?"

"It wasn't easy yet it wasn't hard enough," he warned.

"When did you get out?" I asked Joshua as we packed.

"Two weeks ago . . ." he said.

"Why?" I asked.

"Why what?"

"Why are you here? Why are you putting yourself in the same situation? I'm a fugitive, Joshua. I will never live a normal life."

"Kid, you're all I've thought about for the past few months. I started thinking that I don't have a life in America if you're not in it."

"So you're saying," I paused, "that you love me?"

"I thought you knew how I felt about you," he said.

"I want you to say it!" I demanded.

"I love you, kid," he said and kissed me. I stared in his blue eyes and said, "I love you, too," and my eyes welled up with tears.

"It's not safe here. We have to leave. If I found you, the authorities can," Joshua said, and I immediately jumped into action. We ran around my small hut taking only what we could carry. And the $900,000 I still had left. We crept out quietly and headed to the Republic of China. They don't have an extradition treaty with the U.S. for death penalty cases.

TWO

DETECTIVE OLDHAM

JULY 2003

"Get your passport, Ripton. We got a hit!"

"Nikkisi?"

"Exactly! A snitch told us she's living in Ibiza, Spain."

"Don't you ever get tired of trailing her?" Detective Ripton asked.

"I will not retire until I have her back in America, facing charges for the murders she's committed!"

A READING GROUP GUIDE

THE CRISS CROSS

CRYSTAL LACEY WINSLOW

ABOUT THIS GUIDE

The suggested questions are intended to enhance your group's reading of this book by Crystal Lacey Winslow.

1. Why does Noki resent Nikki so much? Is there more to it than Nikki just being a prostitute? Could the fact that Noki witnessed her sister's indiscretions at such a young age make her despise Nikki? Do you think it was Nikki's responsibility to take care of Noki? If so, do you think she did a good job? Why do you think Noki was ashamed to admit she was halfblack when she dated black men? Noki despised that her mother and sister were prostitutes, yet she was promiscuous. Why do you think Noki was so sexual at a young age?

2. Do you agree with Brian when he said Nikki could have stopped prostituting herself long before she did? Was it reasonable of Nikki to wait until she had someone with money to give her stability before she stopped

prostituting? Why do you think Nikki continued to jostle long after she had married a wealthy man? How do you feel about Jack? Do you think that Brian and Nikki could have worked their relationship out? If not, what made him stop loving her since she was a prostitute when they met? Do you think Brian is a hypocrite?

3. Did witnessing their mother's suicide play a role in the choices Nikki and Noki made? Do you think Nikki loved Joshua? Or did she love him out of desperation and the need to be loved? And if she did love him, what made her fall in love? Do you think that Joshua will be good for Nikki considering his track record with beautiful women?

4. Why do you think Joshua gave up his life to go on the run with Nikki as a fugitive? Do you think he should have considered his son with Kaisha (Kaisha and his son are explored in *Life, Love & Loneliness*)? Do you think that Parker is still in love with Joshua? If so, do you think her love for him will drive her current husband away?

5. Kayla loved Nikki. How does Kayla's knowledge that her best friend is on the run for her life affect her? Will she be able to cope? Do you think Nikki will ever try to contact Kayla?

6. Ivanka displays signs of psychosis at an early age when she bludgeons the dog to death. Although this early sign is often in a serial killer's profile, was her behavior foreseeable?

7. What role did Maurice's suicide play in Madison's commitment into Creedmore Psychiatric Hospital?

8. Kapri used Kareem as a punching bag with the excuse that she wanted to toughen him up. Do you think that Kareem was just a "wimp" or was he just being respectful? What were your feelings when Kareem turned his mother in? Did you agree with his actions? If faced with the same predicament, what would you do? What about the code of the street: Don't snitch? Does that play a part in Kareem's circumstance? What kind of life do you think that Kareem will have with Maximillian? Do you think that Maximillian will ever admit to Kareem that he's not his father? If he does, how do you think that will affect Kareem?

9. What do you think Knowledge's motive was for putting away money for Kapri? Why do you think he didn't go to see her while she was in jail? Did Kapri have a right to resent him? How do you feel about Maximillian representing Estelle, an admitted racist who had murdered a black woman? Was he just doing his job, or do you feel that money was an important factor?

10. Why do you think Noki killed herself? Could her character and the threat of a long jail sentence have played a part in her decision? Or do you think that she really wanted to help her sister, since she had orchestrated the criss cross?

11. Eddie was a womanizer who was playing Noki and Kapri. Do you think he deserved what he got? Do you believe in Voodoo/witchcraft? Do you think that the spell Kapri cast was the reason Noki killed Eddie and his wife?

12. Who do you think was dead in the morgue in 2002, Lyric or Lacey? Could Lyric have craftily orchestrated the criss crossing of her and Lacey's lives?

13. From the long list of characters who do you most identify with? Who do you sympathize with?

14. The premise of the book revolves around the belief that people's lives are pre-ordained. Do you believe in fate?

BAD APPLE

THE FIVE BOROUGHS DON'T KNOW WHO THEY'RE DEALING WITH...

ESSENCE BESTSELLING AUTHOR

NISA SANTIAGO

COMING SEPTEMBER 2011